Undying Love

*Also by Al and JoAnna Lacy
in Large Print:*

A Prince Among Them
Let Freedom Ring
The Little Sparrows
A Measure of Grace
The Secret Place
So Little Time

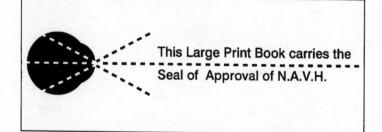

This Large Print Book carries the
Seal of Approval of N.A.V.H.

Undying Love

Shadow of Liberty
Book 4

Al & JoAnna Lacy

Thorndike Press • Waterville, Maine

Published in 2005 by arrangement with
Multnomah Publishers, Inc.

Thorndike Press® Large Print Christian Fiction.

The tree indicium is a trademark of Thorndike Press.

The text of this Large Print edition is unabridged.
Other aspects of the book may vary from the original edition.

Set in 16 pt. Plantin by Carleen Stearns.

Printed in the United States on permanent paper.

Library of Congress Cataloging-in-Publication Data

Lacy, Al.
    Undying love / by Al and JoAnna Lacy.
        p. cm. — (Thorndike Press large print Christian fiction)
    (Shadow of liberty ; bk. 4)
        ISBN 0-7862-7982-6 (lg. print : hc : alk. paper)
        1. Hungarian Americans — Fiction.   2. Fathers and sons
    — Fiction.   3. Immigrants — Fiction.   4. Large type
    books.   I. Lacy, JoAnna.   II. Title.   III. Thorndike Press
    large print Christian fiction series.
    PS3562.A256U54 2005
    813′.54—dc22
                                            2005015900

This book is dedicated to our dear Christian friends and loyal fans, George and Kathy Matrai, and their children, Chrissy and Kenny. Thank you for sharing interesting information on Hungary, which we used in this story.

We love you!

Philippians 1:2

As the Founder/CEO of NAVH, the only national health agency solely devoted to those who, although not totally blind, have an eye disease which could lead to serious visual impairment, I am pleased to recognize Thorndike Press* as one of the leading publishers in the large print field.

Founded in 1954 in San Francisco to prepare large print textbooks for partially seeing children, NAVH became the pioneer and standard setting agency in the preparation of large type.

Today, those publishers who meet our standards carry the prestigious "Seal of Approval" indicating high quality large print. We are delighted that Thorndike Press is one of the publishers whose titles meet these standards. We are also pleased to recognize the significant contribution Thorndike Press is making in this important and growing field.

Lorraine H. Marchi, L.H.D.
Founder/CEO
NAVH

* Thorndike Press encompasses the following imprints: Thorndike, Wheeler, Walker and Large Print Press.

What God Hath Promised

God hath not promised skies always
  blue,
Flower strewn pathways all our lives
  through;
God hath not promised sun without
  rain,
Joy without sorrow, peace without
  pain.
But God hath promised strength for
  the day,
Rest for the labour, light for the way,
Grace for the trials, help from above,
Unfailing kindness, undying love.

Annie Johnson Flint

The Lord hath appeared of old unto
  me, saying,
Yea, I have loved thee with an
  everlasting love.

Jeremiah 31:3

Prologue

In the 1870s a group of French citizens celebrated the centennial of the American Revolution by commissioning the construction of a statue of "Liberty Enlightening the World." The statue was to be presented to the people of the United States to demonstrate the harmonious relationship between the two countries.

The statue, monumental in size, would be the creation of the talented French sculptor, Frédéric-Auguste Bartholdi, whose dream was to build a monument honoring the American spirit of freedom that had inspired the world.

In the United States, government leaders were pleased with the kind gesture and set about raising the $300,000 needed to build a pedestal for the huge French statue, which would be erected on Bedloe's Island in New York Harbor. Promotional tours and contests were organized to raise the money. During these fund-raising campaigns, American poet Emma Lazarus — the daughter of a prominent Jewish family in New York City — wrote the poem "The New Colossus," which was inscribed on the pedestal just prior to the statue's dedication by President Grover Cleveland on October 28, 1886.

Emma Lazarus's immortal words transformed the French statue of Liberty Enlightening the World into the American Statue of Liberty, welcoming the oppressed of the world within its borders to have opportunity to make their dreams come true.

"The New Colossus" on Miss Liberty's pedestal reads:

Give me your tired, your poor,
Your huddled masses yearning to
   breathe free,
The wretched refuse of your teeming
   shore.
Send these, the homeless, the
   tempest-tossed to me,
I lift my lamp beside the golden
   door!

Castle Island in New York Harbor

served as the chief entry station for immigrants between 1855 and 1891, although it was diminutive in size. In order to enlarge the facilities for processing immigrants, New York authorities began considering another site in the harbor. Eyes shifted to Governor's Island, but that was already occupied by the United States Coast Guard. Attention turned to a larger island just a few hundred yards north of Bedloe's Island, where Lady Liberty held high her torch. (Bedloe's Island was later named Liberty Island.)

The choice island was originally called Kioshk, or Gull Island, by Native Americans in the 1600s; Gibbet Island in the early 1700s when criminals were hanged there from a gibbet, or gallows tree; and later Oyster Island because of its abundant population of shellfish. In the early 1780s, the island was purchased by wealthy merchant Samuel Ellis, from whom it derived its present name. New York state bought Ellis Island in 1808 and used it as an ammunition dump until July 15, 1892, when the immigration facility — built at a cost of $500,000 — officially opened its doors. From that time, Ellis Island was the lone entry station for immigrants, and remained so until 1943.

11

The hopeful message on the Statue of Liberty's pedestal has greeted millions of immigrants from countries across the seas who left their homelands behind in search of a better life in the United States of America.

According to the Statue of Liberty–Ellis Island Foundation, today more than a hundred million Americans can trace their roots to ancestors who came into this country through Ellis Island. This means that approximately half of today's Americans are the offspring of pioneering ancestors who registered into the country through that immigration station which stands virtually in the shadow of the Statue of Liberty.

Martin W. Sandler, author of the book *Immigrants*, says, "Our cultural diversity is our greatest strength, for we are more than a nation. Thanks to those who dared to be immigrants, we are a nation of nations. It is a heritage of which we should all be proud."

American historian Oscar Handlin said, "Once I thought to write the story of the immigrants in America. Then I realized that the immigrants were America's story."

They came from many countries across the Atlantic Ocean. For many, the journey was treacherous, and the good life they came for was just a dream. For others, the sailing was smooth, and they prospered in the new land. Both kinds of people created the rich and diverse country in which we live today.

They heard talk about a place where all men were free, a place of compassion. But what about the cost? Not just money for the passage, but the emotional toll. For most immigrants, grandparents, aunts, uncles, cousins, and friends would be left behind. The same was often true of wives and children. The men would have to go alone and send for their families later. Many of the children, who came with their mothers later on, would see their fathers for the first time in months — sometimes years — in the shadow of the Statue of Liberty.

The immigrants were driven by pain and fear and hopelessness; by poverty and hunger; by religious persecution; or by the simple need to survive. They came with nothing but the clothes on their backs, a pocketful of dreams, possibly a flimsy suitcase, trunk, or lidded woven basket, and some crumpled bills carefully stashed in pockets or purses. There are countless stories of new friendships and relationships that were begun while aboard ship or while waiting at the process station to be approved by physicians and government officials to enter into the country.

None who entered this new land and found their place within its borders did so without having their lives changed forever.

A Note from the Authors

It is with great pleasure that we present this series of novels about America's immigrants. We have walked the grounds of both Liberty and Ellis Islands and caught the spirit of those men, women, and children who left their homes in faraway countries, traversed the oceans, and came to the land of the free.

Passing through the same buildings on Ellis Island where they took their medical examinations and their verbal tests in hope of entering this country, we could almost hear the shuffle of their weary feet, the murmur of voices, the laughter of children, and the crying of babies.

The walls of the buildings are covered with photographs of the immigrants, their faces displaying the intimidation they felt, yet a light in their eyes that showed the hope that lay within them for a better life in America.

We have purchased many historical books that have been written about the immigrants. Some tell of statements that were made by them during and after their arrival in New York Harbor. A Cleveland, Ohio, man told of when his mother and her six children arrived on Ellis Island from England. The father, a stone mason, had come to America a year earlier to find a job. "I was five years old at the time," he said. "I remember standing with my mother and five brothers on the ship as it entered New York Harbor. It was very early in the morning. I saw the city's lights and the Statue of Liberty. We were only at Ellis Island for a few hours, and I remember looking up at my mother after we passed through inspection. We smiled and kissed and hugged each other because we had achieved this great thing. We had been accepted into America."

Those readers who know our other fictional series are fully aware that our stories are filled with romance, adventure, and intriguing plots designed to make the books hard to lay down. They are interlaced with

Scripture that will strengthen and encourage Christians, and as always, the Lord Jesus Christ is honored and His gospel made clear.

Since the books in this series are about the people of Europe, which is comprised of many countries and tongues, and because a great number of them spoke several languages, we will not weary the reader by continuously pointing out what language they were speaking. We will simply give it to you in English.

It is our desire that the reader will feel as we did when we walked those hallowed halls, deeply impressed with the courage of those people who helped settle this land we call home.

One

It was Tuesday morning, February 7, 1893, in New Orleans, Louisiana. At the docks on the Mississippi River, a large paddle-wheel riverboat was taking on passengers. The inscription on the sides of the boat read *Hardik Lines #1*. The steam engine could be heard running while billows of black smoke rolled out of the dual smokestacks and floated skyward.

The yellow sun was making a weak attempt to dispel the mist that hovered low to the ground and seemed to float on the surface of the wide river. There was a slight breeze, and the thin fog seemed to dance in circles as it enshrouded the riverboat and the docks in its mysterious haze, giving the whole area a surreal aspect. People on the docks seemed to disappear and reappear rapidly in the swirling mist.

Standing at the open door of the pilot's cabin on the boat's second level was Sigmund Hardik and his lovely wife, Zofia. They were peering through the curling fog, watching the passengers advance slowly up the gangplank, handing their tickets to two of Hardik's crewmen.

Zofia's body shivered a little, both from the view of the ghostly trees, dripping with moss, in the oak grove near the docks, and the sharp bite of the breeze.

The voices of the passengers on the docks and those who stood with them saying their good-byes were a steady thrum when suddenly two sharp male voices pierced it harshly.

"It was a fair duel, Grasile. Now, get off my back!"

"You killed my brother, Veaubien, and I'm going to have my revenge!"

Every eye within earshot of the two men was turned toward them. They were on the back edge of the docks, near the misty oak grove.

"You know where the road is, Philip," said Veaubien. "Get on it before you get hurt. I have no desire to shoot it out with you."

Philip Grasile, who was stocky and a bit shorter than the slender Veaubien, took a step closer. "I'm challenging you, mister! Right in front of all these people. Duel me, or be counted a yellow-bellied coward!"

On the riverboat, Zophia Hardik gripped her husband's arm as Veaubien snapped, "You've got your duel, pal!" The two men walked swiftly off the docks into the oak grove, each pulling a pistol from inside his coat, and vanished from sight. A few people followed and were swallowed by the mists.

Sigmund looked at Zofia, shaking his head. "I've heard how men in this country settle disputes with duels, but this is the first time I've actually seen one about to happen."

Other people on the docks were hurrying into the grove to observe the duel.

Zofia buried her face against her husband's shoulder. "Oh, how awful!"

Suddenly, two shots rang out, almost as one. Zofia jerked at the sound of the shots, burrowing her face farther into Sigmund's shoulder.

He squeezed her hard.

She eased back in his arms, raised her head, and looked toward the spot where Veaubien and Grasile had gone into the grove. "Oh, Sigmund," she said, "what a barbaric way to settle a dispute. Does someone have to die? Can't they discuss it reasonably?"

Sigmund's line of sight was fixed in that direction, also. Then looking down at her, he said, "Apparently it is not in them to discuss it reasonably, dear."

She met his gaze with troubled eyes. "No man is an island. Think of the people connected with these two men who will suffer because of their rash behavior."

Sigmund nodded, and both of them turned their faces toward the shore as people were emerging from the foggy grove. Some were wide-eyed in horror from what they had just witnessed.

At the same time, the sound of pounding hooves filled the air, and two New Orleans police officers came through the fog, drawing their horses to a halt. People gathered around them as they dismounted, telling them about the duel in the oak grove.

Suddenly the man called Veaubien appeared. One of the men who had been filling the officers in on what had happened pointed to the tall, slender man. "That's one of them!"

Both officers rushed up to Veaubien.

"And the other man?" said one of them.

"He's dead," was the calm reply. "My name is Charles Veaubien. The man I just

22

killed was Philip Grasile. These people can tell you that he approached me right here on the docks and challenged me to the duel because I killed his brother, Victor, last Saturday in a duel. They can also tell you that I tried to avoid the confrontation."

Immediately, several voices spoke up, corroborating Veaubien's statement.

The officers looked at each other, nodded. One of them said, "We know about your duel with Victor Grasile, Mr. Veaubien. We also know that our chief cleared you of any wrongdoing. It was a legitimate duel and you won. These people have testified of the same thing, here with Victor's brother. You are free to go."

Veaubien nodded, turned, and headed for the Hardik boat. The officers entered the oak grove, picked up the body, draped it over one of their horses, and rode away.

The riverboat passengers got in line at the gangplank as Sigmund and Zofia looked on from the second level. They watched Charles Veaubien as he handed his ticket to one of the crewmen and stepped on deck. When everyone was on board, a small crowd gathered around Veaubien, commenting on the duel.

The swirling mists that hugged the

ground and the river began to dissipate, and the sun's light was breaking through bright and clear.

Sigmund Hardik signaled to the man inside the pilot's cabin. The man pulled a rope cord above his head. The boat's whistle sounded from the roof of the pilot's cabin, hissing steam.

Sigmund lifted his voice loud enough for all to hear, told the passengers his name, and introduced his wife. Since for most of the passengers this was a pleasure trip, Sigmund assumed a cheerful attitude to help offset the impact of the violent death that had just taken place. He greeted his passengers warmly in his distinct European accent, telling them he hoped they would have an enjoyable ride up the Mississippi, however far they were going. With a bright expression on her face, Zofia also welcomed the people, saying if there was anything she and her husband could do to make their trip more comfortable, to please let them know.

The passengers applauded. Sigmund and Zofia waved at them, smiling, and the whistle blew again. The workmen on the dock released the thick ropes that held the boat to the dock. The Hardik crewmen reeled the ropes in from the side of the boat, and the paddle wheel began churning water. With black smoke roiling from the smokestacks, the boat pulled away from the dock and headed north up the mighty Mississippi.

Sigmund and Zofia descended the metal steps to the main deck and began milling among the passengers. While they were talking to one New Orleans couple, the man said, "Mr. Hardik, have you heard before of that Frenchman, Charles Veaubien?"

"No, sir," said Sigmund. "I haven't."

"He is a well-known gambler in our city. He has been in scrapes before at the casinos, but his duel with Victor Grasile last Saturday was his first in New Orleans. I've been told that he killed several men in duels in France."

"Probably so, since he came out the winner in both duels with the Grasile brothers. He has to be a good shot, and he must have some experience along those lines."

The Hardiks continued to move among the passengers, greeting them and doing everything they could to make them feel welcome on board. Soon they found themselves coming up on Charles Veaubien, who had just turned away from two men with whom he had been talking.

The Frenchman smiled at them. "Ah, Mr. and Mrs. Hardik! I am so pleased to get to meet you." He shook hands with Sigmund, and when Zofia offered her hand, he took it gently, bowed, clicked his heels, and touched his lips to her knuckles.

When Veaubien turned to her husband, Zofia covertly wiped the moisture from her knuckles on the skirt of her dress.

Still smiling, Veaubien said in his pronounced French accent, "I came to New Orleans from Paris almost a year ago, Mr. Hardik. From the very first day I arrived here, I heard about Hardik Lines, and have heard much since. I have been looking forward to taking this necessary business trip up the Mississippi to St. Louis, Missouri, on one of your boats. I did not know I would be so fortunate as to meet the owner of the company and his charming wife."

Sigmund smiled broadly. "Well, we're glad you're aboard, sir."

"Thank you." He ran his gaze between the Hardiks. "I must apologize for the spectacle I became when I was forced to face Philip Grasile in the duel just prior to boarding your boat."

"No apology is necessary, Mr. Veaubien," Sigmund assured him. "It was quite apparent that you had no choice in the matter. You certainly tried to avoid it."

Veaubien nodded. "Even as I tried to avoid the duel with Philip's brother last Saturday. It was over a poker game. Victor accused me of cheating and challenged me to a duel. I was unable to persuade him differently."

Sigmund looked him square in the eye. "Did you cheat him?"

Holding Sigmund's gaze without flinching, Veaubien said, "I did not."

During these moments while Sigmund was in conversation with Charles Veaubien, Zofia stuck close to her husband's side. The gambler left her a bit off balance, and she was still perplexed about the duels, and why they were necessary. She carefully listened to Veaubien's words to Sigmund, but in her heart, she felt there had to be a more civilized way to settle disputes than by two men squaring off and shooting at each other. Even though Sigmund seemed to understand Veaubien's explanation of the duels, she had grave misgivings. She told herself this dueling business must be a man thing. She certainly had never heard of two women squaring off with pistols to settle a quarrel.

The Frenchman's words invaded her thoughts when he said, "Mr. and Mrs.

Hardik, you both have strong accents. Where in Europe are you from?"

"We are from Baja, Hungary," replied Sigmund. "We came to America four years ago to build a new life here in the land of the free."

"I came here — to New Orleans — because the gambling is so profitable. But not because I felt in bondage in France." Veaubien's eyebrows arched. "Things were bad in Hungary?"

"Yes," said Sigmund. "It was the political unrest in Hungary. It is still the same today and has been going on since the Hungarians fought the Habsburgs and lost the battle in 1711. From that time until now, Hungary has not been its own country but a mere province of the Habsburg Empire, which has been the ruling house of Austria since the thirteenth century."

Veaubien rubbed his pointed chin thoughtfully. "Really? I recall hearing something about the Habsburgs and the Hungarians when I was in school, but that's been several years now. Refresh my memory with a little more detail, would you?"

"I don't want to bore you."

"Oh, you won't bore me! I find this interesting."

Sigmund looked at Zofia, shrugged, and

28

looked back at the Frenchman. "Well, in 1849, the Hungarians — longing to be free — revolted against the Austrian Habsburg regime and brought about a bloody battle. Sad to say, the Hungarians were defeated. But this did not break their spirit."

"Ah yes. Some of it is coming back to me now. It was after Emperor Franz Joseph came into power in Austria that something changed."

"Yes. After more years of rebellion by the Hungarian people against Austrian rule, Emperor Franz Joseph conceded to a point, and the Compromise of 1867 took place, which resulted in a dual monarchy of Austria, the empire, and Hungary, the kingdom."

Veaubien was nodding. "And the Austria-Hungary combination is now a federated state of two parliaments and two capitals — Vienna and Budapest."

"Exactly. So in addition to being emperor of Austria, Franz Joseph is also king of Hungary."

"Yes, yes. I recall learning some of this in school, as I said. I am glad to have it refreshed to my memory. So apparently the twenty-six years under the Compromise has not done much to satisfy the Hungarians."

"Only a little. Though the Compromise helped our country to have at least a degree of independence and a remotely better economy, the people still resent the dual monarchy and the serious problems that come with it. They still rise up periodically to show their rebellion, and it makes things worse. Most of the time there is bloodshed."

Veaubien rubbed his chin again. "So there really isn't freedom in Hungary at all."

"Right. It was the lack of real freedom in our country that finally drove Zofia and me to pack up our daughter, Andra — who was fourteen then — and come to America."

A lump formed in Zofia's throat and unbidden tears misted her eyes as she listened to her husband recount the trials and tribulations they had been through in their homeland. For the most part, she had come to love America and their comfortable home in Memphis, Tennessee, but listening to Sigmund speak of Hungary caused a nostalgic longing to fill her for her native homeland and all the loved ones and friends left behind. Giving herself a mental shake, she touched Sigmund's arm. "Dear, will you and Mr. Veaubien excuse me, please? I need to go to our cabin."

"Why, of course," said Sigmund, noting the mist in her eyes. "Are you all right?"

"I'm fine. I just need to sit down for a while." With that, she patted her husband's arm, nodded to the Frenchman, and walked away in what was now clear sunshine.

When Zofia entered the cozy cabin on the second deck, she closed the door softly behind her. She made her way across the room and sat down on the edge of the bed. Allowing her overwrought emotions to spill out, she wept quietly for several minutes. Finally, she took a handkerchief from the nightstand, dabbed at her wet cheeks, and lifted her face heavenward.

"Dear Lord," she said, her voice choking a bit, "You know I love this free land of America, and this is now my home. I don't wish to return to Hungary, but sometimes I do get lonesome for my family and the places that are familiar to me. Please calm my torn spirit and help me to be thankful for Your abundant blessings. After all, my real home is in heaven. Anything on this earth is only temporary."

Picking up her Bible, she turned to one of her favorite passages: Hebrews 13:5. Dabbing at her eyes, she read it aloud:

"Let your conversation be without covetousness; and be content with such things as ye have: for he hath said, I will never leave thee, nor forsake thee."

Drying the last trace of tears from her cheeks, she whispered, "Thank You, Father, for the contentment that only You can give!"

When Zofia had walked toward the metal stairs that would take her up to the cabin, Sigmund continued his discussion with Charles Veaubien. "We had heard repeatedly about the new life thousands of Europeans were finding in America. We began to talk about it a lot, including Andra in our conversations, and after praying much about it, the three of us agreed that we should go to America."

An unpleasant expression shadowed Veaubien's countenance at Sigmund's mention of praying about going to America.

Sigmund noticed it, but went on. "I owned seven tour boats in Hungary, Mr. Veaubien, which carried tourists between Budapest and Baja on the Danube River. I sold my boats, and we came to America. When we arrived in New York City, I did a little research and learned of the paddle-wheel riverboats on the Mississippi River; and after praying about it, we decided to go to St. Louis, where I could look into the riverboat business."

Veaubien put on a smile and said, "Well, St. Louis would be a good place to start."

"It proved to be just that. On the very first day we arrived in St. Louis and I went to the docks, I learned about a man in Memphis, Tennessee, who was retiring and wanted to sell his eight paddle-wheel riverboats. I had enough money from selling the boats in Hungary to purchase the man's boats. Thus, the Hardik Lines of riverboats was established. It is working out well, and my family and I are happy."

"I'm glad for that," said the Frenchman.

"Ah, Mr. Veaubien, I . . . ah . . . noticed that when I mentioned prayer, it seemed to bother you."

The gambler chuckled. "Well, Mr. Hardik, it's just that I believe a man simply has to plow his own way through the fields of life. I met a man in New Orleans a couple of months ago who kept talking like you do. He was a nice little fellow, but he brought up the subject of prayer a lot and things the Bible says about heaven and hell and my need of salvation."

Sigmund let a smile curve his lips. "Heaven, hell, and salvation, eh?"

"Yes."

33

"Well, let me ask you, Mr. Veaubien, if you had been the one to die in that duel back there in the oak grove, which place would you have gone? Heaven or hell?"

Charles Veaubien chuckled nervously, tossed a glance toward the rear of the boat, and looked back at Sigmund. "Ah . . . there's a man waiting back there in the stern to talk to me. I'd better go see him. Please excuse me."

With that, the gambler hurried away.

Two

Friday, February 10, was a cold, blustery, rainy day in Memphis, Tennessee. Bundled up against the driving, icy downpour, eighteen-year-old Andra Hardik hurried along the boardwalk, thankful for the shelter she found beneath the overhanging roof that covered the wooden sidewalk.

When she reached the corner, a gust of wind plucked at her hat. She gripped it, pushed the post office door open, and hurried inside. It took her a few seconds to get the door closed because of the wind gusting against the open door.

Behind the counter, postal clerk Avery Meade smiled. "Good morning, Andra. A bit nasty out there, isn't it?"

"Just a bit," she said, moving toward him and brushing rainwater from her coat. "I'm here to pick up the mail for my family, Mr. Meade. My parents are both

35

on Papa's number one boat, which left New Orleans on Tuesday if everything is on schedule."

"Sure." Meade headed toward a large rack of cubbyholes a few steps behind him.

Andra was given a bundle of mail. She thanked Meade, tucked the bundle under one arm, pushed the door open, and went back out into the inclement weather. Her head down, straining against the wind, she greeted the other brave people along the boardwalk as she hurried past the shops and stores. The rain pelted her face when she left the boardwalk, crossed the muddy street at the intersection, and headed toward home.

Moments later, Andra entered the Hardik house through the kitchen door. A waft of warm air greeted her. She laid the bundle of mail on the table, removed her hat and coat, hung them on wall pegs, and moved up to the stove. Lifting the lid, she dropped another log on the fire, put the lid in place, and set a kettle of water on to heat up. She then held her hands over the stove to warm them, rubbing them together briskly.

When her hands were sufficiently warm, Andra sat down at the scrubbed kitchen table and began going through the mail.

Most everything was for her father, but she was elated to find two letters addressed to her. One was from her closest friend from school days in Baja, Hungary — Maria Pataki. The other was from her cousin Nikola Hardik, also of Baja. She pushed the rest of the mail aside, laid her two letters in front of her, then shoved the chair back and went to the stove.

The kettle was now bubbling. She took a porcelain teapot and teacup from the nearby cupboard. She then placed tea into the strainer and added the hot water. She carried pot and cup to the table and set them down.

Dropping back down on the chair, Andra looked at the two letters. She was always glad to receive news from the homeland. She decided to read Maria's first. She opened the envelope, took out the letter, and began to read.

Tears of joy filled her eyes and began spilling down her cheeks. Andra and her parents had been born again just six months before their departure from Hungary to come to America. In that time, Andra had witnessed to Maria, wanting to see her saved, but Maria had not responded. After settling down in Memphis, Andra had written to Maria, once again giving her the gospel. Maria had written back, but did not refer to Andra's message. Twice more, they had corresponded, both times with Andra quoting Scriptures concerning salvation, but when Maria wrote back, she avoided any mention of the subject.

Andra's fourth letter had gone to Maria in early January, bathed in prayer, and once again giving her the plan of salvation in a loving and kind manner. In this letter, Maria told Andra that when she first talked to her about Jesus in Baja, she had never heard the gospel before, and it was so new to her that she had a hard time grasping it. The letters began coming in the same vein. But in this letter, Maria told Andra that the Scriptures she had been including in her letters had finally opened her eyes to her lost condition, and on January 12, she received the Lord Jesus as her Saviour.

Andra wept jubilantly, praising the Lord for His work in Maria's heart. Wiping tears, she told herself she would write Maria back as soon as she read Nikola's letter.

Taking her cousin's letter out of the envelope, Andra began reading. Excitement showed in her eyes, and the more she read, the more excited she became. Nikola was getting married in June, and she reminded Andra how the two of them had made plans when they were in their early teens that they would be either maid or matron of honor in the other one's wedding.

Nikola was asking if Andra could come to Baja and be her maid of honor. She and her family wanted Andra to come a couple of months early and stay with them until after the wedding.

Andra held the letter close to her heart. "I'll have to talk to Papa and Mama about it, Nikola, but I'm sure they will let me come." She slipped the letter back in the envelope and sighed. "Oh, Nikola, it will be so good to see you again!"

Before answering Maria Pataki's missive, Andra poured herself a cup of fragrant tea, went to the cupboard and returned with a bottle of honey and added a spoonful. She took a few sips of the luscious brew, then went to the parlor and took out pen, ink, paper, blotter, and an envelope from a desk drawer and returned to the kitchen. Sipping tea periodically, she wrote to her friend, rejoicing with her in her newfound salvation in Jesus Christ.

Eager to get the letter in the mail, Andra put on her coat and hat, took a last gulp of the tea, put the letter in a coat pocket, and stepped out into the chilly air. The rain had stopped, and the wind had diminished to a slight breeze.

Even though the air was still chilly, she hardly noticed it as she walked along the street. There was a warm glow coming from her heart over Maria's salvation, and it seemed to flow all the way through her body.

Soon Andra was at the post office. She entered the building, deposited the letter in the mailbox, smiled at Avery Meade, and headed back through the door. As she stepped out onto the boardwalk, she saw her best friend from church just coming out of a store. "Katie! Hello!"

Katie Hubbard smiled and hurried toward Andra. The friends hugged each other, their breath emitting little puffs of vapor on the cold air.

Andra's eyes sparkled. "Oh, Katie, I'm so happy! You remember my telling you about my friend Maria Pataki in Hungary."

Katie's face brightened. "Yes. You've been writing to her, giving her the gospel. Are you going to tell me she got saved?"

"Yes! I picked up the mail a couple of hours ago, and there was a letter from Maria. She told me the Scriptures I have

40

been putting in my letters finally opened her eyes to her lost condition. She received Jesus as her Saviour on January 12."

"Well, praise the Lord! That's wonderful."

"It sure is! I just mailed a letter back to her, telling her how happy I am that she is now my sister in Christ."

Katie chuckled merrily. "I have no doubt she's eagerly waiting to hear back from you."

"Oh yes. That's why I hurried to the post office. I wanted to get it on its way today."

Katie smiled. "New subject."

"Uh-huh?"

"Didn't we have a wonderful time at choir practice Wednesday night?"

"Oh yes! I'm so glad Pastor Richland was able to get Mr. Grady to be our director. He's so much fun, and does he ever know his music! He's going to be such a blessing to the church, and —"

When Andra's words cut off, Katie noticed that she was looking across the street, a shocked expression on her face. Following her line of sight, Katie understood immediately why she was shocked. Brad Fetterman had just come out of a store with Nadine Sellers on his arm.

Andra's features pinched and the hurt

41

she felt showed in her eyes. A trembling hand went to her mouth. Katie took hold of the other trembling hand and squeezed it tightly.

Across the street Brad Fetterman's gaze fell on the stunned Andra. "Uh-oh," he said, his throat tight.

"What's the matter?" asked Nadine, then her own eyes found Andra. "Oh. Well, I guess it's time she knows."

"Wait here," said Brad, leaving Nadine and heading across the muddy street.

When both young women saw Brad weaving his way through traffic toward them, Katie attempted to pull her hand free from Andra's. "I'll leave the two of you alone to talk."

But Andra tightened her grip on Katie's hand. "No. Don't go, Katie. Please stay with me."

"All right," said Katie, moving closer to her friend and planting her feet. Since Andra wanted her to stay for what was about to be an unpleasant confrontation, Katie would let nothing move her away.

Andra bit her lower lip as Brad stepped up on the boardwalk. "Andra . . . can I . . . talk to you alone?"

"No," she replied crisply, gripping Katie's hand. "Whatever you have to say,

42

you can say it in front of Katie. She's my best friend."

Seeing the coldness in both young women's eyes, Brad looked down at his feet and rubbed his hands together. The chill he was feeling was only partly from the nippy air.

Brad cleared his throat nervously, brought his gaze up to meet Andra's, and cleared his throat a second time. "Andra, I . . . I've been trying to find the right way to tell you that . . . well, that Nadine and I have gotten back together. I really thought I was over her, but . . . but last week I found out I wasn't. Y-you're a nice girl, and I don't mean to hurt you, but . . . but I know now that Nadine is the girl for me."

Andra said, "By last week, you mean before Sunday?"

"Well . . . uh . . . yes."

She stared at him incredulously, her long black hair curling softly over one shoulder. "How could you sit with me in church last Sunday after I came down from the choir loft, acting like everything was perfect between us?"

Brad looked down. He glanced at Katie, then at his feet again. Shuffling them slightly, he said, "I . . . I j-just hadn't found the way to tell you, so I . . . kept up the pretense. Nadine didn't like it. She was sitting with her parents two pews behind us, and I could feel her eyes burning into the back of my head. But I told her I had to find a way to let you down easy."

"I guess that problem is solved now," Katie said stiffly.

Andra thought for a moment about the situation. Although she hadn't known for sure that she was actually falling in love with Brad, it still hurt to be rejected. She thought about how she prayed daily for God's leadership in her life, and told herself that He was fully aware of what had happened this past week between Brad and Nadine. Undoubtedly, Brad was not the man the Lord had chosen for her.

Andra said, "Brad, I wish you had been honest with me, instead of acting like I was still your girl."

Deep lines penciled themselves across Brad's brow. "Andra, I'm sorry. I handled it all wrong. And . . . I'm asking your forgiveness."

Sighing deeply, Andra gave him a small smile. "It's all right, Brad. I forgive you. I would rather find out now that you're not the man the Lord has chosen for me."

"Will you hold a grudge against Nadine?"

"Call her over here."

Across the street, Nadine Sellers waited, watching as Brad talked to Andra. But she couldn't hear what was being said. When Brad turned and motioned for her to come to him, a shiver went through her body. Swallowing hard, she stepped off the boardwalk, and with great difficulty she crossed the muddy street, feeling the eyes of the two women on her and avoiding their gaze.

When she approached the boardwalk on the other side, Brad reached his hand out to her. "It's all right, Nadine," he said, gripping her fingers and pulling her to him. "Andra understands. I admitted to her that I handled this all wrong, but she has forgiven me."

Slowly, Nadine raised abashed eyes and encountered Andra's gaze. To her surprise and relief, it was not filled with anger, but rather with understanding.

"Nadine," Andra said softly, "since it appears that Brad and I are not meant for each other, I hope you are the one the Lord has chosen for him."

Nadine was trying to come up with appropriate words and was having some difficulty.

Andra spoke again, running her eyes between Brad and Nadine. "I wish both of you had been honest with me before this moment, but I want you to know that I wish you the best."

"Thank you, Andra," said Nadine weakly. "I . . . need your forgiveness, too. We both should have come to you immediately after we knew we were for each other. We were wrong to go on waiting for a convenient way to break it to you."

"I forgive you," Andra said quietly.

Brad frowned. "Then you won't hold a grudge against either of us?"

"Since I have forgiven you, that means I'll hold no grudges. As a Christian, I am told in God's Word to forgive my brothers and sisters in Christ when they have wronged me. Just like the Lord forgives His children without holding a grudge, we are to do the same."

"Thank you," said Brad. "I still want us to be friends."

"So do I," Nadine said, trying to form a smile on her lips.

Andra's lips curved upward. "We are still friends."

When Brad and Nadine walked away, Katie said, "I admire you for the way you handled the situation. I'm sure the Lord has a very special young man picked out for you. You sure don't want to get the wrong one."

Andra was still having a hard time with the shock of what had just happened. "You're right about that, precious friend of mine. Thank you for being my friend."

"You don't have to thank me for that, honey. You'd stand by me if I had to go through this with Greg."

"I sure would, but you won't. The Lord has made it quite clear that He has chosen you and Greg for each other." She paused to take a shallow breath. "Well, I guess I'd better get home."

Katie touched her arm. "Would you like to come home with me? You're human and this has been a jolt to you, even though you know God is leading in your life. I don't think you should be alone tonight."

Andra patted the hand that lay on her arm. "Thank you, sweet Katie, but I have things to do around the house with both my parents gone. I . . . I sort of need some time to myself, too. I'll be fine. Don't worry. I have no doubt that the Lord had a purpose in all of this. My future is in His hands and not my own."

"All right, honey. It sounds like you've got a grip on it. I'll see you later."

The friends hugged each other and went

their separate ways.

The kitchen had grown cold while Andra was gone. She stirred the embers in the big black cookstove and added two more logs.

By the time Andra had removed hat and coat and had taken time to build a fire in the potbellied stove in the parlor and light two lanterns, the kitchen was cheery and warm. She pulled the kettle over the fire on the stove, then cut some cheese and sliced a thick piece of bread. She bowed her head, thanked the Lord for the food, and began eating.

Her thoughts went first to the incident with Brad and Nadine. There was still a hollowness inside her because of the sudden loss of Brad as a candidate for the man she would one day marry and the disappointment she felt toward him for deceiving her about his renewed relationship with Nadine. But she had forgiven them and told herself the shock and disappointment would fade away with prayer and the passing of time.

She sipped the hot tea between bites of bread, and it did wonders to soothe her jangled nerves.

Her mind then went to Maria's letter, and the joy it had brought to her heart began to show itself again. She had prayed so hard that the Lord would use her witness to bring Maria to Himself. And He had so marvelously answered those prayers.

Then she thought of Nikola's letter. What a happy time she would have, visiting her cousins, aunt and uncle, and being maid of honor in Nikola's wedding!

As she finished the last bite of cheese and bread, Andra was feeling calmer, and much more at peace over the Brad and Nadine shock. She cleaned up the table, washed and dried the dishes, then went into the parlor. The potbellied stove had warmed the room comfortably.

She picked up her Bible from an end table by the sofa and sat down in an overstuffed chair. One of the lanterns she had lit earlier stood on a small table next to the chair. Opening the Bible, she angled it toward the light and turned to one of her favorite passages — Proverbs 3:5–6.

She read it aloud to herself. "Trust in the LORD with all thine heart; and lean not unto thine own understanding. In all thy ways acknowledge him, and he shall direct thy paths."

Silently, she ran her eyes over the words again. "Dear Lord, I certainly trusted You with all my heart to save my lost soul, and I certainly did not lean on my own understanding as to how to obtain my salvation. I leaned on Your precious Word. And now that I am Your child by the new birth, I still must not lean on my own understanding, but continue to lean on Your Word. And I must acknowledge You in all my ways as I walk the path of life here on earth. Help me always to do so, Lord. I never want to take a path unless You direct me on that path."

As she ran her eyes over the two verses once more, it was as if a dark cloud suddenly drifted away, allowing the sun to shine through. She sighed as tears filled her eyes, and said, "Thank You, Lord, that with Brad, You have directed my path. Please direct my path to the man You have chosen for me when it is Your time to do so."

She thumbed the tears from her cheeks, closed her eyes, lowered her head, and yielded herself into the strong arms of her Saviour. In those arms, she found hope and peace.

At ten o'clock the next morning, Andra Hardik arrived at the docks on the Mississippi River. The sun shone down with welcome warmth out of a clear sky.

Knowing that *Hardik Lines* boat number one was scheduled to arrive between ten and ten-thirty, she sat down on a bench, pulled Nikola's letter out of her purse, and began reading it again.

While reading it, from the corner of her eye she saw a man, woman, and two teenage girls draw up, chatting merrily, and sit down on the bench next to her. All four glanced at her.

Folding the letter and inserting it in the envelope, she placed it back in her purse and smiled at them. "Hello," she said cheerfully. "Are you folks here to meet someone who is coming in, or are you to be passengers on the boat?"

The man said, "We are going to be passengers. We're taking the boat as far north as Cairo, Illinois. We'd like to go all the way to St. Louis, since the Hardik boats go there to turn around, but we don't have that much time."

The sisters looked at each other whispering and nodding, then one of them smiled at Andra. "Didn't we see you in church Sunday? You were in the choir."

Andra's smile broadened. "You're right. My name is Andra Hardik."

"Hardik!" said the woman. "You mean

as in 'Hardik Lines'?"

"Yes, ma'am. My father owns the Hardik Lines. I am waiting for him and my mother to arrive from New Orleans. Papa, of course, is piloting the boat. Another Hardik skipper will pilot the boat on up to St. Louis. May I ask your names?"

The man said, "My name is William Allen. This is my wife, Sarah, and these are our daughters, Millie and Lorna. Millie is fifteen, and Lorna will soon be fourteen."

"Well, nice to meet you," said Andra. "And where are you from?"

"We're from Portland, Maine," said Sarah. "We came to Memphis to visit my older sister, who has been quite ill. But thank the Lord, she is doing better now. We wanted to take a ride on a riverboat before we go back home."

"All four of us are Christians, Miss Hardik," said William, "and we very much enjoyed the services in your church on Sunday."

"I'm glad you enjoyed it," said Andra. "Our pastor, Duane Richland, is a wonderful man and a great preacher."

"That he is," said William.

"And your choir is marvelous," put in Millie. "Do you also sing solos, Miss Hardik?"

"Yes, and I'm in a girls' trio, too."

"Oh, how exciting!" said Millie. "Lorna and I sing in a girls' chorale in our church."

"It's a blessing to serve the Lord in music, isn't it?" said Andra.

"It sure is. Miss Hardik, I just love your European accent. Where are you from originally?"

"My family and I are from Hungary. We came to America four years ago, to start a new life in this wonderful country. There has been political unrest in Hungary for a long, long time. It brings so much misery to the people. We grew weary of it, and after much prayer, were led by the Lord to come to America. Papa owned a line of tour boats in Hungary. He was able to sell them for a good price, and the Lord made it possible for Papa to purchase this river-boat line. We are superbly happy here."

"I'm so glad," said William. "So you and your family were saved while still in Hungary?"

"Yes. The pastor of Baja's most aggressive Bible-preaching church knocked on our door one day and gave us the gospel. We didn't get saved then, but we attended the church the very next Sunday, and after a powerful hellfire-and-brimstone sermon, we walked the aisle and received Jesus into our hearts."

"Well, praise the Lord for preachers who will preach those kinds of sermons!" said William. "Our pastor in Portland preaches that kind quite often."

Suddenly the high-pitched sound of a whistle filled the air. Other people had gathered on the dock, and along with Andra and the Allens, were looking up river as the Hardik riverboat was angling toward shore on the sun-kissed surface of the mighty Mississippi. Andra rose from the bench, her eyes fixed on the boat. The Allen family also rose to their feet. Moments later, the whistle blew again, and the churning paddles brought the boat to the dock.

Andra turned to the Allens. "It's been a real joy to meet you folks. I hope you have an enjoyable trip on the river. You can't get on the boat until the other passengers get off, but fortunately I can because I'm anxious to see my parents. God bless you."

The Allens bid Andra good-bye, and watched as she hurried toward the edge of the dock where the crew was already placing the gangplank between the boat and the dock. When she drew up, the crewmen greeted her warmly, and she returned the greeting with a smile. While she waited for them to secure the gangplank in place, she looked up toward the pilot's cabin and saw her parents standing just outside its door.

They waved and she waved back.

Although it had been a relatively short time since Andra had seen her parents, she had missed them as always. She felt an urgent need to be with them and to tell them the news of both letters from Hungary, and also of Brad leaving her for Nadine.

When the gangplank was firmly in place, one of the Hardik crewmen said, "There you go, Miss Andra."

Lifting her long skirt a bit, Andra ran up the gangplank, threaded her way among the passengers who were about to leave the boat, quickly climbed the steps to the second level, and dashed to her waiting parents.

"Mama! Papa!" she cried with elation as she rushed up to them, arms open wide, and hugged them both at the same time.

"Whoa, there, sweet daughter!" said Sigmund. "What has you so excited?"

Taking a step back, Andra ran her gaze between the two people who meant so much to her, and a happy grin spread across her lovely face. "I just missed you both a lot, Papa."

Zofia smiled and tilted her head. "We're glad for that, honey, but we both know you well enough to know that this jubilance you have is more than just having us home. Come on, now. What is it?"

"Well-l-l . . ."

Sigmund took both of his ladies by the hand and said, "Let's go sit down on the bench over here so we can talk and I can watch the passengers getting off. And in case they need me, I can keep an eye on the crew at the same time." When the three of them were seated, both parents each took one of their daughter's hands in their own. "All right, sweetheart, let's hear it."

Andra swallowed hard. "Well, I have some good news and some bad news. Which do you want first?"

"Oh, I'll always take the bad news first and get it over with," said Zofia. *It can't be too bad, or Andra wouldn't be so exuberant.*

"All right," said Andra, a tiny grin playing at the corners of her mouth. "The bad news isn't really that devastating, but it will no doubt shock you as it did me. It broke my heart for a little while, but I talked to the Lord and read my Bible, and I'm at peace with it."

"Whatever are you rambling about?" her

mother said. "Tell us what happened."

"Oh, I'm sorry, Mama. It's just that the good news is so wonderful that I want to get to it quickly. Anyway, what I'm rambling about has to do with Brad."

"Brad?" said Sigmund. "What about him?"

"Well, he broke up with me. You remember that he used to go with Nadine Sellers."

Sigmund frowned. "Yes."

"He's back with her?" said Zofia.

"Yes, Mama. Let me tell you about it." Andra told her parents about the scene that took place on the street downtown the day before. Talking about it brought some of the hurt to the surface, which caused her voice to break a couple of times, but she valiantly maintained her composure and finished the story.

"Oh, baby, I'm sorry," Zofia said, folding her in her arms.

Sigmund laid a hand on Andra's shoulder. "Honey, that young man surprises me. I thought he was really serious about you. This makes me want to have a talk with him, myself."

An errant tear trickled down Andra's cheek. She quickly wiped it away and looked at her father. "I'm really all right,

Papa. It took me by surprise, of course, but I know God's hand is in it, and my future is safe with Him."

Zofia cupped her daughter's face in her hands. "Are you sure you're all right?"

"Yes," said Sigmund. "Are you sure?"

A smile again curved the young girl's lips. "Yes, Mama, Papa. I'm fine because I know God's perfect will has been done. He is in control of my life. I told you about Katie being with me there on the street, but I didn't tell you what she said right after Brad and Nadine walked away. She's so sweet. She said, 'I'm sure the Lord has a very special young man picked out for you. You sure don't want to get the wrong one.'"

"Well, bless her heart," said Zofia. "She's right about that."

"Yes, Mama. Brad would have been the wrong one, so I trust the Lord to lead the right one to me in His own time."

Sigmund kissed her cheek. "That's my girl. You just keep trusting the Lord on this, honey, and it'll be all right."

"That's for sure," said Zofia, patting Andra's face lovingly. "So much for the bad news. What's the good news?"

Andra took both letters out of her purse and handed them to her mother. "Read them to Papa, Mama. Start with Maria's letter."

When Zofia finished Maria Pataki's letter, all three were shedding tears, rejoicing together in Maria's salvation.

When Zofia finished Nikola Hardik's letter, both parents were happy with the news of the wedding, and agreed that their daughter should return to Hungary and do as her cousin wished. They told her it would be good for her to spend some time with her aunt, uncle, and cousins, as well as to take part in Nikola's wedding.

Andra thanked them and said she would begin making travel plans right away.

Three

It was just before midnight in Hungary's capital city of Budapest on Friday, March 10, 1893.

Police officer Laton Strand heard a moan before he opened his eyes and realized it had come from his own mouth. He was lying on his side on the cold, hard ground. Unconsciousness swirled at the edge of his mind like a black shroud, threatening to pull him back into the inky pit that had just given him up. He steeled himself against it. His head felt like it had been split open when his attackers struck him down with a series of blows, but he could not tell if he was bleeding.

Blinking to clear his eyes, he raised his pounding head enough to look across the dark, shadowed capitol grounds. The back side of the capitol building was on fire. Flames were leaping toward the black sky, and he thought he heard the clanging of a fire bell in the distance.

My partner . . . where is he?

Strand looked around him, trying to remember if the small mob of citizens who had jumped them had pounded Officer Byor Gresham down, too.

As he ran his pained gaze in the dull glow of the street lamp above him, he saw Gresham's body slumped against the base of the metal fence that surrounded the grounds. Gresham's eyes were open but staring blankly into space. His head was a bloody mass. He was not breathing.

Suddenly a trickle of blood ran into Laton Strand's eyes. He put a shaky hand to the back of his skull and felt the warm moisture. He was indeed bleeding, and bleeding profusely.

The fire bell. It was clanging repeatedly, and growing louder by the second. His head began to spin. Have to stay conscious, he told himself. Have to tell Chief Serta who did this.

Suddenly, the pounding of galloping hooves met his ears, and he raised his head again to see the fire wagon pulling onto the driveway that crisscrossed the capitol grounds. Four police officers followed the wagon on their horses.

61

Blood was trickling into Strand's eyes steadily, but he struggled to roll onto his stomach. When he had made it that far, he pulled his legs up under him and summoned every ounce of his remaining strength to raise himself to a standing position. Swaying shakily, he wiped blood from his eyes and staggered in the direction of the blazing capitol building.

The flames were spreading and massive dark clouds of smoke lifted skyward.

After a few steps, his legs gave way, and he fell to the ground. With effort, he made it to his feet again, wiping blood from his eyes and blinking to clear his vision. He could see some of the firemen scrambling about with fire hoses, positioning themselves strategically to best attack the fire, while others were at the wagon beginning to work the hand pumps. The four policemen were off their horses, helping the firemen arrange the hoses.

Strand staggered a few more steps, then fell again. His head was spinning, but he managed to get up and stagger on. He heard a second fire wagon's bell clanging, and the thunder of pounding hooves. This wagon passed by him only a few feet away, and the driver noticed him, looking back at him, which caused the firemen on the wagon to look at him, too.

Strand almost fell again, but righted himself. He paused to watch the second wagon draw up to the rear of the blazing capitol building. The men jumped off the wagon, and just before he fell again, Strand saw the driver hurry up to one of the police officers and point back at him.

When he hit the ground, he saw the officer running toward him.

Dawn was breaking in a broad fan shape on the eastern horizon when Wilhelmina Serta heard the pounding at the front door of the house and opened her eyes. Her husband stirred and made a moaning sound.

The pounding continued. Wilhelmina shook him vigorously. "Akman! Akman! Somebody's at the front door."

The police chief opened his eyes, stared at the ceiling, then sat up. Shaking his head to clear the cobwebs from his brain, he threw the covers back and swung his legs over the side of the bed. "This is the one thing I don't like about my job. Too many nights my sleep is interrupted."

Moments later, fully dressed, Akman opened the front door to find Officers Heran Matif and Var Tanca on the porch, their faces telling him something bad had happened before they could get it out of their mouths.

Between the two of them, Matif and Tanca gave Chief Akman the story.

About midnight, a band of some fifteen to twenty male citizens had started a fire on the back side of the capitol building. However, before getting too far, they had been accosted by Officers Laton Strand and Byor Gresham, who were on their regular patrol in that part of the city. Somehow the band of men had overpowered the officers, disarmed them, and pounded them to the ground, using some kind of blunt instruments.

Thinking they had killed both officers, they then went onto the capitol grounds and set fire to the capitol building. They indeed had killed Officer Gresham, but Officer Strand was only unconscious. He came to while the first of three fire wagons was arriving and made his way toward the burning building. When the second fire wagon arrived, the driver noted Officer Strand staggering toward the scene, and alerted Officer Heran Matif. He rushed to Strand just as the officer fell to the ground. Officer Var Tanca joined them and Strand told them the story, naming five of the men in the mob.

Strand told them that when he and Gresham first confronted the collection of angry men, they said they were going to do something to get the government's attention. They wanted their Hungarian language back; they wanted the peasants' right to vote given back to them; and they wanted their tax money to go for helping Hungarians, not the people of Austria.

Serta scratched his temple. "Well, these are the issues that the general public in this country are upset about. Did they get the fire put out?"

"Yes, sir," said Tanca. "The damage is serious, though."

"What about Officer Strand?"

"We took him to City Park Hospital, sir," said Matif, his countenance sagging. "But he died only a few minutes after we got there. The doctor said it was a brain hemorrhage."

Serta's own countenance fell. "That gang of dissidents took the lives of two fine officers. They will pay for this."

"Yes, sir," said Matif. "At least we have five names."

"We'll get all of them," Serta said. "I am in agreement with their cause, but they have no right to batter two of my men to death and set fire to the capitol to get the government's attention. I will go to Burgomaster Zelko's office this morning. King Franz Joseph has got to do something before this situation gets worse."

Budapest's burgomaster had been in his office less than five minutes that morning when his secretary tapped on his door, telling him that Police Chief Akman Serta was there to see him.

Markus Zelko saw the grave look in the eyes of the chief when he came through the door. He stood up, extended his hand, and as he gripped Serta's hand, he said, "Chief, I figured I would see you this morning. I heard about the fire at the capitol building. No details as yet, only that a band of dissident citizens started the fire."

"It is worse than that, sir," said Serta. "Two of my officers are dead. Killed by that mob when they tried to stop them from going on to the capitol grounds. One officer lived long enough to identify five of them, and I have my men going after them. We will hunt down the others, too."

"Do you know if the dissidents are upset about the public's three main issues, or is it something else?"

"It is those three issues, all right. I went

to my office this morning before coming over here. When I arrived, three men were waiting for me. Editors-in-chief of all three Budapest newspapers. They showed me placards the dissidents had lain at the doors of their buildings last night before going to the capitol to start the fire. They listed the same three issues on those placards, and warned that if King Franz Joseph didn't do something about them within a week, they would burn more government buildings."

Zelko sighed, a sigh that came deep from within his husky chest. "All right. I will go to Vienna on Monday and talk to the king. He must bring this problem to a satisfactory solution. Even if you are able to catch all of the men involved in killing the two officers and setting fire to the capitol, there are plenty more out there who will take up where they left off. There'll be riots, too."

"Yes, sir. Shall I see if I can arrange a special boat to take you to Vienna?"

"That won't be necessary. I travel the river enough to know the schedules of most of the boats. I know Miklos Varda's tour boat goes to Vienna every Monday, as well as four other days a week."

"Oh yes. You and Miklos are old friends, aren't you?"

"That we are. I've ridden his boat up to other towns and cities along the Danube, as well as to Vienna, many a time. I wish he also went south of Budapest. I would ride his boat that direction, too, on my business trips. But he only runs between here and Vienna."

Serta stood up. "Well, sir, I'll be going. I have to go see the families of my two dead officers. A task I do not relish."

Also rising, Zelko said, "I don't envy you, Chief. Both of our jobs have unpleasant elements, and when we have to deal with those elements, we wish we did something else for a living."

"You're right about that. Let me know as soon as you return how it went with the king, won't you?"

"Of course."

On Monday morning, March 13, sunshine danced on the rippling waters of the blue Danube River. Forty-year-old Miklos Varda was standing on the main deck of his tour boat at the Budapest docks greeting passengers as they boarded, when he spotted his friend Markus Zelko in line, moving slowly up the gangplank.

Varda was talking to a tourist from the Netherlands when he saw the burgomaster

68

step onto the deck and head his direction. He waved at Varda, who waved back with a smile. The Dutchman made a complimentary comment about the boat and walked away to join friends.

Varda and Zelko shook hands. Varda said, "Are you going all the way to Vienna this time, Markus, or are you stopping off somewhere in between?"

Zelko looked around to see if anyone was close, and noting that no one was within earshot, he lowered his voice and said, "I'm going to Vienna. I wired King Franz Joseph on Saturday and have an appointment with him tomorrow morning."

Matching the burgomaster's voice level, Varda asked, "Does this have to do with those men who killed two police officers and set that fire at the capitol?"

"It sure does."

"Have you caught any of them yet?"

"Seven of them. We're working on the rest. We will get them."

"I'm sure you will. So you're taking this episode to the king."

"Yes. No doubt you read in the papers about the placards that were put at the doors of all three newspapers and their message."

"I did. So you will be talking to the king about those three issues."

"Yes. With the growing unrest in Budapest on these issues, I'm sure the rest of the country feels the same way about them. If the king doesn't do something to appease the people soon, there are going to be riots in the country's larger cities that could kill people and destroy property. Plus, we already have a warning that there will be more such incidents as happened Friday night, as you know."

Miklos nodded, his brow deeply lined. "I sure hope the king will listen to you and do what has to be done to settle this problem."

"Yes. Me too."

Miklos changed the subject, raising his voice to normal level. "So how's your family doing?"

The burgomaster had two married daughters, and a son who was about to get married. He told his friend that everyone was doing fine, and talked about his three grandchildren, saying that at the moment, his wife was at the oldest daughter's home in Trentin, which Miklos knew was in northern Hungary.

The burgomaster then said, "How are Beatrice and the boys?"

"Doing fine," said Miklos. "Beatrice is still putting up with me, and I couldn't ask for a better mother for Stephan and Joseph."

Zelko chuckled. "Takes some kind of woman to put up with you, old pal!"

Miklos laughed. "About the same as your wife, huh?"

They laughed together. "Is Stephan still as fascinated with his little brother as always?" Zelko knew the Vardas thought for years that the only child they would have was Stephan, who was now nineteen. Then, nine years after Stephan was born, along came Joseph, who had recently had his tenth birthday.

"Yes, he is," said Miklos. "Joseph has been such a joy to all of us, and we cherish him more every day. Stephan loves his little brother more than ever and caters to his every whim."

Zelko shook his head in wonderment. "You know, Miklos, that is highly unusual. Most teenage boys cannot be bothered with little brothers."

"I have to say, Markus, that both of my boys are very, very special."

The one-hundred-fifty-mile trip to Vienna, Austria, took nearly seven hours.

The next morning, Markus Zelko left his hotel in downtown Vienna and took a hired buggy to the capitol building.

Entering the building, he was greeted by a uniformed guard. "Good morning, Mr. Zelko. I was told that you have an appointment with Emperor Franz Joseph, and I am supposed to escort you upstairs to his office."

"Fine, Rakoz," said the burgomaster. "Then I will be in good company all the way up the stairs, won't I?"

When Zelko was accompanied into the outer office of Franz Joseph's complex by the armed guard, he was greeted by his secretary, Julius Szabo, who told him the monarch was ready to meet with him.

The burgomaster was then ushered by the secretary into the plush office of the man who was at the same time emperor of Austria and king of Hungary. The silver-haired Joseph rose from the chair behind his desk, shook hands with Markus Zelko, and they sat down facing each other in overstuffed chairs near the fireplace.

Hot tea was brought in by Julius Szabo, and after taking a sip, Franz Joseph said, "I assume from your wire, Burgomaster, that this meeting is quite urgent."

"Yes, sir. We are having a tremendous amount of unrest in Budapest, and I know it is as bad in the rest of the country. I fear that devastating riots will take place in many of our major cities unless the people are appeased in three specific areas."

The king of Hungary adjusted himself on the large chair and took another sip of tea. "I know the language change is one of them."

"Correct, sir. But let me tell you what happened this past Friday night in Budapest, then I will tell you the other two issues."

Franz Joseph listened intently as Markus Zelko told him of the small mob who had brutally battered two of his police officers at the capitol grounds, leaving one dead, and the other unconscious; then set fire to the capitol building. When he had completed the story, telling him of Officer Laton Strand dying of a brain hemorrhage after providing information which had led to the arrest of seven of the mob, and of the placards left at Budapest's three newspapers, Franz Joseph shook his head. "This is serious, Burgomaster. Indeed, very serious. Let's talk about the language problem, first."

They began to discuss the situation. Several months previously, King Franz Joseph and the Hungarian Parliament replaced the Hungarian Magyar language with the

German language as the official legal language of Hungary. The people opposed it vehemently, sending letters to Joseph in Austria and making themselves heard all over Hungary. The newspapers printed their comments since Hungary was supposed to have free press. The opinion of the people was that Magyar had been Hungary's language for nearly a thousand years and it should remain the same.

"The people feel strongly enough about it, sir," said Zelko, "to burn the capitol building and beat two police officers to death. I know this was only a small mob, but they were also acting on behalf of a great number of others. If this language problem isn't changed, there is going to be much more trouble, believe me."

Hungary's king nodded silently. "Go ahead with the second point of controversy."

"That, sir, is the change that was made in Hungary's law last year, making it so that peasants are no longer allowed to vote on issues the rest of the populace can vote on. The people at large feel that just because the peasants are poor and pay little or no taxes, that that should not make them less than citizens of their country. I have heard a great deal from the people of

Budapest about this, but from what I've learned by talking to other burgomasters, the opinion is widespread."

Franz Joseph thought on it a moment, then said, "And what is the third point of controversy?"

"Well, sir, the general public is very upset because much of their tax money is used to help Austria with its financial problems. They are vehement about this, believe me. This issue, also, is spread all over the country. It isn't isolated just in Budapest. They believe this money should go to aid Hungarian peasants, providing food, clothing, shelter, and medicines for them. They deeply resent paying tax money that ends up aiding Austrians."

Franz Joseph let his mind take in what the burgomaster had told him, thinking on it for a long moment. Then he spoke. "I want to think these things over, Burgomaster Zelko. A man in my position must not do anything rashly. As I said, this is very serious. But there are many things to consider here. Making changes could cause other serious problems. I will let you know what action I am going to take, if any, within a couple of days."

Markus Zelko stared in open-mouthed astonishment. A red flush crept across his cheeks. He struggled to control the ragged emotion that stirred within him. "If any, sir? Have I not made my point here? Two officers are dead because of these issues I have just pointed out. Budapest's capitol building has been burned and will cost a great deal to repair. I respectfully advise you to take action on all three and to do it very soon. Hungary is sitting on a bomb, and the fuse, King Franz Joseph, is already lit."

On Thursday, March 16, Burgomaster Markus Zelko was at his desk when his secretary entered his office, holding a sealed envelope.

"Telegram for you, sir," she said. "From King Franz Joseph."

Zelko thanked her, and she left the room as he was slitting the envelope open. The message read:

March 16, 1893
Burgomaster Markus Zelko
City and County Building
Budapest, Hungary
Burgomaster Zelko,
    In regard to the issues which have the people of Hungary upset, and which you and I discussed in my office on

76

March 14, I have decided to change them, at least to a degree.

I will come to Budapest by boat on Friday, March 24, and will make a speech to the people on the capitol grounds at ten o'clock on Saturday morning, March 25.

Please advise the Budapest newspapers of this, so the people of the city, surrounding towns, villages, and rural areas will know of the speech and can attend.

I am confident that you will provide sufficient police protection in case of troublemakers.

Regards,
King Franz Joseph

Zelko read the telegram over again. He was glad to hear that the king would make the speech concerning the changes that would come on the three issues, but he was worried about the king's words: "at least to a degree."

He immediately left the building and personally visited the offices of the editors-in-chief of all three Budapest newspapers. He told them of his visit with King Franz Joseph on Tuesday, what subjects were discussed, and of the king's reply by wire.

The next morning — Friday, March 17 — all three newspapers used bold headlines to announce the king's upcoming speech to be given in front of Budapest's capitol building on Saturday morning, March 25.

It was early afternoon on Sunday, March 19. On Budapest's west side, in the affluent Buda Hills section, Bela and Ravina Bartok greeted Pastor Varold Tivadar and his wife, Gerda, at the front door of their lovely home.

Ravina had a delicious meal prepared. The Bartoks sat down at the dining room table with their guests, and Bela asked the pastor to lead them in prayer, thanking the Lord for the food.

As soon as they started eating, Bela looked across the table. "Pastor, that was a tremendous sermon this morning. It seems that every time you center a message on Calvary, I learn something new about it."

The preacher smiled. "That's the wonder of our Lord's suffering and death on the cross, Bela. The more we study the Scriptures on the subject, the more we realize how much more there is to learn. And it has depths that our earthly, finite minds will never fathom. I'm sure we will learn much more about it when we get to heaven."

Ravina smiled at the preacher. "Do you recall, Pastor, that you preached about Calvary on that Sunday morning when Bela and I were saved fifteen years ago?"

"I most certainly do. I preached that morning on our Saviour's cry from the cross, 'My God, my God, why hast thou forsaken me?'"

"Oh yes," said Bela. "You dwelt on the fact that Jesus was forsaken by God the Father so sinners like us would not have to be forsaken by Him in hell if we would only repent and put our faith in Jesus to save us." He looked at Ravina, then back at the pastor. "We could hardly wait for you to finish the sermon and start the invitation so we could come to the altar and be led to the Lord."

"That's for sure," said Ravina.

There was a brief silence while they continued to eat, then Gerda ran her gaze to Ravina. "Are you getting anywhere with Miklos and Beatrice?"

"No, we're not. As you know, we continue to witness to them. Even though my brother and Beatrice were upset way back there when we were saved and baptized in your church, and left the 'mother' church, they still stay close to us. We will keep praying for them and trying to win them to the Lord."

Ravina started to say something else as the pastor said, "You both are aware — Oh, I'm sorry, Ravina."

She smiled. "It's all right, Pastor. Go ahead."

Tivadar grinned. "You both are aware that I have been on their doorstep several times, but so far, they have not let me in, nor will they let me talk to them. There is another family in their neighborhood that I'm trying to reach, so I always knock on both doors when I'm there. Gerda has been with me on two or three occasions."

Gerda nodded. "The Vardas have a nice home there on Pozsony Street, but as often as the Danube goes over its banks, I would be nervous every spring and summer if I lived just two blocks from it."

"That area on the river's east side has been damaged by floods many times," said Bela, "but so far the Vardas have had only minimal damage each time."

The pastor looked at Ravina. "Now, what were you going to say a moment ago when I interrupted you?"

"I was going to tell you and Gerda about my nephew, Joseph. He's ten years old now. Both boys have come and stayed overnight with us on occasion over the years. We have given Stephan the gospel repeatedly, and he has shown interest at times, but we both can see that he fears going against his parents, so he just won't make the move. However, just two weeks ago, Joseph was staying with us, and we had the joy of leading him to the Lord."

"Well, praise God!" said the pastor. "At least that's a step in the right direction."

"The last we knew," said Bela, "Joseph had not yet told his parents that he got saved. There's an element of fear there."

Tivadar nodded. "I can understand that. We'll just keep praying that the Lord will save the whole family."

"Yes, we will," said Gerda. "How old is Stephan now?"

"He's nineteen," Bela replied. "He'll be twenty come August."

"I just have to believe the Lord will answer our prayers and honor our witness to them," said Ravina. She noticed that the pastor's cup was empty. She picked up the coffeepot from next to her on the table and poured him a fresh cup.

The preacher smiled. "Thank you, Ravina." He paused, then asked, "How is Miklos's tour boat business doing?"

"Seems to be doing fine," said Bela. "He makes his regular runs to Vienna and has the boat pretty well loaded with passengers both ways. Of course, he does well hauling freight back and forth, too."

"Well, I'm glad for that." The pastor's eyes strayed to a newspaper lying with the front page up on a small table nearby. The headlines of the *Budapest Herald* told of the king's forthcoming speech on the capitol grounds next Saturday. He looked back at Bela. "What do you think about the king coming to make his speech concerning the three big issues?"

"I'm glad he's coming, but from some of the articles I've read in the papers, I fear he may not give in fully to the demands of the people. There could be trouble."

"That is my opinion, too."

"It frightens me," put in Gerda. "Especially after that incident at the capitol grounds a week ago Friday night. I'm afraid of what the dissident citizens will do if the king hedges on fully making the changes that he should."

"We're all nervous about that," said Ravina. "There's been so much unrest in this country for so long. I sure hope things settle down pretty soon."

Four

On Monday evening, March 20, the sky was inky black and a brittle winter moon hovered over Budapest. Bisecting the city, the Danube River flowed slowly southward, ice crusting along its banks. Moonlight glimmered off the river's surface with a luminous purity.

At the Varda home some two blocks east of the river, the kitchen was alive with the delicious aromas of a thick potato soup and black bread as the family sat down for supper. Immediately, Miklos, Beatrice, and Stephan began discussing King Franz Joseph's upcoming speech, while ten-year-old Joseph listened, his eyes running from father to mother to brother.

"I really don't think he's going to give in to letting the peasants vote," said Beatrice.

Miklos frowned. "Well, he might, but if he does, it will be only the peasants who at least pay some taxes. There are so many who pay none at all."

"Well, if he listens to the majority of the men of parliament, there will be no change at all."

"I think you're right, Mama," said Stephan, who had thick black hair and a handsome, angular face. "Most of the men of parliament don't seem to care at all about the poor people of this country."

"On the other hand," said Miklos, "the king may not let them influence him at all. He knows how serious all three of these issues are. Today is about gone, so it's only four days, now. We'll have the answers to our questions when he makes his speech."

"Papa," said Joseph, "I want to go and hear King Franz Joseph next Saturday." The boy looked a great deal like his brother, except his hair was light brown and there was a generous sprinkle of freckles on his face.

Wiping his mouth with his napkin and swallowing a gulp of strong coffee, Miklos set steady eyes on his youngest son. "No, Joseph. You are not going. It could be very dangerous. You will stay home where you belong and where no harm can come to you."

The boy's face pinched. "But . . . but I

really want to go, Papa. Please? I have learned so much about the king in school, and since I have never seen him, I want to. I want to hear his speech, too." A sly grin spread over his face. "I like the king because his name is Joseph, like mine."

Beatrice took a sip of coffee, ran her gaze to Stephan, then looked at her husband as he said, "No, son. Not this time. Perhaps another time when there is not so much turmoil in this country, you can go and see your namesake when he is here to make a speech. There are so many people in this city and the surrounding areas who are upset about the very things the king is going to discuss on Saturday, there could be real trouble if he doesn't say what they want to hear. It is best that children do not attend the speech."

"But, Papa, I really want to see him, and —"

"I don't want to hear another word about it, Joseph," Miklos said. "Do you understand me?"

Joseph lowered his eyes to his plate, dismay written on his ten-year-old freckled face. "Yes, Papa," he muttered in a barely audible voice.

"Good," said Miklos. The matter was closed as far as he was concerned.

Beatrice reached across the corner of the table and patted Joseph's head. "Your father is right, honey. Children shouldn't be at the speech. Papa and I will go. We'll tell you boys about it when we come home."

Stephan set tender eyes on her. "Mama . . ."

"Mm-hmm?"

"Since it could be dangerous, it would be best if you stay home, too. I'm not a child, so I will go with Papa."

"He's right, dear," said Miklos. "You can stay home with Joseph while Stephan and I attend the speech."

Deep lines penciled themselves across Beatrice's flawless thirty-nine-year-old brow. "Maybe nobody from this family should go. I don't want either of you to get hurt."

Miklos shook his head slightly. "As a citizen of Budapest and as a citizen of Hungary, it is my duty to go, sweetheart. And since Stephan will soon be twenty years old, he needs to get involved in the country's politics."

"Well, you're right about that, but I still have the fear that you and Stephan could get hurt if a riot breaks out."

"Now, sweetheart, don't you let it worry you. I realize, as I already told Joseph, it could get dangerous, but Stephan and I can handle it better than you or Joseph can. And besides, it may go just fine. I really think the king knows the delicate situation he is dealing with, and will act accordingly so there won't be any violence."

Beatrice bit her lips. "I hope you're right."

They finished supper, and afterward, Joseph was helping his mother do the dishes and clean up the kitchen while Miklos and Stephan sat in the parlor and talked further about the three issues the king would be addressing in his speech.

They were talking about the Hungarian tax money that was going to the Austrians when there was a knock at the door. Stephan jumped out of his chair, hurried to the door, and pulled it open. His eyes lit up and he smiled. "Aunt Ravina! Uncle Bela! Come in!"

Beatrice and Joseph had just finished their work in the kitchen, and the ten-year-old dashed to his Aunt Ravina. With her arms wrapped tightly around Joseph, Ravina bent down, put her mouth close to his ear, and asked in a low whisper, "Did you tell your parents yet?"

"Not yet," he whispered back. "I have to find just the right time. I haven't told Stephan, either."

Joseph then hugged his Uncle Bela, who pinched his ear playfully. "Boy, you are growing like a weed!"

"That he is!" said Beatrice, laughing. "He is outgrowing his shoes and his clothing faster then he can wear them out."

Milos chuckled. "If Joseph is like his brother, it will get worse by the time he is thirteen."

"Can you stay for a while?" Beatrice asked.

"Sure," said Ravina. "We're here to make an evening of it, if you have the time."

"Of course we do," said Miklos. "Let's go into the parlor. We've got a nice fire going in the fireplace."

The fire had the parlor warm and cozy, and soon the guests were sitting comfortably, enjoying its warmth.

"It's a cold night out there for being almost the end of March," said Bela.

"Yes," said Miklos. "It seems that old man winter wants to hang on past his usual time."

"I'm sure it will start warming up any day, now," put in Ravina. "Old man winter has got to let go pretty soon."

Miklos looked at his wife. "How about some hot chocolate all around, honey?"

"Sounds good to me," said Beatrice, rising from her chair. "I have some fresh-baked molasses cookies to go with it."

Ravina stood up. "Let me help you, Bea."

The two women hurried out of the parlor and chatted on their way to the kitchen, where Beatrice mixed cocoa powder, sugar, and milk in a large pan and placed it on the cookstove, which was still warm. She opened the lid, tossed a log on the fire, replaced the lid, and pushed the pan to center it over the fire.

At the same time, Ravina was taking crockery mugs down from a shelf, arranging them on a flowered tray. "Mmm. That hot chocolate smells wonderful on a cold night like this."

"Yes, indeed," said Beatrice. "It will be even better when you get some down inside where it can warm you from the inside out."

In the parlor, Bela stretched himself on his soft overstuffed chair near the fire. "Well, Miklos, I assume from what Stephan was telling me that your tour boat is carrying as many passengers as usual for this time of year."

"Yes, it is. But of course, it will get better come mid-May. I'm glad for the income I make by also transporting freight. Really helps when the tourists aren't coming in full force like in the warm time of the year."

Bela nodded. "I'm sure that's true. It's good that you have the freight business, too."

There was a brief silence, then Miklos said, "When you and Ravina knocked on the door, Stephan and I were discussing the speech King Franz Joseph is going to make next Saturday."

Bela raised his eyebrows. "Oh yes. The speech. I am wondering just how much pressure the king will let parliament put on him when it comes to those three issues. I think if he made the decision without worrying over their reaction, he would bring them in line with what the people of this country want and deserve. But you know parliament."

"Yes. They're the ones who changed the laws on these issues in the first place. The king just went along with the changes to keep peace in the government."

"Uncle Bela," spoke up Stephan, "did you know that Burgomaster Zelko rode on Papa's boat to get to Vienna so he could meet with the king?"

"No, I didn't. Did you get to talk to him, Stephan?"

"No. I wasn't on the boat on Monday. I stayed home to do some work around the house that needed to be done. I get paid my regular crewman wages when I stay home, if it's to do work Papa wants done. But Papa told us that he got to talk to Mr. Zelko."

"Briefly, at least," said Miklos. "He shared with me privately that he was going to Vienna to talk to the king about the country's problems, principally the three big issues. He took another tour boat home, apparently. He wasn't on mine."

In the kitchen, Beatrice was stirring the steaming hot chocolate in the pan. "You know, Ravina, I'm a little anxious about all the unrest in our country. I sure hope these problems the king is going to discuss on Saturday don't get out of hand and end up in bloodshed."

"I sure hope not, either," said Ravina. "Bela and I have discussed it at length. We've prayed about it and committed it to the Lord. He has a plan for each of our lives, and we're leaving it in His hands."

"Well, I suppose that's the thing to do," said Beatrice as she began pouring hot chocolate into the mugs Ravina had placed on the flowered tray.

Ravina piled a mound of fragrant

cookies on a blue and white plate.

Beatrice filled the last cup. "All right. Let's get this into the parlor while it's hot."

Soon everyone had a steaming cup in their hands and cookies with it.

The men had been discussing the issue of the peasants not being able to vote, and with everyone settled, Bela brought it up again. The adults gave their opinions on what they thought the king would say about it on Saturday.

Joseph listened silently, then at an opportune moment, he spoke up.

"Papa, I really would like to go to the speech with you and Stephan. I want to see King Franz Joseph real bad."

Miklos was fixing hard eyes on the boy as Beatrice said, "Joseph, it has already been settled that you are not going because of the danger involved if a riot should break out. You and I are staying home."

The Bartoks had their attention on Joseph. They turned it on Miklos when he explained, "We decided that Beatrice would stay home with Joseph so Stephan can go with me. I feel that since Stephan is almost twenty years old, he should attend the speech."

Joseph ran his gaze between the Bartoks. "Uncle Bela, Aunt Ravina, don't you think

Papa and Mama should let me go see King Franz Joseph, since I have never seen him?"

"No, Joseph," said Bela. "Your parents are right. With the potential for trouble at the speech, children should not be there."

"That's right," put in Ravina. "Even your uncle and I aren't going. We decided that we will just read the king's speech in the newspaper and find out what happened that way. Most certainly, children should not be there."

Joseph's countenance fell.

Miklos said, "I don't think the king will say anything to incite the people's anger, but since I can't be absolutely sure, it is best that children not be in the crowd. Now, Joseph, brighten up. Your mother and I are doing what's best for you."

"As long as I can remember, there hasn't been real peace in Hungary," Stephan said. "I wish things could get settled down so there was no more unrest and no more threat of riots and people trying to burn down the capitol building." In a dismayed tone, he added, "Why can't this country just have some peace?"

Bela set gentle eyes on his oldest nephew. "Actually, Stephan, there is little peace in the whole world. Threats of violence or all-out war seem to hang over every country like dark storm clouds."

Beatrice put fingertips to her mouth. "I don't understand why the world is like this."

"The answer is in the Bible, Bea," said Bela. He knew the Vardas kept a Bible in their house, though they never read it. "If you will get your Bible, I'll show you."

Miklos was wishing his wife hadn't made her statement, but it was too late now. He looked at his youngest son. "Joseph, go get the Bible. Where is it, Beatrice?"

"It's in the third drawer from the top in the bureau in our bedroom."

Joseph obediently hurried away to fetch the Bible. Secretly, he was glad Uncle Bela was going to read his parents and his brother something from the Scriptures.

The boy was back in less than a minute and handed the Bible to his uncle. Bela thanked him and began flipping pages.

Bela had everyone's attention as he quickly found the passage he wanted. "I'm going to begin here in Isaiah chapter 59. Through Isaiah's pen, God is speaking to the people of Israel concerning the salvation of their souls, explaining that His hand is not shortened that it cannot save them, nor His ear heavy that it cannot hear. First, I'll read verses 1 and 2 to you. 'Behold, the LORD'S hand is not shortened, that it cannot save; neither his ear heavy, that it cannot hear: But your iniquities have separated between you and your God, and your sins have hid his face from you, that he will not hear.' "

Bela looked up at Beatrice, then ran his gaze to Miklos and Stephan. "So you can see that it was their iniquities and their sins that stood between them and God. Only by repentance of sin and faith toward Him to save them, could the people of Israel have salvation. And nothing has changed. It's the same with sinners today. Ravina and I have talked to you about it many times.

"God sent His only begotten Son into the world to pay the price for sin by dying on the cross of Calvary. In that death, He shed His precious blood to provide the way for sins to be washed away. They buried Jesus that day, but a dead Saviour cannot save anyone. Just as He said He would, He rose from the dead and is alive, looking down from heaven, inviting lost sinners to come to Him for salvation. But, sad to say, the bulk of humanity rejects Him today, unwilling to repent of their sin, even as did the Israelites.

"Now, let me show you the results of their rejection of God's truth and only way of salvation. In the following verses, He speaks of the bloodshed, violence, and destruction in their paths, then says in verse 8, 'The way of peace they know not; and there is no judgment in their goings: they have made them crooked paths: whosoever goeth therein shall not know peace.' "

Bela looked at his oldest nephew. "So you see, Stephan, there is no real, lasting peace in the world's nations because they will not turn to Jesus Christ, believe His gospel, and be saved. They walk crooked paths that lead to violence, destruction, and death. And God says right here that those who walk the crooked paths shall not know peace. Do you understand that?"

"I think so, Uncle Bela."

Bela nodded, then ran his gaze to Miklos and Beatrice. "The human race — except for warmongers — wants and desires peace, especially in their individual hearts and lives." He turned back in the Bible to the New Testament. "Let me show you about this personal peace that the human heart desires. No person can have real, genuine peace unless he or she has peace *with* God. Real, genuine peace can only come *from* almighty God. And unless people have the peace *of* God, they cannot have the real, genuine peace their hearts desire.

"I am going to read you three verses that say exactly what I have just stated. First, we must have peace *with* God. Romans chapter 5, verse 1. Speaking of saved people, it says, 'Therefore, being justified by faith, we have peace with God through our Lord Jesus Christ.' Please note that we can only have peace *with* God through Jesus Christ. Not religious systems or rites. Just Jesus Christ."

Bela flipped farther back in the New Testament. "Now, let's deal with peace *from* God. Colossians chapter 1, verse 2. This is addressed to people who are saved. In God's Word, they are often called saints. 'To the saints and faithful brethren in Christ which are at Colosse: Grace be unto you, and peace, from God our Father and the Lord Jesus Christ.' Did you get that? Peace only comes *from* God our Father and the Lord Jesus Christ. Not from religious systems or rites. This peace from God can only be given to saints — saved people."

Miklos and Beatrice glanced at each other.

Bela turned back one page. "Now, let's

see about the peace *of* God. Philippians chapter 4, verse 7. 'And the peace of God, which passeth all understanding, shall keep your hearts and minds through Christ Jesus.' This book of Philippians is also addressed to the saints. Born-again people. Blood-washed people who have repented of their sin and received the Lord Jesus Christ as their personal Saviour. Note again, that this peace *of* God is keeping their minds through a Person. Not a religious system. Not through religious rites. A Person. That Man who died for the sins of the world on Calvary's cross and came back from the grave — Jesus Christ. So, as I said, peace *with* God, peace *from* God, and the peace *of* God can only be experienced by those who know Christ as personal Saviour. Unless Jesus lives in your heart, you cannot know real peace."

Miklos's features showed the irritation he felt. "Our church teaches differently, Bela. Before our relationship becomes strained, let's talk about something else."

"I think we'd better," agreed Beatrice.

Stephan sat in silence, pondering what he had heard.

Ravina looked at Joseph and smiled at him. Joseph smiled back, saying with his eyes that he was glad Jesus lived in his heart. And Ravina understood the message.

On Thursday morning of that week, Miklos Varda was working on his boat with two of his crewmen. One was his son, Stephan, and the other was Ervin Lujza, who was in his late twenties. Stephan and Ervin were swabbing deck, washing windows, and doing other small jobs.

Miklos was in the pilot's cabin putting a new drive wheel in place, when his attention was drawn to a figure coming up the gangplank from the dock. His muscles tensed. It was Banton Hunyard, and the man's anger showed plainly on his face. Banton Hunyard owned a tour boat that also ran between Budapest and Vienna. He had never been friendly to Miklos.

Not wanting his son or Ervin Lujza to hear whatever Hunyard had to say, Miklos left the pilot's cabin and hurried down to intercept him. He made it just in time. When Hunyard halted at the end of the gangplank, Miklos drew up. "What can I do for you, Banton?"

Hunyard stood immobile, his cold gaze fixed on Miklos. "I want to talk to you!"

"Well, I will talk to you, but not here. Let's go down on the dock."

Hunyard regarded him icily, pivoted, and walked back down the gangplank with Miklos on his heels. They threaded their way among the people milling on the dock, and when they found a relatively private spot, Miklos said, "You're obviously upset, Banton. What's wrong?"

Hunyard was slightly smaller than Miklos. He narrowed his eyes and pressed his lips into a thin line. "You're stealing customers from me in an underhanded way, Miklos, and I want it stopped."

"And just how am I doing that?" demanded Miklos.

"By cutting your prices at times to lure them to your boat and away from mine."

Miklos resisted the desire to unleash his own anger. "I am not trying to take customers from you. It is simply good business to cut the ticket prices now and then. It brings passengers who would not normally ride the tour boats. You should do the same thing. Once those passengers have ridden our boats, they like the trip better than taking the trains, so they come back again and again. If you will join me in it, we can work together and cut our prices at exactly the same time. It will be profitable for both of us."

Hunyard gave him an incredulous look, a

dark scowl lining his brow. "I wouldn't work with you if my life depended on it." He clenched his fists till his knuckles were white ridges.

Keeping cool in spite of his own anger, Miklos Varda warned him in a soft but level voice, "Don't swing at me, Banton. You'll wish you hadn't."

The look in Miklos's eyes was enough to cool Banton Hunyard down a bit. "Your price cutting is hurting my business."

"Are you deaf? I just suggested that we work together and cut our prices at the exact same time. If we did, I wouldn't be hurting your business at all."

"You must be the deaf one," growled Hunyard. "Didn't you hear me say I wouldn't work with you if my life depended on it?" With that, he wheeled and stomped away.

Miklos returned to the pilot's cabin and resumed his work. He was glad that neither Stephan nor Ervin was aware of what had happened.

Late the next day, when Miklos and Stephan entered the Varda house, having made a run to Vienna, they found Beatrice sitting at the kitchen table, weeping. Joseph was at her side, his arm around her.

They both looked up as the two men entered the room. Miklos said, "Sweetheart, what's wrong?"

With shaky hand, Beatrice handed him a telegram as Stephan looked on. "It's from Vivian and Matthias," she said, sniffing and putting a handkerchief to her nose.

Stephan and his father exchanged serious glances, then Miklos read it silently. Stephan waited to hear its message.

Vivian Burtan was Beatrice's younger sister. She and her husband lived in the city of Heviz, which was in western Hungary. The telegram said that Beatrice's widowed father, Edmund Mahart, who lived with the Burtans, had become very ill, and his doctors were saying he might not get better. They were urging Beatrice to come, even if Miklos could not make it.

Miklos finished reading it and handed it to Stephan. Miklos turned to Beatrice, whose features were very pale. As he put his arms around her, she said, "I must go to Papa's side immediately, Miklos."

"Of course," he said, drawing back and looking into her reddened eyes. "I will go with you. Fenyo and Ervin can take the boat on its trips to Vienna and back until I return. Stephan can stay home, walk Joseph to and from school, and do some more odd jobs around the house. You and I can catch the night train to Heviz this evening and be there in the morning."

"Couldn't Joseph and I go with you, Papa?" asked Stephan.

"We don't know how long we'll be gone, son," said Miklos. "It's best that Joseph not miss any school. You know some of the things I was going to have you do around here between trips to Vienna. Just work on them."

"All right," said Stephan. "I sure hope Grandpa gets better fast, and you and Mama can come home."

Miklos and Beatrice quickly packed a couple of suitcases, and Stephan drove them toward the railroad station in the family buggy with Joseph at his side.

While the buggy moved down the dark streets, Miklos said, "Stephan, after you see us off at the depot, I want you to go by Fenyo's house and Ervin's house and tell them what has happened. They are to make the regular runs as usual until I return."

"I will take care of it on the way home, Papa," Stephan assured him.

Soon they were at the railroad station, and the boys stood on the platform next to the train as their parents were about to enter their coach. The whistle blew, and the conductor called for all passengers to board.

The parents hugged their sons, and as they were moving toward their coach, Miklos called over his shoulder, "Joseph, you mind your big brother. Understand?"

"Yes, Papa," called the boy. "I will."

"Tell Grandpa I love him!" called Stephan.

"Me too!" cried Joseph above the din of the depot.

They watched their parents board and saw them sit down near the rear of the coach. Within a few minutes, the whistle blew again, and the big engine hissed steam as it lurched forward and began chugging out of the depot.

Miklos and Beatrice waved at their sons, and the boys waved back.

Five

Ervin Lujza and his wife sat in their parlor
with Stephan and Joseph Varda and listened as Stephan told them of his grandfather's illness having become seriously
worse. He explained that his parents were
on the night train to Heviz, and that his father had asked him to come to the Lujza
home and tell Ervin that he and Fenyo
Mozka would have to make the regular
runs to Vienna as usual. He said that he
would not be able to be on the boat with
them because he had to stay home and take
care of Joseph.

Ervin assured Stephan that he and
Fenyo would keep the boat operating.

The Lujzas both expressed their concern
over Beatrice's father and offered to let the
boys stay with them until their parents returned.

Stephan thanked them for the offer, but

declined, saying it would be best if they were in their own home. The Lujzas said they understood, but as they walked the boys to the door, they told Stephan to let them know if there was anything they could do for them while their parents were away.

At the Mozka home, Fenyo and his wife made the same offer to keep the boys in their home, and assured Stephan they understood when he politely declined. Fenyo told Stephan that he and Ervin would keep business as usual.

As the buggy pulled away from the Mozka house and headed down the street in the direction of the Varda home, Stephan noticed that his little brother was unusually quiet. Joseph sat motionless beside him, staring straight ahead, blankly.

Stephan put his arm around him and pulled him close. "Missing Papa and Mama already, eh, little pal?"

"Uh-huh," said Joseph.

"That's why you're so quiet? You usually have a lot to say."

"I miss Papa and Mama," said Joseph, "but that's not why I'm quiet."

"Oh? Then what is it?"

Joseph looked up at him by the dim light of the street lanterns along the way. "I . . .

well, I was trying to —"

"Trying to what?"

"Well, I was trying to figure a way to ask you something."

Stephan squeezed him tightly. "You don't have to figure a way to ask me *anything*. Come on. Out with it. What do you want to ask me?"

Joseph swallowed hard, glanced at the starlit sky for a moment, then looking back at Stephan, said, "Would . . . would you take me to the capitol grounds tomorrow morning so I can see King Franz Joseph?"

Stephan regarded him with a frown. "Joseph, I can't do that. You heard what Papa and Mama said about your going to the speech. They don't want you there."

"Are *you* going to go?"

"No. I can't. I have to stay home and take care of you."

"But you should be there so you can hear what King Franz Joseph says, Stephan."

They turned the corner onto Pozsony Street, the horse's clopping hooves sending echoes into the night. "I will just have to find out what the king said from someone who goes to hear him. Or I can read about it in Sunday's *Budapest Herald*."

Joseph shook his head. "No, Stephan,

you should really hear him yourself. Papa said you're almost twenty, and you ought to know what's going on. And Papa also said he really didn't think there would be any trouble. So when you go, you should take me with you."

They were nearing the Varda house.

"Little brother," said Stephan, "I know Papa said he thought King Franz Joseph wouldn't say anything that would start trouble, but he also said that he could be wrong. And even if I decided to go, you would have to stay home. Papa and Mama made it clear that you were not to go. But since that would leave you home all by yourself, I won't be going, either."

Joseph thought about Uncle Bela and Aunt Ravina, who said they would not be going to the speech, but kept it to himself. They would keep him at their house, he was sure. Stephan had not thought of them, and Joseph was not about to bring them up.

Stephan turned the buggy into the driveway and guided the horse past the house to the barn at the rear. The horse and buggy were put away, and the boys moved across the yard and mounted the steps of the wide back porch. Joseph was ahead of his brother. He turned the knob, opened the door, and noted that the house was very still and shadows loomed eerily in the kitchen. He stopped and Stephan bumped into him.

"What are you doing, little brother?" asked Stephan.

Joseph shook off the weird feeling the stillness and the shadows had put on him, and moved inside without answering his brother's question.

Stephan stepped to the cupboard, took the glass chimney off the lantern, felt around for a match, and striking it, lit the fuse. The kitchen was immediately aglow and most of the shadows vanished.

But the house was still quiet as a tomb.

Eyes wide, Joseph turned to Stephan. "Boy, it's just not the same with Mama and Papa gone. Especially Mama. She always has a hug for me, and the kitchen is a warm and happy place when she is here."

"You're right," said Stephan. "It won't be the same with Mama not here to cook supper for us either, but she and Papa trust me to do the cooking, so I'll do the best I can. I'll get a fire going and have something on the stove in no time."

"All right. I'll set the table while you're fixing supper."

In a short time the cookstove was putting

off welcome heat, and Stephan had food cooking. Once the simple fare was on the table, the Varda brothers sat down, filled their plates, and began wolfing it down.

Between bites, they talked about their grandfather, and the concern they had that he might not live much longer.

When they were finishing up, Joseph swallowed the last of his mashed potatoes. "Stephan, I really do want to go see King Franz Joseph tomorrow. Won't you please take me? There isn't going to be any trouble. The king will make everybody feel better when he tells them he is going to make changes that will bring them happiness. Please, Stephan? Please?"

Stephan's heartstrings were disturbed by the pathetic look in his little brother's eyes, and he had to check himself when he felt the temptation to give in. There was a lengthy moment of silence, then he shook his head. "No, Joseph. Papa and Mama said they didn't want you to go."

Joseph sensed the weakening in his big brother and was determined to push it further.

A short while later, when the boys were getting ready for bed in their room, Joseph was buttoning his nightshirt and working up tears. When they began to spill down his cheeks, Stephan noticed them. "Hey, little guy, what's wrong?"

Joseph's chin quivered and his voice trembled. "I . . . I really want to go see King Franz Joseph, Stephan." He sniffed, wiped tears from his cheeks with the sleeve of his nightshirt, and released a tremulous sigh. "Ple-e-ease? I've studied so much about him in school. I'm a citizen of Hungary, even though I'm only ten years old. Don't I have a right to see him in person and hear his speech?"

Joseph could see that his big brother was touched by his tears, and this time it took Stephan even longer to find his voice. "Joseph, I can't take you to hear the king. Papa would beat me good, and Mama would really be angry with me, too. Now get in your bed. It's time for both of us to get to sleep."

Head hung low, Joseph pulled back the covers on his bed, slid beneath them, and laid on his side, with his back toward his brother.

Stephan doused the lantern, climbed into his own bed, and said, "Good night, Joseph."

Silence.

"I said good night, Joseph."

A squeaky voice said, "Good night."

Stephan could hear his little brother sniffling in the darkness, and it tore at his heart. Since Joseph was old enough to reach for something he wanted, or even point a finger at it, Stephan had gone to the limit to see that he got what he wanted. He yearned to satisfy him this time, agreeing with the child's reasoning that even though he was only ten years old, he still was a citizen of Hungary and had a right to see the king in person and hear his speech. There probably wouldn't be any trouble, either, but his parents had laid down the directive. Joseph was not to attend the king's speech.

Big brother tossed and turned while little brother continued to sniffle. Making sure Stephan could hear him, Joseph kept it up for almost an hour, hoping that Stephan would give in and tell him he would take him to see King Franz Joseph. But there was no response from Stephan, and finally, Joseph cried himself to sleep.

Only then did Stephan slip into slumber.

As the westbound train thundered through the night, Miklos Varda held his wife's hand. "Sweetheart, please don't cry. Maybe your father will rally and live longer."

Using a handkerchief to dab at her cheeks with her free hand, Beatrice said, "I know it's possible because he has rallied three times before when we thought he would die, but how many times can he do that? I'm afraid this time he won't make it."

Miklos squeezed her hand. "Don't give up. There's still hope."

Beatrice nodded and wiped tears again. "I wish we could have brought the boys with us."

"Me too. But since we don't know how long we will be gone, it's best that we left them home. We wouldn't want Joseph to miss out on his schoolwork."

"You're right, honey," she said. "But I miss both of them already."

"Me too."

Miklos looked out the window at the twinkling lights of a small farm community the train was passing while the click of the wheels filled their ears. "I've been meaning to tell you about the unpleasant confrontation I had with Banton Hunyard yesterday morning. I didn't bring it up last night because I — well, I just forgot about it."

Beatrice looked at him, her brows pinching together. The mention of Hunyard's name brought a sour look to her face.

113

"What did he do?"

Milklos knew that his wife had only met Banton Hunyard on three occasions. She did not like him on the first occasion, but with each following one, she liked him less. "He accused me of stealing customers from him by dropping my ticket prices periodically."

Her frown deepened. "What? That's ridiculous. Doesn't he do the same thing? As far as I know, the other tour boat owners do it the same way you do."

"Well, he doesn't. I simply told him it is good business to drop the prices now and then to draw people to the boat who ordinarily use other means of transportation. I pointed out that once they make the trip north by boat, they get to liking it and come back. I suggested that he do the same, and that he and I even work together so we drop the prices at the same time."

"And?"

Miklos chuckled. "That made him madder yet. I thought he was going to take a swing at me. I put a steely look in my eye and warned him not to do it, and he backed off. Then he stomped away in a huff, saying he wouldn't work with me if his life depended on it."

Beatrice met her husband's gaze with serious eyes. "I don't trust him, Miklos. Keep an eye on him."

"Honey, Banton is a bit strange, but I really don't think he'd do anything to cause trouble."

"Watch him," she said.

Miklos nodded. "I think both of us need to get some sleep, sweetheart." With that, he picked up the two pillows that lay beneath the seat in front of them and handed her one. Both of them settled back and soon fell asleep to the steady rocking of the coach and the rhythmic sound of the clicking wheels beneath them.

Beatrice awakened sometime in the middle of the night with a strange sense of uneasiness pervading her heart. She thought on it a moment, then said in a low whisper, "It's probably because Papa is so sick. I've got to take Miklos's approach and think positive on this."

Both Vardas were fully awake long before dawn on Saturday morning, and the train chugged into the Heviz railroad station just after sunrise. They hired a buggy to take them to the Burtan home, and when they knocked on the door, Matthias and Vivian welcomed them warmly.

When the hugging was done, Beatrice

asked about her father.

"He's still sleeping," said Vivian. "I hate to tell you this, but I'm afraid he's getting even worse than he was when we sent the telegram. We have him under the care of both Dr. Mohosz and Dr. Ralaton. At times like this, I wish Heviz was large like Budapest, so we would have a hospital. But at least one doctor or the other comes to look in on him every day." Tears misted her eyes. "I . . . I'm just afraid he's not going to be with us very long."

"Both doctors say Grandpa could rally again," said Matthias. "You know, like he's done before. I keep telling her he will do it again."

Beatrice managed a weak smile. "Miklos keeps telling me the same thing. We just have to keep hoping."

"Of course, sis, we'll just keep hoping," said Vivian, putting an arm around her waist. "How long can you stay?"

"We'll stay till we see how Grandpa's doing for sure. If . . . if he doesn't rally, we want to be here when — well, you know."

Vivian looked at her husband. "Honey, I'll take them to their room, then I'll head for the kitchen and get breakfast started."

Matthias nodded. "I'll get the fire going in the cookstove."

Vivian led the tired travelers down a long hall into a sunny bedroom. "You can wash up and refresh yourselves," she said. "I'm so glad you're both here. It helps to have loved ones close in a time of heartache."

"It relieves my mind to be here with you," Beatrice said, kissing her sister's cheek.

Vivian headed for the door. "I'll get breakfast going. It'll be ready in about half an hour." She closed the door.

When Vivian was gone, Miklos placed their small pieces of hand luggage on the bed and began opening them. Beatrice removed her bonnet and travel-wrinkled dress while Miklos took out a fresh shirt from his overnight bag along with his shaving soap, cup, brush, and razor.

Beatrice took the pins from her hair and finger combed it in front of the mirror. She recoiled it into a tight bun at the nape of her neck and put the pins in again. Bathing her face at the washstand also helped relieve some of the tension and weariness.

Deciding he would go ahead and shave with the cold water in the washbowl, Miklos did so hurriedly. When he was finished, he put on the shirt he had taken from the travel bag.

Beatrice took a plain cotton dress from

her bag, shook the wrinkles out of it, and after putting it on, smoothed it down. When they opened the door, they were greeted with the aromas of breakfast cooking, and followed them to the pleasant kitchen where Vivian had the meal ready.

Matthias came in, saying he had just checked on Grandpa and he was still sleeping.

While the foursome was eating, Matthias said, "We read in the Heviz newspaper that King Franz Joseph is making a speech on the capitol grounds in Budapest this morning. It said he is going to deal with the country's three main issues of discontent: the language change, the peasants' right to vote, and the large amount of our tax money that is going to the Austrians. Do you know of anything else?"

"That's it," said Miklos. "He knows if he doesn't do something in all three of these areas, he's got real trouble on his hands."

"I'm worried, though," said Matthias.

Miklos swallowed a mouthful of scrambled eggs. "About what?"

"I'm afraid the king has too much pressure from men in parliament who put these issues into law to begin with. I really wonder if he will go far enough with these issues to pacify the people and to keep those who have a bent toward dissidence from rioting."

"Matthias, I'm sure the king understands the delicate situation, and I feel reasonably sure that he will act accordingly." Miklos took a sip of hot coffee.

Matthias raised his eyebrows. "*Reasonably* sure?"

Miklos shrugged, cocked his head sideways. "Well, I sure hope he will act accordingly. Certainly Franz Joseph doesn't want riots on his hands."

"I don't think he would choose riots, Miklos," said Vivian, "but I'm wondering if he has the fortitude to go against parliament's grain to the point that the dissidents will be satisfied."

"I sure hope he does," put in Beatrice. "The last we heard, the police haven't caught all of those men who started the fire at the capitol building. If they are still on the loose, I guarantee you, there's going to be trouble if the king doesn't come across with good news about these issues at hand."

"Could be real trouble," mused Matthias.

Beatrice nodded. "Our Joseph very much wanted to go to the speech and see the king, but Miklos and I agreed that he shouldn't go, just in case there is trouble."

"That's good," said Vivian.

"Until we received your telegram about Grandpa being so ill, Stephan was going to attend the speech with me, and Beatrice was going to keep Joseph home with her," said Miklos.

"Well, I guess you will have to read the newspapers to find out what happened," said Matthias. "Just like the rest of us."

Miklos chuckled. "You're right about that."

When breakfast was over, Matthias left the kitchen to check on the patient. He returned, saying they could go in. Matthias and Vivian took Miklos and Beatrice into Grandpa Edmund Mahart's room, where they found the ailing old man with a faint smile on his face. He set his bleary eyes on Beatrice, and she rushed to the bed, bent over, kissed his wrinkled cheek, and embraced him.

Tears filled Beatrice's eyes as she looked at her father, and though she did not voice it, she realized how feeble he had become since she saw him only three months ago. She gave him Stephan and Joseph's message of love, which made him smile again. When she stepped aside so Miklos could embrace Grandpa, she could tell he was thinking the same thing about his fragility.

Edmund Mahart talked to Beatrice and Miklos briefly, while Vivian fed him what little breakfast he felt like eating. Soon his eyes were drooping, and he fell asleep.

The two couples left the room, and while they walked down the hall, they discussed Grandpa's serious condition. Both Vivian and Beatrice were weeping, and their husbands tried to comfort them.

At sunrise in Budapest, Stephan Varda rolled over in his bed and ran his gaze to his little brother. Joseph had his back toward him with the covers up to his ears and lay perfectly still. Stephan slipped out of his bed quietly. Wanting to let his little brother sleep as long as possible, he picked up his clothes and shoes and tiptoed out of the room to dress in the kitchen.

However, Joseph was just playing possum. As soon as Stephan closed the door, Joseph bounded out of the bed. While putting on his clothes slowly, he tried to come up with a plan that would successfully convince his brother to take him to the king's speech.

In the kitchen, Stephan soon had breakfast almost ready and was about to go to the bedroom when he heard footsteps at the kitchen door and turned around to see Joseph standing there, fully dressed.

"Well, good morning, little brother," Stephan said with a broad smile on his lips. "I was about to come and wake you up. Breakfast is almost ready."

Joseph looked at the clock on the wall. It was a few minutes after seven. Moving closer to his big brother, he said, "Stephan, when you and Papa were planning on going to King Franz Joseph's speech, I heard Papa say that you should get to the capitol grounds at least an hour and a half early so you could find a good spot close to where the platform will be. I know you won't want to take the horse and buggy, so since we'll have to walk, if we eat breakfast right away, we can still be there by eight-thirty."

Stephan shook his head, blinking his eyes, then set them on his brother. "You just don't give up, do you? I told you that I'm not taking you. It could be dangerous, and that's why Mama and Papa don't want you to go. Come on. Get up to the table. It's time to eat."

Joseph was quiet when they first started eating, then looked across the table at Stephan. "Tell me something."

"What?"

"If it's supposed to be so dangerous at the speech, why would Papa want to go? And especially, why would he take you with him?"

Stephan laid his fork down and scrubbed a palm over his face. "Chances are pretty good that nothing bad is going to happen, little fellow, but there's no guarantee. Papa felt good enough about it that he didn't worry about going himself, nor did he worry about taking me with him."

"See there! Nothing bad is going to happen. I want to go."

Stephan picked up his fork and stabbed a slice of sausage. "Eat your breakfast, Joseph Varda. I'm not taking you to the speech."

Joseph's gaze was unflinching. "You just don't want me to have any happiness at all."

Stephan frowned and looked at him with puzzlement. "It's not that at all, Joseph. Don't you understand? I just don't want something bad to happen to you. Neither do Mama and Papa."

Joseph burst into tears and shoved his chair back from the table. Putting his hands to his face, he sobbed like his heart would break in two.

Stephan shook his head and bit down on

the inside of his cheek.

"Please, Stephan," sobbed Joseph, putting a plaintive, heartrending sound in his voice and letting the tears stream down his face. "Please, please, please take me. Nothing bad is going to happen. I'll never ask you to do anything for me again. Ever! You just have to understand how important this is to me! It would make me so happy to get to see King Franz Joseph. I'm sure other children in my class at school will get to go."

Stephan shook his head again, wiping a palm over his eyes.

Seeing that his brother was weakening, Joseph sniffed and let tears drip off his chin. "I'm going to be so embarrassed when I go to school Monday, and many of my classmates tell about getting to see and hear the king. Please, Stephan! Ple-e-e-e-ease!"

Stephan swallowed the lump that had risen in his throat. He thought about the last ten years of his life. In all that time, he reminded himself, he had never denied his little brother anything. From the day Joseph was born, he had been the apple of his big brother's eye. During the last six years, especially, the brothers had spent countless hours together, and Stephan had taught him and trained him in many, many ways.

As Stephan beheld his little brother's tearstained face and listened to his piteous pleas, something collapsed within him. He breathed a huge sigh. "All right, all right, Joseph. I may live to regret this, but I will take you."

Joseph's eyes widened and he drew a shuddering breath.

"You will?"

Stephan closed his eyes and nodded. "Yes. I'll take you. The chance of something bad happening at the speech is pretty small. Papa said so himself."

Joseph leaped off his chair, jumped up and down, and shouted for joy. He dashed to his brother, threw his arms around him, and cried, "Oh, Stephan, thank you! Thank you! You're the best big brother in all the world!"

Stephan rose from his chair, gripped Joseph by the shoulders, and looked square into his eyes. "You must never tell Mama and Papa that I took you. Understand?"

"Oh yes! I understand. I promise. I will never tell them," vowed Joseph.

Six

A few white clouds littered the azure sky over Budapest, and the morning sun was lifting higher, shortening the shadows of trees and buildings.

It was just after eight o'clock when a police wagon drew up in front of the Savoy Mansion Hotel, which was the city's finest. It stood five stories high and was within half a block of the Danube River.

Two uniformed officers were on the seat of the enclosed wagon. The driver hopped down, hurried to the rear, and opened the door. "Here we are, sir."

Markus Zelko stepped out. "I shouldn't be more than a half hour or so."

As Zelko headed for the large double doors that led to the hotel's lobby, he noted the king's royal carriage parked close by. Two royal guards stood at its side in their impressive red and black uniforms.

They both nodded at him politely and he nodded back.

Entering the lobby, Zelko made his way toward the winding staircase. He climbed to the fifth floor and moved down the wide hallway toward the king's special suite. Two more royal guards stood at the suite door, one on each side and their backs to the wall.

They noted Zelko's presence on the floor instantly and watched him as he came toward them. When he drew up, one of the guards said, "Good morning, Burgomaster Zelko. The king is ready to see you."

The other guard opened the door and spoke to another guard inside. "The burgomaster is here."

The inside guard ushered Zelko through a large, beautifully furnished room to a second door. He tapped on it, and another guard opened the door. When he saw the burgomaster, he said, "Good morning, sir. Please come in. King Franz Joseph is waiting for you."

When Zelko stepped in, he ran his admiring gaze over the spacious room to the large windows, where the king stood. The windows offered an excellent view of the city and the beautiful blue Danube.

Franz Joseph told the guard to leave

them alone, and he stepped back and closed the door.

Zelko noted the plush Mediterranean furniture and the thick carpeting on the floor that ran from wall to wall. There were expensive paintings on the walls, blending richly with the luxuriant tapestries.

Franz Joseph gestured toward a nearby chair. "Please sit down, Burgomaster Zelko. I will remain standing if you don't mind. I love the view of the river from here."

"Certainly, sir," said the burgomaster, removing his hat as he sat down.

The king let his gaze rest on the river for a moment and finally turned around to face Zelko. "You're wondering about the approach I will be taking in my speech."

"Yes, I am, sir. I have heard much talk here in the city, and the people are divided in their opinions as to whether you will grant their wishes or not. About half say you will let the majority of parliament dictate your decisions on the issues, and the rest have confidence that in spite of parliament's feelings in these matters, you will stand with the people."

Franz Joseph rubbed his chin. A moment passed, then he looked at Zelko. "I have it worked out so that both government and the people will be satisfied."

Zelko stared at him, his mouth pulled into a thin line. "Sir, I mean no offense, but it sounds like a compromise to me, and I strongly advise you not to cut corners. I have a hard time believing that you can satisfy both the people and parliament."

"I have worked hard on this, Burgomaster," the king said evenly. "My speech is ready, and I believe the people will accept what I have to tell them."

"I hope so, sir, because if the people are not satisfied, there will be trouble. I mean *serious* trouble. We have now apprehended every man who was in the dissidents who set fire to the capitol building and killed those two officers. They are behind bars and will be facing murder charges. But believe me, there are plenty more of their ilk out there on the streets. They will be on the capitol grounds, waiting to hear what you have to say."

Franz Joseph turned his back toward Zelko and set his eyes on the rippling waters of the Danube. "I do not foresee any trouble, Burgomaster, but just in case — you *are* prepared to squelch any troublemakers, aren't you?"

"Yes, sir. In addition to these palace guards who have accompanied you from Vienna, there will be a mounted police unit with your royal carriage. At the capitol grounds, there will be a large number of police officers moving about the crowds with nightsticks and rifles, as well as sidearms. Chief Serta and I have also alerted the commandant of the army camp outside the city that there could be trouble, and he will have troops ready to act if needed. He will have two men at the capitol grounds prepared to ride to the camp and call for help if the occasion arises."

"Good. We most certainly need to be prepared, but I feel quite confident that the people will accept my proposals on these touchy issues."

Zelko rose to his feet and moved toward the king. "All right, sir. I hope you are right. But I have arranged with Chief Serta to be at your side, along with a good number of officers positioned next to the platform. If trouble should raise its ugly head, they will quickly usher you and your palace guards to the royal carriage and see that you are taken from the scene immediately. I trust this meets with your approval."

Franz Joseph smiled. "Of course. I very much appreciate your looking out for me."

"Good. Then I will be going, sir. You will see me hovering close to you, also, upon your arrival at the capitol grounds."

The king walked with Zelko toward the door. "I will be glad when this speech is over and done with so I can put my mind on other things. With the people of Hungary and their government leaders both happy, I can tend to some more pressing problems in Austria."

Markus Zelko had serious doubts that both the people and the government leaders were going to be happy with the compromise King Franz Joseph had worked out, but he said no more. He had already stated his feelings on the matter.

It was almost eight-thirty when Stephan and Joseph Varda arrived at the capitol grounds in downtown Budapest. Stephan's right hand lay on his little brother's shoulder as they moved across the grounds toward the spot where the makeshift platform stood.

Running his gaze around them, Stephan said, "We didn't get here any too early, Joseph. There's already quite a crowd. I see a place close by the platform. Let's get over there quick."

As the boys threaded their way through the crowd, Joseph's eyes were wide. He noted the large number of policemen and focused on the rifles they carried, as well as the holstered revolvers on their belts and the nightsticks.

Stephan listened closely as they passed by small groups of men and women, trying to pick up what they were saying about the issues to be discussed by the king. He heard comments on both sides. Stephan was a bit disturbed that so far, he had seen no children in the crowd at all. Apparently their parents were being cautious. He told himself that certainly King Franz Joseph was not going to do anything that would bring trouble.

Abruptly, Joseph pointed to a small group of people. "See there, Stephan? Two of my friends from school are here."

When Stephan spotted the two boys, he felt better. Not everybody was expecting things to get dangerous.

A brass band was assembling on one side of the platform as the Varda brothers drew near.

Stephan led Joseph to a spot beside a man and woman who both had gray hair. "Hello, boys," said the man. "Are your parents with you?"

"No, sir," replied Stephan. "They had to go to Heviz to see our grandfather. He is very sick."

"Oh. I'm sorry to hear that. So you boys are here alone?"

"Yes, sir."

The stately gentleman smiled. "My name is Lajos Suddard. And this is my wife, Trina."

"Hello, boys," said Trina. "And what are your names?"

"I am Stephan Varda, and this is my little brother, Joseph. He is ten years old."

Lajos Suddard smiled at the child. "Joseph, eh? Sort of like the king."

"Uh-huh. That's why I like him. I have never seen the king before, and this is why Stephan brought me."

Trina set admiring eyes on Stephan. "You're a good big brother, son. Most big brothers your age wouldn't have time for a ten-year-old little brother."

Joseph's eyes brightened. "He's the best big brother in all the world, ma'am!"

Stephan blushed and messed up Joseph's hair. "That might be stretching it a bit."

"You brought me here today to see the king. That shows what a good big brother you are."

Lajos was studying Stephan's handsome features. Stephan felt it and met his gaze.

"I've seen you somewhere on more than

133

one occasion. I'm trying to think where it was."

Stephan grinned. "Do you ever ride the tour boats up to Vienna?"

"Tour boats! Yes, we do. That's it. You are a crewman on Miklos Varda's — Oh, sure. *Varda*. It didn't sink in until now. You're Miklos's son."

"Yes, sir."

Lajos started asking questions about the boat, and while Stephan was answering them, Joseph looked around at the growing crowd, once again eyeing the police officers and their weapons with awe. While doing a panorama of the capitol grounds, his attention was drawn to a new office building that was under construction east of the imposing capitol building with its huge pillars and golden dome.

Joseph could not remember ever seeing a building of such size under construction. The framework was up and the roof was on. Building materials of various descriptions were stacked around, including three huge piles of bricks. People were moving about the construction site, looking it over.

Turning to his brother, who was explaining something to Lajos Suddard about the boat's steam engine, Joseph

134

tugged at his sleeve. "Stephan . . ."

"Excuse me, sir," Stephan said to Lajos. "Joseph, haven't you been taught not to interfere when adults are talking?"

"Oh. I'm sorry."

"Well as long as you have my attention, what is it?"

The child pointed to the construction site. "Do we have time for you to take me over there so I can see what it looks like when a big building is being built? I've never seen one before."

Always wanting to please his little brother, Stephan said, "There's time, Joseph, and I would take you, but we would lose our places here. You want to be close to the platform, don't you?"

"Tell you what, Stephan," spoke up Lajos, "Mrs. Suddard and I will save your places for you. Go ahead. Take him over there."

"Thank you, sir," said Stephan. "I'll finish telling you about the engine when we get back. We won't be gone long."

Stephan took Joseph by the hand and led him through the crowd to the construction site. When they reached it, many others were looking it over. Stephan explained that it was to be a brick building, pointing out the three huge piles of bricks. He also showed him the stacks of lumber and window frames, explaining how it all went together.

Joseph was impressed with what he saw, and asked other questions. Some Stephan could answer, and others he could not. After a few minutes, he said, "We'd better get back to our places, Joseph. It won't be long till the king arrives."

Joseph smiled up at his big brother. "Thanks for bringing me over here, Stephan."

He messed Joseph's hair up. "You're welcome. Let's go."

Joseph pointed himself in the direction of the platform and darted ahead of his brother into the crowd.

"Joseph!" called Stephan. "Slow down!"

Already amid a group of people, the child paused, looked over his shoulder between them, grinned, and let his big brother catch up to him.

"Joseph," scolded Stephan, "don't be running ahead of me. You could get lost in this crowd. Give me your hand."

Reluctantly, Joseph extended his hand, allowing Stephan to take it, and together they threaded their way through the tightly pressed throng toward their reserved spot. As they were pushing and shoving, Joseph suddenly pointed ahead. "Look, Stephan! It's Janos!"

Following his little brother's finger, Stephan saw the face of his close friend Janos Kudra. They had gone through school together since both were six years old. Janos was with three other young men and happened to look Stephan's direction just as he and Joseph drew near.

Smiling broadly, Janos said, "Well, if it isn't Joseph Varda and his aging big brother!"

Laughing, Stephan playfully swung a fist at his friend's chin, missing it by a fraction of an inch. "Aging big brother, eh?"

"Well, you'll turn twenty almost three weeks before I do. You're the old man!"

Being acquainted with Janos's three friends, Stephan spoke to them, then turned his attention to his little brother and Janos as the latter clipped Joseph playfully on the chin. "Hey, little pal, you're really growing fast, aren't you?"

Joseph giggled and punched him in the stomach the same way.

Janos bent over, forcing a breath from his mouth as if the boy had hurt him, then raised palms forward. "Please, Joseph, I give up! Don't hit me anymore!"

Joseph laughed. Janos put an arm

around his shoulder and said to Stephan, "So how do you think the speech is going to affect this crowd?"

"Favorably, I hope."

"Me too. Are your parents here?"

"No. They're in Heviz with our grandfather. He's pretty sick."

"Oh. Sorry to hear that. So it's just you and Joseph."

"Mm-hmm. I wouldn't have brought him, but he is a great admirer of King Franz Joseph and has never seen him in person. We had better be going. Some people are holding our places right up there by the platform."

Janos grinned. "You two must have come plenty early to get a spot that close. What did you do, get up before dawn?"

Stephan chuckled. "Not quite. But we did come early so my little brother could see the king close-up."

"Well, I wish I could get that close to him," Janos said, squeezing Joseph's arm. "How about trading places with me?"

Joseph lightly punched him in the stomach again, laughing. "No way, Janos!" Then he said to Stephan, "We'd better get going."

Janos told the Varda brothers he would see them later, and watched as Stephan took his little brother's hand and led him forward, weaving through the tight press.

The brass band struck up a lively tune as Stephan and Joseph finally drew up to Lajos and Trina Suddard. Lajos pointed in the direction of the street. "Look, Joseph! It's the king!"

All eyes in the crowd were now turned that direction. The royal carriage was coming across the capitol grounds with the mounted escort of palace guards, plus one in the driver's seat and another sitting inside next to the king. Surrounding the carriage and the mounted palace guards were a dozen policemen on horseback. Ten coaches followed, bearing the men of parliament. At the spot near the platform where the carriage and coaches would draw to a halt, a unit of police officers stood ready for the king to arrive. With them were Burgomaster Markus Zelko and chief of police, Akman Serta.

The royal carriage drew up and the band raised the volume of their instruments as King Franz Joseph stepped from the carriage, preceded by the guard who had ridden inside with him. There were cheers and boos from the crowd as Zelko and Serta quickly flanked the king and let him stay a half step ahead of them as he mounted the steps of the platform.

Joseph Varda's eyes were dancing with joy as he grabbed his brother's arm. He jumped up and down. "Stephan! He looks just like his pictures! Oh, this is so neat!"

Stephan was pleased to see his little brother so excited. He thought of his parents and felt a stab of guilt because he had gone against their orders. But the elation he saw in his little brother at that moment quickly dispelled his guilt feeling. Joseph had now seen the king, and when the speech was over and Stephan took his little brother home, no harm would have been done. Joseph could secretly treasure his memory and would always be grateful to his big brother for it.

The cheers and boos continued coming from the crowd as King Franz Joseph stood between Chief Serta and Burgomaster Zelko while the men of parliament formed an arc behind the platform. The band reached its climax, closed off with a drumroll, and those in the crowd cheering the king went quiet. The dissenters continued to vocally show their disdain for the king.

Chief Akman Serta stepped forward to the podium, raised his hands, and in a loud voice, commanded them to be quiet. The noise continued, and the policemen in the crowd began waving their rifles and night-sticks while scowling menacingly at the dissenters.

Stephan Varda was surprised to see the dissenters so vocal.

Joseph observed the scene in puzzlement. He looked up at Stephan. "Why don't those people like the king?"

Stephan shrugged his shoulders, seeing no need to go into it at that moment.

As the dissenters continued their booing and hissing, one policeman moved up to a man who was among the loudest and raised his nightstick in a threatening manner. The man suddenly went quiet, and within a few seconds, all the dissenters followed suit.

Chief Serta said loudly, "There is to be no more such demonstration! We will have order here!" With that, he stepped back.

Burgomaster Markus Zelko moved up, spoke a few loud words backing Chief Serta's warning, then asked the king to come to the podium and speak to his subjects.

An obviously nervous King Franz Joseph stepped to the podium, greeting the people in the name of the crown, then speaking in Magyar, said loud enough for all to hear,

"As all of you know, I am here today to clarify three items of law in this country, which have been a subject of debate ever since they were introduced into law several months ago.

"I will speak to you first concerning the change made by parliament, with my approval, in replacing the Magyar language with the German language as the official legal language of Hungary."

A few boos were heard, and the policemen moved toward the guilty parties, raising their nightsticks. This quieted them, and King Franz Joseph proceeded, saying that second, he would address the issue of peasants no longer being able to vote, followed with some explanations as to why much of the Hungarian tax money was being used to aid Austria.

There was relative silence as the king went on.

"Let me first speak about the language change. Parliament and I have agreed to concede in certain areas where the legal language will go back into Magyar." He smiled.

Hearing the words "certain areas," the dissenters in the crowd began looking at each other, frowning and shaking their heads.

"These areas," said the king, "will be in personal matters as follows. Magyar once again will be the official language for marriage licenses, wills, and adoption papers. In all other matters of law, including court records, government documents, newspapers, books published, and business papers, German will remain the official language."

The dissenters immediately began shouting at the king, saying they wanted the official language changed back in all matters to Magyar and the German language thrown out.

The smile left Franz Joseph's face as the dissenters' voices grew louder.

Chief Akman Serta moved up beside the king and told them to get quiet.

A man in his late twenties who stood near the platform took two steps closer and shook his fist at the king. "You're crooked and underhanded, Franz Joseph! You don't care about the people! All you care about is pleasing parliament!"

Quickly a policeman moved up and struck the man with his nightstick, knocking him down. Another man close by screamed at the policeman, clenching his fists. A policeman stepped up quickly, cracked him over the head with his nightstick, and the man fell face down, unconscious. A dissenter swore angrily at that policeman, calling him a vile name. The officer sidestepped him and dropped him with the nightstick.

Loud voices erupted from the crowd, which now was in an uproar.

Stephan Varda leaned close to his little brother, who was showing fear. "It's looking dangerous, Joseph. I'm taking you home."

Joseph nodded. "Let's go."

As the Varda brothers pushed their way through the crowd toward the street with Stephan holding Joseph's hand, the people were milling about, shouting at each other angrily. Stephan caught sight of King Franz Joseph being escorted to his carriage by Chief Serta and Burgomaster Zelko, with policemen and palace guards surrounding them.

Suddenly a gunshot was heard. People began running every direction. Everything was tight, and the Varda brothers were jostled repeatedly by the frightened, enraged crowd. Just ahead of Stephan and Joseph, a big man was shoved hard by two men equally as large who were railing at him. He staggered backward, slamming into Stephan.

The impact of the body blow caused Stephan to go down, losing his grip on Joseph's hand. The big man fell on top of him, yelling at the men who had shoved him. Stephan struggled to free himself of the man's weight.

On his feet after a moment, Stephan looked around while the sound of another gunshot split the air. There were more screams and shouts as people continued to stampede in every direction like wild, frightened animals.

Joseph was nowhere to be seen. Panic rose in Stephan's mind. Crying out Joseph's name, he frantically fought the crowd, trying to catch sight of him in the mad mixture of dashing bodies. Battling his way forward, he continued to cry out his little brother's name, but his progress was slow. Once more Stephan was knocked to the ground by men fighting each other. Fists were flying and men were on the ground wrestling. Policemen battled with dissenters, some of them on the ground with their opponents, still swinging their nightsticks.

Scrambling to his feet, Stephan caught a glimpse of Joseph, who was wailing in terror while being carried along by the press. He was some forty or fifty feet ahead of Stephan. Joseph disappeared from Stephan's view again as he continued to struggle against the maddened crowd.

Seconds later, Stephan saw Joseph once more, but instantly, the boy was swept from his sight. "Jose-e-e-eph!" he cried. "Jose-e-e-eph!"

There was another gunshot, and the roar of the crowd beat in Stephan's ears as he struggled to get to his little brother. Soon he caught another glimpse of him. Joseph was looking back at his big brother, wailing and terrified.

Suddenly, Stephan was knocked off his feet again, and a man and two screaming women fell on top of him. Ejecting wordless cries, Stephan tried to free himself. After what seemed a lifetime, he was finally on his feet again, pushing in the direction where he last saw his little brother.

But he could not see Joseph anywhere.

There were more gunshots. The police were clubbing dissenters as fast as they could. The crowd was totally out of control.

Intense fear and icy hysteria had Stephan Varda in their grip. He knew he was in the midst of a full-fledged riot.

Seven

As Stephan Varda thrust himself through the wild crowd toward the last spot where he had seen Joseph, it seemed he was enmeshed in a nightmare. It was like he was having one of those terrifying dreams in which the sleeper is trying to reach a certain place and can only move in slow motion.

Except this was not a dream. It was real.

A wordless whimper escaped his lips. "Oh, Joseph, where are you?"

Gasping for breath and fighting his way amid the boiling horde, he ran his anxious eyes from side to side. Soon he was almost to the construction site on the east side of the capitol grounds.

Suddenly, Stephan saw a mob of dissenters at the brick piles in front of the framed-up office building, throwing bricks at policemen and others in the crowd.

Men, women, children, and police officers were falling under the barrage of hurling bricks.

There was more rifle fire, and dissenters began to go down. Others were being clubbed to the ground with police nightsticks. It was bedlam. Screams, cries, and shouts filled the air. People were running every direction.

Stephan was frantic to find Joseph. A tight band squeezed his heart as he dodged running people and cried out Joseph's name repeatedly. Suddenly two big men were charging toward him. He was in the path they had chosen to get away from the gunfire. One of them set wild eyes on him and bawled, "Get out of my way!"

Stephan had nowhere to go. He was closed in on the right and left, and someone was shoving him from behind. The big man made a fist and cracked Stephan solidly on the jaw. He landed on his back, stunned, but was aware of people falling on top of him. The coppery taste of blood filled his mouth. He opened his eyes and stared through a blue haze at the legs of people running past him. He started to get up and was struck in the face by a foot as a man stumbled over him.

Stephan shook his head in an effort to

148

clear the haze from his eyes, and rose up on his knees. A trickle of blood touched the corner of his left eye, and he used his sleeve to wipe it away. The man's heel had cut Stephan's forehead. He started to get up and was once again bowled over from behind by someone else who was on the run.

Stephan heard someone shout that the army had arrived, and suddenly, guns were roaring like a string of giant firecrackers. People were stumbling over him, and some were stepping on him. As if by instinct, he rolled into a ball and covered his head with his hands, protecting himself as best he could.

The swarming force of Hungarian soldiers soon had the riot quelled.

From his position on the ground, Stephan tried to stay the thin flow of blood on his forehead with his shirt sleeve while looking around. A large number of dissenters were taken into custody by the soldiers. Most of the crowd left in a hurry, but some stayed because they had loved ones and friends who were lying on the ground. Policemen and soldiers moved about the capitol grounds, checking on the many men, women, and children who were down. Some were injured or wounded.

And some were dead.

There were no deaths among the police officers, but some were injured seriously.

A frenzied Stephan Varda, hands, arms, and face bruised, struggled to his feet and staggered about, in search of his little brother. He asked soldiers and policemen if they had seen Joseph, giving his description. But none could say they had.

He found himself staggering in the direction of the framed-up office building, and suddenly he saw two soldiers bending over a small form near a brick pile. One of the soldiers picked up the limp form, and shock waves bolted through Stephan when he recognized that it was Joseph.

An anguished cry escaped his lips as he stumbled toward them. Joseph lay perfectly still in the soldier's arms. His face was smeared with blood and his eyes were closed.

The soldiers eyed Stephan as he drew up and said in a strained voice, "He's my brother, sir. Is he —"

"He's dead, son. A flying brick struck him in the head."

It was like Stephan was in another nightmare. But again, it was all too real. Fixing his unbelieving eyes on the lifeless form, he broke down and sobbed. The other soldier put an arm around Stephan's shoulders, squeezing tight.

Still sobbing, with tears washing his dusty, blood-caked face, Stephan reached toward Joseph's body. "May I . . . may I hold him, sir?"

The soldier relinquished the small body into Stephan's arms. He clasped the lifeless form close to his chest and slowly sank to his knees, a low moan rising from the depths of his soul. The moan intensified to a wail as he looked down into the beloved face of his little brother, now pale in death.

What have I done? Oh, what have I done? Papa and Mama will never forgive me! I disobeyed them. Now Joseph is dead. Now I must face their wrath. Oh, what have I done?

Suddenly a familiar voice penetrated his thoughts. "Stephan . . ."

He looked up to see his friend Janos Kudra looking down at him, sympathetic sorrow creasing his face and filling his eyes. "What happened?"

Stephan tried to speak, but choked on the first word.

Taking a step closer, one of the soldiers looked at Janos. "The boy was hit in the head with a flying brick, sir. He didn't live long afterward."

151

Janos bit his lower lip and laid a hand on Stephan's shoulder. "I'm sorry."

Stephan raised his tormented eyes to his friend. "Why — why wasn't it me, Janos? I wish it was me. Not Joseph. I will live with the horror of this forever."

Janos was without words.

Tears flooded Stephan's red-rimmed eyes as he lowered his head and pressed it on the breast of his little brother. "Forgive me, Joseph. I'm so sorry!"

As a wail escaped Stephan's lips, one of the soldiers looked at Janos. "What are the brothers' names?"

Janos told him, also giving the Vardas' home address.

The soldier wrote down the information, then asked if he knew where the parents were. Janos explained that Mr. and Mrs. Varda were out of town.

Stephan raised his head, having regained his composure to a degree. The other soldier said, "Stephan, we need to take the boy's body to the chief of police to report his death. Chief Serta is close by, over here."

Stephan nodded and rose to his feet, still clutching the small body to his chest. Shoulders slumped and head bent down, he followed the soldiers with Janos's arm around him.

When they reached the spot where Chief Akman Serta was standing with two of his officers at his side while he talked with a weeping woman whose husband had been killed in the riot, they waited quietly. Janos kept squeezing Stephan's arm in an attempt to show his sympathy.

Soon both of the officers walked away with the weeping woman. As the soldiers stepped up to the chief, Serta's eyes went immediately to the small body in Stephan's arms. He pulled his lips tight. "Oh no. Another child."

"Yes, sir," said one of the soldiers. "This young man is the dead boy's brother. His name is Stephan Varda. The boy's name was Joseph."

Two more police officers drew up and flanked their chief. Serta nodded at them, acknowledging their presence, then moved close to Stephan. "I'm sorry about your little brother. I take it your parents are not here on the grounds."

"No, sir," said Stephan. "Our — my parents are in Heviz visiting my grandfather, who is very ill. He lives with my aunt and uncle there."

The chief patted Stephan's arm. "I really am sorry. Very sorry."

Stephan nodded, biting his lips. Joseph's

body was still nestled close to his chest.

"If you will give me the name and address of your uncle and aunt in Heviz, I will send a wire to your parents and advise them of what has happened."

Stephan's grief and sorrow made it difficult to keep his emotions under control, but he did so while giving Chief Serta the information.

When Serta had it written down, he set compassionate eyes on Stephan. "Do you have any relatives here in Budapest?"

"Yes, sir. My father's sister and her husband. Their last name is Bartok. Uncle Bela and Aunt Ravina live in the Buda Hills section."

"Would they let you stay with them until your parents can get here? I'd really hate to see you go home and be alone at such a horrible time like this."

"Yes, sir, they would. Jos-Joseph and I often stay with them overnight. I mean . . . Joseph did. When he was alive."

"Chief Serta," spoke up Janos, "I am a close friend of Stephan's. I will accompany him to the Bartok home."

"All right. Thank you. I'll need the Bartoks' address, too."

Stephan gave him the information, then Serta looked at him. "Now, Stephan, I need to have these two officers take your little brother's body to the city morgue. Do you understand?"

Stephan's lips quivered. "Y-yes, sir."

One of the officers stepped up and extended his arms. Stephan met his gaze, then kissed Joseph's cold, pallid cheek, and looked at him wistfully. "Good-bye, little brother."

The officer cradled Joseph's body in his arms and quietly walked away with the other policeman at his side. They headed toward a police wagon that was parked nearby.

Chief Serta laid a hand on Stephan's shoulder. "I will send the wire to your parents shortly. And I will have one of my men come to the Bartok home a little later to check on you, all right?"

Stephan nodded. "Yes, sir."

At Buda Hills, Bela and Ravina Bartok were talking to a group of a dozen or more neighbors in their front yard. Two of the couples had been to the king's speech on the capitol grounds. When they described the horror of the riot and gave the gory details, Ravina turned to Bela and gripped his arm. "I'm so glad Miklos and Beatrice refused to allow Joseph to attend the speech."

Bela nodded. "Me too. It's good to know he's home safe with Stephan, and —"

The sudden break in her husband's words caused Ravina to follow his line of sight toward the street. Two young men were coming into the yard. Both Bela and Ravina were surprised to see Stephan.

By this time, the others in the group were eyeing the approaching pair.

Ravina frowned. "Bela, do you recognize the young man with Stephan?"

"No. But I can tell by Stephan's countenance that something is dreadfully wrong."

Ravina had also noted the dismal look on her nephew's face. "Yes, I think so." As Stephan and Janos drew up, Ravina went to Stephan. "Honey, what's wrong?"

Stephan's voice was weak. "Aunt Ravina, Uncle Bela, this is my friend, Janos Kudra. Could — could we go in the house so I can talk to you?"

Ravina frowned. "Of course. But where's Joseph?"

Stephan moistened his lips with his tongue. "I — I'll tell you in-inside."

The Bartoks excused themselves to their neighbors and led Janos and Stephan into the house. As soon as Bela closed the door behind them, tears sprang into Stephan's eyes and he broke into sobs. The Bartoks looked at Janos, then back at their nephew.

"Stephan, what is it?" pressed Bela.

Stephan swallowed a sob and tried to speak, but choked up. With tears streaming down his cheeks, he looked at Janos, asking with his eyes that he tell them.

Face grim, Janos ran his gaze between Bela and Ravina. "Joseph . . . was a . . . a victim of the riot."

Both Bela and Ravina gasped, their eyes widening as they exchanged glances.

Bela cleared his throat. "You . . . you mean Stephan took Joseph to the king's speech?"

Janos, who was not aware that Miklos and Beatrice had forbidden Joseph to go to the speech, looked at his friend, then back at the Bartoks. "Yes. I ran into both of them there. Why?"

"When Ravina and I were visiting in the Varda home a few nights ago, the subject of Joseph's going to see and hear King Franz Joseph on the following Saturday came up. Miklos and Beatrice agreed that Joseph was not to go because of the possibility that there could be trouble. They didn't want him there."

Ravina's features lost color. "Has something happened to Joseph?"

Bela's scalp tightened when he saw Janos

swallow hard. He looked at Stephan, then back to Janos. "What?"

Janos's voice trembled. "In the midst of the riot, many of the dissenters were throwing bricks from brick piles at the site of the new office building that is under construction. Joseph — Joseph was hit in the head with a flying brick. It — it killed him."

Stunned, Ravina's hand went to her mouth. Her eyes bulged in disbelief.

Bela took her into his arms, and as she broke down, he wept with her. After a few minutes, Bela gained control of his emotions and looked at his nephew, wiping tears. "Stephan, why did you take the boy to the speech when your parents forbid it?"

Stephan swallowed another sob. In a hollow, tremulous tone, he explained how after their parents were on their way to Heviz, Joseph began begging to be taken to the speech. He kept it up until this morning, and finally, to make him happy, he had taken him, figuring there really wouldn't be any trouble.

Suddenly, Stephan was sobbing again as he said, "Uncle Bela, I was wrong to disobey my parents, even to try to make Joseph happy. They — they will hate me when they find out. I'm terrified at the thought of facing them."

Bela put an arm around his nephew, and Ravina took hold of Stephan's hand.

"Stephan," Bela said, "your parents are going to be terribly shocked, but they won't hate you."

But Bela soon saw that his words were wasted. Stephan broke into heavy sobs, saying that indeed his parents would hate him. It was his fault that Joseph was dead, and they would never forgive him.

Ravina squeezed Stephan's hand. "Honey, what was done with Joseph's body?"

Since his friend was still choked up, Janos said, "Mrs. Bartok, Chief Akman Serta had Joseph's body taken to the city morgue. Chief Serta is sending a wire to Mr. and Mrs. Varda in Heviz. He will have one of his officers here to check on Stephan a little later today. I really need to be going."

The Bartoks thanked Janos for coming along with their nephew in his time of grief, and Stephan merely nodded.

When Janos was gone, Bela and Ravina took Stephan into the parlor, sat him down, and tried to comfort him further. Their compassion served to bring more tears. When they finally got him quieted some, Ravina said, "Stephan, your Uncle Bela and I want you to stay here with us until your parents get home."

Bela smiled at him. "Will you?"

Stephan nodded. "I would love to. Thank you."

Once again, Stephan's mind went to his dead little brother, then to his parents, and he buried his face in his hands, sobbing.

Bela and Ravina looked at each other, wondering what to do, and suddenly Stephan jumped to his feet, clamping a hand over his mouth. He made a gagging sound, dashed from the parlor, and ran down the hall to the washroom.

The Bartoks stood up, both gazing at the parlor door where they had last seen him.

Ravina sighed. "Oh, if only Stephan were a Christian . . ."

"Yes," agreed Bela. "What a difference it would make."

They discussed the fact that they had talked to Stephan many times about receiving Jesus into his heart, but because of his parents' attitude about what they called fanaticism, he had never done so.

"I'd like to talk to him right now, sweetheart," said Bela, "but he is too torn up over Joseph's death, and over the fact that he must face Miklos and Beatrice. He wouldn't be thinking clearly enough to properly deal with his sin and his lost condition."

"You're right, honey. We'd best wait. A false profession of faith is worse than none at all." Ravina took a deep breath and let it out slowly. "But you and I can rejoice that we were able to lead Joseph to the Lord before this awful tragedy happened."

"Yes. Thank God. We know the boy is now in heaven."

They heard Stephan come out of the washroom, and waited while his footsteps grew louder. When he came through the parlor door, he was pale and his whole body was quivering.

Ravina moved up to him and squeezed his shoulders. "Stephan, I'll make you some peppermint tea. It will help settle your stomach."

Stephan put a hand to his forehead. "I've got a horrible headache, too, Aunt Ravina."

"I want you to go lie down in your room. I'll bring you some salicylic acid along with the tea."

"All right."

Both Bela and Ravina accompanied Stephan to the room which was always his when he stayed with them. Bela helped him remove his shoes, and Ravina made him comfortable as he lay down on the bed.

"You rest now, honey," she said, stroking his cheek. "I'll be back in a few minutes."

Some twenty minutes later, the tea was hot, and its fragrance filled the kitchen. Bela sat at the table and smiled as Ravina poured him a mug of the steaming liquid. She filled another mug for Stephan, poured in a good dose of salicylic acid powder, stirred it, and headed down the hall.

When she stepped into Stephan's room, he was lying flat on his back with an arm thrown across his eyes. Tears were seeping around his arm, flowing silently down his pale cheeks.

She moved toward the bed. "Here's your tea, honey. I put the salicylic acid in it."

Stephan rubbed shaky palms over his eyes and down his face, trying to dry the tears.

"I want you to drink all of this, then give in to it and sleep if you can."

Stephan sat up, managed to give his aunt a weak, trembling smile, and took the mug in his hands. "Thank you, Aunt Ravina. You're always so good to me."

As Stephan began sipping the tea, Ravina sat down on the edge of the bed and looked into her nephew's eyes. "I want to tell you something, Stephan. Maybe it will help ease the pain in your heart."

He swallowed, took another sip, and looked at her with puzzlement.

"You know how your Uncle Bela and I have often talked to you about putting your faith in the Lord Jesus Christ to forgive you of your sins and save you from going to hell when you die?"

He nodded silently.

"You probably know that we talked to Joseph about it, too, over the past few years."

"Yes. He told me each time you did."

"Well, a few weeks ago, when he was staying here with us, we talked to him again and showed him how to be saved. That night, Joseph received Jesus into his heart as his Saviour, Stephan. Because he did, I can tell you that according to God's Word, he is now in heaven. I just wanted you to know that he is safe in the arms of Jesus."

Stephan's lips quivered and tears filmed his eyes. He sniffed and wiped at the tears that began to spill down his cheeks. "He didn't tell me about that. Thank you for letting me know, Aunt Ravina. Maybe someday we can talk more about it."

He put the mug to his lips, tilted it upward, and drained it. Ravina took the empty mug from him and gently caressed his cheek. "We will talk more about it when you're feeling better, Stephan. Now lie down and close your eyes. I'll lower the window shade and you get some rest. All right?"

"Yes, ma'am."

Stephan eased onto his back and laid his head on the pillow. Ravina placed a light coverlet over him, lowered the shade, and quietly left the room. When she entered the kitchen, Bela was still at the table.

"How is he doing?" he asked.

"I think he will sleep, now. I . . . ah . . . I told him about Joseph getting saved here at our house."

"How did he take it?"

"He thanked me for telling him, and even said maybe we could talk about it someday."

"Mm-hmm."

"Did I do right, telling him about Joseph?"

"Certainly. He'll think about it, I'm sure."

Ravina set the empty mug on the cupboard and sat down across the table from Bela. "I told him Joseph is in heaven with

Jesus, and it seemed to help him."

"Wonderful," said Bela, reaching across the table and taking her hands in his. "Let's just take Stephan to the Lord in prayer right now."

They bowed their heads, closed their eyes, and Bela led them in prayer for their hurting, distraught nephew. He prayed for Stephan to be saved and his parents as well. He also prayed for the grieving that they had, but they were thankful that Joseph was with Jesus.

As they prayed, a spirit of peace settled over them.

When Bela closed the prayer, they looked at each other, wiping tears, and Bela said, "We must continue to pray for them, sweetheart."

Ravina sniffed and nodded. "Yes. Miklos and Beatrice are going to be devastated when they get that telegram from Chief Serta. We're going to need wisdom to deal with them properly, and to be the comfort to them that they are going to need."

There was a knock at the front door of the house.

Bela stood up and headed for the hall. "That is probably the police officer that Janos said was coming."

When Bela opened the front door, he

heard Ravina's footsteps behind him. The man in the dark blue uniform said, "Mr. Bartok, I am Lieutenant Kord Utvar. Chief Serta sent me."

"Yes, Lieutenant. Please come in."

Ravina drew up as Utvar stepped inside and Bela closed the door. He introduced her to the lieutenant. "I am pleased to meet you, ma'am."

Ravina smiled. "Can you come in and sit down, Lieutenant? I can heat up some tea."

"Thank you, ma'am, but I can only stay a few minutes. Today's riot has all of us in the police department quite busy. Chief Serta wanted me to tell you that he sent a wire to Stephan's parents at the Burtan home in Heviz. I am to come back and let you know as soon as he receives a return wire."

"We really appreciate Chief Serta taking such a personal interest in this situation, Lieutenant," said Bela.

"That's the kind of man he is, sir. In fact, he would be standing here himself if he didn't have his hands full right now. May I ask how Stephan is doing?"

Bela rubbed the back of his neck. "He is taking his brother's death pretty hard. He even became sick to his stomach and has a severe headache."

Utvar shook his head sadly. "Such a terrible tragedy. I believe the chief said Stephan is nineteen."

"Yes."

"We have Stephan lying down right now, Lieutenant," said Ravina. "He will be staying with us until his parents come home."

"That's good. He will need all the comfort both of you can give him. Well, I must get back to headquarters."

"Thank you for coming," said Bela as he moved toward the door.

"And please express our appreciation to Chief Serta for his kindness in this whole matter, Lieutenant," said Ravina.

"I will, ma'am. And I will be back as soon as Chief Serta hears back from the Vardas."

Eight

At Heviz, the telegraph receiver clicked out its Morse code, and agent Emile Zoda's features slacked as he hastily wrote down the message. "Oh no," he breathed. "Oh no."

His partner, who sat beside him at the long desk, looked up from a stack of papers he was poring over. "What is it, Emile?"

Emile finished the last word, laid the pencil down, then raised his head and met Sigg Galofa's gaze. "You've heard me talk about my next door neighbors, the Burtans."

"Yes."

"And I've told you about Vivian's father, Edmund Mahart, being so sick."

"Mm-hmm. He lives with the Burtans if I remember correctly."

"That's right. A dear old man. Well,

right now, Vivian's sister and her husband are here visiting from Budapest because Mr. Mahart has taken a turn for the worse and might die."

"I'm sorry to hear that. So this wire has something to do with Mr. Mahart?"

"No. But it's bad news for Vivian's sister and her husband. You know King Franz Joseph was to make a speech at the capitol grounds in Budapest this morning?"

"Right."

"Well, by what is said in this wire, there was a riot. Budapest's chief of police informed Vivian's sister and her husband that their youngest son was killed in the riot."

"Oh no."

Emile shook his head sadly. "I have met Miklos and Beatrice Varda on several occasions when they have visited the Burtans in the past. And I've met their two sons, also, Stephan and Joseph. It was Joseph who was killed. It is bad enough that the Vardas are here because Mr. Mahart could be dying. But now, they have to learn that their little boy is dead."

"That's awful."

Emile swallowed hard as he folded the paper and inserted it into an envelope, then set entreating eyes on his partner. "Sigg . . ."

Sigg Galofa met his gaze. "You want me to deliver the telegram for you."

Emile swallowed hard again. "Will you? I'd sure appreciate it. I just couldn't stand at their door and hand them this envelope. Not at a time like this."

At the Burtan home, the two couples were sitting in the parlor talking quietly when they heard Dr. Avery Ralaton come out of Edmund's room. All four stood to their feet, eyeing each other with a combination of hope and anxiety on their faces.

When the doctor came through the door with the medical bag in his hand, he was smiling. "You were right, Vivian. He definitely has shown some improvement."

"Oh, wonderful!" exclaimed Vivian.

"Yes," said Beatrice. "What is your assessment of the improvement, Dr. Ralaton?"

"Well, it's hard to give you anything positive yet, but based on my experience with Edmund, I can say that I believe you are going to have him a little longer than we were thinking a few days ago."

"I guess you can't say how much longer, can you?" asked Matthias.

"No. My guess would be a few more months, but it's hard to predict these

170

things. Elderly people can fool you. You can think they are about to step through death's door, then they rally and sometimes last years longer. I hope this will be the case with Edmund. He's sleeping now. Let him rest until he wakes up on his own."

When the doctor was gone, the two couples sat down in the parlor again, rejoicing in the good news.

Beatrice said, "Miklos, I sure wish our boys could have come with us. Grandpa keeps talking about them. It would have been good for them to see him, too. Especially now that he's doing better."

Miklos started to reply, but was interrupted by a knock at the front door.

Matthias sprang out of his chair and headed for the parlor door, speaking over his shoulder. "I'll see who that is. Be right back."

While Matthias was on his way to the front door, Vivian said, "I hope Grandpa is still alive when school lets out in May, so Joseph can come see him. And Miklos, I hope you will let Stephan off for a few days so he can come, too."

Miklos chuckled. "Well, even though Stephan is my best crewman, and it will probably bankrupt my business to have him gone, I'll give him up for a few days."

All three were laughing as Matthias re-entered the parlor. The laughter faded quickly when they saw him holding an envelope with a disturbed look on his face.

"Honey, what's wrong?" queried Vivian.

Matthias held up the envelope. "It's a telegram for Miklos and Beatrice from police chief Akman Serta in Budapest."

As Matthias handed the envelope to Miklos, a sinking feeling came to Beatrice. Ever since they had arrived in Heviz, something had been troubling her. She had tried to convince herself that it was simply because her father was so ill and maybe was dying. But the uneasy feeling had stayed with her. She watched with bated breath as Miklos opened the envelope and scanned its message. "What . . . is it, Miklos?"

Miklos's face blanched, then seemed to crumple. A faint sheen of perspiration appeared on his brow as he took a shuddering breath to steady himself and turned misty eyes on his wife. "Chief Serta says Joseph was killed when a riot broke out in front of the capitol building this morning while the king was giving his speech."

Beatrice's breath caught in her throat, her heart hanging in mid-beat. Her eyes were wide as she shook her head, unable to find her voice. A numb, icy sickness settled in her stomach.

Vivian left her chair, leaned over, put her arms around her sister, and looked at Miklos. "Does the chief say how it happened?"

"There are no details."

"What about Stephan? Does he mention him?"

Miklos licked his dry lips and nodded. "He does. He says Stephan is bruised some, and has a cut on his forehead, but otherwise is unhurt. He asks that we come home as soon as possible, and requests that we wire him as to when we will arrive in Budapest."

Beatrice found her voice, though it was hoarse. "Th-that's all? He gives no clue as to how it happened or what killed our little boy?"

"No. There is nothing more in the message."

Beatrice went completely to pieces, sobbing uncontrollably. While Vivian was trying to console her, Miklos broke down. Matthias squeezed his shoulders, speaking above his sobs, attempting to comfort him.

After a moment, Miklos thanked Matthias for his kindness, then went to

Beatrice and took her into his arms.

It took several minutes for the devastated couple to bring their emotions under control. When they did, and Beatrice was sniffling into a handkerchief, Miklos thumbed away his own tears. "We will need to get to the railroad station as soon as we can, so we can be on the next train that leaves for Budapest."

"We'll take you as soon as you can get your bags packed," said Matthias. "Vivian and I will help you."

"First I will run next door and see if Leila Zoda will come and watch over Papa while we take you to the station," said Vivian.

She dashed out the door and was back in three minutes, saying Leila would be right over.

While the two couples wrestled with their emotions, they packed the bags. Matthias went to the small barn behind the house and quickly harnessed his horse to the family carriage. As Miklos and Matthias picked the bags up to take them to the carriage, Beatrice said, "We'd best not disturb Papa, Vivian. I'll have to leave it to you as to when you should tell him about Joseph."

"I'll talk to one of his doctors about

174

that," said Vivian. "Of course, he'll have to be told that you and Miklos left before you had planned on it. But I'll take care of that, too. Let's get you to the railroad station. I'm sure Stephan needs you in the worst way."

Minutes later, the Vardas were in the Burtan carriage on their way to the depot, with Leila Zoda taking care of Edmund Mahart. Miklos was on the front seat with Matthias and the women were seated behind them. Vivian had an arm around her sister.

As the carriage moved through the streets, Miklos turned on the seat and looked at Beatrice. "This horrible news has had my thoughts jumbled. But you know what this means, don't you? Stephan disobeyed us and took Joseph to see the king."

Beatrice's lips were quivering as she nodded. "Yes. That he did."

Neither Matthias nor Vivian commented, but they knew Stephan was in trouble.

The Vardas were silent for the rest of the ride, but mixed emotions were building in both of them. Their grief over Joseph's death grew by the moment, along with anger toward Stephan, whose arrant disobedience caused his little brother's death.

When they arrived at the depot, they found that an eastbound train was leaving in just over an hour. Miklos purchased their tickets, then leaving the sisters at the depot, he and Matthias climbed in the carriage and headed for the telegraph office.

Beatrice and Vivian sat down on a bench in the terminal, and once again Beatrice began to wipe tears.

Vivian put an arm around her. "Honey, I'm so sorry this awful thing has happened. I can't even imagine what you're going through."

Beatrice dabbed at her wet face. "I . . . I was just thinking of the day I learned that we had another child on the way. We waited such a long time. And then, I was thinking of the day Joseph was born. It . . . it was such a happy day. And now, because of Stephan's brazen disobedience, Joseph is — Joseph is gone." She released a sob. "Gone forever. Oh, how could Stephan do such a thing? We told him as plain as could be that he was not to take Joseph to the speech."

Vivian was trying to think of something to say when she saw Beatrice's face turn purple with anger. She riveted her eyes on her sister. "Stephan's going to pay for this, Vivian. He's going to pay! I feel nothing but disgust and wrath toward him. He's going to wish he had obeyed us."

Vivian was startled by her sister's ferocity. Taking hold of her hand, she said, "Now, honey, calm down. You haven't heard Stephan's side of the story, yet."

"I don't need to hear it, Vivian! There *is* no other side to it. He disobeyed us, and now Joseph is dead! That young man is in deep trouble."

"Sis, listen to me. Please don't do this. Give Stephan the benefit of the doubt. After all, he is your son, too. Think about the day you found out that you were going to have your first child. Think about the day Stephan was born. Those were happy days, too. And keep in mind that he has to feel terrible about this. Please give him a chance to explain."

Beatrice set her jaw, stared at the ceiling, and said no more.

Emile Zoda was alone in the telegraph office when Miklos and Matthias arrived. He offered his condolences to Miklos in the loss of Joseph before sending the wire to Chief Akman Serta, advising him when the Vardas would arrive in Budapest.

★ ★ ★

Late that afternoon in Budapest, Bela Bartok came into the kitchen as Ravina was putting a steaming bowl of gravy on the table.

She gave him a loving smile. "Just in time, sweetheart. Supper's ready. Did Stephan go to sleep?"

"Yes. That sedative Dr. Rakoz gave him worked beautifully."

"Good. Let's sit down."

Miklos offered thanks to the Lord, and as they began to eat, the setting sun peeped under the back porch roof and painted the walls with gold bars that slowly changed to red. By the time they were finished, twilight had captured Budapest, and Bela helped Ravina clean up the kitchen and do the dishes.

Bela was drying the last plate and Ravina was putting the eating utensils in a cupboard drawer when they heard a knock at the front door.

Bela put the plate on a shelf in the cupboard and hung up the dish towel. "I'll see who it is, honey. Probably Lieutenant Utvar."

When Bela opened the door, he smiled at Utvar and swung the door wider. "Come in, Lieutenant. We've been expecting you."

Ravina greeted the lieutenant. Together they entered the parlor and sat down with Bela and Ravina side by side, facing Utvar.

Utvar ran his gaze between them. "Chief Serta received a wire from the Vardas about an hour ago. They are on a train right now, and will arrive in Budapest at ten-thirty tomorrow morning. There will be a police wagon at the depot to pick them up, and they will be brought here immediately."

Bela nodded. "Good. I'm glad to hear that they can get here that soon."

"Me too," said Ravina.

"So how is Stephan?" asked Utvar.

"Bela had to go for Dr. Imre Rakoz," said Ravina. "He is the Vardas' family doctor as well as ours. In fact, it was Dr. Rakoz who delivered little Joseph when he was born."

"I see. So Stephan got worse?"

"Yes. He is so upset that he has been sick to his stomach repeatedly, as well as having severe stomach pains. And the headache had become so bad it was affecting his vision. Dr. Rakoz gave him medicine to settle his stomach, and another kind of medicine to ease his headache, which contained a sedative to help calm his nerves and put him to sleep. He is sleeping right now."

"I am glad to hear that. I hope this terrible thing doesn't bring on some kind of mental or emotional breakdown. I've seen a lot of it in my sixteen years on the police force. But I haven't seen a case quite like this, where an older teenage brother had to look at his younger brother's body after such a violent and sudden death. I'm glad to hear he is in Dr. Rakoz's care."

"Actually, Lieutenant, there is more to it than just seeing his brother's body. Stephan is terribly afraid of facing his parents."

Utvar's brow furrowed. "Why is that? The riot was certainly not Stephan's fault."

Bela and Ravina exchanged glances, then Bela looked back at Utvar. "So you haven't been informed of the fact that Stephan went against his parents' orders."

"Orders?"

"Yes. Joseph had asked his parents to let him go see King Franz Joseph, and they said no. They made sure Stephan understood that under no circumstances was Joseph to attend the speech. They felt that the possibility of trouble was too high. They didn't want him vulnerable to that kind of danger."

"Mm-hmm," said the lieutenant, nodding his head slowly. "So Stephan wanted to go to the speech so much that he took his little brother in spite of the possibility of such danger, and in spite of his parents' command. I understand."

Bela adjusted himself on the overstuffed chair. "Well, you still don't quite understand, Lieutenant. It wasn't that Stephan wanted to attend the speech that much. I told you that Joseph had asked his parents to let him go to the speech."

"Yes."

"It's like this. Stephan and his parents have coddled Joseph since he was born because he came so late in the family. He had a very special place in their hearts. Miklos and Beatrice babied Joseph a lot, but Stephan did so even more. He couldn't stand to see little brother deprived of anything he wanted. This morning, Joseph begged him repeatedly to take him to see the king, shedding tears, and saying the danger wouldn't be that bad. Finally, Stephan broke down and gave in, wanting to make his little brother happy. Stephan was also convinced that nothing bad would happen. The breach of his parents' command was strictly because Stephan wanted to make Joseph happy."

Utvar nodded. "All right. Now I understand. Thank you for making it clear to me. I will explain this to Chief Serta. He needs to understand it, too. I sure hope Mr. and Mrs. Varda are not too rough on Stephan. He most certainly is suffering enough as it is."

"We are going to do our best to help my brother and his wife see this," said Ravina. "We know they have to be terribly upset, knowing that Joseph was killed. But they also must take into consideration how Stephan looked at the situation when he disobeyed them. Adding to his broken heart with anger will only cause more problems."

"You're right about that," said Utvar, rising from his chair. "Well, I must be going."

The Bartoks walked the lieutenant to the door, thanked him for the interest he had shown in the family, and asked him once again to express their appreciation to Chief Akmar Serta for his interest.

It was almost nine-thirty that night when Ravina stood over her nephew and spooned hot broth into him as he sat up on his bed.

Stephan was pale and haggard. His eyes

held a shadow through which shone a soft, subdued light as he swallowed the last spoonful of broth. "Aunt Ravina, thank you for being so good to me. You and Uncle Bela will never know how very much I love you."

Ravina pressed a smile on her lips as she examined the small bandage Dr. Rakoz had put over the cut on his forehead. "We both love you very much, Stephan. You have been a bright light in our lives."

"As much as Joseph was?"

"Every bit as much."

"Thank you."

She smiled again, laid the bowl aside, and picked up a mug from the nightstand. "Here's another dose of the sedative powders that Dr. Rakoz left for you. I mixed it with milk like before. Drink it all, and then I want you to get back to sleep. Rest is very essential."

Stephan drained the mug and handed it to her. "Thank you, Aunt Ravina. I hope someday I can do something special for you."

"What I want, and what your uncle wants, is that you get over this and go on with your life. That will be special to us."

Tears filled Stephan's eyes. He wanted to speak of the fear that was chilling him concerning facing his parents tomorrow morning, but he slid down on his back in the bed, wiped at the tears, and thanked her for the broth.

Ravina set the mug on the nightstand, then leaned over the chimney on the lantern and blew out the flame. The bedroom door was open, and a small bit of light came from a lantern in the hall. She sat down on the edge of the bed, bent over, and kissed his cheek. "Close those blue eyes of yours and go to sleep."

He looked at her for a long moment, then let his eyelids drop. When she didn't move, he opened them again. "Aren't you going to go to bed yourself, Aunt Ravina?"

"Later. I'm staying here till I know you're asleep."

He tried to smile. "You're the greatest, you know that?"

Her smile was stronger than his. "In your eyes, anyway. Now close them, young man."

As Ravina had thought, it was only a few minutes until Stephan was sound asleep, breathing steadily.

Bela was already in bed when Ravina entered their room, and he looked up at her. The lantern was still burning. "He asleep?"

"Yes. Thanks to the sedative."

Soon the lantern was out and pale moonlight bathed the room in silver. They talked about the tragedy for a while, then prayed together and soon were asleep.

Somewhere in the depths of the night, Stephan Varda was tossing and turning in his bed, in the midst of a bad dream. In the nightmare, he was standing on the capitol grounds alone in the light of a full moon, his eyes taking in the scene where the riot had taken place. Bodies lay all around him — men, women, and children.

Suddenly from behind him, he heard a familiar voice speak his name. Cold chills iced his backbone, and he wheeled about to face the owner of the voice. He found himself staring into the pallid, sharply drawn features and blank, dead eyes of his little brother. Joseph was clad in a black shroud.

"It's your fault I'm dead, Stephan," Joseph said. "It's your fault! If you had not disobeyed Papa and Mama, I would still be alive."

Stephan's feet seemed planted in the ground beneath him. He wanted to run, but was powerless to do so. He opened his mouth and let out a wild, howling scream.

★ ★ ★

In the master bedroom, Ravina awakened and sat up in bed, rubbing her eyes. She threw back the covers, slipped out of the bed, and started putting on her robe by the moonlight that flooded the room.

Bela made a moaning sound and rolled over. Suddenly another scream echoed down the hall from the direction of Stephan's room, and Bela's eyes came open. Blinking, he saw Ravina standing near the window, buttoning her robe.

"That Stephan?"

"Yes," she said, hurrying toward the door. "He must be having a nightmare."

Another scream filled the night, followed seconds later by heavy sobbing.

Bela threw back the covers. "Wait a minute."

Quickly he pulled on his robe and lit the lantern on the small table beside the bed. "Let's go."

When they reached Stephan's room, he was sitting up in the bed, sniffling. He looked at them with wide, wet eyes. "I'm sorry. I woke you up, didn't I?"

"That's all right," said Bela, holding the lantern. "Nightmare, eh?"

"Yes. I dreamed I was at the capitol grounds and Joseph was there. He said it

186

was my fault he was dead, because I disobeyed Mama and Papa."

"It was only a nightmare, Stephan," said Ravina, stroking his sweaty brow. "It wasn't real."

"I know. The dream I had before that was bad, too, but it wasn't real. It sure seemed real, though."

"What was it?" asked Bela.

"I dreamed that Papa and Mama confronted me about Joseph's death. They said it was my fault and told me to get out of their home and never come back. Of course it may be real, after all. This is probably what they will do tomorrow."

"No, they won't," said Ravina. "They will do no such thing."

"But they know by now that I took Joseph to the speech. They probably hate me already. They will never want to see me again."

She shook her head. "No, no. What you did couldn't make your parents hate you, or want you out of their lives. You are their son, too."

"That's right," said Bela. "You're their son as well as Joseph was."

"You need to get back to sleep, Stephan," Ravina said softly. "Now lie back down. You've only had bad dreams.

They weren't real, nor did they represent what is real."

Stephan lay down. Bela tugged the covers up close under his chin while Ravina rubbed his temples lightly. Only minutes passed until Stephan was fast asleep once more.

The Bartoks left Stephan's room and padded back to their bedroom.

As they entered the room, Ravina said, "I wish in my heart that I felt as certain about Beatrice and Miklos as I tried to convince Stephan."

"I know what you mean," replied Bela, setting the lantern on the small table beside the bed. "Joseph was so very special to them, and they doted on him. Probably a lot more than they should have, and more than was good for him. He wouldn't have been so insistent with Stephan that he disobey their parents and take him to see the king if he didn't feel in his mind that should they find out, they would let him get away with it. And they were bound to find out one way or another. These things have a way of surfacing, no matter how well hidden."

The lantern was doused, and the Bartoks were soon back under the covers in the moonlight that filtered through the curtains. "Poor Stephan. Joseph could always get his way with him. And now Stephan is paying such a terrible price for loving his little brother so much."

"We'll do all that we can to smooth the waters and trust the Lord to give us wisdom," said Bela. "They are going to need help. God will guide us."

Bela felt a hand slip into his. "You are such a marvelous source of comfort to me, sweet husband of mine."

Bela took her in his arms and held her in his warm embrace for a few minutes. Then Ravina whispered, "We need to get some sleep ourselves, darling."

With that, she pulled away gently and kissed his cheek. "Good night, my love."

Before Bela could respond, sleep had already claimed him.

Nine

Stephan Varda found himself standing just inside the front door of his home, facing his parents, who stood in the small foyer like menacing beasts. The eyes of both Miklos and Beatrice blazed with wrath.

His father stabbed a finger at him and spat out through clenched teeth, "It's all your fault that Joseph is dead! Do you hear me? It's all your fault!"

"That's right!" said his mother, burning him with accusing eyes. "You disobeyed us, and now your little brother is dead! It's the same as if you threw that brick yourself! Get out, Stephan. Get out of this house and don't ever come back!"

Miklos's features were like granite. "You heard what she said. Get out!"

Stephan's chest constricted. It felt like his heart stopped. He turned and opened the door. Without looking back, he stepped onto the porch.

His father's booming voice seemed to shake the entire house. "Don't you ever set foot on this property! We never want to see you again!"

Suddenly, Stephan's eyes were open, and dawn's early light showed him that he was in his room at the Bartok house. He sat up, wiped sweat from his face, and took a deep breath. "Another bad dream," he said in a low murmur. "Just like the first one I had last night."

Abruptly, the fact that he would be facing his parents for real within a few hours struck him like a slap in the face. He lay back down and closed his eyes. Cold fear was like a wet snake across his chest. His stomach wrenched. *Maybe I should just get up right now and run away. Get out of here before they arrive.*

Then he thought of Uncle Bela and Aunt Ravina. They both assured him that his parents would not take such an attitude. His uncle and aunt had been so good to him. He owed it to them to stay.

Rolling onto his side, Stephan opened his eyes long enough to look through the window and catch sight of the rising sun's rays on the treetops outside, then closed them again.

He did not know how long he was in that position when he heard footsteps in the hall. He opened his eyes and saw that the sun was up and painting his room a bright yellow. Seconds later came the sound of his doorknob turning. He rolled over to see Uncle Bela step in.

He moved up to the bed. "Good morning, Stephan. Any more nightmares?"

"Yes, sir. I had another one just like the first one."

"Your parents saying Joseph's death was your fault, and telling you to get out of their home and never come back?"

"Yes. That one."

"Well, it was just a bad dream. Do you feel like getting up and eating breakfast with us? Your aunt has her special cinnamon-spiced oatmeal cooking and biscuits in the oven. We're not going to church today because we don't want to leave you alone in your emotional condition. How about it? Can you eat some oatmeal?"

Stephan sat up and nodded. "I'll try, Uncle Bela."

"Good!"

As he dropped his legs over the side of the bed, Stephan's brows knitted together. "Uncle Bela, do I remember right? You told me last night that my parents will arrive at the depot at ten o'clock?"

"You remember correctly, my boy," said Bela, moving toward the door. "Breakfast will be ready in twenty minutes."

When the door clicked shut behind his uncle, Stephan left the bed and padded to the mirror above the washstand. He hardly recognized himself. He looked half-dead and needed a shave. His eyes were red-rimmed and his cheeks were hollow. They seemed to have shrunken since yesterday morning. His whole appearance was one of misery.

Stephan decided to bypass the shave. Sighing, he poured water into the wash-bowl from the pitcher that sat next to it and splashed the cool liquid in his face, being careful not to get the bandage on his forehead wet. He took the towel from the rack next to the mirror, dried off, then combed his hair into some semblance of order. While doing so, he noted that the red bruises on his hands, body, and legs had turned purple.

He told himself the bruises would slowly fade away, as would the soreness in his joints and muscles. He met his gaze in the mirror. "What will never fade away, Stephan Varda, is the pain in your bruised heart. Joseph is dead."

He drew in a shuddering breath, closed his eyes, and steeled himself for the confrontation that was coming shortly after ten o'clock. He opened his eyes as he let his breath out slowly.

When Stephan neared the kitchen, the delicious fragrance of breakfast cooking met his nostrils. Other than the bowl of broth he had downed last night, he had not eaten since yesterday morning. His stomach growled and his mouth watered. The medicine Dr. Rakoz had left for him had settled his stomach, and as he entered the kitchen, the strongest aroma was that of hot coffee, which smelled inviting.

"Good morning, Stephan," Ravina said cheerfully. She gave him a hug and kissed his cheek. "Your uncle said you had the nightmare about your parents a second time."

"Yes."

"Well, like he told you, it was just a bad dream." She turned to Bela. "Let's give thanks for the food first; then you men can sit down and I'll dish it up."

They bowed their heads, closed their eyes, and Bela led in prayer, thanking the Lord for the food and asking Him to bless it to the nourishment of their bodies. Before closing off, he said, "And, Lord, watch over Stephan. He means so much to us. We have always loved him in a special way since he came into the world almost twenty years ago."

The Bartoks heard their nephew swallow hard. When Bela closed off his prayer, he and Ravina opened their eyes to see Stephan wiping tears.

He stepped close and put his arms around both of them. "You two have always been so good to me. Thank you for the love you have always shown me. And thank you for praying for me, Uncle Bela."

Ravina looked at him with eyes of love. "Honey, we have prayed for you all of your life. You remember that we have talked to you about being saved many times."

Stephan nodded.

"Well, we are not going to give up. We want you to be saved so you will be in heaven with us and Joseph for all eternity."

Stephan looked deep into her eyes. "I'm so glad to know that my little brother is in heaven. He's as happy as he can be now, isn't he?"

"Yes. Happier than anybody could ever be here on earth. In heaven there are no riots, no heartaches, no troubles, no hospitals, and no cemeteries. Best of all, Joseph is in the glorious presence of the Lord Jesus."

Stephan wiped tears and drew a deep breath through his nostrils, catching the pleasant aroma of the hot coffee. "Well, I would be reasonably happy if I could get a cup of your coffee."

Ravina smiled. "All right. Both of you sit down."

When the men had taken their places at the table, Ravina poured them steaming cups of coffee, then placed bowls of hot oatmeal before them. Golden brown biscuits came next. As Stephan poured milk on his oatmeal, Ravina said, "Eat as much as you can, dear. There's molasses for the oatmeal if you want that, too."

Bela and Ravina watched as their nephew put down the bowl of oatmeal, two cups of coffee, and three biscuits swathed in butter. When he finished, he wiped his mouth with a napkin. "That was very good, Aunt Ravina. Wish I had room for more."

She warmed him with a smile. "You did very well, Stephan. After having the stomach problem you did yesterday, I didn't think you would be able to eat that much. I'm glad. Now, you should go and lie down for a while. You mustn't push yourself too hard. You have been through a tremendous strain."

"That's right," said Bela.

Stephan's countenance sagged. He nodded solemnly. "Yes, and a greater strain is coming later this morning."

The Bartoks exchanged glances, but neither one commented.

When Stephan had returned to his room and Bela went to the backyard to do some work, Ravina worked on cleaning the kitchen. With a prayer in her heart for Stephan and his parents, she worked quickly, then went on to freshen up the rest of the house. She had learned through experience that when her world was disturbed, it was best to stay busy. With her body in action and her mind and soul centered on the Lord, everything went better.

At about nine-thirty, Ravina was sweeping in the hallway when she saw Bela come into the house. A few minutes later, she noticed him entering Stephan's room with his Bible in hand. She smiled, whispered a prayer, and went back to her work.

It was almost ten-thirty when Ravina was doing some dusting in the parlor near the large front window. In her peripheral vision, movement outside on the street caught her attention, and her heart leaped in her chest when she turned to see the police wagon that was pulling up in front of the house.

Moving closer to the window, Ravina watched as Miklos stepped out of the wagon, turned, and gave Beatrice his hand to help her out. Miklos kept his grip on Beatrice's hand and said something to the two policemen in the seat, and they drove away. Miklos and Beatrice turned and slowly headed toward the house.

Tears welled up in Ravina's eyes when she saw the grief and agony etched on the faces of her brother and sister-in-law. She backed away from the window, laid the feather duster on a small table, and ran down the hall.

When Ravina neared the door of Stephan's room, she saw that it was open an inch or two. She could hear Bela's voice as she drew up and quietly pushed the door open further.

Both men were sitting on the bed. Bela had his Bible open in his hands. "That's why Jesus went to the cross, shed His blood, and died. There was no other way for guilty sinners like you and me to be forgiven and spend eternity in heaven with God. You see —" Bela's eyes had strayed to the door. "Oh. Hello, honey."

"Miklos and Beatrice are here," Ravina said. "They'll knock on the door any second."

Stephan's features lost color. "M-maybe I should j-just run out the back door right now and keep on running."

Bela laid a steady hand on Stephan's shoulder. "Running away is not the answer. You must face your parents, tell them the truth, and rely on their good judgment to understand why you took Joseph to see King Franz Joseph. They must forgive you for the honest mistake you made."

Stephan licked his pale lips nervously.

Bela squeezed his shoulder. "Certainly your parents remember how even they bent over backward time and again to please Joseph. They will understand, Stephan, and they will forgive you."

"Yes, they will, Stephan," agreed Ravina as the knock was heard at the front door of the house.

Bela closed his Bible and moved toward her. He paused at the door and looked back at his nephew. "You wait here, Stephan. Aunt Ravina and I will go to the door and meet your parents. We'll spend a few minutes with them, then bring them back to see you."

Stephan nodded, biting his lips. As his aunt and uncle were heading toward the front of the house with a second knock reverberating down the hall, he closed the door and walked to the window, which offered a view of the neighbors' backyard and the alley. He drew several short breaths, feeling the nerves twitch throughout his body. The blood in his veins seemed cold as ice, and his stomach was hurting again.

He ran his gaze across the backyard to the alley and mumbled softly, "Go on, Stephan. Climb through the window and run away while you still have a chance."

With trembling hands, he unlocked the window and pushed it open. He raised one leg, swung it over the sill, and as he ducked his head under the window frame, his uncle's words echoed through his head: *Certainly your parents remember how even they bent over backward time and again to please Joseph. They will understand, Stephan, and they will forgive you.*

He froze in place, shook his head, and eased back into the room. He closed the window and began to pace the floor slowly, his heart pounding.

When Bela opened the front door with

Ravina at his side, the Vardas both burst into tears. Ravina took Beatrice in her arms, and while the women wept and clung to each other, Bela embraced Miklos and said in a broken voice, "I . . . I'm so sorry about your loss of Joseph."

All Miklos could do was weep.

While holding a sobbing Beatrice, Ravina said, "Honey, I love you as much as if you were my sister, rather than my sister-in-law. Bela and I are torn up over our nephew's death, but I know you're hurting more because you have lost a son. My heart bleeds for you and Miklos. And when you two hurt, I hurt."

Ravina's compassionate words touched both Beatrice and Miklos. The freshness of Joseph's death caused both Miklos and Beatrice to weep uncontrollably. Ravina kept her arms around Beatrice as Bela did with Miklos. When both of them had gained control of their emotions, the Bartoks guided them into the parlor, and everyone sat down. Beatrice was seated on the couch between Miklos and Ravina. Bela was in a chair facing them.

Miklos cleared his throat and wiped a tear from his left cheek. "The policemen who picked us up at the depot told us that Stephan was here with you. Where is he?"

"He's in the room where he always stays when he spends the night with us," said Bela. "I might as well tell you that he is terrified about having to face you. He had a bad night, too. Nightmares."

The Vardas looked at each other, but before either could speak, Ravina said, "To put it mildly, Stephan is devastated over what happened to Joseph. Bela had to bring Dr. Rakoz here to see him."

Beatrice's eyes widened. "Dr. Rakoz?"

Ravina nodded. "Yes. Stephan was in bad shape." She went on to tell them the symptoms of Stephan's stress and what medicines Dr. Rakoz had given him.

Miklos scrubbed a palm over his face. "We will talk to Stephan in a little while, but right now we want to know exactly what happened to Joseph."

Bela frowned. "You don't know?"

Miklos shook his head. "Chief Serta's telegram only said Joseph had been killed Saturday morning when a riot broke out at the capitol grounds while the king was giving his speech. He gave no details whatsoever. But then, how could he do that in a telegram? The two officers who drove us here from the depot had not been at the riot, so they could tell us nothing about Joseph, except that his body is at the city morgue. Please. We must know exactly what happened."

Bela and Ravina exchanged glances. The look in Ravina's eyes told her husband that she wanted him to tell the story. Bela nodded. Ravina took hold of Beatrice's hand. Beatrice's face was a mask of misery.

Clearing his throat nervously, Bela began the story by telling Miklos and Beatrice how on Friday night and Saturday morning Joseph repeatedly begged his big brother to take him to the capitol grounds so he could see King Franz Joseph.

Bela absentmindedly pulled at an ear. "You both know how Stephan always wanted to see his little brother happy, and would go to any length to see that Joseph had what he wanted."

Miklos and Beatrice only stared at him.

Ravina sat looking on with bated breath.

Bela went on. "Well, as Stephan told Ravina and me, he finally gave in because he knew it would make his little brother happy. Desiring so much to please Joseph, Stephan convinced himself the chance of there being trouble during the king's speech was minimal, so he took him."

Miklos slammed his palm on his knee. His face went purple with anger and the veins in his neck stuck out. "Well, Stephan convinced himself wrong! He had no business making such a decision just because Joseph was begging him! He blatantly disobeyed our orders!"

"That's right!" Beatrice said.

Down the hall in his room, Stephan stopped pacing when he heard his father's loud flare-up. He looked toward the closed door, swallowed hard, and felt a pain lance his stomach. He closed his eyes and shook his head. Just then, his mother's sharp voice met his ears. Though he could not make out the words of either parent, their anger was unmistakable.

His lips quivered and he looked toward the window. Should he make his escape while it was still possible? He thought on it a moment. No, he owed it to his aunt and uncle to stay.

In the parlor, after both Miklos and Beatrice had ejected their angry outbursts, Bela threw a palm up. "Well, wait a minute. Let me remind both of you that many times Ravina and I have seen you give in to Joseph's whims and desires because he was the baby of the family, and you wanted to please him and keep him happy."

The Vardas glanced at each other, then looked back at Bela, neither caring to comment.

Bela proceeded. "Both of you should be willing to forgive Stephan, since he was only doing the same thing. Yes, he disobeyed you, but behind that disobedience was Stephan's unswerving desire to make his brother happy. Having listened to other people's comments about the upcoming speech, he was persuaded that King Franz Joseph would not say anything that would stir up the dissenters. Stephan did wrong, I agree. But he only wanted to please his brother, convinced that the chance of a riot taking place was very, very small. I am pleading with you to take that young man in your arms and tell him he is forgiven."

Miklos and Beatrice continued to stare at Bela, an iron silence on their tongues.

Bela sighed and sent a glance to Ravina.

She met his glance steadily. "Go ahead and tell them what happened, honey."

Bela drew in a deep breath, nodded, and set his gaze once again on the Vardas. While they kept their eyes on him, he began telling them the story of what happened to Joseph at the capitol grounds when the riot broke out, as related to him by Stephan and confirmed by Lieutenant Kord Utvar.

When the mourning parents heard of Joseph being killed when a flying brick struck him in the head, Beatrice covered her face with her hands and went completely to pieces.

Ravina took Beatrice in her arms while Miklos's anger toward Stephan burned within him.

Bela observed the fierce anger on Miklos's features and the fire in his eyes as he jumped to his feet and looked in the direction of Stephan's room.

Bela stood up. "Now, Miklos, get a grip on yourself. Things will only get worse if you go to Stephan in this frame of mind."

Miklos set his jaw and fixed Bela with hot eyes. "He disobeyed me, Bela. His mother, too. Joseph is dead because of him. He's going to wish he had listened to us!"

With that, Miklos stormed out of the parlor with Bela on his heels.

Beatrice and Ravina clung to each other, eyes wide, faces pinched.

Ten

As Miklos Varda stomped down the hall toward Stephan's room, Bela ran past him and jumped in his path, facing him. Miklos came to an abrupt halt, measured the smaller man petulantly and growled, "Get out of my way."

Bela kept his voice low. "Miklos, I'm begging you. Don't do this. Cool off before you go down there and confront that boy. Stephan is already horribly torn up over Joseph's death. If you go in there fuming like this, you could do irreparable damage. It is unwise to speak or act when you're in the heat of anger."

Miklos's heart was pumping furiously, his muscles bunched. "What makes you the expert on this?"

"I'm not, but God is."

"What do you mean?"

"He has much to say about it in His Word."

Miklos's jaw jutted.

Bela's eyes did not flinch. "God says, 'He that is soon angry dealeth foolishly.' Cool down, Miklos, or you'll play the fool. God also says, 'Be not hasty in thy spirit to be angry: for anger resteth in the bosom of fools,' and 'Let every man be swift to hear, slow to speak, slow to wrath.' God knows what He is talking about, Miklos. I'm telling you, if you go in there with your anger burning, you're going to do something foolish, and like I said, you could do irreparable damage."

"How do you know so much about this?"

"It's fresh on my mind because Pastor Tividar preached on the subject last Sunday night. In his sermon, he told us something I never knew about the Roman emperor Julius Caesar. When Julius was a young man he had a short temper, and twice he destroyed friendships between himself and men who were valuable to him because he was hasty in his spirit to be angry. When it happened the second time, Julius realized what a fool he had been.

"From that time until the end of his life in 44 B.C., when provoked, he always repeated the entire Roman alphabet before he permitted himself to speak or act. He had enough wisdom to cool down first, and it was going through the alphabet that gave him the wherewithal to do it. Now, let's return to the parlor and talk until you get a grip on your temper."

Miklos shook his head stubbornly. "I'm going to that room right now, Bela. Stephan did wrong and his brother was killed because of it! He's going to face me!"

As he spoke, Miklos sidestepped to go around Bela.

However, the smaller man also sidestepped, blocking his way. "Miklos, don't play the fool."

Miklos shifted in the other direction. "I'm going, Bela. Don't try to stop me!"

Again, Bela made a fast move to block his way. "Please don't do it. You'll be sorry."

Miklos's mouth twisted into a brutish expression as he thrust out the heel of his right hand and struck Bela in the center of the chest, knocking him off balance. While Bela was stumbling backward, Miklos dashed down the hall.

Bela regained his balance and ran after him. "Miklos, don't! Wait!"

Inside his room, Stephan was standing at the window, looking out. When he heard

his uncle's cry and the thunderous footsteps of his father, a cold dread clutched
his heart. Gripping the windowsill, he kept
his back toward the door, biting his lips.

The door swung open. Miklos took two
steps into the room. "Turn around and
look at me, Stephan!"

Bela drew up and stood in the doorway
as Stephan pivoted slowly, his features
white and strained. Fear showed in his
eyes. There were tears on his cheeks.

Miklos's voice cut right through to
Stephan's heart as he boomed, "Joseph is
dead because of your fool impudence,
Stephan! If you hadn't disobeyed your
mother and me, Joseph would still be
alive."

Bela moved into the room and stood a
step behind Miklos, concern written on his
face.

Stephan's body quivered and the tears
continued to stream down his cheeks as he
choked on his words. "Papa — Papa, you
— you need to understand —"

"Understand *what?*"

"J-Joseph kept begging me over and over
to take him to see King Franz Joseph.
When I told him that you and Mama had
forbidden it, he begged all the harder. I . . .
I finally gave in, wanting to make him

happy. I . . . I really didn't think there would be any danger. Even you had said, Papa, that you really didn't think anything violent would happen. I thought it would be all right."

Miklos trembled and his face contorted. His bulging eyes reflected his rage as he made a quick move to Stephan and slapped his face, which staggered him back against the windowsill.

"I don't care what you thought! You had been told not to take Joseph to the king's speech. Your disobedience to our command got your brother killed!"

At that moment, Stephan saw his mother come into the room with Aunt Ravina at her side. Anger was burning in his mother's eyes as she moved in farther and stood beside his father, glaring at him.

Stephan sniffed, sucked in a short breath, and looked at his parents through a wall of tears. His voice was a tight squeak. "Mama, Papa, what I did was wrong. I realize that, now. I'm so sorry! So very, very sorry! Please forgive me."

Beatrice's emotions were completely out of control. She could not keep the contempt out of her voice as she snapped, "I can't forgive you, Stephan! You deliberately disobeyed our orders. Joseph is dead because of your disobedience. You're as guilty of killing my baby boy as if you had thrown the brick yourself!"

Stephan thought back to his nightmare, where his mother had said the same thing. His blood seemed to turn to ice, and his face seemed to age right in front of their eyes.

Drawing a shuddering breath, he sobbed, "Mama, Papa, I'm begging you! Please, please forgive me!"

A hand went to Ravina's mouth and tears welled up in her eyes.

Bela felt a pang in his heart.

Miklos slapped Stephan's face again. There was a hot hiss in his voice. "I'll forgive you when you bring your brother back from the dead! And not until then."

Ravina winced as if Miklos had slapped her face. Bela started to move toward the angry man, but Ravina grabbed his arm and pinched down hard. He stopped and looked at her. She gave him a pleading look and shook her head. Bela blinked his eyelids and moved back beside her. They set their eyes on Stephan, who seemed to cave in at his father's curt words.

Stephan's left cheek was bright red with a pair of welts. Wiping tears, he said with a break in his voice, "Papa, you know I can't bring Joseph back."

Both parents stared at him, unblinking, their eyes like coals of fire.

Stephan turned, moved to the bed, and sat down on its edge. His shoulders sagged. His upper body seemed to fold. He buried his face in his hands and wept.

Miklos and Beatrice did not move. They both continued to stare at him.

Bela's whole body was trembling as he observed Stephan's crumpled form.

Ravina's tear-filled eyes fixed on her devastated nephew. The combination of grief and compassion was a constricting band around her head. There was a strange clawlike scratching at her heart. Her chest was tight, her throat narrow. It was difficult to swallow, difficult to breathe, difficult to see for the tears that blinded her vision.

Wiping her eyes clear, she surprised Bela by moving away from him and going to Stephan. She knew that her brother and his wife might turn their anger on her, but she had to do what she could to comfort her nephew.

Under the Vardas' unblinking glare and Bela's astonished gaze, Ravina stood over Stephan, bent down, and wrapped her arms around him. He looked up through his tears to see who it was and rose to his feet, putting his arms around her in return.

Holding him tight, Ravina rose up on her tiptoes and planted a kiss on his welted cheek. "Oh, Stephan, I'm so sorry that all of this has happened. You did wrong in disobeying your parents, yes. But you thought you were doing the right thing for Joseph's sake. I love you, Stephan, and I can't stand to see you hurting like this."

Stephan drew a shuddering breath and looked into her eyes. "I love you, too, Aunt Ravina. I love you so very much. Thank you for loving me."

The scene touched Bela deeply, but Miklos and Beatrice were unmoved.

Ravina kissed Stephan's cheek again, then turned and went to her brother and sister-in-law. "We need to leave Stephan alone, now. He has had enough."

"I agree," spoke up Bela, stepping to the door and turning around. "Let's go." With that, he moved into the hall.

Ravina followed her husband.

Miklos took Beatrice by the arm and guided her toward the door. He looked back at Stephan, his face a mask of fury. When they were in the hall, Bela moved to the door and closed it softly.

In the hall, Miklos and Beatrice clung to each other, their nerves frayed. Bela laid hands on their shoulders. "I want you to come back to the parlor and sit down. Ravina and I want to tell you something about Joseph."

The Vardas both looked at him quizzically.

He patted their shoulders. "Come on."

"I have hot water on the stove," said Ravina. "I will go to the kitchen and make some tea."

"Can I help you?" asked Beatrice.

"No, honey. You go on with Miklos and Bela. I'll be there in a few minutes."

Ravina went toward the kitchen while Bela led Miklos and Beatrice up the hall and into the parlor. As they sat down, Bela looked at them with concern in his eyes. "Listen to me. You have already lost one son. If you don't change and forgive Stephan, you're going to lose him, too. Is that what you want?"

Beatrice's lips began to quiver and tears filled her eyes, but she made no reply.

Miklos looked at the floor and ground his teeth, his jaw muscles rippling beneath the skin, but he did not answer.

Bela took a deep breath and let it out slowly through his nostrils. "Look. I know you're hurting. I haven't even asked about your father, Beatrice. How is he doing?"

Beatrice sniffed and wiped a tear from her cheek. "He is better right now. His doctor says he may be with us a little longer."

"Well, I'm glad to hear that. Now, as to this tragedy, it is true that if Stephan hadn't taken Joseph to the capitol grounds, Joseph would still be alive. I wish this was the case. But it isn't. But can't you find it in your hearts to forgive Stephan? He admits he did wrong. He has asked you to forgive him. Are you just going to ignore this?"

Ravina came through the door, carrying a tray that bore a steaming teapot and empty cups. She poured a cup for each of them, then sat down again beside Beatrice.

Miklos took a sip and swallowed it. "You said you wanted to tell us something about Joseph."

Bela looked at Ravina. "Go ahead, darling."

Bela ran his gaze between Miklos and Beatrice. "Both of your boys have come here periodically and stayed overnight with us since they were quite small. We often talked to them about the Lord when they were here. Not to try to shove Jesus down their throats, but to open their eyes to their need to be saved. So far, we have gotten

216

nowhere with Stephan, but the last few times Joseph was here with us, he began to show interest. He even began to ask questions, which told us he was thinking about it. Well, one night in early February when Joseph was staying with us, he brought the subject up and said he wanted to be saved.

"He said he wanted to be a Christian like us. I went through the plan of salvation with him carefully, having Joseph read the Scriptures to us aloud." Bela's throat tightened and tears misted his eyes. "That evening, Joseph called on Jesus to save him."

Beatrice said, "Joseph never one time mentioned to us that his aunt and uncle were talking to him about salvation, nor did he tell us that he had made this move to be saved."

"Right," said Miklos. "He never mentioned any of it. And Stephan has never told us that you were talking to him about it, either."

"Well, I'm sure you both can understand that. Your church doesn't preach the gospel. It teaches humanistic philosophy and coats it with a semblance of Christianity, but God's Word is not preached. This is why Ravina and I left it when we got saved.

"Of course, we've already been over this

with you many times. But it is your attitude toward the truth of the Bible that has kept Stephan from telling you that we have talked to him about being saved, and this is what has kept him from receiving Christ as his Saviour. He is afraid to.

"Joseph was able to overcome his fear of you enough to open his heart to Jesus, but not enough to tell you what he had done."

Miklos and Beatrice exchanged glances, holding each other's gaze for a moment, then looked away.

"Miklos, Beatrice, Joseph is in heaven with Jesus because he did what God says in His Word a person must do to be saved," Bela said. "He repented of his sin and opened his heart to Jesus, trusting only Him for salvation. Not religious rites and good works as your church teaches."

"Bela is right," Ravina said. "God's Word says that when people die, they either go to heaven or to hell. There is no third place they can go. Those who do as Joseph did, go to heaven. Those who refuse to believe the gospel and to open their hearts to God's Son and trust Him alone to save them, die in their sins and go to hell."

Miklos jumped to his feet and began pacing the floor. "I don't want to listen to any more of this fanaticism."

Beatrice was obviously shaken. "I want to hear more of what the Bible says about it so I can have absolute assurance that my little boy is in heaven."

Miklos stopped and stared at her.

She met his gaze. "I have to know for sure, Miklos. Please allow me this."

Miklos shook his head and began pacing again.

Ravina picked up a Bible from a small end table by the sofa and began flipping pages.

Miklos was now fuming as he paced, and his anger toward Stephan was growing by the minute.

Bela stepped to him and took hold of his shoulders. "Please, Miklos, calm down."

"I don't have anything to be calm about! My son is dead because his brother decided to ignore the orders his mother and I gave him. Stephan took him from us. He's going to be sorry for that!"

In his room, Stephan could hear his father raving, but was unable to make out his words. He thought about what both parents had just said to him. His mother said she could not forgive him. His father said he would forgive him only when he brought Joseph back from the dead.

Stephan walked to the window and looked outside. While focusing on the alley, he mumbled, "There's only one thing to do. I've got to get away from both of them. I certainly can't stay here."

While the sound of his father's raging was in his ears, Stephan opened the window and climbed out. When his feet touched the ground, he dashed to the alley, then ran as fast as he could to the street. There, he turned and ran for several blocks until he reached downtown Budapest.

He stopped on a street corner, contemplating his situation while catching his breath. People on the sidewalk moved past him from both directions. He reached into his hip pocket and pulled out his wallet. Flipping the currency slowly, he totaled in his mind how much money he had on him. He thought on it for a moment, then decided to take a freight boat and get out of Budapest. His father wouldn't want him as a crewman, anyway. He had enough money to take him anywhere in the country if he took a freight boat. They were always glad to carry a few passengers for a price. But the price would beat anything on a tour boat.

He would go somewhere else and get a

job. With his experience, he no doubt could find work on a tour boat in another part of Hungary. His parents would probably not care that he was gone, but just in case they should try to find him for some reason, he would need to take a freight boat where the captain and crew did not know him.

He would have to go south since his father's boat ran north out of Budapest. Chances would be slim that anyone on a southbound boat would know him. He knew he should wait till after dark and take one of the boats that traveled at night. He would decide later where to get off.

With this settled in his mind, he headed down the street in the direction of the river. As he drew near the docks, with the familiar sounds of boat whistles and engines and the loud voices of dock personnel, he realized it would be quite easy to run into someone he knew. He decided to hide in one of the storage sheds and wait for the day to pass. When night fell, he would find the right boat and get on board.

Soon he was at one of the sections on the wharf where a string of storage sheds stood in a straight line only a few yards apart. When he drew up, he looked both ways to make sure there was no one looking his direction.

There were wagons on both sides where dock men were loading or unloading goods at sheds, but they were some distance away and the men were wrapped up in their work. None were looking his way.

The shed doors were metal and slid on metal tracks. Carefully, he slid the door open, allowing minimal squeaking sounds. Stepping inside, he drew it closed. There were small windows on the sides of the sheds, which in spite of the crust of dirt on the glass, allowed some light.

Stephan wriggled his way through stacked boxes and crates to the rear of the shed, where he sat down on the hard wooden floor between two crates.

For the next hour or so, Stephan wrestled with his thoughts. In his mind, he pictured Joseph's dead body that he held in his arms before the police took it to the morgue. He shook his head in an effort to clear away the memory. It did, but was soon replaced with the scene he had experienced at the Bartok house when his parents tore his heart out.

Their cruel words echoed through his head over and over until he put his palms to his ears as if that would keep him from hearing them.

After a little while the harsh words faded, and just as Stephan took his hands away from his ears, he heard male voices. His body stiffened when he heard the door squeak open and the voices grow louder.

He scooted farther back between the crates until his body touched the wall, and he held his breath. He caught a glimpse of both men as they began taking small boxes from a tall stack and carrying them to the wagon. They were talking about Saturday's riot at the capitol grounds and the large number of people who were killed and injured.

Stephan forced every part of his body to remain still, though the muscles of his legs were aching. At one frightening moment, the two men began working on a stack of boxes only inches from him. He couldn't believe they didn't see him, but they took only four of the boxes from that stack and carried them to the wagon. Seconds later, the door screeched in its track and went shut.

Stephan mopped sweat from his brow with his hands, took a deep breath, and heaved a sigh of relief.

He laid his head back against the wall and closed his eyes. Instantly, his mind went to his little brother. Joseph had been dead for only a day, but he missed him terribly. Hot tears surfaced, burning his eyes. Blinking against the tears, he raised his eyes toward heaven.

"Oh, Joseph, I miss you so much! But at least I know you're in heaven. I'm so glad to know that. I . . . I'm sure you're happy. That's more than I can say about me."

Stephan Varda lost control for a moment and sobbed with his face pressed against his knees. As he regained control of himself, he blinked and wiped tears. *Maybe he really can hear me!*

Looking heavenward again, he said with quivering voice, "Joseph, please forgive me for letting you persuade me to take you to hear the king. I'm almost twenty years old. I should have known better. It's my fault you had to die. No, I didn't throw the brick, but that brick couldn't have hit you if you weren't there. I took you! I'm sorry . . . so sorry! Please forgive me."

Stephan drew a shuddering breath. "Joseph, I miss you. I . . . I hope someday we can see each other again."

Suddenly a black thought descended over his mind, and he muttered, "No, I guess not. There's no way God would let me into heaven after what I did."

Eleven

While Stephan Varda was heading for the docks, at the Bartok house his father was becoming angrier by the minute as he paced the floor. Bela was walking beside him, trying to reason with him.

Beatrice was sitting on the couch beside Ravina with the Bible open between them. She was trying to concentrate on what Ravina was showing her, but Miklos's frequent angry outbursts at Bela kept drawing her attention away.

Suddenly, Miklos stopped, stared into Bela's eyes and growled, "Enough, Bela! I'm going back there and giving Stephan a good beating for his blatant disobedience!"

Beatrice burst into tears and jumped up. She stood in front of her husband. "No, Miklos! Beating Stephan isn't going to accomplish anything."

Miklos's mouth pulled down into an om-

225

inous slash. "Oh yes, it will! It will make me feel better."

Beatrice touched his arm, meeting his hard gaze through her tears. "I . . . I've been thinking about the way we treated Stephan. What he did was wrong, yes. But like Bela said, you and I have gone out of our way many times to make Joseph happy." She squeezed his arm. "Stephan asked us to forgive him, and we refused. We were wrong, Miklos. Terribly wrong. Don't go back there and beat him, I beg you."

Miklos's face turned crimson. He drew a breath to speak, but Beatrice cut him off. "Stephan asked us to forgive him, but we said no. What kind of parents are we? He is still our son. I . . . I can't stand this. I must go and tell him I *do* forgive him. Will you come with me and tell him you forgive him, too?"

Miklos set his jaw stubbornly. "You can go ahead if you want to, but I am *not* going to forgive him! Joseph is dead, and it's all his fault!"

Beatrice released her grip on Miklos's arm and ran from the parlor and down the hall. When she reached Stephan's room, she opened the door and burst in. Her mouth fell open and her eyes widened when she saw the window standing open and the room unoccupied. She dashed to the window and looked out, running her gaze across the yard and into the alley. Her face went ashy white.

Her hand muffled the cry that was trying to escape from her mouth. At the edge of hysteria, she turned back, stumbled to the bed, and collapsed on it.

At that instant, Ravina rushed in, and at a glance, she could see that Stephan was gone. She went to Beatrice, sat down on the bed beside her, and laid a hand on the back of her head.

Beatrice rolled over, her entire body shaking. "Oh, Ravina, how terrible Miklos and I have treated that poor boy! We let our grief and anger rule our better judgment. Stephan will always live with those hateful words we hurled at him. We should have listened to you and Bela. We should have waited until our anger had cooled and we were thinking rationally."

With that, Beatrice put her hands to her face. "Oh, dear God in heaven! Please give us another chance with Stephan. Help us to find him!"

Ravina left the bed and stuck her head out the window. Stephan was gone, all right.

Suddenly, Beatrice left the bed and darted out of the room, hurrying up the hall. She burst into the parlor to find Bela still trying to get Miklos calmed down. "Stephan is gone! He went out the bedroom window. Oh, Miklos, we must find him!"

Anger was still burning in Miklos's eyes. "Gone, eh? Well, you're right. We must find him so I can give him the beating he deserves!"

Bela stepped between Beatrice and Miklos and took a firm hold on the man's arms. "Miklos, listen to me! Get a grip on yourself. Hasn't enough damage been done already? We've got to find Stephan so you and Beatrice can reconcile with him. If we don't, he may never come back. Right now you may not care, but Beatrice does. Why go on like this just to satisfy your own stubborn determination? Think of Beatrice. She's a mother. She realizes how wrong she was to treat Stephan as she did. She wants him back. Don't you love her enough to forget your own anger toward Stephan and help her find her son?"

Miklos wiped a palm over his mouth, looked at the pleading eyes of his wife, then set his eyes once again on Bela.

Seeing resignation in Miklos's eyes, Bela

said, "Let's get a plan together. Where do you think we should start looking?"

Miklos took a deep breath. "Janos Kudra. He's probably Stephan's closest friend. No doubt we'll find him at Janos's house."

"You know where that is, don't you?"

"Yes."

"Then, if it's all right, Ravina and I will go with you."

"Of course it's all right," said Beatrice. "It will help to have you with us. You two have shown him love today. All we showed him was anger and contempt."

Janos Kudra was surprised to see the Vardas and the Bartoks when he opened his door in response to the knock. "Well, hello. What can I do for you?"

Miklos stepped up closer. "Janos, is Stephan here?"

A frown penciled itself across Janos's brow. "Why, no. Is he supposed to be?"

"He — well, as you know, he's been staying at his aunt and uncle's house since yesterday. You also know that his mother and I were in Heviz. We arrived by train this morning, knowing only that our Joseph had been killed in the riot yesterday. When we arrived at the Bartoks' house, we were given the horrible details. Stephan's mother and I were pretty rough on him. In our sorrow and grief over Joseph, we blamed Stephan for his death and were pretty cruel about it. Especially me. When he was alone in his room, he went out the window and ran away. We — we want to find him and work things out between us. My first thought was that he might have come here."

"No, sir. But I would like to help you find him. May I?"

"Well, of course. I'm thinking that since he knows a lot of people at the docks, he might have gone there."

"Then let's head for the docks," said Janos, stepping out and closing the door behind him.

The two couples and Janos Kudra climbed into the Bartok carriage, and Bela pointed the horse toward the river. While they rode through the streets, they talked about the best strategy for their search. Bela and Ravina would go one direction on the docks and Miklos and Beatrice would go the opposite direction. Janos would work his way among the dockworkers, while the Bartoks and the Vardas moved among the people on the docks, giving Stephan's description and asking if they had seen him.

When they reached the river, Bela parked the wagon in one of the parking lots. The five of them agreed to meet in front of a nearby shack on the docks where fishing equipment and bait were sold, and went their separate ways.

At the very time the search was being made, Stephan was still in the storage shed. His nerves were stretched tight. A delivery wagon was parked at the open door of the shed, and two men were carrying boxes inside. They were making a new stack directly in front of where Stephan was hidden, and so far, had not detected his presence.

The two delivery men were joking with each other and laughing while they worked. Stephan's head came up when he heard another male voice cut into their laughter. He recognized the voice. It was Janos Kudra, and he was asking them if they had seen Stephan Varda, giving them his description.

When the two men told Janos they had not seen anyone of his friend's description, Janos thanked them and walked away.

Stephan wiped the sheen of sweat from his face, asking himself why his parents would care enough to tell Janos about his disappearance. They hated him because he had killed his brother. It was as if he had thrown the brick that took Joseph's life.

The sun was lowering in the western sky when the two couples and Janos Kudra met in front of the bait shack. Disappointment showed on their faces as they told each other there had been no sign of Stephan and no one had seen him, even the men who worked other tour and freight boats and who knew him.

"What do we do now?" asked Beatrice, her features drawn and bleak.

"I think we should go to police headquarters and talk to Chief Serta," said Bela. "We need to report Stephan's disappearance so the police can keep an eye out for him."

Miklos nodded. "Good idea. Let's do it."

"If you folks don't mind," said Janos, "I'll have you drop me off at home. There's no need for me to see the chief with you."

"Of course," said Bela. "We sure do appreciate your willingness to come down here to the docks and help us in the search."

"More than we can tell you," said

Beatrice. "You're a true friend."

A smile curved Janos's lips. "Stephan has always been a true friend to me. I sure hope you find him."

In Chief Akman Serta's office, he listened to the story as told by the Vardas and the Bartoks. When they finished, he leaned forward and put his elbows on his desk. "I'm really sorry to hear this. I have to tell you — if I were in Stephan's shoes, I would be plenty upset and discouraged. I will advise all the men on the force so they can keep a lookout for him."

"We appreciate that, Chief," said Miklos.

Serta nodded. "One thing I need to explain, though. Since Stephan is nineteen years old and chose to leave the Bartok home, I cannot authorize a thorough search of the city."

"We understand that," said Beatrice. "But we thank you that you will advise your men to watch for him."

The others also thanked Serta for his kindness concerning Stephan and left the police building. As Bela put the carriage in motion, Beatrice said, "Miklos, maybe Stephan will think it over and somehow find it in him to come home. Let's have Bela take us there now."

"It might be good to go to their house first," Miklos said. "He might go back there, since my sister and Bela have treated him so well."

Beatrice swallowed a lump that rose in her throat. "Yes. Let's do that."

When they arrived at the Bartok house and went inside, Beatrice ran down the hall and into Stephan's room. It was just as it had been before: unoccupied.

The others caught up, and Ravina put an arm around her. "Honey, you and Miklos are welcome to stay here. I think that at home there'll be so much to remind you of Joseph."

Beatrice stroked Ravina's cheek. "You're so kind to offer, but I really want to go home. Stephan may fool us and be there."

"Right," said Miklos. "We have to see. We should be going."

Bela laid a hand on Miklos's arm. "If he's not there, but you find that it's too hard to stay in the house — like Ravina said — you're sure welcome to come back for as long as you want."

Miklos patted the hand that was on his arm. "Bela, after the way I've treated you, I'm surprised you would want me back in your house. I'm sorry. I've been an obnoxious nincompoop. Please forgive me."

A smile spread over Bela's face. "You're forgiven. Let's take you home so we can see if perhaps Stephan has gone there."

Bela drove the carriage across the Danube River on the Margaret Bridge from the Buda Hills section to the lower ground on the east side of the river. When they pulled up in front of the Varda house, all was still.

"Maybe he's in there, honey," Miklos said to his wife as he hopped to the ground and gave her his hand.

While Beatrice was getting down with Miklos's help, Bela said, "Don't forget our offer. Our house is open to you anytime."

Miklos managed a smile. "Thank you. We'll keep it in mind if it gets too tough in there."

Ravina told her brother and Beatrice that she loved them as they walked toward the front porch. Both gave her a grim smile.

The Bartok carriage rolled away and the Vardas went inside the house. It was quiet as a tomb.

Beatrice moved into the hall and called, "Stepha-a-a-an! Stepha-a-a-an! We're home! Are you here?"

Both waited for their son to reply if he was in the house.

Silence.

"I'll check the boys' bedroom," said Miklos, hurrying ahead of her.

Beatrice followed slowly, her heart in her throat. She kept her eyes focused on Miklos as he paused in front of the boys' bedroom and called Stephan's name.

Silence.

Miklos glanced back at Beatrice, then opened the door. She hurried toward it, but drew to a halt when he shook his head. "He's not here, honey."

Miklos's broad shoulders sagged as he moved back toward her. There were tears in his eyes. "I went too far, honey. I went too far. I let my hurt and rage rule my thoughts and my tongue. I —" He swallowed a sob and choked on it. "I keep thinking about what Bela said to me before I went into that room after Stephan. 'If you go in there fuming like this, you could do irreparable damage. It is unwise to speak or act when you're in the heat of anger.' But . . . but stupid, foolish me. I went into that room fuming, in the heat of anger."

He wiped tears. "Oh, why didn't I listen to Bela? Why? He reminded me that I had already lost one son, and told me if I didn't change and forgive Stephan, I would lose him, too."

Beatrice took hold of his hand. "Honey,

I also mistreated Stephan. I told him I could not forgive him."

"I know, I know," he said quietly, "but I was worse. I know I cut his heart out when I said the only way I would forgive him is if he brought Joseph back from the dead. How wicked of me! And now, like Bela said, we've lost Stephan, too. Oh, what have I done? What have I done?"

At the Budapest docks, Stephan Varda made his way up the gangplank of a freight boat just before midnight, and scanning the faces of the crew by lantern light on deck, he saw no familiar face. Approaching the captain, who stood near the bow, he said, "Good evening, sir. Someone on the dock told me this boat is going south to Baja. Is that correct?"

"It sure is, son," said the silver-haired captain. "You looking for a ride?"

"Yes, sir."

"Where to?"

"Well, Baja, since that's where you're going."

The captain cocked his head. "You mean you really don't care where you go, just so you go?"

Stephan cleared his throat nervously. "Ah . . . yes. I really don't want to explain my situation, sir. I just —"

"It's none of my business, son. If you've got twenty forints in your pocket, you have your ride to Baja."

Stephan's mouth curved into a smile. He had barely more than twenty forints, but at least he had the fare for the trip. He took out his wallet, paid the man, and was glad to be aboard.

He walked across the deck to the port side of the boat, leaned his tired body on the railing, and looked down at the reflection of the dock's lanterns on the surface of the river. Lifting his eyes skyward to the east, he saw the full moon above the city. The moon was clear and bright and allowed him a view of the outlines of many buildings along the docks, and even the taller ones toward downtown.

Stephan rubbed his chin. *This may be the last time I ever see Budapest,* he thought as a lump found its way into his throat. *I'm on my own now. Not much money left. Baja is almost to the Yugoslavian border. I'll have to decide what to do once I get to Baja. I'll need a job, and all I know is river work. I'll find something. If not in Baja, somewhere else. I just want to work until my mind and body are so tired that I won't have to think or feel. Joseph is dead, and Papa and Mama don't want anything to do with me. I'll just bury myself in whatever job I get.*

Moments later, the boat was loosed from the dock, the engine roared, and they were on their way south. Stephan looked around to see if there were any other passengers. Everyone else looked like crewmen.

In a matter of minutes, the boat was leaving the city behind. Stephan let his eyes stray toward the bow. He took one long, last look at the city he knew so well — the city that claimed the life of his little brother.

A mist of tears covered his eyes. He wiped the tears away, lowered his head, left the rail, and found a bench next to the base of the wheelhouse. Slumping down on the bench, he leaned back, closed his eyes, and let his mind wander to his home and happier times.

The next day was Monday, March 27.

King Franz Joseph was still at the Savoy Mansion Hotel in Budapest. He had been in meetings all day on Sunday with Burgomaster Markus Zelko and the men of the Hungarian Parliament. They were attempting to iron out problems that had arisen because of Saturday's riot at the capitol grounds and to come to an agreement on the three issues the king had been set to address in his speech.

The burgomaster and the men of parliament had agreed with King Franz Joseph that he should leave things as they had been before Saturday until he could let the people of Hungary know what changes he had planned to tell them about in the speech. He would simply put the changes in the newspapers.

After breakfast that Monday morning, Markus Zelko was alone with the king in the royal suite.

Zelko was telling Franz Joseph of comments he had heard from citizens of Budapest and surrounding areas concerning his statements made on Saturday about conceding in only one area about Hungary's official language.

"Sir," said Zelko, "the people of Hungary want their language back, and they are very serious about it. They want the German language thrown out as the legal and official language of the country. If you don't do as they want, the riot we saw Saturday was a picnic compared to what will come next. I implore you — give us our Magyar back."

There was a knock at the door.

The burgomaster jumped up from his chair. "I'll get it, sir."

Zelko opened the door and one of the guards said, "There are two gentlemen here who would like to see the king, sir. They are waiting in the hall. They are from the Danube Printing Company."

Zelko turned and looked at the king. "Two gentlemen are here to see you from the Danube Printing Company, sir."

"Find out what they want," said Franz Joseph.

"Yes, sir. I'll be right back."

The burgomaster closed the door of the inner room and crossed the large, open room.

A second guard was standing at the door. It was open, and when Zelko drew up, he recognized Eiger Bethlen, the owner of Danube Printing Company, Budapest's most prominent printers. They not only did commercial printing, but also printed books.

There was a younger man with Bethlen, whom Zelko had seen around the city but did not know. He set his eyes on the older man. "Good morning, Mr. Bethlen."

"Good morning, Burgomaster Zelko," said Bethlen. "They told us at the desk that King Franz Joseph is in his suite. We

241

would like to see him, if he will receive us."

Zelko stepped into the hall and pulled the door closed behind him.

"What did you want to see him about?"

"A very important matter that is related to the language change. Let me introduce this young man. Burgomaster Zelko, this is Arpad Fulop. Arpad does the typesetting for all the books we print."

Zelko extended his hand. "I'm glad to meet you, Mr. Fulop."

"The pleasure is mine, sir," said Fulop. "I have long admired you, but until now have never had the opportunity to meet."

Zelko gave him a smile, then looked at Bethlen. "I assume this matter is quite important."

"Very important, Burgomaster. And it is urgent. We really need a few minutes with him."

"As you know, the king is not very well acquainted with who is who in this country, Mr. Bethlen, but I will tell him who you are and that you need a few minutes with him."

"I would appreciate it very much. It is indeed very important."

Zelko turned and opened the door. To the guard he said, "These gentlemen have an urgent need to talk to the king. I think he will see them. I will be right back."

The guard nodded, and as Zelko headed for the door of the inner room, he invited Bethlen and Fulop to step inside.

As Markus Zelko drew up to the king, he said, "Sir, are you acquainted with the Danube Printing Company?"

"I've seen the name somewhere, but I really don't know anything about them."

"Well, they are Hungary's largest printers. The owner of the company, Eiger Bethlen, is here, along with the man who sets the type for the books they print. His name is Arpad Fulop. You see, they print books as well as do commercial printing for all kinds of businesses. And most important, sir, they also do all the printing of official papers and documents for the government. They are the only printers in all of Hungary who can do it."

Franz Joseph nodded. "I see."

"Mr. Bethlen says he and Mr. Fulop need a few minutes with you. He says it is urgent and of utmost importance. It has to do with the language change. I urge you to give them their few minutes."

"Certainly. I will be glad to do so. You know this Eiger Bethlen personally?"

"Yes."

"All right. Bring them in. I want you to sit in on it, too."

"Yes, sir."

Markus Zelko was smiling broadly as he headed for the door.

Twelve

King Franz Joseph was standing at the large window, looking down at the boats on the Danube River when Burgomaster Markus Zelko ushered Eiger Bethlen and Arpad Fulop into the room.

Zelko made the introductions, and all four sat down on plush chairs in a small circle.

The king looked at Bethlen and said, "Burgomaster Zelko tells me you have the largest printing company in Hungary."

"Yes, sir."

"And I understand that you print all of the government's official papers and documents."

"That we do, sir. And we feel it is a privilege."

"Burgomaster Zelko said that you requested to see me about something concerning the language change."

Bethlen scooted forward in his chair. "Yes, sir. We wouldn't have bothered you, but it is very important."

Franz Joseph nodded. "What can I do for you?"

"Well, sir, I have a serious problem I need to explain, because I very much need your help."

"Go on."

Bethlen nervously inched a little closer to the edge of the seat. "When the Hungarian Parliament put into law that the German language was to be the official and legal language of Hungary, I was given official papers ordering me to print all government papers and documents in German."

"Yes."

"The papers also made it clear that all books printed by our company must now be in German."

"Correct. And I assume you are doing so."

Bethlen nodded. "We have complied with the edict, but I have one problem in all of this in which I need your help, sir."

Franz Joseph adjusted his position in the chair slightly. "And that is?"

"Several months before parliament put the language change into law, Danube

Printing Company had made a contract with the Federated Bookstores of Hungary to print Bibles in the Hungarian mother tongue."

The king nodded, meeting Bethlen's gaze.

"Immediately upon signing the contract, we started setting up a Bible to be printed in Magyar. Arpad, here, who has proven to be the best typesetter in all of Hungary and Austria, has labored hard on the Old Testament, working long hours." Bethlen paused, smiled at Arpad, then turned back to the king. "Since Arpad is Jewish, he has been thrilled to work on the Old Testament."

Franz Joseph looked at Arpad. "I'm sure that is so. Do you have a problem with setting type for the New Testament, since Jews do not believe it should be in the canon?"

"Not really a problem, your majesty. I am just not as thrilled. I have already begun setting type for the New Testament. In fact, I am almost halfway through it."

Eiger Bethlen eased back in his chair slightly. "One week before the new law went in, King Franz Joseph, Arpad finished setting the type for the Old Testament. It is ready to print now. And as he just told you, he has been working on setting type for the New Testament. Believing that you would announce in your speech last Saturday that the new law had been rescinded, I told Arpad to keep setting the New Testament type. Since the riot broke out, and you were not able to finish the part about the language problem, I need to know if we can go ahead with our plan to print the Bibles in Magyar."

"We will talk about that in a moment, Mr. Bethlen," said the king. Then setting his eyes on Arpad, he said, "In my formative years, Mr. Fulop, I lived in a community that was heavily populated by Jews. I know what the Jewish people believe and how they think. Tell me, how can you, as a Jew, justify setting type for the New Testament?"

"I can do it for two basic reasons, sir," said Arpad. "The first is that I believe the New Testament does have much literary value. There is a great deal of Jewish history in the New Testament. And second, Mr. Bethlen has treated me in such a wonderful way ever since I came to work for him six years ago, I will gladly do it for him."

"I greatly admire you for this, Mr. Fulop."

"Thank you, sir. I can understand how the Hungarian people feel about their mother tongue being replaced by the German language. The Jews of the world would love to have our mother tongue back."

"Hebrew."

"Yes. But we have been forced to use the Yiddish language since the ninth century. And you probably know that Yiddish is of German descent."

Franz Joseph nodded. "I do. Yiddish is a fusion of Hebrew and German, which was done by the Germans in the ninth century."

"You learned a lot from your Jewish neighbors, didn't you?"

"I sure did. And I can appreciate how the Jews feel. They naturally want their mother tongue back."

"And that is exactly the way it is with the Hungarian people, sir," said Eiger Bethlen. "We want our mother tongue back in every facet of our lives. And let me say right here, it will cost my company heavily in a financial way if you say we must print the Bibles in German. We would have to start all over, and this would bring about a giant problem."

"Oh? A giant problem, Mr. Bethlen?"

"Yes."

"And that is?"

Bethlen glanced at Arpad, then back to the king. "Arpad and his wife, Sarai, are scheduled to immigrate to America in early May. He is being given a job in a large printing company in New York City by his uncle, who owns the company. It will put him in a position to one day be owner of the company when his uncle retires. I hate to lose him, but I cannot offer that kind of opportunity to him. I can't blame him for accepting his uncle's offer. However, it will be devastating to my company if Arpad has to start all over and put the Bible into German. He would not be here to finish it, and finding another typesetter as proficient as he is would be next to impossible. My company has a deadline in the contract with the Federated Bookstores when the Bibles have to be off the press. If everything stays the same, Arpad will be done in another three or four weeks, and we can begin printing the Bibles. Otherwise, we will never make the deadline."

The king glanced at Markus Zelko and saw the pleading in his eyes.

He then smiled at Bethlen. "Mr. Bethlen, I am in full sympathy with your dilemma. I am giving you permission to continue with the Bibles in Magyar."

Bethlen and Fulop exchanged happy glances, then Bethlen looked at the king. "Thank you, sir. Thank you so much."

Franz Joseph left his chair and went to a small table where his valise lay. He opened it, took out a sheet of paper, pen, ink, and blotter, and sat down at the table. Looking at Eiger Bethlen, he said, "I am going to write a letter stating that I have given you permission to proceed printing your Bibles in Magyar. You need to have it in writing so if there is ever any question about it, you will have this letter as your authority."

"Thank you, sir," Bethlen said. "I appreciate this more than I can ever tell you."

The king dipped the pen in the inkwell and scratched out the letter. When he finished, he looked at the burgomaster. "Mr. Zelko, I have made a place here where you can sign as witness to this document."

When it was done, a relieved Eiger Bethlen folded the paper, slipped it inside his coat pocket, thanked the king once more, and left with his typesetter.

The keeper of Budapest's City Morgue looked up from his desk as two well-dressed men came into his office. He glanced at the clock on the wall, noting that it was barely five minutes after eight o'clock in the morning. He looked back at the men, and it took him only a second to recognize one of them. He rose from the chair, smiling. "Well, look who's here! Bela Bartok! How are you, old friend?"

A surprised expression came to Bela's features. "Dom! The last I knew, you were morgue keeper up in Miskolc. How long have you been here?"

"Almost three months. Marla wanted to come back to Budapest, and I heard that they were looking for a new morgue keeper here, so I wired Chief Serta and asked him to put in a good word for me."

"Well, I'm glad. Let me introduce you to Miklos Varda. He is Ravina's brother. Miklos, shake hands with Dom Ruda. He and I went to school together."

When Miklos and Dom had greeted each other and shaken hands, Dom looked at his friend. "Well, tell me, Bela, are you still running those lumber camps in the mountains of the Northern Uplands?"

"Well, yes and no," said Bela. "I had some health problems five years ago and just couldn't handle it anymore. Commuting between here and there two or three times a week simply became too much. I still own the business, and it's doing well. I hired a man to oversee it for me. He does the work, and Ravina and I still enjoy a good income from the business. I spend a great deal of my time working for my church now."

"Oh yes. I remember. You got really tied up with that church several years ago, didn't you?"

"Yes, and I love every minute of it."

Dom glanced at Miklos and noted the grave look in his eyes. "Bela, I got so excited when I saw you that I didn't think to ask why you and your brother-in-law are here. I'm sorry."

"Miklos's son, Joseph, was killed Saturday in the riot, Dom. The police brought the body here."

Dom's hand went to his forehead. "Oh yes, of course. Joseph Varda. I think my brain needs repair. I apologize, Mr. Varda. I should have known who you were when Bela introduced us. I am so sorry about your little boy. Ten years old, I believe."

"Yes," said Miklos, his voice tightening. "We're here to let you know that we will be making arrangements for Joseph's body to be picked up by the Baross Funeral Home. We're going there next."

"All right," said Dom. "Ah . . . Bela . . ."

"Yes?"

"I . . . I want to suggest that —" He

looked at Miklos. "Mr. Varda, I think it would be best that you tell the people at Baross that you want a closed-coffin funeral."

Miklos's face blanched. "You mean because —"

"Yes, sir. The brick did extensive damage. I don't think the undertakers can do enough cosmetic work to — well, you know . . ."

Miklos swallowed with difficulty and nodded. "I understand what you're saying, Mr. Ruda."

"If you would rather take a look before you make a decision about it, it's your right and privilege, sir."

Miklos's features lost more color. "Ah . . . no. I'll take your word for it."

"Would you feel better if your brother-in-law viewed the body?"

Miklos turned his sad eyes to Bela. "Would you mind?"

"I think you and Beatrice will both feel better about it if I do."

Miklos sat down on a wooden chair and watched as Dom led Bela through the office door and down the hall.

Less than five minutes had passed when they returned. "Miklos, you don't want to see him," Bela said. "It would be even

254

worse for Beatrice. I strongly advise you to tell the people at Baross that you want the casket closed and sealed."

On their way back to the Danube Printing Company building, Eiger Bethlen and Arpad Fulop were making their way along the busy street, drawing near the Baross Funeral Home. Their attention was pulled to two men who were coming out the door.

"Look, Arpad," said Eiger. "That's Miklos Varda coming out of the funeral home."

Both Bethlen and Fulop knew Miklos Varda, for they had often ridden his boat when traveling with their wives to Vienna on weekends.

The dismal look on Miklos's face brightened a bit when he spotted the printer and his typesetter coming toward them. He greeted them as they drew up and introduced them to Bela, explaining that he was married to his sister, Ravina.

"Has . . . has something happened, Miklos?" Eiger said.

"Yes. Something horrible," said Miklos, then told him and Arpad of Joseph's death during the riot at the capitol grounds on Saturday. "Bela and I were just making funeral arrangements."

Both men spoke their condolences.

"This has to be tough on Mrs. Varda and Stephan, too, Miklos," said Arpad. "How are they holding up in their grief? I was impressed with how close Stephan was to his brother and the love he showed him."

Miklos felt his mouth go dry. He cleared his throat. "Yes, Arpad. My boys were very close. Stephan and his mother are both taking it very hard."

Eiger laid a hand on Miklos's arm. "If there is anything I can do, my friend . . ."

"I appreciate that, Eiger. And if there is, I will sure let you know."

"Good. When is the funeral?"

"Ten o'clock Wednesday morning."

Eiger squeezed his arm. "Myra and I will be here."

"Sarai and I will be here, too, if Mr. Bethlen will give me the time off," said Arpad.

"Of course," responded Eiger. "All four of us will be here. And you pass my condolences along to Mrs. Varda and Stephan, won't you?"

"Certainly." Miklos wished with all of his heart that Stephan was home.

"For me, too, Mr. Varda," put in Arpad.

"I will, thank you."

With that, Eiger and Arpad hurried on

to the Danube Printing Company, eager to share the good news of their meeting with the king.

Eiger quickly called for a meeting of all his employees and told them about the king giving permission for them to proceed with printing the Bibles in Magyar. There was much rejoicing.

Arpad went right back to work on his typesetting.

At the Varda home, Ravina and Beatrice were sitting side by side at the kitchen table. Ravina had her Bible open and showed Beatrice several passages on salvation. "So you see, honey, that night at our house in February, Joseph did exactly what I just showed you. God's Word makes it clear that Joseph is in heaven."

Beatrice used a handkerchief to dab at the tears in her eyes. "Thank you for showing me this, Ravina. It's so different than what our church teaches, as you well know."

"Yes. Bela and I thank the Lord every day for getting the real gospel to us. It's so wonderful to know Jesus and to have the absolute assurance that heaven is our eternal home. Religion cannot give this assurance, Beatrice, because it involves human works and religious rites. Salvation is by grace and not of works, as I showed you in Ephesians chapter 2."

Beatrice sniffed and kept dabbing at her eyes.

"Beatrice, I believe you understand that unless you turn to the Lord like Joseph did, you will never see him again. He is in heaven. You will end up in hell if you die like you are." Ravina prayed, *Precious Holy Spirit, please work on her by Your mighty power. I want to see her saved so badly.*

Beatrice was about to say something when they heard footsteps on the back porch and the door came open.

When Beatrice saw her husband enter with Bela behind him, she left Ravina's side and hurried to Miklos. "Honey, have all the arrangements been made?"

"Yes. The morgue keeper is a friend of Bela's. He . . . he told us that we should tell the people at the funeral home that we want a closed-coffin funeral."

Beatrice's face pinched. "Wh-why?"

"The brick did quite a bit of damage to Joseph's head. I asked Bela to take a look at it. And he said neither you nor I should see it. I didn't want anyone else to see it, either. So I told the undertaker to seal up the coffin."

Beatrice's eyes filled with tears. Miklos took her in his arms. "I'm sorry, honey, but it's best this way."

"I understand," she said, sniffling.

Ravina looked at Bela. "Who was this friend at the morgue?"

"Dom Ruda. They've been back here for almost three months. I'll tell you about it later."

Ravina nodded.

"The funeral is set for Wednesday morning at ten," Miklos said. "We stopped at the church and told Reverend Lukacs. He said that would be fine. Then we went to the telegraph office and sent a wire to Matthias and Vivian. I'm sure they will be here for the funeral if they feel they can leave Grandpa."

"I hope they can," Ravina said. "It will help if they are here."

Suddenly, Beatrice drew a shuddering breath and began weeping. "I don't know how I'm going to get through the funeral! It would help me immensely if Stephan would come back and I could get things reconciled with him. Oh, I never should have talked to him like I did — especially saying that I could not forgive him."

Ravina stepped up and laid a hand on Beatrice's shoulder. "Honey, don't torture yourself over it."

Beatrice clung hard to her husband and looked through her tears at Ravina. "But I tore Stephan's heart out, Ravina! Once such words leave our mouths, they are gone and we can never take them back, no matter how sorry we are that we spoke them. I would give anything if I could make them disappear as if they had never been spoken, but it's impossible."

She sucked in a sharp breath then cried, "Oh, the horrible damage and heartache the wrong words spoken in hurt and anger can cause! I want so much the chance to ask my precious son's forgiveness and to give him mine. The pain I'm feeling over what I said and did to Stephan is almost as awful as the pain of losing Joseph."

She looked up into her husband's eyes. "Miklos, somehow we must find Stephan. I will never give up searching for that boy! I need him so desperately."

Easing back in Miklos's arms, Beatrice put her hands to her ravaged face. The tears spilled through her fingers and ran down her arms.

"Honey, I want above all else to find our son, too," said Miklos fervently. "Nothing in life matters as much as being able to have Stephan back and beg his forgiveness."

Bela stepped closer. "Miklos, Beatrice, I realize you don't believe in prayer the way we do it, but the Lord knows where Stephan is. Would you mind if right now we bow before Him and ask Him to send that boy home?"

Beatrice removed her hands from her face. "Oh, please do, Bela! I wouldn't mind at all!"

Bela met Miklos's stern gaze. "Is it all right with you? After all, this is your house."

A stone-faced Miklos Varda thought on it a moment. "It's all right, Bela."

Beatrice bowed her head and closed her eyes as did Ravina and Bela.

While Bela led in prayer, Miklos stood silently looking on, wondering to himself if God was really listening.

Thirteen

As dawn was breaking in Hungary's eastern sky, Stephan Varda was standing on the deck of the freight boat, leaning on the rail as it chugged southward on the Danube River toward Baja. Foggy wisps, which were normal for that time of year, floated in the air a few feet above the surface of the river.

Just then, Stephan heard a grumble in the vicinity of his belly and realized he needed food. Shortly after they had pulled out of Budapest, Stephan had used the last of his money to purchase an apple and some coffee from the captain. At the time it helped to ease the hunger, but the long night was over and once again the organ in his midsection was sending unmistakable signals.

He murmured, "Somehow I'll feed you when we get to Baja."

He leaned harder on the rail and thought

about his situation. He must decide soon where to settle himself so he could find a job.

A lump rose in his throat as a deep loneliness filled his heart. He must start his life all over again. Alone. His parents didn't love him nor want him, and his little brother was dead.

I know disobeying Papa's firm command was wrong, he thought, *and I have paid the price and I will always carry the guilt. Joseph wouldn't be very proud of his big brother if I totally succumb to my grief and heartache and don't try to go on. I'll find the right job in the right place and will make something of myself.*

With a new resolve coursing through him, Stephan put his mind on the task before him. He told himself once again that with the experience he gained on his father's tour and freight boat, it would be best to seek work in that direction. However, as a boat crewman on the Danube River, he could easily run into men who knew him, who would report to his father where they saw him. Since his parents wanted him out of their lives, he didn't want them to have any idea where he might be.

He thought of Hungary's other river, the

Tisza, which also was heavily trafficked by tour and freight boats. Located in the eastern part of the country, the Tisza River ran south all the way from northeast Hungary and emptied into the Danube in southern Yugoslavia. On the Tisza, he would not be known by men in the tour and freight boat business.

The city of Szeged was on the Tisza River some seventy miles due east of Baja. He had been to Szeged once, when he was thirteen years old. Uncle Bela and Aunt Ravina had gone there on a brief vacation and had taken him with them. He remembered Szeged as being a friendly place, and it was exceptionally clean — like Budapest.

As Stephan contemplated going to Szeged after he arrived in Baja, he realized he would have to walk. He had no money with which to purchase a train ticket to Szeged. He told himself that possibly as he walked the road eastward, he would be able to catch rides with farmers who were driving their wagons from the small towns that went along the road.

Still leaning on the rail, Stephan's attention went to a tour boat that was coming from the south and no doubt headed for Budapest. To make sure no one on the approaching boat could recognize him if they knew him when it passed by, he walked across the deck to the other side and studied the cattle in the fields a few hundred yards away.

His stomach growled at him again.

It was almost noon when the city of Baja came into view. Seated on one of the deck's benches, Stephan rose and walked toward the bow, letting his eyes take in the skyline of Baja. He would stay there long enough to make an attempt to beg some food from someone. Then he would begin his seventy-mile trek to Szeged.

A deep loneliness gripped him as he thought about starting life all over again without his family.

Soon the boat veered from the center of the wide Danube River and angled toward the docks. The crewmen were readying themselves for the task of unloading the freight.

Stephan's stomach was an empty pit in his middle. He had been to Baja on several occasions and knew the city well. He decided to walk into the business district and see if a fruit merchant might take pity on him and give him something to eat.

When the boat was secured to the dock, Stephan thanked the captain for letting him travel on his boat and walked down the gangplank. He moved quickly from the docks and made his way to Baja's main street. As he headed for the business district, he came to a spot on Baja's east side where the street intersected with the road that led to Szeged. A sign on a pole had an arrow painted on it, pointing east. Below the arrow, the sign said: *Szeged, 112.63 kilometers.* It was seventy miles.

He paused for a moment and looked eastward along the Szeged Road. He saw wagons and buggies moving both directions on the road and thought that certainly he would be able to get rides along the way, which would prevent him from having to walk the entire distance.

As he moved on toward the business section, Stephan's attention was drawn to dark clouds that were gathering in the western sky. *Well,* he thought, *snow season is over in Hungary. This is the last week of March. The clouds are definitely darker than snow clouds. It looks like a good rain is in the offing. I sure hope the storm will not last long. As soon as I find something to eat, I must get on the road.*

In Baja's business district, two young women sat on a bench outside a small café in the marketplace, eating sandwiches and drinking coffee they had purchased in the café.

Both were noting the gathering clouds to the west. Andra Hardik looked at her cousin and said, "I think we're going to get a good downpour, don't you, Nikola?"

Nikola, who was nineteen, nodded. "Sure looks like it. We ought to be home before it hits, though."

"Mm-hmm. Good thing. Your mother doesn't have her raincoat with her, either."

Nikola ran her gaze both directions along the sidewalk. "Don't see her yet, but here comes Alice Berman — I mean Wadford. I'm still not used to her being married."

Andra leaned forward so she could see her lifelong friend. Although Alice was almost five years older than Andra and came from an extremely wealthy family, they had been close since their early school days.

The cousins both took the last bites of their sandwiches and drained their coffee cups while watching Alice thread her way among the busy shoppers toward them.

As she came near, Alice's eyes widened when she spotted the Hardik cousins. A smile spread over her face, and she hurried to them. "Hello, Andra, Nikola! You never know who you will run into in this place! Shopping?"

"We bought a couple of small things," replied Nikola. "We're just waiting for my mother." She scooted closer to Andra. "Here, sit down."

Alice did so, then looked at her friend. "Andra, I was hoping to get to see you some more while you're here for Nikola's wedding. Those few minutes last week when we ran into each other at the park weren't enough. I sure was glad to see that you could come home for the wedding, and that you were able to come this far ahead so you two could have some time together."

Andra smiled. "As soon as I received Nikola's letter with the wedding date in it, I showed it to my parents. They were happy to let me come right away. And I'm sure glad because the time is fleeting. June 2 will be here before we know it."

Nikola giggled. "Yes. And finally, I will be Mrs. Nathan Cheny!"

Alice smiled. "I know you and Nathan will have a wonderful marriage and will be very happy together."

Nikola smiled back. "So how's it going with you and Gene? Any better since that day we saw you in the park?"

Alice's countenance sagged. "It's about the same. I'm beginning to think he married me for my money. If I don't buy him everything he wants, he gets real hard to live with. We've been married a year and a half now, and his greed is only getting worse. Last week I finally decided there was only one way to handle him. I put him on a monthly allowance. Each month when he has spent his allowance, he will get nothing more until the next month rolls around."

Andra shook her head. "Alice, you and I talked about this before you married Gene. I told you then that with his coming from a middle-class family, you might have problems with him."

Alice sighed. "You did. And so did some of my other friends — and my parents. But I was so blindly in love, I couldn't see anything like that happening. I still love Gene, and I think he has some love for me, but his greatest love is for my money."

"I'm so sorry," said Andra. "I was hoping that in spite of everything, you and Gene would be happy together. What do you think? Is there a chance your marriage will get better?"

Alice shrugged. "Hard to say, but I'm going to give it everything I've got. Maybe when Gene gets to see his parents, he'll handle things better."

Andra's eyes widened. "You and Gene are going to America?"

"Yes. He misses his parents so. They've been gone almost a year now."

"Where do they live?"

"In Chicago, Illinois."

"When are you going?" asked Nikola.

"Probably early June. Gene does have a job, in spite of the fact that he is married to me, and has vacation time coming then. It will be after your wedding, though, so we'll be there to see you become Mrs. Nathan Cheny."

"Good. I'm glad for that."

Alice rose to her feet. "Well, ladies, I need to be going. It's been nice to talk to you. I hope, Andra, we can see each other again before you go back to America." She chuckled. "Who knows? Maybe we'll be on the same ship."

Andra stood up, as did Nikola.

Embracing Alice, Andra said, "Wouldn't it be nice if we *did* end up on the same ship?"

Alice kissed her friend's cheek and hurried away. Both young women looked around and, seeing no sign of Nikola's mother, sat down again.

"Honey, we've been so busy since you arrived, talking about my wedding," Nikola said. "Let's talk about you for a change. Any handsome young men in Memphis you're interested in?"

"There are three in my church who are nice young men, and I've dated all three several times but nothing serious has developed."

"Well, tell me about them."

Arriving at the marketplace, Stephan Varda approached the first fruit stand he came to. The merchant was just finishing a sale, and when the customer walked away, he looked at Stephan with a smile. "What can I do for you, young man?"

Stephan moved up to the counter, his nerves tingling. "Ah . . . sir, I'm traveling. I'm on my way from Budapest to Szeged to find a job. I . . . I've had some misfortune, and my money is gone. I was wondering if you could spare a couple pieces of fruit."

The merchant's smile was quickly replaced with a scowl. "Get out of here! If I fed every tramp with a sob story who begs for food, I'd be out of business. On your way before I call a policeman!"

Frustrated, Stephan moved on down the street. In the next block he saw three café signs and his stomach growled again. Wouldn't it be wonderful to sit down to a nice meal? But his money was gone. Though he hated to have to do it, he would try another fruit merchant.

Before reaching the end of the block, he came upon another fruit stand. He made the same approach and was angrily told the same thing. He walked away disappointed, reached the corner, and crossed the street.

While he made his way down the next block, he looked at the café signs again, wishing he had the funds to buy a meal. His eye fell on another fruit stand, which stood next door to one of the cafés. He would try once more.

As he neared the fruit stand, he noticed two young women about his age who were sitting on a bench, talking. They happened to look up at him. Both smiled in an amicable manner. Stephan smiled back as he stepped up to the fruit merchant's counter. He explained to the merchant that he was on his way from Budapest to Szeged to find work and was out of money, and asked for a couple pieces of fruit.

The two young women were once again engaged in conversation, but the merchant got their attention when he angrily refused to give Stephan any fruit.

Stephan walked away, his shoulders slumped, and headed for a nearby bench.

One of the young women said to the other, "Nikola, did you hear that? He certainly doesn't look like a beggar. He looks so sad."

Stephan sagged down onto the bench. *If the farmers are like the fruit merchants, how am I ever going to survive the long walk to Szeged? I'm already feeling a bit weak.*

He sighed and stared into space as his stomach cramped from hunger.

If I make it to Szeged and find a job, when I see someone in need, I will certainly share with them.

Suddenly, in his peripheral vision, he saw one of the young women moving his way, looking directly at him. When she drew up, he did the gentlemanly thing and rose to his feet. Meeting her gaze, he pressed a smile on his lips.

There was a warm, compassionate look in her eyes. "Sir, I saw what happened a moment ago, and I'm sorry for the way that merchant treated you."

Stephan nodded. "Would you like to sit down?"

"Thank you."

He sat down beside her and gave her another smile.

"May I ask you something, sir?"

"Of course."

"How long has it been since you've had a meal?"

Stephan was taken with the lovely brunette's kindness and her exquisite beauty. "Well, I had breakfast yesterday and an apple and a cup of coffee last night. I came from Budapest on a freight boat. I'm on my way to Szeged to look for a job."

"But you have no money."

Stephan cleared his throat lightly. "Right. It's a long story."

"My name is Andra Hardik. I used to live here in Baja, but my parents and I moved to America four years ago. We live in Memphis, Tennessee. I'm just here for a visit and a little family business. May I ask your name?"

"Stephan Varda."

"And you are from Budapest, you said."

"Yes, Miss Hardik. I was born and raised there."

"But you're relocating to Szeged to find a job."

"Yes."

Andra opened her purse, counted to herself, and took out several bills of Hungarian currency. "Here's three hundred forints."

Stephan raised a palm. "Oh, Miss Hardik, I can't —"

"Stephan, listen to me," she said, giving him a steady look. "You don't look like a beggar. You are dressed well and clean and are properly groomed. I have plenty of money left. I want to share this money with you. I give it to you in the name of my Saviour, Jesus Christ."

Tears filmed Stephan's eyes. He still felt he should not take the money, but he didn't want to insult her kindness and generosity. Even more, he was touched that she was giving the money to him in the name of Jesus Christ. His mind flashed to Uncle Bela and Aunt Ravina. This is the way they would have done it, too.

Blinking at the tears, he accepted the money. "Miss Hardik, I don't know how to thank you. Please know that this is deeply appreciated."

Andra smiled, showing a perfect set of snow white teeth. "I can see that."

At that instant, the other young woman stepped up.

"Stephan Varda, I want you to meet my cousin, Nikola Hardik."

When Nikola and Stephan had greeted

each other, Andra said to him, "You recall I said that I'm here on a little family business."

"Yes."

"Well, Nikola is getting married in June, and I am going to be her maid of honor in the wedding."

Stephan noted that the dark clouds had now covered the sun and the smell of rain was in the air. "Congratulations on your upcoming marriage, Miss Nikola. I hope you will be very happy."

Nikola did a slight curtsy. "Thank you, sir. It looks like that rainstorm is getting close."

Andra glanced westward. "I wonder what's keeping your mother."

Stephan moved his admiring gaze back to Andra. "Thank you, again, for your kindness and generosity. Your giving the money to me in the name of Jesus Christ really makes it special. I have an aunt and uncle in Budapest who would also have given the money in the name of Jesus Christ."

Andra's eyes lit up. "Do you know Jesus as your Saviour?"

Stephan shook his head. "Ah . . . no. You see, I —"

"Nikola, Andra," came a woman's voice

as she rushed up. "We have to hurry before we get caught in the storm that's coming."

Tiny raindrops were beginning to fall.

"Oh, hello, Aunt Kiraleen," said Andra. "I want you to meet Stephan Varda from Budapest. Stephan, this is Nikola's mother, Kiraleen Hardik."

Stephan nodded. "Glad to meet you, ma'am."

Kiraleen gave him a quick smile. "Come on, girls. We must go right now." As she spoke, Kiraleen took both of them by the hand and tugged on them.

Andra set her warm eyes on Stephan. "Good-bye. I'm glad I got to meet you."

"Thanks again for the money."

Andra smiled and was hurried away by her aunt.

Stephan watched as the three women disappeared in the milling crowd. *That girl has to be a born-again Christian like Uncle Bela and Aunt Ravina.*

The rain was coming down harder and the wind was picking up. Stephan turned and hurried toward the café that stood next door to the fruit stand where he had been refused.

When he stepped into the café, the delicious aromas in the air almost overcame him. Shivering a little from the chill of the wind and rain, he wiped the raindrops from his face and brushed them from his glistening hair. Looking around, he found that every seat at the counter and every table were occupied. A middle-aged man whom he assumed to be the owner stepped up. "Welcome, sir. There should be some space momentarily. Would you like a seat at the counter, or would you prefer a table?"

"Either is fine, sir," said Stephan.

"All right. I'll let you have whichever comes first."

"Thank you."

While waiting, Stephan tried to sort out the different aromas in the air and decide what he would order to eat. *I think I could eat a horse. But I've got to be frugal and just order enough to get me by. I don't know how long it will be before I manage to get a job and receive my first pay. Right now, a couple slices of bread and a cup of hot coffee would seem like a feast to me.*

He thought about the long walk ahead of him if the farmers in this part of Hungary were like the fruit merchants, and considered using some of the money for a train ticket to Szeged. Seconds later, he decided against it. In case it took him a while to find a job, he'd best keep the money in his pocket. Certainly there would be farmers out there on the road who would let him ride in their wagons or buggies. It wasn't like it would deprive them of income as it would be with the fruit merchants.

The angry flicker of lightning lit up the street outside, followed by a cannonade of thunder. The wind was blowing even harder and the rain was coming down in sheets.

Stephan watched it for a moment, then ran his eyes over the café. Still, every seat at the counter was occupied and so was every table.

He sighed and folded his arms across his chest. Suddenly his thoughts went to his dead little brother and his unforgiving parents. Grief swooped like a dark bird into his heart. Furious wings seemed to batter the inside of his chest.

Oh, Joseph, I'm so sorry I took you to the king's speech. I should have used my good sense. Mama, Papa, I'm sorry. If . . . if only you could have forgiven me.

The owner stepped up from behind Stephan. "Sir, I'm sorry that nothing has freed up, yet. Nobody wants to go out into the storm."

"I understand. Can't blame them for that. I'll wait."

His stomach growled once again.

A middle-aged man, who sat alone at a table nearby, overheard the conversation between the owner and the young man. Swallowing a mouthful of food, he raised his fork. "Mr. Kodaly?"

The owner stepped to the table under Stephan's gaze. "Yes, sir?"

"I couldn't help but overhear what you were saying to the young man. He is welcome to sit here at my table with me if he wishes."

Kodaly looked at Stephan questioningly.

Moving to him, Stephan said, "I will gladly accept the offer." Then he said to the man, "Thank you, sir, for your kindness."

The man smiled and gestured toward the chair across the table.

"Yes, thank you," said the owner.

Stephan pulled back the chair, sat down, and scooted it up to the table. He then reached out, offering his hand. "My name is Stephan Varda, sir. I am on my way to Szeged to try to find a job."

"Glad to meet you, Stephan. From where?"

"Budapest."

"I see. Well, Stephan Varda, my name is Szeren Braun. I am a farmer. My place is some five miles east of here. Are you taking the train to Szeged?"

"Ah . . . no, sir, since I don't know how long it will take me to find a job. My finances are limited, so I'm planning on walking to Szeged. Of course, I'm sort of hoping there will be some farmers who will come along and offer to let me ride with them for whatever distance."

Braun grinned. "Well, you just met your first farmer on that list. I'll be glad to let you ride with me in my wagon as far as the turnoff to my farm."

Stephan's eyes lit up. "Sir, I am delighted to accept your offer! Thank you."

At that moment a waitress stepped up to the table, notepad and pencil in hand. "May I take your order, sir?"

"Oh! I haven't even looked at the menu yet."

"The roast chicken, mashed potatoes, chicken gravy, hot bread, and sweet pickles are really good, Stephan," said Braun.

Immediately, there was excessive moisture inside Stephan's mouth.

"Sounds good to me! I'll have that."

The waitress scratched it on the pad. "And to drink?"

Lightning fluttered outside, sending its dancing light inside the café.

"I'll take coffee. Black."

Thunder boomed, rattling the windows as the waitress hurried away.

While the farmer continued eating his meal, Stephan looked toward the windows, watching the rain splatter against them.

Braun swallowed his food and glanced that way. "I sure hope it lets up pretty soon. I'd rather not get soaked on the way home."

Stephan nodded. "Me too. It's a long way to Szeged. I don't want to have to travel in a downpour like that."

Other customers seated nearby were also looking at the storm as it lashed the windows. Many were talking to each other from table to table. When the word *flood* was used two or three times, farmer Szeren Braun shook his head and looked at Stephan. "The word *flood* puts a chill down my spine. I've gone through enough floods to last a lifetime."

"Tell me about them."

"Well, I was raised on a farm about thirty miles south of here in Yugoslavia. I guess my father's farm was flooded at least a half-dozen times in my growing up years. It was about eight miles from the Danube. And since I moved here just after marrying and bought this farm, the Danube has gone over its banks several times in the past thirty years. Five of those times, it has come close to wiping me out. Of course, my farm is three miles closer to the river than my father's was."

"I can see why the word would send chills down your spine. I was born and raised in Budapest, so I know, of course, what floods are."

Braun nodded. "You sure do. You're how old?"

"Nineteen. Almost twenty."

"Then you can remember some floods that almost wiped the city out."

"I sure can. I've seen Budapest severely damaged by floods. I remember floods when my parents' house and many neighbors' houses were nearly destroyed. Sometimes the water was three or four inches deep."

"Where did they live?"

"On the east side of the river, where the land is relatively low. I have an aunt and uncle who live in Buda Hills, which is on the high ground west of the river. Only people well-off financially can live there. They have never had floodwater inside their house."

"I can understand that," said Braun. "I've been to Budapest many times, and I can say that Buda Hills would be a good place to live when a flood hits that city."

"For sure."

"I've heard that the mountains in Germany and Austria — which as you know, feed the Danube — have had massive amounts of snow this past winter. Some people are saying the Danube is no doubt going to go over its banks when the snow thaws."

"I've heard that, too."

Braun shook his head. "It could really be bad if we get rain like this at the same time the snowmelt is filling the river."

"Yes. *Very* bad."

"You say you're going to Szeged. Since the Tisza River flows through there, it could flood the city this year, too. It gets its water from those northern mountains."

Stephan nodded solemnly. "I know."

"I remember a flood back in eighty-eight that almost destroyed Szeged. What kind of work will you be doing there?"

"I hope to get a job on a tour and freight boat, which is where my experience lies."

Braun chuckled. "Well, good. At least aboard a boat, you will be *on* the Tisza River if it floods and not *under* it!"

Stephan laughed. "You're right about that!" Suddenly he realized that he had not laughed since Joseph was killed.

It felt good to laugh again.

Immediately he was flooded with guilt and a look of sadness crossed his countenance.

The change did not escape the farmer's eye. He frowned. "Something wrong, son?"

Stephan swallowed hard, and just then the waitress arrived with a tray bearing his food.

Fourteen

As the waitress set the tray on the table and began unloading the steaming plate of chicken and gravy-soaked potatoes, a plate of hot bread, a dish of sweet pickles, and a steaming cup of coffee, she smiled at Stephan Varda. "You look hungry, sir. If you need more, just let me know."

"I'll do that," Stephan said. "Thank you."

When the waitress walked away, Stephan picked up his fork and dived in. While wolfing the food down, he grinned at Szeren Braun. "Sure is good!"

"I eat here just about every time I come to town. The food is always good." With that, the farmer stuffed the last piece of bread in his mouth.

Stephan made sure he had a lighthearted look on his face, hoping Szeren Braun would think he had misread his countenance a moment ago and not ask any questions. He didn't want Braun to know the real reason he was so far from home and on the road alone.

When Braun swallowed his bread, he drained his coffee cup and studied Stephan's features. Stephan was afraid the same question would be asked again, but Braun let his eyes stray to the café's large front window. "Well, look at that, Stephan. The rain is letting up."

Stephan turned his attention to the scene outside. The falling rain was a mere mist, and the clouds were losing their dark look. "Sure enough. I'm glad to see that."

"Me too."

The hungry young man continued to put down his meal. Soon the waitress returned carrying a coffeepot and asked if they needed refills. When she had filled both cups, she asked Stephan if he wanted more food. He told her no, though he would like to have had more. But the storm was over, and he sensed that the farmer was eager to head for home.

When Stephan had finished eating, clouds were breaking up and little slivers of sunshine were peeking through.

Braun glanced out the window once again. "Looks like we can head east without getting wet."

"That's good," said Stephan, pushing his chair back and rising to his feet.

Both men walked to the counter. The farmer paid for his meal, and as Stephan stepped up to the cashier, he pulled out his wallet. When he took out the proper number of forints, he looked at the bills and thought of Andra Hardik. Warmth flowed through his heart as he thought of her generosity, her pleasant smile, and her sweet personality.

He handed the cashier the money, and as he slipped the wallet back in his hip pocket, Andra's beautiful face seemed to hang like a portrait on the wall of his mind. *What a dunderhead you are, Stephan Varda! You should have asked Andra for her address in America so when you are making wages, you could send her the money and pay her back. Oh, well, it's too late now. I'll just remember to do for someone else in need like she did for me.*

When Stephan and the farmer moved outside, there was more blue showing in the sky and the sun was shining brightly, giving off its welcome warmth.

Szeren Braun led Stephan a short distance down the street to the spot where his wagon was parked. A pair of muscular bay geldings was hitched to the wagon. Braun climbed into the seat from the boardwalk to avoid stepping into the muddy street. Stephan waited till the farmer had sat down and scooted over, then climbed up and sat down beside him.

Braun released the brake, snapped the reins, and put the wagon into motion. Immediately the thick brown mud coated the wheels, and the horses found themselves slipping a bit in the thick mire.

As Braun guided the wagon onto the Szeged road, he said, "That was some riot at the capitol grounds in your city on Saturday, wasn't it?"

Stephan felt his heart leap in his chest. His jaw set, then loosened. "Yes."

"Several people were killed, from what I read in the *Baja Daily News* — even children."

A pang struck Stephan's stomach. This time it was not from hunger, but from grief. His voice was barely audible. "Yes. Even children."

Braun gave him a sidelong glance, then set his eyes once again on the road ahead. There were two wagons some distance ahead, coming toward them. "Parliament should never have put in those foolish laws, anyway. Especially the one that replaced Magyar with German as our official and legal language. No wonder the people in this country are upset. And that includes me. Franz Joseph should have known there was going to be trouble unless he threw German out."

"Yes, sir. He should have known that."

Braun went on, expressing his views on the other two issues. Periodically, Stephan commented in order to keep the conversation going.

When they met the two wagons on the muddy road, Braun waved and the drivers waved in return. Shortly thereafter, they met another wagon, and about a mile farther down the road, they approached a farmer who had pulled his wagon off to the side of the road, and was bent over, working at the left front wheel.

Braun pulled rein and halted his wagon. "Need help?"

The farmer straightened up, smiled at both Braun and his passenger. "An axle bolt was loose. Got it, now. But thanks for the offer."

Braun nodded and put the team back into motion.

Soon they were nearing a spot where a narrow farm road angled up to the main road, and Braun tugged on the reins to slow the team. "Well, my friend, this is where I turn off. Wish I could take you all the way to Szeged, but I've got chores to do and cows to milk."

"I don't expect that, Mr. Braun," said Stephan.

Stephan had enjoyed his time with the farmer and felt a little reluctance when he realized they would now come to a parting of their ways.

"I hope you're able to find a job real soon, Stephan."

"Thank you, sir," said Stephan, throwing his leg over the edge of the seat. When his feet touched the mud, he slipped and had to grab the side of the wagon to keep from going down. "Whew! This mud is really slick!"

"It may be slow going for you, lad, so take it easy."

Stephan released his hold on the wagon. "I will. Good-bye, sir, and thank you. I hope the rest of your day is a pleasant one."

Braun nodded with a smile and snapped the reins. He turned off the main road onto the narrow one and drove away.

Stephan took a few tenuous steps until he got the feel of it, then moved a little faster down the road that stretched out in front of him, looking like a shiny ribbon in the afternoon sun.

Moments later, he heard the rattle of a wagon behind him and turned to look over his shoulder. It was the farmer who had stopped to tighten an axle bolt farther back. Stephan kept walking and when the wagon drew close, he paused and raised a hand.

The farmer stopped. "Need a ride, son?"

"Yes, sir."

"Weren't you in the wagon that passed me a while ago?"

"Yes, sir. Mr. Braun gave me ride from Baja as far as he was going. I'm on my way to Szeged."

The farmer's thick gray eyebrows arched. "Szeged? Well, I'm only going some seven miles east of this spot, but I'll be glad to carry you that far."

"That would be great, sir. Thank you."

Stephan rode the seven miles, then was on his feet in the mud again as the farmer pulled off the road and headed across a miry field toward a farmhouse, barn, and outbuildings.

Stephan's mind went to his dead little brother and his unforgiving parents once more as he continued plodding along the muddy road.

The sun was lowering in the sky behind

him, making his shadow a long one when another wagon came along and stopped. It was a farmer, his wife, and three small children. When Stephan explained that he was on his way to Szeged to find employment on a tour and freight boat, the farmer told him to climb aboard.

This time, he was invited to spend the night with the family on their farm. He was fed a good supper and given a nice clean bed in a spare bedroom. The next morning he ate a huge breakfast, then was given a ride to the main highway, where once again, he plodded his way eastward. It was Tuesday, March 28.

Stephan had walked about four miles when he was offered another ride. He walked several more miles after that ride was over, and it was late in the afternoon before another wagon driver stopped and offered him a ride. This one carried him all the way to a midsized town called Myor, where the farmer advised him was a good eating place and an inn where he could stay for the night.

Before he entered the café, Stephan counted the money in his wallet. *If I'm very careful, this should last me until I can get a job on the Tisza.*

Entering the café, he found a small table

in the corner by a window that was covered with a sheer lace curtain. He noted that the place was shiny clean, which reminded him of his mother's spotless kitchen at home.

A lump found its way into his throat. Swallowing hard several times, he was able to get rid of it.

The waitress who approached his table was about his mother's age and reminded him of her. He told himself she was as clean and spotless as the café. He ordered a bowl of lamb stew, hot bread, and black coffee.

Presently the waitress returned with a large steaming bowl of delicious smelling stew along with a huge chunk of bread slathered in melting butter and a fragrant cup of black coffee.

As he watched her walk away, his eyes misted again. She really did resemble his mother.

The next morning, Stephan was on the road once more by six-thirty. He had walked some two or three miles when he heard rattling wheels behind him.

When the sound told him the wagon was drawing close, he looked over his shoulder. This was not a farmer, but a delivery wagon.

He lifted a hand to get the driver's attention. The driver drew rein. "Needing a ride, son?"

"Yes, sir."

"Well, climb in."

As Stephan moved up to the wagon, he saw by the lettering on the side that the driver was delivering packaged food from Baja. When he settled onto the seat, the driver asked, "How far you going?"

"Szeged. I'm going there to see if I can find a job on a tour and freight boat. That's my background."

"Well, all right. It just so happens that Szeged is my destination."

Stephan heaved a sigh of relief. "That's the best news I've had all day!"

In Budapest at ten o'clock that Wednesday morning, the sky was heavy, and a steady mist was falling.

At the cemetery, the Vardas' minister, Gyorg Lukacs, stood at the head of the sealed coffin, which rested on a wheeled cart beside the open grave. One of the men from the church held an umbrella over Lukacs as he spoke in low tones, quoting a few humanist philosophers on the subject of life and death, which offered no comfort or hope to the listeners.

Under a thin canvas-covered wooden framework, Miklos and Beatrice sat on a bench with Bela and Ravina Bartok flanking them. Seated on a bench beside them were Matthias and Vivian Burtan. The soft rain pattered on the canvas cover.

Standing in the rain, holding umbrellas, were a few neighbors and friends, including Janos Kudra and Miklos's two crewmen, Fenyo Mozka and Ervin Lujza.

While the soft rain came down and the minister droned on with the opinions of renowned philosophers, Ravina held Beatrice's hand and glanced at her periodically. Her heart went out to her. Beatrice looked haggard. What few lines she normally had in her face were deeper, but there were lines where Ravina had never seen them before, patterning her pallid skin.

Beatrice stared at the coffin, which was no more than five feet long. She visualized the body of her youngest son lying inside — cold and still. Her tongue was thick and dry and clung to the roof of her mouth. There was an ever-tightening knot in the pit of her stomach as Lukacs continued in his monotone. His empty words meant nothing to her.

For a moment, Stephan's handsome face swam into focus in Beatrice's mind. How could she have been so cold and blunt as to tell him she could not forgive him? And now he was gone. Maybe forever. The knot in her stomach became a sharp cramp, stabbing into her like a jagged knife.

She chewed on her lower lip, suffering the memory of her words to him when he needed her most. *I failed you, my precious boy. I'm your mother, and I failed you!*

Ravina saw Beatrice's drawn and pale features twist up, and tears fill her eyes. She tightened the grip on her hand. Miklos felt Beatrice's body stiffen and saw her head bend down. He had an arm around her and squeezed her more snugly. At the same moment, Vivian looked up on her bench, reached past Miklos, and patted her sister's hand.

Beatrice looked at Vivian through her veil of tears and nodded her appreciation. Her entire body was not only rigid, but was trembling.

As Lukacs continued in his dismal tone, Ravina leaned close to Beatrice. "Honey, it isn't at all like he is saying. We are not left to the man-made ideas of metaphysics and the emptiness of idealism. God is real. His Son is real. His Spirit is real. Heaven is real, and Joseph is there right now. If you will let Jesus speak to you through His Word, you can become a child of God and know it. You can know you're going to heaven and that you will see Joseph again and hold him in your arms."

The minister called for everyone to bow their heads and led the small group in a hollow prayer that had no feeling. When he finished, he walked to the parents, holding his own umbrella, and told them he was sorry for their loss, but that Joseph would ever live in their hearts.

He turned away and the rest of the small group began to file by Miklos and Beatrice to offer their condolences. When that part was over, Ravina wrapped her arms around Beatrice and whispered in her ear, "Remember, honey. God's Word is true."

It was early afternoon that same day when the delivery wagon pulled into Szeged. The driver asked Stephan if he knew how to get to the docks, and Stephan assured him he did. He thanked the man for the ride and hurried down the street toward the docks.

When Stephan reached the Tisza River, he ran his gaze up and down the docks. Three tour and freight boats were anchored at the docks, as well as two freight boats. He noted that the river seemed to be higher than normal as he moved toward the first tour and freight boat. He knew it had rained hard on this side of Hungary.

As he approached the boat, he saw emblazoned on its side near the bow: *Fuzer Lines Number Seven*. Seeing the name, he realized it was familiar. He had heard of Fuzer Lines on the Tisza.

Stephan mounted the gangplank and stepped on deck. Several crewmen were busy moving freight into place. He stepped up to a pair. "Good afternoon, gentlemen. My name is Stephan Varda. Could you tell me where I might find the Fuzer office here on the docks?"

"What did you need?" asked one.

"I wanted to apply for a job. I have tour and freight boat experience on the Danube."

"Well, Mr. Fuzer just happens to be on this boat at the moment. He's up there in the wheelhouse. Go on up."

Stephan thanked him and headed for the narrow stairs that led up to the second deck. When he reached the top, he looked through the window of the wheelhouse and saw two men inside. As he stepped up to the door, one of the men was coming out.

He smiled at Stephan. "May I help you?"

"Yes, sir. I was told by a couple of the crewmen that Mr. Fuzer was up here in the wheelhouse."

He made a turn and pointed with his chin. "That's him right there. Mr. Fuzer, someone here to see you." With that, the man headed for the stairs.

Fuzer smiled at the young man. "Come in. I'm Visgrad Fuzer."

Stephan extended his hand and Fuzer gripped it in a friendly shake. "Mr. Fuzer, my name is Stephan Varda. I have moved here from Budapest and am looking for a job. I have experience on boats exactly like this, on the Danube. Do you happen to have any openings?"

"As a matter of fact, I do. You look pretty young. How old are you?"

"Nineteen, sir. Almost twenty."

"And how many years have you been working tour and freight boats?"

"Almost seven years, sir. I started when I was thirteen. It was only part time until I finished school, but once I graduated two years ago, I went on full time."

"Well, you look husky enough. It so happens, Stephan, that one of the crewmen on this very boat quit to take a job on another boat line. How soon can you start?"

"Would tomorrow morning be all right? I need to find a place to stay."

"We're pulling out about seven-thirty in the morning. Could you be here at seven?"

A sense of pure relief flooded through Stephan Varda. His features beamed. "Yes, sir!"

"The pay is seventy-five forints a week to start. Is that all right?"

Stephan's smile broadened. "Yes, Mr. Fuzer. That will be fine."

"Good! I'll be glad to have you."

"Thank you, sir. I wonder if you could recommend a place to stay."

"Sure can. There is a nice boarding-house just four blocks south of the docks, on the same street. Right-hand side. It's called Anna's. Nice lady owns it. Nothing fancy. But I've been told that the rooms are clean and the rent is reasonable. I'm sure I saw a vacancy sign there when I came to the docks this morning."

"Thank you, sir. I'll be on my way. And I'll report for work right here at seven o'clock tomorrow morning."

"See you then."

Stephan Varda made his way off the boat and headed down the street in the direction Visgrad Fuzer had indicated. A few people nodded to him as he walked briskly.

When he crossed a side street and entered the fourth block, he saw a large-frame, two-story house with a sign out front about halfway down the block. It was light gray with white trim. A covered porch wrapped around the front and sides of the house. A few comfortable looking chairs with bright flowered cushions were set together near the front door. A porch swing was swaying in the breeze near the chairs. The whole place had a homey look.

Stephan read the black and white sign that hung on a porch post.

ANNA'S BOARDINGHOUSE
Clean Rooms for Rent
Vacancy

Stephan made his way up the porch steps. Through the white screen door, he could see that the front door was open. He rapped on the doorframe and through the screen he saw a tall, slender woman coming. A crown of snow white hair was pulled up tightly into a bun that sat regally on top of her head. He guessed her to be in her late sixties or early seventies.

Swinging the screen door open, she showed him a wide smile and sparkling dark eyes. "Yes? May I help you?"

"Are you the proprietor, ma'am?"

She nodded. "I am Anna Polzin."

"My name is Stephan Varda. I just came here from Budapest. I am looking for a room, ma'am. I was told by Mr. Visgrad Fuzer that yours are quite nice. He just hired me and said I should come here."

"Ah, yes, Mr. Fuzer. Fine man, I've been told. Come in, young man. I have one room vacant right now. It's on the second floor. Follow me and I will show it to you."

As Stephan stepped through the door, his eyes fell on the parlor off to his right. He was at once transported back to the house where he was raised. It was almost identical to the parlor in the Varda home at 1124 Pozsony Street in Budapest. He stopped and stared.

The woman was already mounting the stairs. She paused and looked back at him. "Come along, Stephan."

Stephan took another quick look at the parlor, and with homesickness clutching his heart, hurried up the stairs behind her.

Anna led him down a narrow hall with windows at each end where yellow sunshine was filtering in. He noted paintings on the walls. Some were still life and others were pastoral scenes with cattle and horses in open fields and around barns and corrals.

At the third door from the staircase, Anna stopped, turned the knob, and swung it open. Taking a step to the side, she motioned for him to enter ahead of her.

"Thank you," he said, and entered the bright, sunny room.

It was not a large room, but it was immaculate. A double bed stood in one corner. It was covered with a multicolored quilt and looked inviting to his travel-weary body. A small chest with a water pitcher and bowl stood in another corner. There was a comfortable looking over-stuffed chair by the window, and next to it was a small table polished to a high gloss. A coal oil lantern sat on the table.

Anna looked at Stephan's empty hands. "Do you have luggage, Stephan?"

"Ah, no, ma'am."

"You brought no clothing with you?"

"I . . . ah . . . had to leave Budapest earlier than planned and was not able to pack any baggage. I will buy new clothes here in Szeged."

"Well, when you do," she said, moving to an armoire, "this is where you will hang them."

"Yes, ma'am," he said, nodding.

Anna moved to the window, which was adorned with muslin curtains that were pulled back and tied on either side, letting the sunshine in. She gestured toward the overstuffed chair. "You will find this very comfortable."

"I'm sure I will, ma'am."

Stephan stood in the center of the room and slowly turned in a circle as Anna watched him. When he came around and met her eyes with his own, he said, "I would very much like to rent the room, Mrs. — it *is* Mrs. — Polzin?"

"It is. I am a widow. The room rents for five forints a week."

"Sounds reasonable enough to me."

"Good! I assume since you are going to be working for Visgrad Fuzer that it will be on one of his boats."

"Yes, ma'am."

"So you will sometimes be gone for several days at a time."

"Yes."

"Well, when you're here, breakfast is at six. Supper is at six-thirty. These meals, of course, are included in the price of the room. I believe you will find the food tasty and filling."

Stephan smiled. "I have no doubt of that."

As he spoke, he removed his wallet from his hip pocket, opened it, and took out ten forints. Placing them in her hand, he said, "I'll pay two weeks at a time, Mrs. Polzin, so if I happen to be gone on the day the rent is due, it will be covered until I return from a river trip."

"I appreciate it, Stephan. Thank you. Now, I will leave you to get settled. I will bring you some towels in a few minutes. Remember — supper is at six-thirty. Don't be late."

"Yes, ma'am," Stephan replied, a smile in his voice.

Fifteen

It was early in the second week of April when Police Chief Akman Serta looked up to see Miklos Varda enter his office. Serta rose to his feet behind the desk. "Hello, Mr. Varda. Do you have any news for me?"

"No, sir. I was hoping maybe you had some for me."

Serta shook his head. "No. I'm sorry. I would have contacted you immediately if there was any word about Stephan at all. My men are still on the alert for any sign of him. They will stay that way until I tell them differently. I believe that after this much time has passed I can safely say your son has left the city." He gestured toward the chairs in front of his desk. "Please sit down."

When both men were seated, Miklos said, "I agree with you, Chief. I think Stephan has definitely left Budapest. Certainly if he were still here, someone who knows him and is aware that we are looking for him would have seen him, or your officers would have spotted him. I have no idea where he might have gone, but both my wife and I have a feeling that he is still in the country. We don't think he would leave Hungary."

"I hope you are right," said Serta, "but if he is still in the country, there is nothing I can do to help you find him. It would be different if he were a child, especially if there was evidence that he was kidnapped, but because he is almost twenty years of age, no other law enforcement would put forth the effort to track him down. He is old enough to be on his own, and it is quite evident that he left of his own free will."

Miklos nodded. "I understand, Chief. I know Stephan hasn't contacted any of his relatives in the country, because they would let us know immediately if he did."

"Of course." Serta's brow furrowed. "How is Mrs. Varda handling Stephan's disappearance?"

Miklos wiped a palm over his face and sighed. "Not well at all. I'm really concerned about her. She isn't sleeping well, she hardly eats enough to keep a sparrow alive, and her nerves are shot. I took her to our doctor a few days ago. He gave her some powders to help ease her nerve problem, but it hasn't helped much. She wants Stephan to come home, and I think she is going to pine for him until he does. I miss him, too, of course, but it is all she can think about. I am taking her with me on all the trips to Vienna. I can't and I won't leave her alone. Her brother and his wife have offered to let her stay with them, but she wants to be with me. I just don't know what else to do. If I could come up with some way to track Stephan down, I would do it. I fear she is going to have some kind of emotional breakdown."

Serta leaned forward in his chair and placed his elbows on the desktop. "There is one thing you can do."

"What's that?"

"Since you and Mrs. Varda feel strongly that Stephan is still in Hungary, you should put ads in the major newspapers all over the country, telling him that you want him to come home."

Miklos's eyes lit up. "I never thought of that! Thank you for the idea. I will go home right now and talk to Beatrice about it."

At the Varda home, Beatrice was in the

boys' room lying on Stephan's bed when she heard the front door of the house open and close.

Quickly, she sat up and dabbed at the tears on her cheeks with her hankie. She had sobbed over her loss of both boys for quite some time, and just in the last few minutes was gaining control of herself.

She touched fingers to her hair, trying to erase the evidence of her emotional episode as much as possible. She could hear Miklos's footsteps as he moved through the house, looking for her. It was too late to rush to some other room.

The sound of his footsteps grew closer, and Beatrice heard him sigh as he stopped at the open door. She looked up at him, knowing her eyes were red.

Miklos stepped in, noting that the spread on Stephan's bed where she sat was messed up. A glance at Joseph's bed indicated that she had been on it, too.

Beatrice watched him glance at Joseph's bed, and as he set his eyes on her, she said defensively, "Yes, I've been on both beds, crying. Somehow I feel closer to them by touching the beds where they slept."

Miklos moved to the bed, sat down, and put an arm around her. "Honey, you don't have to explain. I understand. I wish I could bring them both back."

She looked at him with tired eyes. "I assume Chief Serta had no news for us."

"No. But he suggested something neither one of us have thought of."

"What do you mean?"

"Something to do that might bring Stephan home."

"What?"

"He suggested we put ads in major newspapers all over the country, telling Stephan that we want him to come home. I told the chief both of us feel that Stephan is still in Hungary."

Beatrice let the idea take root in her mind, then her eyes brightened. "Yes! That might do it! It's certainly worth a try."

"All right, we'll proceed in that direction. I was thinking on the way home that since you are going with me on each trip to Vienna, when we put the ads in the papers, we will tell Stephan to contact Bela and Ravina if we're not here when he comes home. We'll explain that you are on the boat with me."

Beatrice nodded. "Stephan will understand why I need to be on the boat with you. And the way he loves his aunt and uncle, there will be no problem in contacting them. That is an excellent idea,

Miklos. I'm glad Chief Serta came up with it."

"Since the *Budapest Herald* is our largest newspaper, we'll go there. Pelso Galton is one of the top executives. He and his wife have been on the boat several times, and I've gotten to know them well. We'll go straight to him. He can help us put the ads in the other papers all over the country. Are you up to going right now?"

Beatrice dabbed at her hair. "Let me freshen up a little. I think we should probably go tell Bela and Ravina what we're doing, since we are involving them."

"Right. You freshen up. I didn't put the horse and buggy away. They're at the front of the house. I'll wait out there for you."

"Oh, I think that is a marvelous idea!" said Ravina as the two couples sat in the Bartok parlor. "If Stephan sees the ad and knows you both want him to come home, I feel certain he will."

"An excellent idea," put in Bela. "Wherever Stephan has gone he is meeting people, and even if it's some person who knows him that sees the ad, he or she will tell him about it."

Ravina patted Beatrice's arm. "And both of you know that we're happy to be a part of it. If Stephan comes home while you two are somewhere between here and Vienna, we will keep him right here at our house until you return."

Miklos rose to his feet. "We thank you both. Well, Beatrice, we'd better get going. I'm eager to talk to Pelso Galton so we can get the wheels rolling."

Beatrice hugged Ravina and kissed her cheek. "Thank you for always being here when we need you."

Ravina warmed her with a smile. "That's because we love you."

Beatrice hugged Bela, and the Bartoks stood on the front porch and watched as they climbed into the buggy and drove away.

In the buggy, Beatrice turned and waved. Bela and Ravina waved back, and the buggy turned the corner, taking them from her view.

Beatrice sighed. "I really feel good about this."

"Me too."

While the buggy moved along the streets to the rhythmic patter of the horse's hooves, Miklos noticed Beatrice in deep thought, counting something slowly on her fingers. "Honey, we need to decide what we want to say in the ads before we sit down with Pelso."

"Mm-hmm. I was thinking about what should go in the ad, myself."

"Well, let's hear it."

"All right. As I see it, we need to get five things across to our boy."

"I'm listening."

"First, we need to tell him that we were wrong to treat him as we did. Second, that we are sorry for it and are asking his forgiveness." She paused. "Right so far?"

"Absolutely."

"All right. Third, we need to say that we indeed have forgiven him for taking Joseph to see the king."

"Yes."

"Fourth, we will tell him we want him to come home, and fifth, we must tell him that our love for him can never die."

"Honey, you are right on every count. All five points will be made clear in the ads."

At his office in the *Budapest Herald* building in downtown Budapest, Pelso Galton welcomed the Vardas and sat them down in front of his desk. The newspaper executive talked about how much he and his wife always enjoyed themselves when traveling to Vienna on Miklos's tour boat, then said, "What can I do for you?"

Miklos told him of Joseph's death in the

314

riot at the king's speech. Galton had not known that Joseph was one of the many casualties. He expressed his sincere condolences.

Miklos explained that while he and Beatrice were out of town, Stephan had taken Joseph to see the king against their orders. Upon arriving home, in their anger they had mistreated Stephan, and he had secretly left home. Miklos went on to tell Galton that Chief Akman Serta had his men alerted to watch for Stephan, but since there was no sign of him in Budapest after all this time, he decided that Stephan had gone elsewhere. When Miklos told Serta that he and Beatrice felt confident that Stephan was still in Hungary, the chief had suggested that ads be placed in all of Hungary's major newspapers telling him his parents wanted him to come home.

Galton agreed that it was a wise thing to do. Taking out paper and pencil, he asked them to dictate what they wanted to say in the ad.

When it was done, Galton said, "All right. The ad will be in tomorrow's edition of the *Herald*, and I will wire it to the other major newspapers all over the country today. The ad should be in those papers day after tomorrow."

"Fine," said Miklos. "We don't care about the cost. We want the ad to run for two solid weeks in each paper."

"And so it shall be," said Galton.

The next morning, Bela Bartok drove away from his bank in downtown Budapest. The smell of rain was in the air. When he reached Buda Hills, the trees along the parkway were steel blue shadows beneath a slate gray sky.

The rain came down in a sudden rush, drenching the hills and sending rivers down the steep streets toward the low ground at the Danube River.

When he pulled into his driveway, Bela quickly guided the carriage to the barn at the rear of the house and led horse and carriage inside.

Moments later, with a folded newspaper under his coat, he hurried into the house. Pausing in the kitchen, he shed his wet hat and coat, took the paper in hand, and made his way up the hall toward the front of the house. "I'm home, sweetheart! Where are you?"

Ravina's voice came back. "In the parlor, honey! Looks like a real drencher," she said as he entered the parlor.

"Uh-huh. Coming down pretty good."

He unfolded the newspaper. "Here's to-day's edition of the *Herald*. Take a look in the classified section."

She took the paper in hand. "Oh. Miklos and Beatrice's ad for Stephan."

"Uh-huh. I read it while I was waiting to see Mr. Norvon at the bank. See what you think."

There was a knock at the front door. Bela left the parlor while Ravina was opening the paper.

Ravina quickly found the ad and concentrated on it while hearing Bela welcome Miklos and Beatrice. It read:

Stephan Varda: We are sorry. Please forgive us for the way we treated you. We were wrong. We have forgiven your disobedience. Please come home.

With undying love, your parents.

The note mentioned contacting his aunt and uncle if his parents were away from home at the bottom of the ad.

At the door, Bela was folding their umbrellas while Miklos was helping Beatrice remove her hat and coat.

"Some rain, eh?" said Bela. "I just got home from downtown. Came out of the sky like it was being poured from a giant bucket."

"You're right about that." Miklos hung Beatrice's hat and coat on pegs.

While Miklos was removing his own hat and coat, Bela said, "I bought a copy of today's *Herald* while I was downtown and read your ad. Ravina's reading it right now in the parlor."

Miklos nodded. "We put the ad in all of Hungary's major newspapers. We wanted to see you and Ravina again before we climb on the boat at noon and head for Vienna."

"I hope the rain lets up before then," said Bela. "I really like the way you worded the ad."

As they moved into the parlor, every eye went to Ravina, who was wiping tears with her sleeve with the open newspaper on her lap. She looked up at her brother and sister-in-law. Laying the newspaper on the table, she left the sofa and put her arms around both of them at the same time. "I appreciate what you said in the ad."

"We meant every word," said Beatrice.

"I know that. Did I hear you say you're leaving for Vienna at noon?"

"Yes."

"I'm so glad you came to see us first."

"Me too," said Bela. "I'm really encouraged with the ad. I'd really like to have prayer right now and ask the Lord to get the ad in Stephan's hands, wherever he is."

Beatrice's drawn features brightened. "Oh, Bela, I would appreciate that. I want our son home as soon as possible."

Bela looked at Miklos. "Is it all right with you if we pray about this together?"

A little less enthused than his wife, Miklos nodded. "Sure. That would be fine."

When Bela finished his prayer, both Beatrice and Ravina were dabbing tears from their faces.

Beatrice ran her wet gaze to Bela, then Ravina. "Thank you both for caring so much about your nephew."

"We love Stephan very, very much," said Ravina. "And we want him to come home."

"We sure do, on both counts," said Bela as he stepped to the end table and picked up the newspaper. "I want to especially commend you for two words in this ad."

Ravina was nodding with a smile tugging at her lips. Bela knew she felt the same about the two words.

"What two words?" queried Beatrice.

Bela held up the folded paper so it was facing them, pointed to the words, and repeated them: "Undying love."

Ravina said, "I noticed them, too, Bela."

While Beatrice and Miklos were smiling

and nodding, Bela said, "It made me think of God's undying love for sinners — including all four of us — in sending His only begotten Son into the world."

Miklos's smile faded as Bela laid the paper down and picked up a Bible from the same end table. "Let's sit down so I can show you."

Ravina and Beatrice sat down on the sofa. The men each took an overstuffed chair, facing their wives.

Bela opened the Bible and turned back toward the end of the New Testament. "Listen to this. I'm reading from the fourth chapter of 1 John. Verses 9 and 10. 'In this was manifested the love of God toward us, because that God sent his only begotten Son into the world, that we might live through him. Herein is love, not that we loved God, but that he loved us, and sent his Son to be the propitiation for our sins.'"

Miklos was staring at the floor, but Beatrice had her eyes glued on Bela.

"Propitiation," said Bela, "is appeasement. God loves sinners, but He hates our sin. His righteousness and His holiness demand that sins be punished. And that punishment is for the sinner to spend eternity in the lake of fire. However, He loves sin-

ners like us so much, He sent His only begotten Son into the world to pay the price
for our sins. Jesus did that when He shed
His precious blood on Calvary's cross and
died to provide the one and only way of
salvation. He raised Himself from the
grave three days later and is alive to save
all who will believe His gospel and let Him
save them.

"As it says here, God manifested His
love toward us by sending His Son to become our propitiation. Jesus *is* the propitiation. The one and only propitiation for
our sins. Only He can save us from an eternity in the lake of fire.

"Verse 9 says that God sent Jesus into
the world that we might live through *Him.*
No one else. Nothing else. Over here in
verse 14, it says, 'And we have seen and do
testify that the Father sent the Son to be
the Saviour of the world.' *The* Saviour.
Jesus is the one and only Saviour for all
mankind. There is no other. God's manifested love is an undying love. He never
stops loving lost sinners and wanting them
to come to His Son for salvation.

"In 2 Peter chapter 3, verse 9, God says
He is 'not willing that any should perish,
but that all should come to repentance.'
Repentance is simply turning from our sin

and unbelief to Jesus, acknowledging that we have sinned against Him, but at the same time, opening our heart to Him and receiving Him as our own personal Saviour.

"In the first chapter of the gospel of John, we are told that only by receiving Jesus can we become the children of God. We've shown both of you before that Jesus said we must be born again to go to heaven. We are not children of God automatically. We are God's creation when we are born into this world, but not His children. We must *become* His children by the new birth. God loves you with an undying love, Miklos. And you, too, Beatrice. He loves Stephan the same way. He wants to save all three of you like He did Joseph."

Bela saw tears glistening in Beatrice's eyes. He knew the Lord was dealing with her. He fixed his eyes on Beatrice. "In Romans 10:13, it says, 'Whosoever shall call upon the name of the Lord shall be saved.' When we believe His gospel, repent, and call on Jesus to save us, He says He will do it."

Beatrice drew a shuddering breath. "Bela, I want to be saved. I want to open my heart to Jesus and take advantage of that undying love of God for me."

Ravina was weeping for joy.

Suddenly, Miklos jumped to his feet, frowning. "Our church teaches something different than this. It has stopped raining. I'm going outside and getting some fresh air."

All three watched Miklos leave the room.

Beatrice drew another shuddering breath. "I am disturbed that Miklos has taken this attitude, Bela, but I know what you have shown me from the Bible is true. I want to be saved right now."

Bela sat down on Beatrice's other side, and while Ravina held her tight, he guided her in calling on the Lord to save her.

While Ravina and Beatrice were embracing, Bela rose to his feet and said, "I'll go see if I can find Miklos."

When Bela stepped out onto the front porch, he found Miklos sitting on a porch chair. The sun was shining, but more black clouds were gathering in the sky.

Miklos looked up at Bela as he moved to him.

"You all right?" asked Bela.

"Yes. I'm fine."

"Come on inside. Beatrice just received Jesus into her heart. She's saved, Miklos. She's a Christian, now. Ravina and I know we can't cram salvation down your throat and we won't try to do that."

Miklos let out a small sigh and stood up. "Let's go in."

Bela opened the door and followed his brother-in-law into the parlor.

Miklos went right to Beatrice and knelt in front of her, taking her hand. "Honey, Bela told me what you just did. If getting saved helps you in carrying this burden over Stephan, I will be glad for you."

Beatrice wiped happy tears. "Miklos, I know that whenever I die, I will go to heaven. I will be with Jesus foremost, but I will also be with Joseph. I will hold him in my arms again." She paused, swallowed hard. "Don't you want to see Joseph again?"

Miklos's face took on a stony look. "I'm not sure either of us will ever see Joseph again, and right now I don't want to talk about it. We need to get going, anyhow. I have work to do on the boat before we leave for Vienna."

As the Bartoks walked the Vardas to the front door, they assured them that if Stephan came back before they returned, they would keep him at their house.

The Vardas thanked them, and Beatrice added her thanks to Bela and Ravina for leading her to Jesus.

As the days passed, Stephan Varda found that he fit in well with Visgrad Fuzer and his crewmen, and he enjoyed his work on the tour boat as it traveled the Tisza River between Szeged and the city of Kisvarda in the north.

Late one afternoon, when the boat docked at the city of Csongrad in a heavy downpour, Stephan and two other crewmen — Varos Hegy and Lugza Petofi — sat in Hegy's private quarters and discussed the fact that the heavy rains they were having almost daily had caused the Tisza to swell up close to its banks.

Hegy, who was some twenty years older than Stephan and Lugza, said, "One of the passengers on the boat today told me he heard that it has been raining heavily on the west side of Hungary, too, and the Danube River is also rising."

Lugza Petofi shook his head. "I hope it isn't going to mean that both rivers will go over their banks when the spring thaw begins filling them with water in the northern mountains."

Stephan thought of his parents' home. No matter how they had treated him, he wouldn't want their house damaged by flood waters.

"Well, boys," said Varos Hegy, "it looks like the rain is letting up some. We'd better head into town and get us some supper."

That night, with the boat docked at Csongrad, Stephan crawled into his bunk in his private quarters. Lying there in the darkness as the boat bobbed on the troubled surface of the Tisza, his thoughts went to his little brother.

He wept, his chest heaving. "Joseph, I miss you so much. I hope you have forgiven me for letting you talk me into taking you to the king's speech. Somehow I feel since you are in heaven and superbly happy, that you have. Don't forget me, will you?"

Then, with tears still flowing, he said, "Mama, Papa, I miss you so much, too. I love you. No matter how you feel about me, I will always love you."

Miklos and Beatrice Varda arrived at the Budapest docks from Vienna on Friday afternoon, April 14, in a driving rain that seemed to be letting up. Beatrice waited under a shelter on the dock while Miklos went to a stable close by where he always left the horse and buggy while on the river. As the rain pattered on the roof over her head, she felt warmth deep inside. She had enjoyed the trip to Vienna. There was a soft glow on her cheeks. Her newfound salvation had brought a measure of sweet peace to her heart, and she had been learning daily to lean on the precious Saviour.

She was thinking about Stephan, wondering if he had seen one of the ads and had come home, when Miklos pulled up in the buggy. He hopped out, umbrella in hand, guided her to the buggy, and helped her climb in.

The rain was getting lighter as they rode through the streets, crossed over the swollen Danube on Chain Bridge, and headed up the steep road toward Buda Hills.

"Now, honey," said Miklos in a steady tone, "please don't get your hopes up. I don't want you coming apart if Stephan isn't here."

"I won't come apart," she assured him. "I'll be disappointed, yes, but the Lord is giving me strength. But just think how wonderful it will be if he has come back!"

Moments later, Miklos pulled the buggy into the Bartok driveway and drew rein in front of the house.

Beatrice's heart was beating rapidly as Miklos rounded the buggy to help her out.

As he took her hand, he looked into her eyes and saw the hope reflected there. "Oh, Miklos, I want so much to hear that even if Stephan isn't here, that he has contacted his aunt and uncle."

While guiding her to the porch under the umbrella, he said, "I'm hoping this will be the case, too, but let's try not to get our hopes too high. Remember, it has only been a few days since the ads went into the newspapers. If there's no contact from him yet, we'll keep waiting and hoping."

The door came open just as the Vardas stepped up onto the porch. Bela and Ravina smiled at them. Before Beatrice could ask, Bela said, "Wish we could tell you we had Stephan in here, but so far there's been no word from him."

Feeling keen disappointment, Beatrice tried not to show it. She folded Ravina into her arms. "Well, as Miklos just reminded me, it has only been a few days since the newspapers began carrying the ad. We'll just have to give it more time."

"We know you're probably wanting to get home," said Bela, "but come in for a moment. We have something we want to give Beatrice."

The Vardas looked at each other questioningly as Bela led them toward the parlor while Ravina hurried ahead of them. When they entered the room, Ravina picked up a beautifully wrapped package from an end table, smiled, and handed it to her sister-in-law.

"What have you two been up to?"

"Just a special gift to our sister in Christ," said Ravina.

Beatrice's eyes widened and a smile broke across her face. "A Bible? Did you get me a Bible?"

"Well, open it and see," said Ravina, giggling.

Beatrice tore the paper off and found a beautiful Bible with a deep red leather cover, which was edged in a bright gold piping.

She opened it and noted that both Bela and Ravina had written something to her on the flyleaf. She read their loving and encouraging words and thanked them both, then flipped through the pages.

She extended it to Miklos. "Would you like to look at it, darling?"

Miklos's mouth pulled into a thin line as he took the Bible, turned it front to back, and handed it to her. "Mm-hmm. It's nice."

"Beatrice," said Bela, "after you received the Lord the other day, we showed you that you need to be baptized, and you said you wanted to do so."

"Yes."

"We told Pastor Tividar about your being saved, and he was thrilled to hear it. Is it all right if we have him and his wife visit you tomorrow, so you can plan to be baptized Sunday?"

"Oh yes! I would love to have them come."

"All right. You can plan on their being at your house sometime tomorrow."

On Sunday morning, Bela and Ravina picked Beatrice up and they headed for church under a sunny blue sky.

Ravina was sitting between Bela and Beatrice. "Did you enjoy pastor and Gerda's visit?"

"I sure did."

"Well, they came by to see us after they had been to your house, and said they sure enjoyed spending the time with you." She paused. "They said Miklos wasn't there."

Beatrice smiled. "Well, he was until he saw their buggy pull up in front of the house. Then he hightailed it out the back door. He didn't come back until they were gone."

Bela glanced past Ravina at Beatrice.

"All we can do is keep praying for him and let the Lord work in his life."

"Yes. I know the Lord can bring him to the place that he will stop fighting Him and open his heart to Him. He did that to me, and I'm so happy to be a child of God. I'm thrilled about being baptized this morning, too!"

"We're thrilled about it, too," said Ravina.

Beatrice took a deep breath and let it out slowly. "I'm looking forward to going to church regularly. I told Miklos that."

"And what was his reaction?" asked Bela.

"He said he won't stand in my way, but he won't go with me, either."

Ravina chuckled. "He will go with you once the Lord gets hold of his heart."

"Oh yes. What a wonderful day that will be!"

Sixteen

On Thursday, April 27, Beatrice Varda was on the dock in Budapest with Miklos. The sun shone in all its brilliance from the morning sky. The Vardas looked at the river, which ran choppy and deep. Small white waves lapped the banks. Heavy rain had fallen twice more since Sunday.

Deep lines creased Miklos's brow. "I sure hope the rainstorms diminish before the snow melts in the mountains up north."

Beatrice nodded. "What we don't need is a flood."

"Well, let's get on the boat. It'll soon be time to leave."

As they were moving toward the gangplank to board the boat, Beatrice's attention was drawn farther up the dock and she stiffened.

"Uh-oh."

Miklos looked at her, then followed her line of sight. His eyes narrowed when he saw an angry Banton Hunyard approaching them.

Beatrice said in a low voice, "He looks like he's spoiling for a fight."

"To say the least."

Hunyard drew up, breathing hard. The red blood of rage was on his cheeks and a thick vein at the side of his forehead throbbed.

Beatrice squeezed her husband's arm. "Honey, be careful."

Hunyard fixed Miklos with fiery eyes. "You're still at it! Every time you drop your prices for a day or two, I lose business to you! I don't like it, you hear? I don't like it!"

"Cool down, Banton," Miklos said. "I told you why I do that. It brings new business from people who otherwise take a train to Vienna."

"Well, it also brings business that otherwise would have been mine!"

"I'm not trying to do that. May I remind you that I offered to work with you in lowering prices periodically so we would both benefit? But you ignored my offer. So what have you got to be mad about?"

"I'm not obligated to work with you in

any way, shape, or fashion! If you don't stop this price cutting immediately, you're going to be sorry!"

People moving by on the dock were stopping to observe the scene.

Miklos's back arched. "Are you threatening me?"

"It's more than a threat, Varda!" spat the angry man. "It's a promise!"

With that, Hunyard swung his fist at Miklos's jaw.

Miklos ducked the blow and took a step back. "Banton, this isn't something to fight about."

Hunyard leaped forward, swung again, and connected. The blow staggered Miklos backward. He quickly found his balance, and Beatrice put a hand to her mouth when she saw her husband's temper give his cheeks a wicked tautness.

With fire in his eyes, Miklos went after Hunyard, fists pumping.

Hunyard lifted his arms to ward off the two punches that came at his face. Miklos's fists bounced off his arms and Hunyard countered, throwing out a wild punch that grazed Miklos's cheek.

Miklos came back with a stiff blow to the jaw, causing Hunyard to stagger backward toward the edge of the dock. Rushing up, he hit him again. Hunyard's knees did a slight buckle, but he came back with another blow that caught Miklos on his right ear. There was an instant ringing that only served to heighten Miklos's wrath. He landed a solid punch on Hunyard's nose, then followed with a blow on the jaw that whipped the man's head to the side.

The crowd was growing rapidly, and they were moving closer to the combatants. Beatrice felt the pressure of their bodies crowding her.

Hunyard grunted, shook his head to clear it, and came swinging.

Miklos hooked a hard left under his heart and caught him flush on the jaw with a chopping right. Hunyard went down as if a scythe had cut his legs out from under him. They were barely more than three feet from the edge of the dock as Miklos pounced on top of him, straddling him on his knees. He delivered a series of hard blows to his face, then put a choke hold on him.

Beatrice looked on, eyes wide, holding her breath.

Miklos pressed his thumbs against Hunyard's Adam's apple. The stunned man was gasping for breath while clawing at Miklos's wrists. He was turning blue. Beatrice released a tiny whimper and ran toward her husband. The crowd was pressed so close, she had to move around the combatants to get to them. "Miklos! Miklos! Let go of him! You'll kill him! Stop it!"

Hunyard's nose was bleeding, and a bubble of blood appeared at the corner of his mouth as Miklos continued to squeeze his throat. The bubble broke and a thin red ribbon trickled down his chin.

From behind him, Beatrice seized her husband's shirt collar with both hands, shook him hard, and screamed, "Stop it! Stop it, Miklos! You'll kill him!"

This time her voice broke through the wall of fury. Miklos turned his head and looked up at her. His grip on the man's throat relaxed. Then looking down at Hunyard, who was still gasping, he said in a level tone, "You can thank her for saving your life, Hunyard."

As he spoke, Miklos started to get up.

Suddenly, Hunyard kicked him in the stomach, sending him reeling backward. He slammed into Beatrice, knocking her over the edge of the dock. Miklos gained his balance without falling and watched her fall toward the choppy water. As she fell, her head struck a protruding wooden post, then she dropped into the river.

Miklos dived into the river after her. He surfaced quickly and grasped her limp form. When he pulled her close, he saw a deep gash on the back of her head. Holding her head out of the water, he began swimming toward the dock with the crowd looking on.

When he drew near the dock, Miklos saw two men come down to a small platform just above the river's surface. They bent over and extended their hands toward him.

"Swim right up here!" one of them called to him. "We'll take her!"

Seconds later, Miklos relinquished Beatrice's slack body to the men, and they pulled her out of the water. He climbed onto the small platform, breathing hard. "Thank you . . . gentlemen. Thank you. I'll . . . take her, now."

Cradling Beatrice's limp form in his arms, Miklos carried her up the narrow stairs that led to the dock. When he reached it, he saw two uniformed policemen running toward him as people in the crowd pointed his direction.

As they drew up, one of them asked, "Is she alive?"

Miklos nodded. "Yes. She's alive."

"Here," said the other one. "We need to

lay her facedown. We're trained for this. If you will support her head to keep it off the rough wood, it will be a help. Turn her face to the right."

With the aid of the officers, Miklos gently laid the unconscious Beatrice facedown, supporting her head. As the officers knelt down, he said, "She's got a bad gash on the back of her head."

"I see," said one. "We'll take her to the hospital, sir, as soon as we pump her lungs. We have a police wagon right over there."

Miklos looked on — as did the crowd — while the policemen pressed on her back on both sides in rhythm. Immediately, water began to gush from her mouth. She coughed, gagged, and coughed again; then her breathing became a hoarse gasping as the water continued to come from her lungs and spread out in a pool on the dock.

At that moment, Miklos's attention was drawn to his two crewmen pushing through the crowd to get to him. When they drew up, Fenyo Mozka looked down at Beatrice and saw that she was breathing. "People in the crowd told us what happened, Mr. Varda."

Ervin Lujza laid a hand on Miklos's wet

shoulder. "I'm so glad you got to her in time."

"She's got a gash on the back of her head. We're taking her to the hospital as soon as these officers say she's ready to go." As he spoke, Miklos focused on the spot where he last saw Banton Hunyard.

"If you're looking for Hunyard, sir," said Mozka, "those people told us he left."

"I'll talk to these officers about him on the way to the hospital. You two will have to make today's run to Vienna without me."

"Don't you worry about that, sir," said Lujza. "We will take care of it."

Miklos nodded. "You'd best be getting to the boat."

"We will," said Mozka. "If it is all right, we will come to your house to check on Mrs. Varda when we get back."

"Of course."

The crewmen hurried away.

Soon Beatrice was conscious. The officers introduced themselves as Nicholas Darrah and Everd Stigal, and told Miklos they were ready to take her to the hospital.

As Miklos picked Beatrice up, cradling her in his arms, a woman stepped out of the crowd and offered him a white handkerchief. "Here, sir, use this to press against the gash on her head. It's clean."

Miklos accepted the handkerchief. "Thank you, ma'am."

Officers Darrah and Stigal cleared the way through the crowd to the enclosed police wagon. Stigal climbed in the back with the Vardas, and Darrah soon had the team moving at a fast pace through the streets.

Beatrice lay on the floor of the wagon with a thin blanket beneath her. Miklos knelt on one side of her, pressing the handkerchief to the bleeding gash, and Stigal knelt on the other side.

When Miklos saw how quickly the handkerchief was covered with blood, he was on the edge of panic. He was glad Officer Nicholas Darrah had the horses almost at a gallop.

The dullness in Beatrice's eyes was beginning to clear. She looked up at her husband. "Wh-what happened?"

"You fell into the river, sweetheart."

Puzzlement showed on her face.

"Banton Hunyard and I were fighting. Remember?"

She looked blank.

"I was strangling him. You were behind me, trying to get me to let go of him before I strangled him to death."

Suddenly it came back to her. "Oh. Yes.

I remember. You let go of his throat, and when you started to get off him, he kicked you."

"Yes." Miklos took hold of her hand with his free hand.

"You stumbled back into me. I . . . I fell over the edge of the dock. That's all I remember."

"Your head struck the end of a post as you were falling. I dived in and pulled you out of the river. You were unconscious. This officer and the one who's driving the wagon pumped water out of your lungs. We're on our way to the hospital. There's a gash on the back of your head where it struck the post. We've got to have a doctor tend to it."

Tears were building in Beatrice's eyes. She ran her slow gaze to Stigal. "Thank you."

Stigal nodded with a thin smile. "We're just glad you didn't drown, ma'am. If it hadn't been for your husband's courage and quick thinking, you sure would have. The way that river is churning, he was risking his own life to go in after you."

Miklos's features tinted.

Beatrice looked back into Miklos's face. The tears that had been building in her eyes welled over and made a transparent tracery down the plane of her cheeks. "Thank you, my darling husband, for risking your life to save mine."

Miklos checked the handkerchief and it was soaked with blood. Trying to keep the panic from showing in his voice, he said softly, "No thanks needed, sweetheart. I love you. You're my everything. I didn't have to think twice about diving in after you."

Beatrice kept her gaze on him, her eyes still a bit glassy, but full of trust. Miklos lifted the hand he was holding to his lips and kissed it gently. She squeezed his fingers in response and closed her eyes.

Miklos was still burning inside with fury toward Banton Hunyard. As he gazed down at his wife's colorless features, his fury intensified. He turned his eyes on Everd Stigal. "Are you going to arrest the man who caused this?"

Hearing the question, Beatrice opened her eyes and looked at the officer.

"People in the crowd told us that you and Banton Hunyard were fighting, Mr. Varda, and in the midst of the fight, your wife was knocked off the dock into the river. Is this correct?"

"Yes."

"And Hunyard did not intentionally

knock her into the river?"

"No. He kicked me, and I stumbled back into her."

"That's the way it was told to us, Mr. Varda," said Stigal. "Therefore, he cannot be charged. He was simply fighting back at you."

Miklos nodded solemnly. He had wicked thoughts about Hunyard but crowded them aside to concentrate on his injured wife.

They arrived at the hospital. Miklos carried Beatrice inside with the officers flanking him. When the nurses who were on duty at the emergency desk saw the blood and heard the story, they called for an intern. They quickly explained to the intern what happened to Beatrice, and he immediately had her placed on a cart and wheeled away by an orderly to one of the surgical rooms. He told Miklos to sit down in the waiting room. One of the surgeons on duty would see to her immediately. With that, the intern hurried after the cart.

Darrah and Stigal went to the waiting room with Miklos, saying they would stay with him until they found out the doctor's diagnosis of Beatrice's head injury.

The three men sat down, but Miklos was too agitated to sit still, both with worry over Beatrice and anger toward Hunyard. He jumped up from the chair and began pacing the room like a caged lion. Darrah and Stigal exchanged glances, but both knew there was no use to try to get him to sit down.

As he paced, Miklos ran splayed fingers through his hair. Each time he heard footsteps in the hall, he looked toward the door, anticipating the sight of a man in a white frock. Other people came and went from the waiting room, but as yet, there was no surgeon.

Miklos had been pacing for just over an hour when he heard footsteps in the hall, and once again looked toward the door. His fragile patience was running thin. But this time, a middle-aged man in a white frock stepped in, ran his gaze over the room, then settled on Miklos. "Mr. Varda?"

"Yes, Doctor."

Darrah and Stigal left their chairs and stood beside Miklos.

"I'm Dr. Lenton Josmind," said the physician, letting his eyes run over all three faces. "Let's sit down."

When the police officers and Miklos were seated, Josmind drew up a wooden chair and sat down facing them. "I stitched up your wife's head gash, Mr. Varda. As far as I could tell, there was no damage to her skull at all. Her mind seems clear, and my prognosis is that she will recover from the blow without complications. However, I want to keep her in the hospital for a couple of days for observation. If there has been any damage to her brain, we will know it by then. We can't be too careful with a head injury."

Miklos ran fingers through his hair again. "Of course. I appreciate that, Dr. Josmind. May I go in and see her?"

"You may, but you shouldn't stay very long. She needs to rest. She is in room 212. Ten minutes maximum. Any other time you come, please keep the visit to no more than ten minutes."

"We'll wait for you, Mr. Varda," said Officer Nicholas Darrah. "Then we'll take you home."

"Actually, I need to go to Beatrice's brother's home in Buda Hills. I need to let him and his wife know what has happened. They will take me home." Then Miklos turned to the surgeon. "Doctor, will it be all right if my wife's brother and sister-in-law come to see her?"

"Yes, but again, a maximum of ten minutes."

"All right. Thank you."

"If you will come to the hospital at ten o'clock on Saturday morning, Mr. Varda, I will tell you how she is. If everything is all right, you can take her home at that time."

"Fine, Doctor. I'll see you Saturday morning."

The doctor passed through the door and hurried down the hall.

Miklos told the policemen he would be back in ten minutes and walked briskly to the stairs, climbed to the second floor, and soon found himself at room 212. The door was open, so he walked right in.

A nurse was leaning over Beatrice, listening to her heart with a stethoscope. She glanced up at Miklos and put a vertical index finger to her lips.

He drew up beside the bed quietly and smiled down at Beatrice, whose head was encircled with a bandage just above her forehead. She smiled back, weakly.

The nurse removed the microphone at the tip of the stethoscope tube from Beatrice's chest and took the earpieces from her ears. "Are you Mr. Varda?"

"Yes, ma'am."

"Well, sir, I've been monitoring her heart every few minutes, and I'm glad I can tell both of you that the heartbeat is normal.

Dr. Josmind wants me to check it again in an hour, so I will leave you two alone. However, Mr. Varda, you should stay no longer than ten minutes."

"Yes, ma'am. Dr. Josmind said the same thing."

As the nurse left the room, Miklos took hold of Beatrice's hand. "Honey, I'm so sorry for what happened."

Beatrice's speech was still a bit dull. "Darling, it was Hunyard who started the fight. It was not your fault. But I'm glad I stopped you before you choked him to death. Otherwise, it would be me visiting you . . . in jail."

Miklos dipped his head. "I know."

She squeezed his hand. "Thank you for risking your life to save me from drowning."

"Honey, I told you no thanks is needed. You are my wife, and I love you."

Beatrice closed her eyes, swallowed hard, then looked up at him again. "Miklos, if somehow you had been unable to get to me in time to save me from drowning, I would be in heaven with Jesus. I know this without a doubt. And, of course, I would be with Joseph, too."

Miklos nodded. "The police officers who brought us to the hospital are waiting downstairs for me. They are going to take me to the Bartok house so I can let Ravina and Bela know what has happened. I know they will want to come and see you."

"I'm sure they will."

He bent over and kissed her hand again. Tears were visible in his eyes when he stood up straight once more. "Oh, what would I ever do if I lost you?"

She smiled. "Now, precious husband of mine, get that worried look off your face. In a few days I'll be fine."

"Dr. Josmind feels confident of that. But I guess you are aware that you're staying here for observation for a couple of days."

"Yes. I'm thankful for that. Just in case there is something wrong that hasn't made itself known yet, Dr. Josmind says they will know by then. But don't you worry. I'm going to be fine."

Miklos wiped the tears from his eyes and kissed her cheek. "I will go now so you can rest. I'll be back later with Bela and Ravina."

At the Bartok home, Bela and Ravina were sitting on the front porch enjoying the sunny day and the warm air. Bela was reading the day's edition of the *Budapest*

Herald, and Ravina was knitting him a pair of socks. Her eyes happened to stray down the street and she saw a police wagon come around the corner and head their direction. "I wonder what that police wagon is doing in our neighborhood."

Bela lowered the paper and followed her line of sight. They sat in silence and watched the enclosed wagon as it came closer, then as it angled toward the curbing in front of their house, Bela said, "They're stopping here, Ravina."

Her eyes were wide. Laying aside her knitting, she stood up.

Bela put the newspaper down and rose to stand beside her while they both focused on the wagon as the uniformed driver reined it to a halt.

The door at the rear opened. An officer stepped out, then the Bartoks looked on, stunned, as Miklos got out.

"What in the world?" muttered Bela.

The Bartoks looked on as Miklos said something to the officers. When he turned toward the house, both policemen climbed into the seat and drove away.

As Miklos drew near the porch, they both saw that his hair was messed up and there were deep lines of distress visible on his face.

Ravina frowned. "Miklos, what has happened?"

"Let's sit down, and I'll explain."

When they were seated, Miklos told Bela and Ravina about his fight with Banton Hunyard at the dock, and how Beatrice was knocked off the dock into the river. He explained about his diving in, about the stitches in her head, and that she was to be kept in the hospital for two days for observation.

"Oh, Miklos, will they let us in to see her?"

"I asked the doctor. He said you can come and see her. But the visit has to be no more than ten minutes. She needs to rest."

"Well, let's go," said Bela.

Bela hurried to the barn, hitched the horse to the carriage, and they headed for downtown with Ravina riding between the two men.

On the way to the hospital, they discussed Beatrice's fall into the river and the blow to her head.

Miklos scrubbed a palm over his mouth. "I'm so glad the doctor feels she will be all right. I don't know why this horrible thing had to happen, but I'm so thankful that she's still with me."

Bela let a few silent seconds pass, then looked past Ravina at his brother-in-law. "Miklos, hasn't it really sunk in?"

Miklos frowned. "Hasn't *what* sunk in?"

"That God is trying to get your attention."

Miklos's frown deepened. "God? Why is He trying to get my attention?"

"He wants you to do as Joseph and Beatrice did. He wants you to come to Jesus and be saved."

Miklos looked away, saying nothing.

Bela gave Ravina a little smile and said, "Miklos, Ravina and I have tried for years to get you to listen to the Word of God. We've told you how He loves you and wants you in heaven with Him when your life is over here on earth. He wants you saved so much that He is attempting to get you to listen to His Word. Joseph was killed and now is in heaven. Stephan is gone and you almost lost Beatrice. What will it take to get you to let Jesus save you and have His way in your life?"

Miklos said nothing.

Ravina met Bela's gaze and blinked at tears that were now filming her eyes.

Soon they arrived at the hospital and made their way to Beatrice's room. Ravina bent down and embraced her sister-in-law.

When Bela had hugged Beatrice, he looked deep into her eyes and said, "Praise the Lord you're still with us."

"Yes, praise His name. He used Miklos's bravery to save me from drowning."

Ravina put an arm around Miklos. "That was a very brave thing to do. The way the Danube is right now, there was a good chance you would drown."

Miklos blushed. "It really wasn't bravery, Ravina. It was just my love for my sweet wife."

Well, if you love her so much, why don't you want to spend eternity with her? "Bela and I will go to the parsonage after we take Miklos home, Beatrice, and let Pastor Tividar know what has happened. You are a member of the church now, and Pastor would want to know about this so he and Gerda can come and see you."

Beatrice smiled. "I will be glad to have them visit me."

"Before our time runs out," said Bela, "let's have prayer and thank the Lord Beatrice is still alive."

When Bela had finished praying, Beatrice thanked them for coming, and after all three had embraced her and kissed her cheek, they left.

Lying there alone, Beatrice closed her

eyes and said, "Dear Lord, thank You for sparing my life. I ask You to keep working in Miklos's heart. I so desperately want him to be saved. And I pray for Stephan. Please let him see one of the ads and bring him home. I want him to be saved, too, Lord. Now that I am a Christian, my greatest desire is to have the assurance that one day Miklos and Stephan will be together with Joseph and me in heaven."

Seventeen

As the Bartok carriage moved through the streets toward the Varda home, Ravina said, "Beatrice has been through a very difficult ordeal today, but in spite of it all, she still shows a peace and contentment about her that she never had before she opened her heart to Jesus. I can tell that she is already learning to draw strength from Him."

"Yes," said Bela. "I noticed that, too. As young as she is in the Lord, she shows remarkable maturity."

Ravina turned to Miklos. "Can you see a difference in her?"

Miklos was staring straight ahead and seemed oblivious to her question. Leaning forward a bit so she could look into his face, she saw tears in his eyes — something that was rare with her brother.

Her brows knitted together. "Miklos, are you all right?"

Bela glanced past her to focus on his brother-in-law. Miklos kept his line of sight straight ahead as the tears began to spill down his cheeks. "I — I'm just having a hard time with all — all that has happened."

Ravina laid a tender hand on his arm.

He turned his head slowly, glanced at Bela, then set his watery eyes on his sister. "Memories of Joseph haunt me day and night. They are stirred just by being in the house and around the yard where that precious boy brought so much happiness to me."

A man in front of a store called out Bela's name and waved. Bela waved back, then looked at Miklos. "Sorry. Go ahead, Miklos."

Miklos sniffed and blinked at his tears. "Hardly a moment passes, no matter where I go, but that a room or a piece of furniture or some other thing reminds me of something Joseph said or did." He drew a shaky breath and shook his head. "In fact, if I go to the park, the stores Joseph liked downtown, or the . . . the capitol grounds. And now my little Joseph is gone."

The grieving father's hand went to his eyes, and he bent his head down.

Bela wanted to tell him that getting saved would help him immensely in his grief, but remembered that Jesus said Christians should be wise as serpents and harmless as doves. It would be unwise to overdo it, and could do great harm. He had preached to Miklos already that day, saying the Lord was trying to get his attention by all that had happened of late. Bela knew Ravina shared the same feelings, for they had discussed it that very morning.

Ravina patted her brother's arm. "If you want to talk about it, Bela and I are here."

Miklos palmed tears from his cheeks. "It helps to talk about it, especially to you and Bela."

Bela and Ravina exchanged a quick glance, giving each other a fleeting smile.

Miklos drew another shaky breath. "There are more memories to haunt me. Like how callously I talked to Stephan that day at your house before he ran away. The guilt is almost more than I can bear. And like with Joseph, it seems that no matter where I go, there is something to remind me of my oldest son." He swallowed hard. "And . . . and then there is the awful memory of my sweet Beatrice going over the edge of the dock into the river and striking her head on the way down. I will never look at the Danube without thinking of that horrible moment."

Ravina squeezed her brother's arm. "At least you still have Beatrice, Miklos. What a blessing that is."

"Yes. I have been blessed. I still have my sweetheart."

They were pulling into the Varda driveway. Bela was tempted again to preach to Miklos, but he checked himself. As he drew rein in front of the house, he said, "Miklos, please don't forget that Ravina and I love you. We're here for you. Anything we can do, no matter what it is, please don't hesitate to let us know."

Ravina hugged him and kissed his cheek. "I love you. And please give us the privilege of helping in any way we can."

Miklos stepped out of the carriage.

"I love both of you, too. You've already been more help than you can ever imagine, but I promise when I need more help, I will let you know. Thank you for all that you've done for my family and me over the years. You're the best."

Bela smiled. "We'll go to the parsonage and let Pastor Tividar know about Beatrice."

"And thank you for that, too. I'm sure he

and his wife can be a source of strength to her."

Miklos stood at the base of the steps that led up to the porch and watched as his sister and brother-in-law drove away in the golden light of the lowering sun. Ravina looked back and waved just before they turned the corner. Miklos waved in return, then moved up the steps, his mind going to Beatrice.

The house was silent as a tomb when he stepped inside and closed the door behind him. He paused and took a deep breath, letting his eyes roam over what he could see of the house from that spot.

Everything was so still.

There were no sweet aromas of food cooking on the stove for supper. There was no familiar sound of Beatrice humming in her cheery kitchen.

No little Joseph running to hug his papa and welcome him home. No Stephan at his side to share in telling his mother and little brother of their journey up and down the Danube.

Miklos moved slowly down the hall toward the parlor. Haunting shadows were everywhere. He entered the parlor, noted the shadows in the room, and sank tiredly into the softness of his favorite overstuffed chair. He lowered his head into his hands and looked at the floor. "How suddenly one's life can change," he said in a whisper. "One day everything is going along smoothly, and the next day, total chaos has taken over."

Miklos breathed out a long sigh, eased back, closed his eyes, and let his head rest on the back of the chair. Instantly, precious memories began to flood through his mind — memories of happy days with his wife and sons.

Coming all at once, the memories were too much for him. He broke down and sobbed.

When he had regained his composure, he dried his face and laid his head back once more. His eyes roamed to the fireplace. He thought of how Stephan, as a little boy, used to want to help his papa build a fire. Time flashed past those moments, and suddenly in his mind's eye, he saw Joseph doing the same thing when he was the same age.

Miklos sat up straight in the chair. "I've got to do something," he said. "Maybe I should sell the boat, move Beatrice and me elsewhere, and start anew where there aren't places and things to keep stirring the memories."

Suddenly he remembered Sigmund Hardik, whom he had first met on the docks in Baja, Hungary, in June of 1887.

Miklos had taken a load of freight to Baja on a special trip for a merchant in Budapest. He was impressed with Sigmund, who was running a line of tour and freight boats from Baja into Yugoslavia until it joined the Tisza River, then all the way across Romania until it emptied into the Black Sea.

Leaning back in the chair again, Miklos smiled. "Oh, Sigmund, I was so envious of you. I could tell you had made yourself a fortune with those boats. I don't mean that you were filthy rich, but it was evident you were quite well off. And yet, you weren't like so many people with money. You were warm, friendly, and down to earth. Why, even that first time we met, you took me to lunch at Baja's nicest restaurant. And by the time lunch was over, I felt like I had known you all of my life."

Miklos touched his chin and shook his head, pondering on his times with Sigmund Hardik.

In September of 1888, Miklos had hauled another special load of freight to Baja for that same Budapest merchant. *Hoping that you were in town, I went to your office there on the docks. And sure enough, you were there. You welcomed me so warmly. That time, I tried to buy your lunch when you took me to that same restaurant. But you're generous to a fault, Sigmund. You told me in no uncertain terms that if you had to whip me, you were paying for the meal.*

A dry chuckle escaped Miklos's lips. *You paid for the meal, all right. And it was during that meal that we became even better acquainted, and we agreed that we were now friends.*

His mind went back to Baja once more. This time, it was February 1889, when he hauled a load of freight to Baja for that same merchant.

We met up on the docks. I was planning on going to your office to look you up, but there you were, grinning at me as you hurried my direction on the docks.

Time slid back, and the cherished moment was fresh in Miklos's mind . . .

Miklos Varda and his two crewmen, Fenyo Mozka and Ervin Lujza, were just finishing unloading the freight onto a large wagon with the help of three men who were employed by the warehouse that was receiving the freight.

When the last crate was loaded onto the wagon, one of the warehousemen said to Miklos and his crewmen, "It is almost noon. How about you gentlemen eating lunch with us? There's a new café just a block away. We tried it last week and the food is excellent."

Ervin grinned and looked at his boss. "Sounds good to me. How about it, Mr. Varda?"

Miklos was about to answer in the affirmative when his attention was drawn to Sigmund Hardik, who was coming toward him on the dock, a big smile on his face. He knew Sigmund would want to buy him lunch at the fancy restaurant, as usual. With his eyes still on the approaching Hardik, he said, "Tell you what. My friend Sigmund Hardik is here, and as you know, he always wants me to eat lunch with him when I'm in Baja. You two go ahead with these men and meet me back here at the boat at one-thirty."

"Sure, boss," said Ervin. "We'll see you then."

The five men walked away. Sigmund drew up and shook Miklos's hand. "A fellow ought to let his friend know when he is going to be in town. If I hadn't already been on the docks, I wouldn't know you were here."

Miklos chuckled. "Oh yes, you would. I was going to eat lunch with my crewmen and men from the warehouse, then come to your office and see if you were in town."

Sigmund arched his eyebrows. "Why not look me up before lunch so we could eat together?"

"Because you always buy lunch. I don't want to be a leech."

Sigmund laughed and clamped a hand on Miklos's shoulder. "Would you feel better if I let you buy lunch this time?"

"Yes, I would."

"All right. There's a new café just a block away. We'll eat there."

"Oh no, you don't! I'm buying your lunch at our favorite restaurant. Besides, if one of your staff people should need you, they would look for you at the restaurant. Let's go."

When the food was delivered to their table at the restaurant and they started eating, Sigmund looked at his friend. "I have some big news."

"Big news? What is it?" Miklos took a bite of bread.

Sigmund took a sip of coffee. "I just sold my line of boats."

Miklos's eyes widened. He stopped

chewing, started to speak, then realizing he had a mouthful, chewed some more and swallowed. "You sold your boats? You mean you're getting out of the business?"

Sigmund grinned. "Well, as far as freight boating, yes. But not out of the boat business. I'm relocating."

"To where?"

"America."

Miklos's eyes grew wider yet. "America! Really?"

"Yes. I just got back from there. I bought a successful line of tour boats from a man who was retiring. Actually, they call them riverboats. This is on the Mississippi River. You've heard of the Mississippi?"

"Yes. They use paddle boats, don't they?"

"Right."

"Well, tell me why you're doing this."

"Because of the continual political unrest in this country. In America, there is no monarch and no parliament to control the people. They have a president and a congress, but the people get to vote on who will be their president and who will sit in congress. I want my family to enjoy the freedom America offers."

Miklos wiped his mouth with a napkin. "Well, this is a surprise, my friend, but I can't say that I blame you. It's obvious that with this dual monarchy thing between Hungary and Austria, the political unrest is only going to get worse. I worry about it a lot. I'd like to get my family on happier turf if I could."

Sigmund smiled. "Tell you what — if you should ever decide to move to America, I would give you a job if you needed it. Look me up."

Miklos was about to ask where along the Mississippi River Sigmund was going, when one of the men of Sigmund's office staff came through the restaurant door. "I'm sorry to bother you, Mr. Hardik, but we need you at the office immediately. The attorneys are here to do the legal work for your sale, and they are pressed for time."

Sigmund nodded and rose to his feet. "You gave me your mailing address the last time you were here, Miklos. I'll write you when I get settled in America."

Miklos stood up. They shook hands, and Sigmund rushed out of the restaurant with his employee . . .

Still in his parlor, Miklos Varda held onto the mental picture of the last time he saw Sigmund Hardik for a long moment. He then turned his thoughts to Beatrice, who lay in the hospital with the stitches in her head. "Sweetheart, you and I just may be going to America."

Miklos recalled the letter that came to him from Sigmund some four or five months after he had last seen him in Baja. He couldn't remember where along the Mississippi River Sigmund and his family had settled, but he clearly recalled that in the letter, Sigmund repeated his offer: "If you should ever decide to come to America to live, I would give you a job if you needed it. Look me up."

His fingertips went to his forehead. What did I do with that letter? *I know! It's still in a drawer on the boat in the pilot's cabin. I'll look at it tomorrow afternoon, when Fenyo and Ervin return from Vienna. Maybe Beatrice and I can go to America and get away from everything here that drums up these heartwrenching memories. Sigmund no doubt would pay me well. When Beatrice gets better, I'll talk to her about it. Come to think of it . . . I've never even mentioned Sigmund to her or the boys.*

Miklos put his head back and closed his eyes. He thought about America and the things he had heard and read about the land of the free. His mind went to the Statue of

Liberty. He remembered reading about how the people of France had presented the colossal statue to the people of the United States several years ago. Many times since, he had talked to people on his boat who had been to America and had seen it. Every one of them spoke of how impressive it was, towering over New York Harbor, and welcoming immigrants and visitors alike with the torch of freedom held high.

In his thoughts, Miklos imagined Beatrice and himself sailing into New York Harbor to start a new life in a place where there were no places to remind them of happy days with Joseph — and with Stephan.

After a few minutes of optimistic contemplation, he became drowsy and fell asleep.

It was the barking of a neighbor's dog that stirred him awake.

Opening his bleary eyes, Miklos found that he was enveloped in darkness. He yawned, rose to his feet, and felt for the lantern that stood on the small table next to his chair. One hand went to a small dish where the matches were kept. He struck a match, lifted the glass chimney, and touched flame to the wick.

Replacing the chimney with a soft glow of light filling the parlor, he picked up the lantern and headed down the hall toward the kitchen with hunger scratching at his stomach.

The night nurse finished checking Beatrice's heart with the stethoscope and smiled down at her. "Sounds good. Dr. Josmind will be glad to hear this."

Beatrice smiled up at her. "One step closer to being released Saturday morning."

"Mm-hmm. If your heart does as well tomorrow as the record says it has done today, that will be a definite plus in your favor."

They heard footsteps in the hall. The nurse turned to see Miklos standing in the doorway.

"Yes, sir?"

"I'm Miklos Varda. May I come in?"

"Of course, Mr. Varda. Your wife has been expecting you. I just checked her heart, and she's doing fine."

A smile broke over Miklos's features. "Good. I'm glad to hear it."

The nurse told Beatrice she would be in to check on her later and left the room.

Miklos moved up to the bed. "I didn't

mean to be this late, honey. I sat down in the parlor, and before I knew it, I woke up in the dark."

"I'm glad you got some rest. Let's have a kiss."

Miklos bent down and kissed her softly on the lips. "I love you."

"And I love you. Did you eat some supper?"

"Yes. Ate some leftovers."

"Did you get enough?"

"Plenty. Other than your heart, how are you doing?"

"Fine, as far as I can tell."

"Any pain in the back of your head?"

"A little, but nothing bad. You haven't said anything about hearing from Stephan."

"Nothing, honey. I'm sorry. Maybe tomorrow."

Beatrice nodded, disappointment showing in her eyes.

Miklos took hold of her hand. "You're talking clearer now. That's a good sign."

"Dr. Josmind was in to see me before he went off duty. He still wants all day tomorrow to keep me under observation. He said if all goes well, I can go home Saturday morning as planned."

"That's what I'm hoping for."

"Pastor and Mrs. Tividar came to see me

this afternoon. They are such sweet people. I really love them."

Miklos nodded. "That's good." His mind went to Sigmund Hardik and the job offer in America, but he told himself he must wait until Beatrice was out of the hospital and feeling strong again.

After they talked for a while, Beatrice's eyes showed the weariness she was feeling. Miklos told her he would leave so she could get her rest and kissed her good-night. He would see her tomorrow.

On Friday, Miklos visited Beatrice twice, once at midmorning and again in the evening. He learned in the evening that Bela and Ravina had been there in the afternoon, as well as Pastor Varold Tividar and his wife. On both visits when Miklos entered her room, she had asked about Stephan, and when he had to tell her that there was still nothing, sadness captured her eyes and it took her a few minutes to be able to talk about other subjects.

Another heavy rain came just after Miklos went to bed that night, and it poured down for several hours.

By Saturday morning, the sky was clearing as Miklos climbed into his buggy at nine o'clock. He was allowing himself time to drive by the Danube and see if it had risen any higher on its banks. When he reached the river, the white foam from the Danube's water was lapping over the banks at the low spots, spilling down the streets and into yards.

With his mouth set in a grim line, Miklos gave the reins a snap.

It was nine-forty-five when he arrived at the hospital. When he reached the door of Beatrice's room, it was open. Beatrice was dressed and sitting on a chair while Dr. Lenton Josmind stood over her. Miklos noted that her features still had little color.

The doctor turned and smiled at him. "Good morning, Mr. Varda."

"Good morning, Dr. Josmind." He let a crooked grin form on his mouth as he set his gaze on Beatrice. "Well, my sweet, you look like you're going somewhere."

Her eyes brightened. "I'm going home! Now, please understand, Dr. Josmind, that I am very grateful for this good hospital, the capable nurses, and your excellent care. But I miss my home, and I'm needed there."

"That you are without a doubt, sweetheart," said Miklos. "There is nothing so empty as a house without a wife in it. I've been strongly reminded of that fact the past couple of days."

"Good. I'm glad you missed me."

The doctor set his gaze on Miklos. "Don't let her overdo herself when she gets home, though, will you?"

"Absolutely not. She is going to rest and get well."

"Excellent! I was telling her just before you came in, Mr. Varda, that I want to see her a week from today. I want to look at her stitches at that time and check her over. You can stop at the desk and make the appointment."

"We will, Doctor. Thank you for giving her such good care."

In the parking lot, Miklos helped Beatrice into the buggy, then moved around and climbed into the seat beside her. He took the reins in hand. "You haven't asked if there's been any contact from Stephan."

She managed a faint smile. "I know you would have told me by now if there was. But that day will come, darling. Maybe he will come home today. Let's hurry so we'll be there."

As Miklos guided the buggy along the streets, Beatrice talked about what a wonderful day it would be when Stephan came home. They would redecorate his room and make it exactly as he wanted it. She would prepare all of his favorite meals when the three of them weren't traveling on the boat.

Beatrice laid a hand on his arm. "And when Stephan comes, I think you should give him a raise in pay for his work on the boat."

Miklos glanced at her. "I would be glad to, but —"

"But what?"

He drew in a deep breath. "Well, I think we both had better prepare ourselves. Stephan may never come home."

"Oh, but he will, Miklos. I know he will."

"And how do you know?"

"Because God is going to answer my prayers and the prayers of his aunt and uncle. I have absolute confidence that one day soon, our boy will come home."

Miklos felt a coldness seep into his stomach. He knew Beatrice would balk if he brought up Sigmund Hardik's verbal and written job offer in America and what he had been thinking. She would say they couldn't go to America. They must be there when Stephan came home.

Though he wanted to put the boat up for sale as soon as possible, Miklos told himself he would have to give it a little time. One day Beatrice would see that Stephan wasn't coming back.

When they arrived home, Miklos helped Beatrice from the buggy at the front porch and gave her his arm as they climbed the steps and entered the house.

The rainy weather had brought a decided chill to the air. Before leaving the house that morning, Miklos had banked the fire in the parlor's potbellied stove. As they entered the room, Beatrice felt the welcome warmth. "Oh! That feels good."

"I thought you might like that. Let's get you into your favorite chair."

Guiding her to the chair, Miklos took the heavy shawl from her shoulders that Ravina had brought to the hospital and the small hat that she had loaned to her.

Beatrice set soft eyes on him. "Honey, before I sit down, I just want to take a little walk around the room."

"All right, but let me add a couple of logs to the fire first."

When that was done, he let her hold onto his arm as she moved slowly around the parlor, running a hand over her cherished possessions. When they returned to the chair, she ran her gaze over the room. "We never completely appreciate what we have until we come close to losing it. I'm so very thankful that God, in His mercy, spared my life and has allowed me to return to our home."

Miklos put his arms around her and drew her close.

Beatrice hugged him tight, then drew back enough to look into his eyes. "I've been thinking as I've prayed about Stephan coming home. I believe the Lord would have us to put another ad in the country's leading newspapers. Apparently, Stephan did not see the ad. Would you go to the *Herald* and do that?"

"Of course. You sit down, and I'll go right now and talk to Pelso Galton. This time we'll run the ads every day for a month."

"Thank you. You're such a wonderful husband." She rose up on her tiptoes and planted a kiss on his lips.

Beatrice settled into the soft chair and looked up at Miklos. "I know that wherever he is, Stephan will come home when he sees the ad."

Miklos smiled and headed toward the parlor door. As she watched him go, she thought, *And something else I know. One of these days, my darling, the Lord is going to bring you to the place where you will open your heart to Him.*

375

Eighteen

On Sunday morning, Miklos Varda looked across the breakfast table, concern showing in his eyes. "Honey, are you sure you're up to going to church? You look a bit peaked to me."

Clad in her robe, Beatrice smiled at him. "When Bela and Ravina were here last night and expressed their concern about how I would feel this morning, you heard me tell them that being in church would do me good. Of course I'm not feeling as strong as I normally do, but I want to be in the house of God and hear His Word preached."

"Well, I'd feel better about it if you had let me cook breakfast. I could've done it, you know."

"I know, but as long as I felt up to it, I wanted to fix breakfast for you. Since Ravina is having us over for dinner after church, I won't have to cook a big meal today."

Miklos fixed his eyes on the bandage that encircled her head. "Are you sure you want people to see you with that on your head?"

"I'll wear one of my larger hats. It will cover most of it. And even if it didn't, I would still go." She met his gaze. "How about going with me? I'd love to have you sitting in church at my side. You would really love the people. They are so friendly and warm. And Pastor Tividar is really a wonderful preacher. His preaching really holds a person's attention."

Miklos's facial muscles stiffened. "No offense, but I've had enough preaching from Bela."

Beatrice nodded. "Just thought I would ask." *Lord, I'm trusting You to do whatever is necessary in my husband's heart to bring him to Yourself. I'll keep trying to get him to church so he can hear the Word preached, but You know what it will take to get him to come to You.*

When breakfast was finished, Miklos said, "You go get dressed for church. I'll do the dishes and clean up the kitchen."

Beatrice started to object, but refrained when he gave her a mock stony look. She smiled. "All right, Mr. Varda. I will do as you say."

Beatrice had just come into the parlor, Bible in hand, when Miklos rose from his chair. "They just pulled up."

She turned and looked out the window. "That's your sister and brother-in-law. Always punctual."

Miklos and Beatrice made their way to the front door, and Miklos opened it just as Bela and Ravina topped the steps onto the porch. He smiled. "Good morning, sis and sis's husband."

They both greeted him, then Beatrice stepped around Miklos.

"Oh, how lovely you look!" exclaimed Ravina.

"Thank you, but can you see the bandage?"

"A little, but it's all right. Nobody at church is going to care. They will just be glad to see you. Did Pastor tell you he had alerted the entire membership on Friday about your fall, so they could pray for you?"

"No. He didn't mention that. But what a wonderful thing for him to do."

"He's such a kind and caring man."

"You really ought to come and hear him

preach, Miklos," spoke up Bela. "He will hold your interest."

"I . . . I've got some things I need to do around the yard today. Have to get them done because the boat heads out for Vienna again tomorrow morning."

Ravina looked at Beatrice. "Do you want to come and stay at our house while Miklos is gone?"

"Oh, I'm going with him. But thank you for the offer."

Ravina's eyes widened. "You're going with him? But after what you've been through, it may be too much."

"No, it won't. I'll stay in the pilot's cabin. Miklos always lets me sit on the pilot's chair. It's quite comfortable. I'll be fine."

Bela smiled at Beatrice. "Well, if you should find that you're not up to it in the morning, let us know. You can stay with us, or if you'd rather, Ravina will come and stay here with you till Miklos gets back."

"I appreciate that, Bela. And if that should be the case, I'll let you know. Well, we'd best be going, or we'll be late for church."

Miklos kissed Beatrice's cheek and helped her into the Bartok carriage. He watched the carriage until it passed from view, then busied himself in the yard, doing odd jobs that spring brings about. As he was pruning in both the front and back yards, memories of Joseph and Stephan kept coming back to him, ripping at his heart. He told himself that if Stephan had not returned by the time the new ads ran out in the newspapers in a month, he would use Stephan's silence to convince Beatrice that he was not coming back. He would then tell her about Sigmund Hardik's job offer and put the boat up for sale.

When church was over, the Bartoks came by the Varda house and picked up Miklos. Ravina had prepared a nice dinner, and during the meal, Beatrice couldn't keep quiet about the pastor's inspiring sermon and how loving the people of the church were toward her.

After dinner, Bela took Beatrice and Miklos home while Ravina cleaned up the dining room table and did the dishes.

When the Vardas had thanked Bela for the ride and watched him drive away, Miklos put an arm around Beatrice. "Sweetheart, you're looking a little tired. It's time for you to take a nap."

"I am a bit weary, darling. I'll just do that."

"Good. And while you're napping, I'll go down to the docks. Fenyo and Ervin should be back from Vienna by now. I need to do some things on the boat for a while."

When Miklos arrived at the docks, he saw that his boat was in. The river was rough, and the boat was bobbing heavily as the last of the passengers were going down the gangplank, holding onto the side ropes to steady themselves. His two crewmen were helping an elderly couple down the gangplank. They touched the dock just as Miklos drew up. The couple thanked Fenyo and Ervin and shuffled away, holding on to each other.

"Hello, boss," the two men said in unison.

Miklos smiled. "Welcome back."

"How's Mrs. Varda?" asked Fenyo.

"Doing quite well. I brought her home yesterday morning. The doctor wants to see her in a week. She's planning to be on the boat with us tomorrow."

"Well, I'm glad she's up to it," said Ervin. "Any word from Stephan?"

"No. So how was the trip?"

"A bit rough," replied Ervin. "The river is spilling over at the low spots and doing some mild flooding."

"There's some of that here, too, as I'm sure you've noticed."

Fenyo lifted his cap and ran splayed fingers through his hair. "There's much talk in Vienna about the big snow melt-off in the mountains of Austria and Germany, Mr. Varda. They're expecting the river to rise even more in the next few days. Some of the towns between here and Vienna are already preparing for a flood."

Miklos rubbed his chin. "I'm not surprised, but even with the flood threat, we've got to keep the boat in service. As both of you know, we're booked up solid well into June. We must stay on schedule."

Both men agreed, then told their boss they needed to get home to their families. They would see him in the morning.

Miklos made his way up the gangplank, holding on to a side rope. He had to extend both arms to keep his balance as he made his way across the bobbing deck to the stairs. Mounting them quickly, he entered the pilot's cabin, opened a drawer on the right side of the instrument panel, and took out Sigmund Hardik's letter.

Sitting down on the pilot's chair, he opened the letter and read it again. *All right, Sig, so your line of paddle-wheel boats runs from New Orleans in the south to St. Louis in the north. The Hardik Lines' offices and your home are in Memphis, which, of course, is on the Mississippi River.*

Well, even if Stephan does come home in the next month, Beatrice and I will just bring him with us. You probably have a job you can give him, too. But I really doubt he will ever come back. The best thing would be for me to sell this boat right away, take Beatrice to America, and accept the job you have offered. I know if I bring it up before the new ads have run their course, Beatrice will say no. She will insist that we must be here when Stephan comes home. So . . . I'm putting this plan on hold till that month is over.

On Monday, which was the first day of May, the Danube was still rough and choppy. Miklos helped Beatrice up the gangplank with both of them clinging to a side rope, with passengers who were also struggling to get aboard. Beatrice was wearing the same hat she had worn on Sunday to disguise the bandage on her head.

Fenyo Mozka and Ervin Lujza were on deck at the top of the gangplank, taking tickets. When they saw their boss and his wife coming toward them, they both smiled and greeted Beatrice, telling her how glad they were that she was feeling well enough to come on the trip.

"Boss," said Ervin, "most of the passengers booked on the trip are already on board."

"Any cancellations?"

"Not so far, sir. It looks like we're going to have a full load."

"Good." Miklos glanced up at the black smoke billowing from the smokestack. "Steam's up, I assume."

"Yes, sir. We're ready to roll."

"All right. I'll go ahead and take Beatrice up to the pilot's cabin. Let me know when we're ready to cast off."

"Will do, sir."

As Miklos and Beatrice moved across the bobbing deck toward the stairs, they heard some of the passengers talking about the dark clouds that were gathering in the north. Both of them looked that way. "Sure enough, we're going to get another rainstorm."

Miklos sighed. "I hope it doesn't last long."

They climbed the narrow steps, and when they entered the pilot's cabin, he moved the pilot's chair away from the drive wheel and helped her up into it. The chair had widespread legs, which kept it from tipping over when the boat was on rough water. "There you are, sweetheart. Comfortable?"

"Yes, thank you."

Miklos stepped to the starboard window and looked down at his crewmen on the deck below. They had welcomed the last passengers on board and were fastening the metal railing section in place while four dockworkers were swinging the gangplank against the dock. When the gangplank was secured, the dockworkers divided up and went to the thick posts at bow and stern where the ropes were looped that held the boat against the dock.

The ropes were released from the posts, and when Miklos's two crewmen had reeled in the ropes, they looked toward the pilot's cabin and waved. "Full speed ahead!" shouted Fenyo.

While Beatrice sat in the pilot's chair hanging on to its arms, Miklos stepped to the drive wheel. He checked the gauges on the instrument panel, then pushed the throttle forward. The boat veered away from the docks, and seeing that the coast was clear, Miklos spun the wheel, turning the vessel around on the choppy river and heading north.

They were little more than an hour out of Budapest when a heavy rainstorm hit. The rain continued to fall for the rest of the day and was still coming down the next morning when it was time to leave Vienna, taking a new crowd of passengers to Budapest. The passengers were showing some nervousness as they talked about the fast-melting snow up north and the continual rainstorms that had the Danube already spilling over its banks in places.

When the boat was about halfway between Vienna and Budapest, a howling north wind bore down on them, driving the rain even harder and building huge waves on the river. While Miklos held the wheel and battled the rough waters of the Danube, Beatrice seemed unaffected as she talked about the day Stephan would come home, saying she knew the Lord would bring him home one day soon.

Miklos secretly marveled at her faith. He hoped she was right, but he doubted it. He thought of Sigmund Hardik and told himself it wouldn't be long until he and Beatrice would be going to America.

Late in the afternoon, when the boat neared Budapest, the river was spilling over its banks in many places. The rain was still pouring down.

When they entered Budapest and Miklos steered the boat toward the docks, the waves were so high that the passengers questioned how they were going to get off. Fenyo and Ervin assured them that by hanging on to the side ropes of the gangplank, they could make it.

Miklos watched from the pilot's cabin as the dockworkers labored furiously to anchor the boat to the dock and get the gangplank in place, but after some twenty minutes, they had it done. He cut the engine, told Beatrice to stay in the chair, and hurried down to the deck to help his crewmen get the people safely to the dock.

Beatrice watched her husband and his two crewmen through the rain-streaked window on the starboard side. They were helping people as they made their way down the gangplank. It was wet and slick and everyone's feet slipped as the gangplank rocketed up and down while the boat pounded in the trough of the violent waves.

A half dozen times people slipped and fell, including two elderly women who were injured. Beatrice bit her lips when she saw them go down and prayed for them as people on the dock carried them away.

When all the passengers were off, Beatrice was watching her husband and his crewmen as they clung to the boat's railings, talking. She could not hear what they were saying, but she had a feeling they were discussing how to get her off the boat safely.

Only a brief moment had passed when she saw Fenyo and Ervin turn and head down the gangplank, clinging to the side ropes as they went. Miklos was making his way across the bouncing deck.

He was panting when he finally came through the door. "Honey . . . I told Fenyo and Ervin . . . I didn't want to try taking you off the boat with the . . . wind and waves so bad. Did you see the . . . struggle everybody had getting off?"

"Yes. I saw those people fall. I'm really not eager to try it if you think things will get better."

Miklos caught his breath. "They will once this storm blows out. The wind is causing those high waves."

Suddenly the boat lurched and leaned dangerously to one side. Miklos lost his footing and stumbled back against the instrument panel. Beatrice's eyes bulged with fear as she gripped the chair arms.

The boat lurched again, raised high, then dropped down. Beatrice let out a shrill cry. "Miklos! The boat is going to sink!"

Groping his way to her, he took hold of her shoulders. "It won't sink, honey. Just hang on."

The waves rose then tapered into sharp whitecaps just before the wind tore the tops off and sent them flying into the air. The fierce wind drove raindrops like bullets against the cabin windows, and the boat tossed wildly.

Beatrice clutched her husband with all her might. Miklos lost his footing and fell away from her. Her chair slid across the floor of the cabin. Miklos bounced off a wall, stumbled, and fell.

Beatrice gripped the chair arms, her knuckles turning white. The tinny odor of terror was burning her nostrils and coating her tongue. Miklos clambered to his feet and lunged toward her.

Suddenly a massive wave struck the boat, causing it to rise, fall, and lean dangerously, as if it would turn over.

Miklos fell again and saw the abject fear on his wife's face as she clung tenaciously to the arms of the pilot's chair. Summoning all his strength, he found his feet and lunged for her once more. This time he got his arms around her and felt her fingernails digging into his back.

One of the heavy ropes that held the boat to the docks snapped, and when the boat swung hard toward the river, the other rope did the same. The boat was swept downstream, swaying, rocking, and twisting in the ravaging tide.

"I've got to slide the chair over by the wheel so I can get hold of it!" Miklos shouted.

The boat's planks creaked and groaned as if they were struggling to hold together. The wheel was spinning freely. Miklos grasped it, and while hanging on to the chair with one hand and gripping the wheel with the other, he tried to bring the boat under control.

Beatrice gripped the chair for dear life as the boat plowed into the white-capped swells. Other boats were being tossed about on the wild river in the same manner.

Another powerful wave smashed into the boat. It tilted precariously, and with the impact of the wave spinning the boat, Miklos was thrown against the wall and bounced against the instrument panel.

Beatrice flew off the chair and hit the floor. More waves broke over the boat as it rolled about, everything in it making a fearful noise, like it was going to split apart.

On the floor, Beatrice was dizzy and felt a wave of nausea wash over her as she tried to get up. Miklos was in front of the drive wheel, his back tight against the instrument panel. He was trying to break free of the gravitational force that held him there so he could get to Beatrice.

One of the other boats crashed into the side of the Varda boat, tearing a huge hole in its side. The cabin partially collapsed and the door flew open. The wind caught it, ripped it off its hinges, and carried it away.

The impact had also buckled the floor, causing Miklos to be pinned between the drive wheel and the instrument panel. He let out a cry as the boat listed far on the port side, and more powerful waves broke over it. The boat spun around, flinging Beatrice across the floor toward the open doorway. She screamed, her heart thundering, as she sailed out the door on to the deck. The boat was taking on water and sinking slowly as it swirled down the river.

Miklos felt panic rise in his stomach as she slid on her back across the slanting deck. He peered through the front window of the cabin and saw Beatrice being swept overboard by a huge wave. He screamed her name as he watched her go under.

Miklos Varda lost all sense of time as he struggled to free himself, knowing if he didn't, he would soon drown when the listing, sinking boat went under the surface.

Suddenly the Varda boat collided with another vessel and ripped apart. Two walls of the cabin and its roof were carried away by the wind. The impact freed Miklos from his pinned position and he felt himself sailing through air. Seconds later, he was in the raging river. He plunged deep into the ice-cold water, but fought his way to the surface and managed to grasp a shattered piece of the boat and hang on.

Miklos wailed and cried out his wife's name over and over until he was out of breath. Soon he saw the south edge of Budapest pass from view. He was now in open country, moving downstream. Kicking his feet, he was able to drive the heavy piece of wood toward the east bank. It took extreme effort, but in time, he was able to grab a branch of a tree. He let the piece of wood drift away and pulled himself up onto the bank. He crawled a few feet farther inland and lay there shivering.

The river still rushed southward, but the

wind was dying down, and a glance toward the sky told him the storm was passing.

Miklos gritted his teeth and sobbed. Beatrice was dead. Joseph was dead. Stephan was gone and would never come home. His boat was gone. He told himself it would have been best if the river had claimed him as well.

After a while, he was able to pull himself together enough to stand up and head back toward Budapest. The rain had now stopped, as had the wind. The clouds were breaking up and patches of blue sky were visible.

He found that he had to move inland more than two miles in order to evade the floodwaters that covered the farmers' fields. He wondered how much damage had been done to Budapest.

Stumbling along he muttered aloud, "I have never been so alone in all my life. I wonder if my house is gone. I don't even care. I could never live there without my precious Beatrice."

Tears coursed down his cheeks and he let them fall.

Soon his knees buckled, and he dropped to the cold, wet ground. He lay there a long time, unwilling to move. Soon the frigid dampness penetrated his senses. "I have nothing to live for."

He lay there shivering while his tired mind went over all he had lost. Slowly, from somewhere deep within him, arose the desire to live. He shook his head and sat up. *I would be a disgrace to my beloved Beatrice if I just lay down and died,* he thought. *I can't do that. I can't give up. I won't do that to her precious memory.*

Once again, Miklos was on his feet, stumbling northward toward Budapest.

The sun went down and soon twilight was on the land. There were farms all around him. He could see lantern light coming on in the windows of the farmhouses. Even though Miklos had not eaten for many hours, he had no appetite, nor did he feel up to talking to anyone.

Soon he found himself drawing near a farmhouse. But he skirted the house and went to the barn behind it. Slipping inside, he was barely able to make out the interior by what little light was coming through the dusty windows.

He climbed a ladder into the hayloft and lay on his back in the soft hay. He sank into the fragrant pile of hay and closed his eyes.

His thoughts went to his family, and soon tears began to leak around his eyelids and drip into his ears and down his neck. He wept, sobbing out the names of his wife and two sons. After an hour or more, he finally cried himself to sleep.

The light of dawn made its way through Miklos's eyelids, and he sat up, still feeling the emptiness of his loss. He descended the ladder, left the barn, and stepped out into the clear sunrise. With his stomach growling, he continued his trek back to Budapest.

It was almost ten o'clock that morning when Miklos arrived at the outskirts of Budapest. The river was lowering on its banks and its swift current was slowing some, but there was utter devastation in the city along the Danube.

Topping a small rise, he cast a glance toward the Buda Hills district. It was untouched by the flood. *At least Bela and Ravina's house has not suffered from the flood.*

Moving on, Miklos thought about his plans to go to America. Even if his house had been destroyed, it wouldn't matter.

An hour later, he arrived at his neighborhood and found that the worst of the floodwater had gone down, but many houses had been completely swept away in the flood — including his own.

Some people were in their yards, heads bent low, and paid him no mind.

Making his way through thigh-deep water to the spot where his house once stood, he wept. Not for the house but for those who once lived there: his dead wife and youngest son . . . and the older son, who, though he still lived, had gone away for good.

Slowly, Miklos turned and waded away, his shoulders slumped and his head down. His family was gone. His boat was gone. His home was gone. He had nothing left.

He pondered the situation. If he went to the Bartoks' house, they would say they warned him not to fight God. He could not face them.

Miklos always carried a good amount of money in his wallet, which was in his buttoned hip pocket when the boat was struck and went down yesterday. In spite of his having been in the river, the money was still in his pocket. He would take a train to Rijeka, Croatia, on the Adriatic Sea and board a ship for America. He would go to Memphis, find Sigmund Hardik, and take him up on his job offer.

Nineteen

It was almost noon on Friday, May 5, when Miklos Varda moved his way slowly up the gangplank among the crowd of excited passengers at the docks in Rijeka. The sky was clear and a cheerful sun was shining down on him, but Miklos's heart was heavy as he stepped aboard the S.S. *Saale* and handed his ticket to one of the agents. The agent gave him directions to his cabin, which was located on the ship's first level.

He threaded his way through the milling passengers, hearing many of them talk with elation about going to America. When he reached his cabin, he stepped inside, closed the door, and stretched himself out on the bed. Hot tears burned his eyes as he wept over the deaths of Beatrice and Joseph and the disappearance of Stephan.

As he wept, he heard the ship's whistle give off a shrill blast, and he felt the vibration as the big engines were put to full throttle. Seconds later, the *S.S. Saale* pulled away from the dock.

Miklos wiped tears and for a moment, put his mind on the journey that was ahead of him. The ship would soon be on the Adriatic Sea. It would head due south toward the Mediterranean. Once it was south of Sicily, the ship would turn west and sail along the North African coast until it passed through the Strait of Gibraltar and into the Atlantic Ocean. From there, it was almost a straight line across the Atlantic to New York Harbor.

Even though Miklos was going to America to get away from everything in Hungary that would stir up memories of his family, there was an ache in his heart as he thought of them. Beatrice's body was no doubt somewhere along the bottom of the Danube River. Joseph's body was buried in the cold, unfeeling ground at Budapest's cemetery. Stephan was probably still alive, but wherever he was, he was gone from his father's life forever.

The ache in his heart was like the sharp blade of a knife, and the pain of it all caused Miklos to break into sobs. Over and over, tormenting pictures flashed into his mind. There was the ghastly look on

Stephan's face the last time Miklos saw him in the Bartok house. There was the small coffin beside the yawning grave in the cemetery. And there was the horrible scene as Beatrice was swept helplessly from the listing deck of the boat into the angry river.

Miklos's mind suddenly flashed back to that moment at the Bartok house last Thursday when Bela looked past Ravina at him. "Miklos, hasn't it really sunk in?"

"Hasn't *what* sunk in?"

"That God is trying to get your attention."

He remembered how he scowled at Bela. "God? Why is He trying to get my attention?"

"He wants you to do as Joseph and Beatrice did. He wants you to come to Jesus and be saved."

"Miklos, Ravina and I have tried for years to get you to listen to the Word of God. We've told you how He loves you and wants you in heaven with Him when your life is over here on earth. He wants you saved so much that He is attempting to get you to listen to His Word. Joseph was killed and now is in heaven. Stephan is gone and you almost lost Beatrice. What will it take to get you to let Jesus save you and have His way in your life?"

Suddenly, Miklos Varda found himself praying as he lay facedown on the small bed. "Oh, dear God, I'm so sorry!" he sobbed. "I've been such a stubborn fool! I realize how wrong I've been. It was my senseless defiance against You, Your Word, and Your gospel that has cost me my entire family, my boat, and my home. I'm sorry, God! So sorry!"

Miklos sobbed uncontrollably for several minutes. When he finally gained control of his emotions and was sitting up on the edge of the bed, drying his tears, he tried to remember what Bela and Ravina had told him about how to be saved.

But he drew a blank.

He had so stubbornly shut out what they had said, and now he couldn't remember.

Drawing a shuddering breath, he shook his head. "I want to be forgiven for my sins. I want to be saved. I want to be in heaven forever with Beatrice and Joseph. I know I'm supposed to call on the Lord, but . . . but I can't recall just what I'm supposed to say. Maybe . . . maybe there's a preacher on the ship who believes the Bible like Bela and Ravina, and will help me. I'll go to the captain and see if he knows if there is a preacher on this ship!"

Leaving the bed, Miklos went to the washstand. He poured water into the washbowl and splashed it into his face. While drying his face, he looked into the mirror. "Miklos, you look awful."

He hung up the towel, smoothed his hair a little, and hurried out the door.

The sea was smooth and the brilliant sunshine was glistening on its surface. While crossing the main deck, Miklos ran his gaze up to the third level toward the wheelhouse. He could see two men inside, and one of them was probably the captain.

When he reached the third level and was moving toward the wheelhouse, one of the men came out. He was in a white uniform. As Miklos drew up, he smiled and said, "May I help you, sir?"

"Are you the captain?"

"Oh. No, sir. I'm one of the captain's mates. Did you want to see him?"

"Yes, please."

"Well, right now, sir, Captain Howden is in his quarters." He pointed to an open door a few feet away on the third level. "That's it right there."

Miklos's brow furrowed. "It's all right for me to see him there?"

"Certainly. From the captain on down, we are here to serve our passengers and do our best to make their journey a pleasant one."

Miklos thanked him and headed toward the captain's door. As he drew up, he saw a small sign on the open door that read: *Captain Lambert Howden.*

The white-uniformed captain appeared, coming out the door. He stopped and smiled. "May I help you?"

"Captain, my name is Miklos Varda. I . . . I need to know if there might be a preacher on board. I need some spiritual help."

"If there is a minister aboard, I am not aware of it, Mr. Varda. But let's go to the wheelhouse. My passenger list is there."

"I'm really sorry to bother you, Captain, but —"

"You're no bother. That's what I'm here for. Come on."

Captain Howden led Miklos to the wheelhouse, and when they entered, he introduced Miklos to the man at the drive wheel. He then opened a drawer and took out papers that were clipped together. Scanning page after page, he shook his head. When he had looked at the last page, he shrugged. "There is no indication here that any of the men are ministers. I'm sorry."

Miklos's heart suddenly felt like it was

made of lead. "Well, thank you, Captain, for your time."

Howden frowned. "Is there anything I can do for you, Mr. Varda?"

"You don't happen to be one of those born-again, blood-washed Christians, do you?"

The captain's face twisted slightly. "Ah . . . no."

"Well, thank you again for your time."

Miklos's heart seemed to grow heavier yet as he left the wheelhouse, descended the stairs to the main deck, and wove his way through the milling crowd toward his cabin. Suddenly, he spotted two familiar faces. He had not seen Arpad and Sarai Fulop since the day they attended Joseph's funeral.

Arpad's line of sight fell on Miklos, and he called Sarai's attention to him. Her eyes widened, she nodded as she said something to Arpad, and they moved toward him, both smiling.

Miklos's attempt to form a smile was unsuccessful.

Arpad offered his hand, and as Miklos grasped it weakly, Arpad said, "It's nice to see you, but are you not feeling well?"

Miklos bit his lower lip. "No, I . . . ah . . . I'm not."

"Is Mrs. Varda with you?" asked Sarai.

Miklos's countenance sunk. His eyes filled with tears, and he choked on his words. "She — she's dead — ma'am."

While Sarai was attempting to speak, Arpad laid a hand on Miklos's shoulder. "It has only been a few weeks since your little boy was killed. What happened?"

Miklos started to speak, choked, swallowed, and choked again. His voice took on a strained sound. "On Tuesday . . . when the flood hit Budapest, Beatrice was with me on the boat. We had just arrived at the docks from Vienna when the swells were getting huge and the wind was becoming fierce. My crewmen were able to get the passengers and themselves off, but I didn't want to take a chance with Beatrice, so we stayed on the boat to wait until the river settled down some. A huge wave hit the boat, snapping the deck ropes, and we were suddenly being carried downstream.

"Another boat smashed into us. Beatrice was thrown out onto the deck. I was helplessly pinned to the instrument panel inside the pilot's cabin by the drive wheel. I couldn't get to her, and —"

He took a deep breath. "A big wave took her overboard. That — that was the last I saw of her. Another boat collided with mine. My boat split apart, and I was thrown into the river. I — I was more fortunate than my precious wife. I lived to crawl up on the bank."

Arpad squeezed Miklos's shoulder. "I'm so sorry for your loss, Miklos."

Sarai said, "Please know that our hearts go out to you in this terrible tragedy."

Miklos blinked at his tears. "Thank you."

"Are you traveling alone?" Arpad asked.

"Yes."

"Are you going to America, or one of the ports where the ship will stop along the North African coast?"

"I'm going to America."

"What about your son, Stephan? I assume he is staying in Hungary."

Pain showed in Miklos's face. "Ah . . . well, yes."

"We noticed Stephan wasn't at the funeral, Miklos," said Arpad. "Is something wrong?"

Miklos bit his lips but didn't reply.

Sarai set her eyes on her husband. "Arpad, I think this dear man could use some company. Let's take him to our cabin."

Arpad nodded and looked at Miklos.

"Would you like to come to our cabin for a while?"

"I would like that very much."

The Fulop cabin was on the second level. When the three of them sat down, making themselves comfortable, Miklos asked, "Are you going to America?"

"Yes," replied Arpad. "I have a job waiting for me with my uncle, who owns a large printing company in New York City."

Miklos nodded. "Was there some kind of problem between you and Eiger Bethlen?"

"Oh no. When I explained to Eiger that my uncle was setting it up so one day I would become owner of the company, Eiger understood and said he couldn't blame me for going."

"Actually, we would have gone to New York some time ago," put in Sarai, "but Arpad was setting type for Eiger to print Bibles for the Federated Bookstores of Hungary, and in good conscience, he couldn't leave him until that project was finished."

"That was noble of you, Arpad," said Miklos. "So you were setting type for the entire Bible? Both testaments?"

"Yes. I already had the Old Testament done in Magyar and was just beginning on the New Testament when Parliament put through that law that made German Hungary's official and legal language and demanded that all books and periodicals be done in German."

Miklos shook his head. "Mmm. That threw a wrench into the works, didn't it?"

"It would have, but Eiger and I went to see King Franz Joseph when he was in Budapest and talked to him about it. He signed a paper allowing us to publish the Bibles in Magyar. I told Eiger I would stay until I had finished typesetting the New Testament. It's done, so here we are on our way to America."

Miklos rubbed his chin. "I'm curious about something. Could I ask you a personal question?"

"Of course."

"As a Jew, did it bother you to set type for the New Testament? I have several Jewish friends, and I know how they feel about the New Testament. That's why I ask."

Arpad smiled at Sarai, then looked at Miklos. "At first I was bothered about it, but Eiger Bethlen has always been very good to me, and I would do anything for the man. Besides, I did feel that there was some excellent literature in the New Testament."

Suddenly tears welled up in Arpad's eyes. Puzzled, Miklos waited for him to speak.

Arpad brushed at the tears. "Miklos, while I was setting type in the New Testament, and of course having to read every word, something strange and wonderful began to happen in my mind and heart. While working in the Gospels, I began to question what the rabbis had taught about Jesus Christ being a good man, but not the Messiah. When I got to the book of Acts and saw that hardheaded Jew, Saul of Tarsus, become a Christian, along with many other staunch Hebrews, it did something to me.

"Then as I set type in the Epistles, more light began to shine into my darkness. When I saw in the eleventh chapter of the book of Romans that Israel had been blinded in part because of their rejection of Jesus Christ, I realized that very blindness had been on me. By the time I got to the book of Revelation, I was convinced beyond a shadow of a doubt that Jesus Christ is the true Messiah and Saviour. Miklos, I did exactly what the Bible said I had to do in order to be saved. I repented of my sin and received Jesus into my heart, believing His gospel. I am a Christian now,

Miklos. A very happy Christian."

Miklos's heart was pounding. He was going to get the help he was seeking, right here and now — from Arpad Fulop.

"And I am now a Christian, too," said Sarai, a bright smile lighting up her face. "All the time that Arpad was setting type in the New Testament, he kept coming home each evening and telling me what it said, quoting it to me verbatim. Then one evening he came home from work and told me that he had called on Jesus, asking Him to come into his heart and save him. By then I was already convinced that Jesus Christ was the virgin-born Son of God and the true Messiah and Saviour. I knew He had died for me on the cross. Right then and there, in Arpad's presence, I called on Jesus to save me."

By this time, Miklos Varda's burden was lifting. "I . . . I haven't told you about Stephan."

The Fulops listened intently as Miklos told them about Stephan running away from home. He then went on to tell them how Bela and Ravina Bartok had led Joseph to the Lord shortly before he was killed, and had led Beatrice to Him shortly before she was killed. He went on to explain how the Bartoks had talked to him many times, trying to get him to come to the Lord, but he had blocked out their words, even when they were explaining exactly what he needed to do to be saved.

Miklos wiped away more tears. "Arpad, Sarai, the Lord has been working on me in a powerful way since Tuesday. I realize what a fool I've been to reject Him all these years. I want to be saved, but I can't remember what I have to do in order to be saved."

Arpad smiled, left his chair, and went to the small dresser. He picked up his Magyar Bible and looked Miklos square in the eye. "Let me show you."

While Miklos Varda talked with Arpad and Sarai Fulop aboard the S.S. *Saale* on the Adriatic Sea, Stephan Varda arrived in Szeged on Fuzer Lines tour boat number four, having been in Romania all the way to the Black Sea.

When Stephan and his fellow crewmen had watched all the passengers walk down the gangplank onto the dock, they stepped off the boat themselves and heard people talking about the terrible floods up north along the Danube River, and how Budapest had been flooded on Tuesday. Some were saying that over three hundred citizens of Budapest had drowned or were missing.

While the other crewmen headed for their homes, Stephan decided to purchase a copy of the *Szeged Daily News* and read about the Budapest flood. Going to the newsstand right there on the docks, he bought the latest edition of the paper and sat down on a nearby bench. He wanted to learn what he could before heading for the boardinghouse.

He read every word in the front-page article, which was a daily update since the paper had been carrying the story of Budapest's flood for the past four days. The details were sketchy, but he could tell that the flood was bad. The paper confirmed what he had heard people on the dock saying; that over three hundred of Budapest's citizens were dead or missing.

Stephan was immediately concerned for his parents and Aunt Ravina and Uncle Bela, hoping none of them were among the dead or missing.

Since Anna Polzin wouldn't have supper ready at the boardinghouse for two and a half hours yet, Stephan eased back on the bench and casually flipped through the rest of the paper. Soon he was in the classified section, which did not interest him. He started to turn to the next page when his own name caught his eye in one of the columns. His head bobbed and his eyes widened as he focused on the small ad before him:

Stephan Varda: We are sorry. Please forgive us for the way we treated you. We were wrong. We have forgiven your disobedience. Please come home. With undying love, your parents.

Stephan's eyes filled with tears. Even though it had been a short time since he had seen his parents, it seemed like an eternity of memories quickly flooded his mind. The words *undying love* gripped his heart. Sniffling while the tears began to spill down his cheeks, he read the ad again. People passing by were gawking at him. Not wanting to be a public spectacle, he folded the newspaper, put it under his arm, hurried off the docks, and headed down the street toward the boardinghouse.

When Stephan reached the boardinghouse, he was still weeping. He moved through the front door, hoping he wouldn't run into any of the tenants or Mrs. Polzin. He hurried down the hall and bounded up the stairs to the second floor. When he reached his room, he was thankful that no one had seen him. He moved inside, closed the door behind him, and broke into joyful sobs. "Oh, Mama, Papa! My love for you is an undying love, too!"

Immediately, Stephan determined that he would go home to his parents. His mind went to the citizens of Budapest who were dead or missing and his nerves tightened. "Oh, Mama, Papa — you just can't be among that number. You have to be all right. You put this ad in the paper, didn't you? It's dated May 5. It would take a few days to set up the ad here in Szeged from Budapest. You had to be alive and well in order to do that. Yes! You have to be all right! I imagine you put ads in several Hungarian papers, didn't you? Your son is coming home!"

Stephan glanced at the clock on the wall of his room. Suppertime was still an hour away. Mr. Fuzer would still be in his office. He dashed out the door, ran down the stairs, and hit the street at a full run.

Visgrad Fuzer was indeed at his office when Stephan knocked on his door. He opened the door and smiled. "Well, hello, Stephan. I figured you had gone home to the boardinghouse by now. I didn't think I would see you till tomorrow morning."

"Well, sir, that's the way it would have been except for an ad I found in the classified section of today's *Szeged Daily News.*"

Puzzlement captured Fuzer's features. "What about it? Did you find a better job in there?"

"Oh no, sir! I love my job. But . . . but there's something I never have told you. Could I have a few minutes of your time?"

"Why, of course. Let's sit down."

When they were both situated on a couch, Stephan told Visgrad Fuzer his whole story, beginning with Joseph's death. He told him of how his parents had refused to forgive him for taking Joseph to hear the king's speech, and of his running away from home and coming to Szeged to find work. He then showed him the ad in the newspaper.

Fuzer saw the elation in the young man's eyes. "So you're going home."

"Yes, sir."

"How soon?"

"Tomorrow, if it's all right with you."

Fuzer smiled. "Of course. I hate to lose you. You're a good worker, but I understand."

Stephan was given the wages due him, and after sincerely thanking Fuzer, he hurried to the railroad depot. He was able to purchase a ticket for Budapest and secure a seat on the train that was scheduled to leave at ten o'clock the next morning.

When he arrived back at the boarding-house, it was fifteen minutes before suppertime. He stepped into the dining hall, which was adjacent to the kitchen, and while the sweet scent of fried chicken made his mouth water, he called, "Mrs. Polzin! Mrs. Polzin!"

The kitchen door came open and Anna Polzin came bustling into the dining hall, drying her hands on her starched white apron. "Well, hello, Stephan. I'm glad you're back. Did the trip go all right?"

"Yes, ma'am," he said, breathing in short breaths, his eyes sparkling.

Anna cocked her head and frowned. "Are you all right, son?"

"Oh yes, ma'am. Better than I've been in some time."

"Well, tell me about it."

"You remember I told you about my little brother dying?"

"Yes."

"Well, what I didn't tell you was that my parents disowned me because it was my disobedience to them that caused his death."

Anna frowned.

Drawing a deep breath, Stephan took the

newspaper from under his arm, opened it to the classified section, showed her the ad, and explained about his brother's death. Anna read it and tears glistened in her eyes. "Oh, Stephan, I wasn't aware of this, of course, but I'm so very happy for you. You will be going home then, won't you?"

"Yes, ma'am. I have a ticket for the Budapest train that leaves at ten o'clock tomorrow morning. I wish there was a train going tonight, but I'll just have to wait till morning."

Other tenants were now filing into the dining hall.

Anna patted his cheek. "You haven't been here in the boardinghouse for very many days since I rented you the room, but I've become quite attached to you. You're a fine boy, and I will miss you."

Stephan grinned. "I'll miss you, too, Mrs. Polzin, but at least you won't have any trouble renting my room. I know you've had people in, looking for rooms every time I've been here. Tomorrow, you can put up your vacancy sign, 'cause I'm going home!"

Anna patted his cheek again. "I'm glad for you, son. Sit down, now. It's time to eat."

That night, Stephan readied for bed early, hoping he could fall asleep right away, which would make the time pass more quickly.

After tossing and turning for over four hours, he realized he was too excited to sleep. He got up, washed, shaved, combed his hair, and dressed. He stuffed the new clothes he had bought into a knapsack, then sat down in the overstuffed chair. For the rest of the night, he stared out into the darkness beyond the window, willing time to hurry by.

His mind went to his family repeatedly. Each time he thought of Joseph, sadness filled his heart. He wondered what it would be like around the house without his little brother.

He scrubbed a shaky hand over his face. "I can't undo what has happened, but I will be the best son I can to Mama and Papa and make their lives as happy and pleasant as possible."

When dawn came, Stephan yawned, stretched, and rose from the chair. Picking up the knapsack, he stepped out into the hall and moved toward the staircase. He could smell breakfast cooking. Mrs. Polzin, as always, was right on time. Breakfast would be at six-thirty as usual.

He hurried down the stairs, passed through the dining hall, and knocked on the kitchen door. "Mrs. Polzin, it's Stephan."

"Come in," she called.

Stephan pushed the door open and stepped into the kitchen. Anna was busy at the stove, working over steaming skillets. She smiled at him. "Breakfast isn't ready yet, son, but if you want to sit down, I have some hot cinnamon rolls."

"Thank you, ma'am, but I'm much too excited to eat. I just wanted to tell you good-bye and thank you for taking this stray in."

Anna left her cooking for a moment. "I've enjoyed having you here, Stephan." She planted a warm kiss on his cheek. "Go home to your loving parents. I know they need you."

"Yes, ma'am. I'm heading to the depot right now. Maybe the time will pass faster if I'm right there where the trains come and go."

A smile graced her soft features again. "May God go with you."

Twenty

It was just after nine o'clock on Monday morning, May 8, when Bela and Ravina Bartok stepped out of Chief Akman Serta's office at police headquarters in downtown Budapest.

"Again, folks, let me say how sorry I am about your loss," Serta said. "I wish I could have given you some hope, but I had to be honest with you."

"We understand that, Chief," said Bela. "We thought it best to talk to you about it before we totally gave up. Thank you for talking to us."

Ravina gave him a slim smile. "Yes, thank you, Chief Serta."

As Bela helped Ravina into the carriage in the parking lot, he said, "Well, honey, at least we can have closure on it. Miklos and Beatrice met the same fate so many others did when the flood hit."

Ravina settled on the seat, her face set in grim lines. "It's so much easier to let Beatrice go because we know she's in heaven. But my brother —"

"I know, sweetheart. Try to keep your mind on Beatrice. Just think: She and Joseph are in each other's arms now, in the presence of Jesus and the angels."

"I'm so thankful we have that fact to cling to."

Bela rounded the rear of the carriage, climbed up onto the seat, and guided the horse on to the street. As they drove toward the Danube River, Ravina said, "Oh, Bela, if only Stephan would come back. It would help so much to have him with us. He's — well, he's all we have left of the Varda family."

"He will be back, honey. Our prayers will not go unanswered. The Lord knows where he is and how to work in his mind and heart to get him to come home."

"If he would just see that ad, I believe that what Miklos and Beatrice said in it will be enough to bring him home."

"It would sure be enough for me if I were Stephan, I'll tell you that. Especially those last words — undying love."

"They sure leave no doubt as to how they felt about him. I can hardly wait to

420

put my arms around him."

"Me too."

They rode in silence while looking at the damage the flood had done in the downtown area. Water was still pooled in the low places.

Soon they reached the Chain Bridge, and amid a large number of buggies, carriages, and wagons, made their way slowly across the bridge. Ravina glanced down at the river below them. "Hard to believe it was so furious just six days ago, isn't it?"

"Mm-hmm. Sure looks better now. I hope it doesn't get bad again as the snow continues to melt up north."

"It won't be that bad if we don't get more heavy rains and wind like last week."

"Right."

Soon they were off the bridge, moving through the Castle Hill area. When they drew near the Mary Magdalene Tower, which was tall enough to be visible from all over the city, Ravina said, "It looks like the water came up a couple of feet on the tower, but no more."

Bela set his gaze on the tower. "No damage as far as I can see."

"I've told you this before, but I'm so much looking forward to meeting Mary Magdalene in heaven. I want her to tell me what it was like to be the very first person to see Jesus after His resurrection."

Bela nodded. "What a wonderful experience that must have been!"

Ravina was quiet for a moment, then took hold of her husband's arm. "Just think, honey. Beatrice and Joseph have no doubt already met Mary Magdalene."

"I'm sure they have. And Moses and Abraham and Paul and Peter and James and John and — Oh, honey, just the thought of it has goose bumps crawling all over me!"

An hour later, Bela was trimming shrubbery in his backyard while Ravina was sitting on the back porch of the house, knitting.

As Bela bent over a bush, clipping away some dead ends on the slender branches, movement in his peripheral vision caught his attention. He looked up and saw Pastor Varold Tividar coming alongside the house from the front yard. He stood and waved. "Hello, Pastor!" Then to Ravina, "Honey, our pastor is here."

Bela laid his shears down and went to Tividar. As they shook hands, Ravina was on her feet, standing at the end of the porch. "Pastor, how nice to see you!"

As the two men headed for the porch, Tividar said, "I knocked on the front door, and when I didn't get an answer, I figured you might be out back."

"Just doing a little yard work. And Ravina's knitting me a sweater for when the cold weather comes back in the fall."

They stepped up on the porch, and Ravina offered her hand. "To what do we owe this pleasant visit?"

"Well, as you know, we had many tragedies among other families in the church. I couldn't help but notice how sad both of you looked in the services yesterday, but I just couldn't get to you then. I know you are grieving over the disappearance of Beatrice and her husband, and I just wanted to come by and spend some time with you."

"We're glad to have you," said Ravina. "Come. Sit down."

When all three were seated on porch chairs, the pastor said, "So I assume you've had no word as yet about the Vardas."

Bela shook his head. "None. Ravina and I went to police headquarters this morning and had a talk with Chief Serta. He was honest with us. He said if Miklos or Beatrice were still alive, we would know it by now."

Tividar nodded. "I only know that they

were both on his boat here in Budapest when the flood struck so violently last Tuesday. Fill me in, would you?"

"Certainly. Ravina and I only know what we've been told by Miklos's two crewmen, Fenyo Mozka and Ervin Lujza. They explained that the river was really rough when they arrived from Vienna on Tuesday. The boat was bouncing so much that it was difficult getting the passengers down the gangplank and onto the dock. When that was done, Fenyo and Ervin offered to help Miklos get Beatrice to the dock. But because of the injury to her head, he didn't want her to try it. She was still somewhat unsteady on her feet. Miklos told them he would wait and take her off when the river settled down some."

"I see."

"Fenyo and Ervin told us that they both live on the same block over in the Watertown area. They were more than halfway home, when they agreed they should go back and stay with their boss and his wife to make sure they got safely off the boat whenever Miklos wanted to try it.

"By the time they got back to the docks, the Varda boat was gone. Two men told them that a giant wave had hit the docks, and they saw the Varda boat's mooring ropes break. The boat was carried down-river very fast. The two men confirmed that they saw Miklos and Beatrice in the pilot's cabin when the boat was carried away."

The pastor shook his head sadly.

"And then," said Bela, "Fenyo and Ervin told us that someone else they talked to a bit later had seen the Varda boat and another tour boat collide. Both boats were severely damaged. This morning, Chief Serta told us the men in the other boat survived. They came and reported the crash to him and said the last they saw the Varda boat, it was sinking as the roaring river carried it farther south."

The pastor shook his head again. "That does sound bad. I assume there hasn't been any sign of the boat since."

"Yes, there has."

"Oh?"

"Mm-hmm. I talked to an officer on the desk at police headquarters on Wednesday. He told me that both police and port authorities were searching the banks of the river for survivors, and they had found a large section of a bow from a tour boat that had the Varda name on it. So, they knew the boat had to have sunk with that much of the bow missing."

"Oh. So that pretty well tells the story."

"Yes. That part of the boat was found snagged on a bush on the bank some four miles south of the city. He told us we must face the fact that since there has been no appearance of either Miklos or Beatrice in all this time, they had to have drowned. Like so many victims of the flood, their bodies had to have been carried downstream by the huge waves and will probably never be found."

Ravina adjusted her position on the chair. "It's hard to think of them dying in such a violent way, Pastor, but the Lord has given us peace about Beatrice. We know she's with Him in heaven. It's knowing Miklos died lost that makes our hearts ache."

"I understand. It's so tragic. I know you two witnessed to him faithfully over the years. And when I tried to visit him in his home after Beatrice was saved and baptized, he wouldn't let me in. We can only find solace in the Lord. I would like to have prayer with you before I go."

"Of course," said Bela.

Pastor Varold Tividar prayed with the Bartoks, asking the Lord to give them comfort as only He could do. He thanked God that Beatrice had come to Jesus shortly before this tragedy, and that she was now in heaven with her little Joseph.

When the amen had been said, Ravina smiled at the pastor through her tears. "Thank you so much for your compassion and understanding in a time like this."

Tividar wiped tears from his own cheeks. "As your pastor, I love you both very much. When you hurt, I hurt."

When the pastor was gone, Miklos folded Ravina in his arms, and they clung to each other with their hearts heavy over the deaths of Miklos and Beatrice — especially Miklos, whom they were sure died without Jesus.

It was early afternoon as the train from Szeged rolled northwest toward Budapest. Stephan Varda, alone on the seat, pressed his face close to the window. His heart skipped a beat when he noted the familiar rolling hills and patches of forest. He was getting close to home.

He said in a whisper, "I'm coming home, Mama! I'm coming home, Papa! I love you! I'm almost home!"

Suddenly a nervous tingle slithered down his spine and his pulse thudded in his ears. *How am I going to approach them? What will I say? Should I just rush up to*

Mama and hug her, then turn and hug Papa? Or . . . should I just stand there and see what they do?

He ran his tongue around inside his dry mouth. *Guess I'll just take it as it comes.*

At that moment, the conductor came into the coach and moved down the aisle. "Budapest, twenty minutes! Budapest, twenty minutes!"

Stephan's heart skipped another beat.

Soon the city came into view and Stephan waited to see what the flood had done to the city. Finally, the train was within Budapest's city limits, and he ran his gaze over the streets and buildings. He could tell that the Buda Hills district was still intact, but the devastation in the low-lying areas along the Danube River was evident.

Slowing down, the train chugged across the railroad trestle that spanned the river. Stephan's heart sank at the sight of more destruction. Moments later, the brakes squealed as the train came to a halt in the station.

Stephan picked up his knapsack and filed out of the coach with the other passengers, who were talking about the extreme damage the flood had done to the city.

428

When he came out on to the street, he hurried toward the neighborhood of his home on the low ground, fearful of what he might find. It took him some twenty minutes to reach Pozsony Street, and he was saddened to see so many homes completely gone. The houses that were still there had been severely damaged. When he turned onto Pozsony and looked up the block, his heart sank even lower.

The Varda house was gone.

Broken sections of the fence around the yard lay on the wet ground, entangled in the trees, which still stood. The floodwaters had also carried away the small barn that once stood at the rear of the property.

A floodgate opened inside Stephan's brain, washing old memories and feelings to the surface. "Oh, Mama, Papa. It's all gone."

He recalled the note at the bottom of the ad, telling him if his parents were away from home on the boat, he should contact his aunt and uncle.

Stephan took a deep breath and wiped a palm over his eyes. *Mama and Papa are no doubt staying with Uncle Bela and Aunt Ravina. And even if they are in the boat on the Danube, they will be coming back to the Bartok home. I'll go there.*

Taking a last longing look at the empty spot where his home once stood, Stephan turned and hurried back to the river. He crossed over the Danube on the Elizabeth Bridge and made his way to the high ground of the Buda Hills district. His heart picked up pace as he turned into the Bartok yard. He hoped his parents were there and not on the boat.

Bounding onto the porch, he moved toward the door, his mouth dry with excitement.

Bela and Ravina were in the kitchen, where she was busy preparing cake batter at the cupboard and he was doing a little repair work on a cabinet drawer.

When a knock was heard at the front door of the house, Bela laid down his screwdriver. "I'll see who it is, honey."

Ravina nodded. "Good. I might smear up the doorknob with these hands if I answered it right now."

Bela was almost to the door when a second knock came. He turned the knob and opened the door.

His heart stopped, then restarted with a skip as his eyes widened. "St-Stephan!"

Stephan's voice was tight. "Hello, Uncle Bela."

Tears welled up in Bela's bulging eyes. "Oh, my boy, thank God you've come back!"

With that, the stunned uncle wrapped his arms around his nephew and called toward the rear of the house, "Ravina! Ravina! Come here, quickly!"

Stephan clung to his uncle, who was telling him how glad he was to see him, as they heard a squeal, followed by Ravina's pounding footsteps in the hall. Bela let go of Stephan so his aunt could get to him. When she reached them, she flung her arms around Stephan's neck, and broke into sobs of joy.

Nephew and aunt held each other tight and their tears mingled as Ravina pressed her cheek against his.

When emotions had settled some, Stephan said, "I've been working on a boat line out of Szeged on the Tisza River."

Not knowing what to say next, Bela blurted, "Wh-what brought you back, Stephan?"

Stephan's trembling fingers went to his shirt pocket. He pulled out a folded piece of newspaper and handed it to his uncle. "This!"

"Oh, the ad!" said Ravina. "You saw the ad!"

"Yes. I saw the ad."

Having unfolded the paper, Bela smiled as he looked at the ad. "We know about this, boy. The same ad was in the *Budapest Herald*. In fact, your parents put the ad in every major newspaper in Hungary. They felt sure you wouldn't leave the country."

As Bela handed the piece of paper back to him, Stephan said, "I went home first and found — found that there is no home anymore. I assume Mama and Papa are staying with you. Are they here, or are they somewhere upriver on the boat?"

The two exchanged painful glances.

Bela laid a hand on Stephan's upper arm. "Let's go sit down in the parlor."

Ravina said in her heart, *Dear Lord, help us.*

A frown lined Stephan's brow. "Something's wrong. Where are my parents?"

Still grasping the arm, Bela guided his nephew toward the parlor. "We should sit down first. Then we'll tell you."

Ravina was still praying as she followed her husband and nephew into the parlor. All three sat down on the large sofa, with Stephan between his aunt and uncle. Ravina took hold of Stephan's hand.

Stephan's frown deepened as he looked

432

at her, then at his uncle. "What is it? What's wrong?"

Bela cleared his throat nervously. His voice trembled as he said softly, "Stephan, your mother and father drowned in the flood."

Bela's words went through Stephan like a bolt of lightning. He stared at him in utter disbelief. "H-how can this be?" His fingers went to his shirt pocket and produced the folded piece of newspaper. "I saw this ad in the May 5 edition of the Szeged paper. They had to have been alive when they put it in the paper. It takes a few days to —"

"Your father put the ad in all the papers a second time just before the flood hit, Stephan. They drowned on Tuesday."

Stephan's features were white. "This can't be, Uncle Bela! It just can't be!"

Ravina squeezed the hand she was holding. "I know this is a terrible shock, Stephan. It has devastated us, too. Let your uncle explain how it happened. You need to know."

Stephan's hand went to his face. He drew in a shuddering breath, swallowed hard, then set his eyes on his uncle.

"The reason we know the details I am about to give you, is because they were told to me by Fenyo and Ervin. I talked to them on Wednesday."

Stephan sniffed and nodded.

"Your mother was on the boat with your father, Stephan. Since you've been gone, she has gone with him on every trip because she needed his presence. You understand."

Stephan closed his eyes. "I . . . I understand."

"On Tuesday, just before the flood peaked and sent the Danube into a rage, your father's boat pulled into Budapest, having been on its regular run to Vienna. Though the boat was bouncing hard, making the gangplank do the same, they got all of the passengers off. We'll tell you more about it later, but your mother had fallen off the dock a few days earlier and struck her head on a protruding post on the way down. Your father rescued her from the river. She spent some time in the hospital, and on the day of the flood, still had a bandage wrapped around her head. She was somewhat unsteady on her feet, so your father told Fenyo and Ervin to go ahead and get off the boat. He would wait until the water settled down some before attempting to take your mother off the boat."

Miklos told the story to Stephan as he had told it to Pastor Varold Tividar earlier that day.

When Stephan heard that the bodies of his parents were never found, he said, "Uncle Bela, maybe they're still alive."

Bela shook his head. "As much as I wish they were, they can't be. Your aunt and I had a long talk with Chief Akman Serta about it just this morning. He said since they haven't shown up alive after almost a week, and since the bodies have never been found after this much time, they have to be considered dead. No doubt their bodies, like many others who had been in the river, will never be found."

Stephan sucked in a tremulous breath, bent over, and broke into sobs. Ravina squeezed his hand. "Stephan, I'm so sorry. I love you."

Bela laid a hand on his shoulder. "I love you, Stephan. More than you will ever know."

When the sobbing had diminished to quiet weeping, Ravina squeezed her nephew's hand again. "Stephan, you remember that we told you about Joseph being saved?"

"Yes."

"Well, before your mother took that last

boat ride with your father, we had the joy of leading her to the Lord, too. Your sweet mother is in heaven now, Stephan. She and Joseph are together."

Stephan looked at her almost blankly, then shook his head. "I'm glad to know that Mama got saved. It helps to know that she and my little brother are together." He took another shaky breath, anguish showing in his eyes. "What about Papa?"

Ravina and Bela looked at each other, then Bela said, "Stephan, I — I wish your papa had listened when we tried to give the gospel to him, but he always turned a deaf ear. I have to be honest with you. God says in His Word that those who die without Jesus Christ as their Saviour go to hell."

A chill tore through Stephan. His breath refused to lengthen into more than gasps as his face contorted. "No! Oh no! Please tell me Papa's not in hell!"

"Stephan, I wish I could, but we have to believe God. The same Bible that tells of a wonderful place called heaven, tells of that horrible place called hell. The only way to miss hell and go to heaven is to turn to God's only begotten Son for salvation. To refuse is to put one's self in hell."

Again, Stephan was sobbing.

Bela wanted to talk to him about his own

need to receive Christ as Saviour, but Stephan Varda was too overwhelmed with grief. He would never be able to get through to him as long as he was in this condition.

Ravina saw the longing in her husband's eyes. "Honey, he is far too upset right now."

Bela nodded. He wrapped his arms around his nephew and held him tight while he continued to sob. Ravina kept a tight grip on his hand.

The love and compassion of his aunt and uncle gave Stephan comfort, but he sobbed on for several minutes. When he finally gained control of himself, Bela eased back and looked into his reddened eyes. "Stephan, you're welcome to make your home here with us."

Ravina kissed her nephew's cheek. "We would love to have you. Our home is your home."

Stephan wiped tears from his face. "I don't have the words to thank you properly, but I accept. With deep appreciation."

"Good!" said Bela.

Stephan swallowed hard and cleared his throat. "I'm sure I can get a job on one of the tour boats right away. I'll pay you room and board."

Ravina patted his cheek. "That's not necessary."

"Oh yes, it is. I can't just move in here and take advantage of your kindness and generosity. I must pay room and board."

"All right, if it will make you feel better," said Bela.

Stephan managed a weak smile. "Thank you. I'll go to the docks first thing in the morning."

Twenty-one

Stephan Varda awakened with a start and sat up in bed, gasping for breath. The sounds of his father's wailing from the dark regions of hell echoed through his head. Making fists, he pressed them to his ears, trying to shut out the horrid sounds.

This was the second nightmare since he had first fallen asleep. He had no idea how much time had passed since he had awakened the first time, being snatched from his sleep by the haunting sight of his mother. He had found himself staring into the pale face and blank eyes of his mother, standing at the foot of the bed, whispering his name. The memory of it made his skin crawl.

Only when he recalled that his aunt and uncle had assured him his mother was in heaven had the horrible feeling faded away.

He lay back down, his mind fixed on his

father, and used the sheet to wipe sweat from his face. "Oh, Papa, it just can't be. I can't stand the thought of you in — in that awful place."

Stephan closed his eyes, trying to clear his father's eternal state from his mind and just go to sleep.

But sleep eluded him.

His mind was too alert to permit sleep. It was keeping the parade of thoughts alive, which persisted in marching through his brain.

As he lay there, he tried to convince himself that Aunt Ravina and Uncle Bela's beliefs about death and eternity were too narrow. Maybe God had let his father into heaven in spite of his attitude about Jesus Christ and His death on the cross. Maybe God wasn't as narrow-minded as his aunt and uncle believed.

Something at the back of his mind seemed to be telling him it was *he* who was wrong, but he managed to push it from his thoughts. Having some hope for his father, he became drowsy and soon was asleep once again.

Pale sunlight was streaking the walls of his bedroom when Stephan awoke.

His mind went to his dead parents, and

the pain that had lanced his heart since he learned of their drowning in the flood was there again. He put both hands to his temples, pressed hard for a few seconds, then rubbed his eyes. When he opened them again, he glanced at the window. *What time is it? As feeble as the sunlight is, it can't be more than six-thirty.*

He sat up, threw the covers back, and swung his legs over the side of the bed. He stretched his arms, yawned, and got to his feet. Making his way to the washstand, he used the cool water and grooming utensils to shave and comb his hair.

He took a clean pair of trousers and a clean shirt from his knapsack, put them on, then picked up his wallet from the dresser, where it lay next to some coins and the folded ad from the *Szeged Daily News*. Before slipping the wallet into his hip pocket, he let a smile curve his mouth. He pulled two folded forint bills from a special compartment and gazed at them with a faraway look in his eyes. This was the last of the money Andra Hardik had given him that day in Baja. He had saved them as mementoes to remind him of that sweet, generous young lady.

Suddenly, he was reliving the treasured moments spent with Andra . . .

He was sitting on the bench with his stomach cramping from hunger. One of the two young women he had walked by only minutes before was coming toward him. When she drew up, he rose to his feet, met her gaze, and pressed a smile on his lips.

There was a compassionate look in her expressive, dark eyes. "Sir, I saw what happened a moment ago, and I'm sorry for the way that merchant treated you."

Stephan nodded. "Would you like to sit down?"

She thanked him, and as he settled down beside her, she spoke softly.

"May I ask you something, sir?"

"Of course."

"How long has it been since you had a meal?"

"Well, I had breakfast yesterday and an apple and a cup of coffee last night. I came from Budapest on a freight boat. I'm on my way to Szeged to look for a job."

"But you have no money."

Stephan cleared his throat lightly. "Right. It's a long story."

"My name is Andra Hardik. I used to live here in Baja, but my parents and I moved to America four years ago. We live in Memphis, Tennessee. I'm just here for a visit and a little family business. May I ask your name?"

Suddenly there was a knock at his bedroom door. Bela called, "Stephan, you're up, aren't you?"

"Yes, sir," he called toward the door, while slipping the two bills of currency back into their special compartment.

"Your aunt said to tell you that breakfast will be ready in five minutes."

He slid the wallet into his hip pocket. "I'll be there, Uncle Bela."

As the sound of Bela's footsteps faded away in the hall, Stephan hurried and put on his socks. While tying his shoes, he thought of how Andra placed the three hundred forints in his hand, saying she wanted to give it to him in the name of her Saviour, Jesus Christ. He recalled his thoughts at that moment as he told himself this was the way Uncle Bela and Aunt Ravina would have done it.

A coldness came over him as he remembered thinking to himself while Andra walked away: *That girl has to be a born-again Christian like Uncle Bela and Aunt Ravina.* Andra would no doubt take the same position about heaven and hell as his aunt and uncle. She would tell him that without Jesus Christ as Saviour, a person absolutely would not be allowed into heaven. This would make the nightmare about his father absolutely true.

Stephan shook his head to clear his mind, stepped to the dresser, and picked up the folded ad. He opened it, read it again, and said softly, "I love you, Mama. I love you, Papa. With an undying love."

He folded it again and slipped it into his shirt pocket, where he now carried it at all times — close to his heart.

When Stephan entered the kitchen, Bela was already seated at the table. Ravina left the stove and kissed his cheek. "Did you sleep all right, honey?"

He sighed. "Not real well. But I guess that's to be expected in view of all that's happened."

"Sure. I understand."

Bela set compassionate eyes on him. "When the shock wears off, you'll do better."

Stephan nodded. "I'm sure that's true." Then he said to Ravina, "I've got some clothes that need washing. Would that be covered under room and board?"

"Absolutely. Did you leave them out so I can find them?"

"Mm-hmm. They're on the bed."

"I'll take care of them. Sit down. It's time to eat."

When Ravina was seated, Bela led in prayer, asking God to help Stephan through his grief and sorrow.

As they began eating, Bela set his eyes on his nephew. "You have someone in mind to approach for a job?"

While trying to swallow some oatmeal past the lump in his throat, Stephan said, "Yes, sir. There are three or four boat owners that I know quite well. They are — they were friends of Papa's. I feel certain that with the normal continuous turnover of crewmen, I should be able to get a job with one of them right away."

Ravina gave him an assuring smile. "You will, honey."

"I sure hope so. Except for you and Uncle Bela, I don't have much to live for. Work is about all that remains. I figure if I work long and hard every day, maybe I'll be so tired at night that I can sleep and blot out the sadness."

Bela and Ravina exchanged furtive glances, each knowing what the other was thinking.

Soon the Bartoks were rising from the table as Stephan stood up and said, "Well, I'd best be getting down to the docks."

"How about I drive you down there?" asked Bela.

"Thanks, Uncle Bela, but it'll be good for me to walk. I'll be back in time for supper, if not before."

When Stephan was gone, Bela and Ravina talked about their burden to see Stephan come to the Lord. They agreed that in a few more days, when the effect of his grief had eased, they would sit him down and talk to him again about being saved.

It was almost noon when Stephan entered the house and made his way to the kitchen, where he found his aunt preparing lunch. When she set her gaze on him, she saw it in his eyes. "You got a job, didn't you?"

His face was almost beaming. "Where's Uncle Bela? I'll tell you both about it at the same time."

She pointed at the back door with her chin. "He'll come through that door in about three seconds."

Stephan heard footsteps and the door came open.

Bela's eyes widened as he stepped through the door and closed it behind him. "You're back already. You must've found a job."

"Yes, sir. I landed a job on a freight boat owned by Hamor Telek. He was a close friend of Papa's."

"Well, good! And you seem happy about it."

"I sure am. Hamor seems happy to have me, too. He —" Stephan's features tightened.

Bela frowned. "He what?"

"Well, he told me about talking to Papa a few days before — before the flood."

"Uh-huh?"

"He commented on how grieved Papa was because I had run away."

Ravina took hold of Stephan's arm. "Sweet boy, you can't let the past destroy your future. Pull yourself together. Lunch is almost ready."

"So when do you go to work?" asked Bela.

"I have to be back to the docks by one forty-five. The boat is due to pull out at two o'clock."

"Well, that gives me about fifteen to twenty minutes to get some lunch into your stomach," said Ravina. "Get your hands washed."

As Stephan wolfed down his lunch, he told the Bartoks that he would be gone about a month. Hamor Telek had several freight-hauling jobs lined up, which would keep them on the river without a break.

When he finished his lunch, he hurried to his room and picked up the knapsack. He thanked his aunt and uncle for taking him in, hugged them, and hurried away.

As they stood on the porch and watched their nephew pass from view, Bela and Ravina agreed that they must pray earnestly for him and ask the Lord to watch over him until he came home and they could talk to him about his need to be saved.

On Monday, June 12, Bela and Ravina were about to leave the parlor and head for the bedroom to retire for the night when they heard footsteps on the front porch, followed by a knock on the door.

Bela headed for the hall, saying over his shoulder, "You go on to bed, honey. I'll see who this is, and I'll be with you shortly."

Ravina rose from her overstuffed chair, and as she was blowing out the flame in the lantern on the small table, she heard Bela say, "Well, Stephan! Come in, boy. You look tired."

Ravina hurried into the hall. Bela and Stephan were hugging each other as she drew up. Stephan smiled at her, let go of his uncle, and folded her into his arms. Ravina kissed his cheek, eased back in his grasp, and studied his face. "You *do* look tired, honey."

Stephan grinned. "I am tired, Aunt Ravina, but it's a good tired. I very much enjoyed the trips with Hamor and the other men in his crew. It's hard work, but I really like working for Hamor."

"Well, I'm glad to hear it," said Bela. "It always helps when a man likes his job."

Ravina squeezed Stephan's hand. "Are you hungry?"

Stephan shook his head. "No, Aunt Ravina. I ate a late supper with Hamor at one of the cafés near the docks right after we pulled in. All I want to do right now is go to bed. I have to be at the boat first thing in the morning to help Hamor and the other crewmen do some repairs."

"I understand. Have you still been having nightmares about your parents?"

"Only a couple of times. It's getting better."

She planted another kiss on his cheek. "Good. You get to bed now, and I'll have a nice breakfast for you in the morning."

While eating breakfast the next morning, Bela looked across the table at Stephan.

"Your aunt asked you last night about the nightmares. I'm glad you're doing better in that area. How about your grief on the whole? You know, even in your waking hours."

"Each day it gets a little easier, Uncle Bela. I appreciate the concern that both of you have about me. If the world were filled with people like you, it sure would be a better world."

Ravina took a sip of coffee and set her cup back in the saucer. "I'm glad you feel that way about us, Stephan. We have concern for you because we love you."

"I know that, and I appreciate it more than I could ever tell you."

Bela set loving eyes on him. "Stephan, you know that we are also concerned about your eternal destiny. We've talked to you about it many times before."

Stephan swallowed the bite of biscuit he was chewing. "Yes, sir."

"I know you are in a hurry right now, but one of these days when you have some time, we want to talk to you about it some more."

"Yes, sir."

"You want to be with your mother and Joseph when you leave this world, don't you?" asked Ravina.

Stephan's eyes scrunched up with anguish. "I want to be in heaven, yes, but isn't God full of love and forgiveness?"

"Of course."

"Then couldn't He have let Papa into heaven because of His love and forgiveness?"

Bela cleared his throat gently. "Stephan, God's love and forgiveness can only be experienced in Jesus Christ. Unless a person repents of his sin and opens his heart to Jesus, receiving Him as his personal Saviour, there is no salvation. If a person does not receive Jesus, he rejects Him. To die as a Christ rejecter is to die lost. Lost people cannot go to heaven. This is made plain and clear in the Bible.

"And Jesus said in John 12:48 that those who reject Him will be judged by the Word of God when they face Him in eternity. Whether we go to heaven or hell all depends on what we do with Jesus. To receive Him is to spend eternity in heaven. To reject Him is to spend eternity in hell."

Stephan glanced at the clock on the kitchen wall. "Oh! I've got to get going!" He jumped up from the table and headed for the door. "Thanks for the breakfast, Aunt Ravina. I'll be home this evening in time for supper."

There was cold sweat on Stephan Varda's brow as he started down the street toward the river. His uncle's words at the table kept echoing through his mind. As much as he tried to steel himself against what Uncle Bela had said, Stephan knew in his heart that the Word of God was right. His father could not possibly be in heaven. The thought of where his father was at that moment put a shudder through his body.

Soon Stephan was out of Buda Hills on lower ground, hurrying along a busy street toward the docks. There were stores and shops all along the street. He was approaching a men's clothing store when he saw his friend Janos Kudra come out the door, carrying a package.

Before Stephan could utter a word to get his attention, Janos saw him. "Stephan!" They hurried to each other. Janos said, "Stephan, it's so good to see you again!"

"You, too, ol' pal!"

"Where did you go?"

Suddenly, Stephan remembered the day he was hiding in the storage shed on the docks and heard Janos ask the deliverymen if they had seen Stephan Varda. He couldn't bring himself to admit that to Janos. He blinked, putting a blank look on his face. "You know I was gone?"

"Of course. And I know why."

"You do?"

"Yes. When you ran away, your parents and your aunt and uncle came to my house to see if you were there. They told me the whole story. We decided that you just might be at the docks, so all five of us went down there. Of course, we didn't find you. So where did you go?"

Stephan swallowed hard. "I . . . uh . . . went to Szeged. Got a job on a boat on the Tisza River."

"Oh." A grim look came into Janos's eyes. "I was so sorry to hear about your mother's death in the flood. You see, I've been in America."

"Oh?"

"I left on March 27, the day after you ran away from home. I just got back a few days ago. I was visiting relatives in Braddock, Pennsylvania."

"I see."

"It really was a jolt to learn of your mother drowning in the river. I'm sorry, Stephan."

"Are you not aware that my father drowned, too?"

Janos's jaw slacked and his eyes widened. He drew a sharp breath. "Stephan, it was your father who told me that your mother drowned in the flood."

For a few seconds, Stephan stood in stunned silence. "S-say that again."

"It was your father who told me of your mother's death in the river."

Stephan's brows knitted together. With suddenly dry tongue, he muttered, "H-how can this be? Papa drowned with Mama on May 2." The last words came out choked and uneven.

Janos shook his head. "No. I talked to him on Friday, May 5, Stephan."

Stephan's heart was thumping like it was going to shake loose in his chest. "Where d-did you talk to him?"

"On the docks at Rijecka, Croatia. I had come in from America on the *Steamship Saale* and was one of the last passengers to get off. We were several hours late arriving, and by the time I came down the gangplank, they were getting ready to board passengers for the next journey to America. There was your father, among the passengers."

Stephan stared wide-eyed, his mouth open.

"I was in a hurry to catch my train, and your father was about to board, so we only had two or three minutes to talk. When I asked about you, he choked up and told me that you had never come home. Then he told me about your mother being swept from the boat into the raging river at Budapest after it had collided with another boat. He explained that the collision caused him to be pinned between the drive wheel and the instrument panel, which left him helpless to save your mother when she went overboard. He was then freed when his sinking boat collided with a second boat. He clung to a piece of the boat to save his life."

"Janos, Papa never let anybody here know that he was alive — not even my Aunt Ravina and Uncle Bela," Stephan said. "Did he say why he was going to America?"

"He said he had to get away from Budapest, where he was constantly surrounded with so many haunting memories. He was going to America to take a job that had been offered to him by a Hungarian friend of his who used to live in Baja."

"Did he say where he was going in America?"

"No. Nor did he name the friend who was going to give him the job. Like I said, we only had two or three minutes."

Stephan's countenance fell. "Oh."

Janos touched his arm. "I have a pretty good idea where he was going, though."

"You do? Where?"

"Exactly where I was. Braddock, Pennsylvania. The city has a large Hungarian settlement and several steel mills that employ them. That's where all the men among my relatives work. I sort of expect that's where your father went. Many of the Hungarian men have worked their way up into executive positions. That's probably what happened."

Suddenly Stephan's eyes brightened. "I've got to go to America, Janos! I have to find Papa. Thank you for the information."

"My pleasure. I sure hope you find him."

Stephan was panting hard when he reached the railroad depot, pushed the door open, and made his way toward the ticket counter. There were three people ahead of him, which gave him time to catch his breath.

While he waited in line, the exhilaration he was feeling produced goose bumps on his skin. *Oh, Papa!* he thought. *You're alive! You're not in hell. You're in Braddock, Pennsylvania. And I'm coming to America to find you!*

Soon it was Stephan's turn to approach

the ticket agent at the counter. As he stepped up, the agent said, "Yes, young man. What can I do for you?"

"I need to make a reservation on your next train to Rijeka, Croatia, sir, and if I understand correctly, you can also book me on a ship to the United States."

"I sure can. The next train to Rijeka leaves at noon. Just three hours from now."

"All right. How about the ship?"

The agent opened a large notebook, flipped a few pages, then put his finger on the page. "I can put you on the S.S. *Friesland*, which leaves for New York Harbor on Friday morning. You will arrive in Rijeka on Thursday afternoon."

"Great! Can you book me on both and hold the tickets for me? This is sort of sudden, and I don't have the money on me at the moment."

The agent picked up a pencil. "Certainly. Your name, please."

"Stephan Varda. That's S-T-E-P-H-A-N V-A-R-D-A."

The agent then asked for his address. Stephan gave him the Bartok address.

When that was written, the agent looked up and smiled. "Now, on the ship, in which class do you want to travel?"

Stephan's brows knitted together. "Pardon me?"

"You haven't traveled by ship before."

"No, sir."

"Well, there's first, second, and third class, and steerage."

"Oh. I assume steerage is the cheapest."

"Yes, sir. That's where they put the poorest immigrants who are going to America. It's down in the bottom of the ship, below sea level. It's the least expensive, but it is also the least comfortable and with so many children, it is also very noisy. Just thought I should tell you that."

"What about third class?"

"Third class will put you in a small cabin on the ship's main deck. Second class has larger cabins, and is on the ship's second level. First class has larger cabins yet, and is on the third level. The furnishings in the cabins get nicer the higher you go."

"I see. Well, what would it cost for me to travel in third class? I'll need the figure for the train fare in there, too."

The agent looked back at the page, scribbled an amount on a slip of paper, then added the train fare. "Total comes to six hundred thirty-nine forints, Mr. Varda."

"All right, sir. Put me down for it. I'll be

back by eleven-thirty."

The Bartoks were on the back porch and were shocked to see the back door open and their nephew come out with a wide smile on his face. Both stood up from their chairs, noting the sparkle in Stephan's eyes.

Ravina drew a quick breath. "Stephan, what are you doing home so early? And what has you looking so happy?"

"I just found out that Papa did not drown! He's alive, and he's in America!"

Both the Bartoks looked at him, eyes wide, mouths open.

Bela found his voice first. "Stephan, are — are you sure?"

"Positive! I ran into Janos Kudra on the way to work. He told me he talked to Papa on the docks in Rijeka, Croatia, on Friday, May 5. Janos had been in America and got off the same ship Papa was about to take to America. Papa is alive! Janos thinks Papa went to Braddock, Pennsylvania, to work in the steel mills there. He said there is a large Hungarian settlement in Braddock."

Bela hugged Stephan. "Praise the Lord! Oh, thank You, dear Lord, for Your never-ending mercy."

"Amen to that!" squealed Ravina, also hugging Stephan.

"Let's sit down and I'll fill you in on the details," said Stephan.

Talking fast, Stephan told them of his entire conversation with Janos, and what his father had told Janos about his survival in the flood. When he had given the full details, he then told his aunt and uncle that he had already been to the railroad station and made a reservation on the train that was to leave for Rijeka at noon. He had also booked himself on a ship that was leaving for New York Harbor on Friday.

The Bartoks stammered their agreement that he should go and find his father in America.

Stephan then told them that he had already gone to the docks and talked to Hamor Telek. He explained the situation to Hamor, and Hamor understood and was very kind about it.

Running his gaze between them, Stephan said nervously, "Ah . . . Uncle Bela, Aunt Ravina, I need to ask if you will loan me the money for the trip. It will cost a total of six hundred and thirty-nine forints. I'll pay you back as soon as I can."

Bela and Ravina exchanged smiles, then Bela looked at his happy nephew.

"Stephan, we won't loan you the money, but we will *give* it to you."

Tears filmed Stephan's eyes. "Oh, I don't expect you to —"

"We know that, honey," said Ravina, "but we want to give it to you. All we ask is that you let us know just as soon as you find your father."

"I will. You can count on that."

Bela rose to his feet. "I'll get you the money. We keep some stashed in the bedroom."

"Your clothes are all clean," said Ravina as Bela rushed from the room.

"Thank you, Aunt Ravina. I'll go pack my knapsack right now. I have to be at the depot in thirty-five minutes."

"Then we'll have to leave right away. While you're packing your knapsack, I'll fix you a little lunch to take on the train with you."

"That will be great, Aunt Ravina," said Stephan, trying to hide a grin. His aunt had always thought that food would help in any situation.

Thirty minutes later, Stephan purchased his train and ship tickets from the same ticket agent, while Bela and Ravina looked on. They spoke in whispers to each other, both expressing their desire to talk to

Stephan again about being saved, but there wasn't time. They agreed that they would keep him before the Lord in prayer and ask God to lead him to someone who would speak to him about his need of a Saviour.

The Bartoks walked him to the train and found the conductor already calling for all passengers to board.

Stephan hugged his aunt and uncle and thanked them again for the money and all their kindnesses. He assured them he would let them know when he found his father, then hopped on the train.

Twenty-two

they were so ...

On Friday morning, June 16, Stephan
Varda left the covered waiting area on the
Rijeka docks where he had spent the night
on a bench, and got in line to board the S.S.
Friesland.

Children laughed, giggled, and played in
the line. Most of them were clad in obviously inexpensive clothing. Stephan
matched them with their parents, who
were dressed the same way. He was sure
they were destined for steerage. Some of
the mothers were holding crying babies.

While moving slowly toward the gangplank, Stephan let his eyes roam over the
huge ship. He looked at the dual smokestacks that towered over the vessel. Thin
tendrils of dark smoke rose lazily from
them, drifting toward the cloudless sky.

He let his gaze take in the two upper
decks and the bridge, where the pilot's

cabin and the captain's quarters over-looked the rest of the ship. He had seen pictures of steamships as far back as he could remember, but he had not realized they were so large.

Glancing beyond the passengers ahead of him, who were on the gangplank, he noticed four uniformed crewmen who were taking tickets on board and obviously giving the passengers directions on how to find their cabins. He noted the thick ropes that ran along both sides of the gangplank. Some of the children were playing with the ropes and were being scolded by their parents for it.

Soon, Stephan was on the gangplank and feeling the press of the crowd around him. While moving slowly upward, his thoughts ran to his father, causing his heart to quicken pace. Tears of expectant delight welled up in his eyes. What a moment that would be when he and Papa would first lay eyes on each other! There was no anxiety about it. His father loved him with an undying love. There was nothing to fear. He put his hand over the left shirt pocket where the ad was kept close to his heart.

He was still daydreaming about the reunion with his father when a male voice said, "Your ticket please, sir."

Suddenly he realized he had arrived on the deck. He quickly reached into his right shirt pocket. "Oh! I'm sorry."

The crewman smiled, took the ticket, and looked it over. "No problem, Mr. Varda. You're not the first passenger to be in awe of our ship. First time to sail on a steamship?"

"Uh . . . yes. It's a big one, all right. How many passengers can you carry?"

"The *Friesland* is equipped to carry about eight hundred. We have six hundred ninety-seven booked for this journey, so it won't be as crowded as sometimes." He looked into a small notebook, penciled something on the ticket stub, then tore it off and handed it to Stephan.

"As you know, you are traveling in third class. That is the main deck, sir. I wrote your cabin number on the stub, here. You are in cabin number twenty-eight, which is on the port side, about halfway between the bow and the stern. Have a nice trip, Mr. Varda."

Stephan thanked him and moved across the wide deck amid the milling crowd. He would find his cabin, deposit the knapsack, then go to the railing somewhere to watch the ship pull away from the dock.

When he reached the port side, it took

only a moment to find cabin number twenty-eight. He found a sparkling clean room with a double bed and two padded chairs. There was a small table and two chairs next to a sink with a washbowl and water pitcher on a counter beneath a cupboard.

He laid the knapsack on the bed, then stepped to the porthole on the outside wall and ran his gaze over the harbor. A tingle of excitement washed over him. Soon he would be looking at the sea!

Stepping out of the cabin, he glanced toward the side of the ship where he had boarded and saw the crewmen releasing the gangplank. All the passengers were on board, and the ship would soon be pulling out.

He moved toward the stern of the ship. When he passed the cabins, he angled toward the railing, where many other people were standing and looking out across the harbor. As he reached the railing, an elderly couple smiled and greeted him. He returned the smile and the greeting, then leaned on the railing and looked down at the water.

Suddenly the ship's engines came to life. The entire vessel began to quiver, and thick billows of black smoke curled skyward from the smokestacks. The ship's bell resounded across the harbor, and when the clanging died away, the captain appeared on the bridge with a megaphone and shouted to the crew on the main deck at the bow to weigh anchor.

Moments later the engines revved even more, and the S.S. *Friesland* was in motion, pulling away from the dock. Many of the passengers stood at the railing, waving good-bye to loved ones and friends, who stood on the dock waving back.

Stephan threaded his way through the crowd and wound up at the railing on the stern. He watched the white wake of the propellers shining in the sun as the ship headed out onto the Adriatic Sea. Soon the shoreline fell away, and the S.S. *Friesland* was surrounded by pale blue water with the sunlight sparkling off its dancing waves.

Weary from the hectic trip, Stephan made his way to his cabin. He poured himself a cup of water from the water pitcher on the small counter, drained it, and lay down on the bed. His thoughts ran to his father, anticipating the pleasant moment they would meet again . . . and soon he was asleep.

Stephan was not sure what awakened him, but when he sat up on the bed and looked through the porthole, he could tell by the color of the sky that the sun was setting. He yawned, stretched his arms, and left the bed.

When he stepped out on the deck and looked off the starboard side of the ship, the brilliant sun was dropping down in the west with magnificent splendor. Its top rim was barely peeking over the edge of the watery horizon, and it looked like red fire on the waves. Stephan was enthralled at the beautiful sight and stood in awe as the sun sank away, leaving a crimson flame above it.

Stephan awakened just before sunrise the next morning and heard excited voices as the passengers were already heading toward the dining rooms for breakfast.

He bounded out of bed, shaved, combed his hair, and stepped out onto the deck, planning to eat breakfast in the same dining room where he had eaten supper the night before. The ship was rolling gently over the waves, steaming its way south toward the Mediterranean Sea. When his eyes caught sight of the eastern horizon, he was once again in awe as he took in the purplish pink rays of the magnificent sunrise.

When Stephan finished breakfast, he left the dining room and returned to the sea air. He took a deep breath and let it out through his nostrils, deciding to take a walk around and get a good look at the ship.

He decided to go to steerage first, then come back to the main deck and work his way up to the second and third levels. He was especially interested in the third level because he had known very few rich people in his life. He wanted to get a look at those who could afford to travel first class.

When he went through the opening on the main deck that led down the wide metal stairs to steerage, he found himself surrounded by poorly clad families going both ways. As he moved lower into the bowels of the S.S. *Friesland*, he found himself making his way along a catwalk over one of the cavernous boiler rooms. The roar of the huge engines was almost deafening.

When he reached the bottom of the ship, he took in the crowded, uncomfortable situation occupied by the steerage passengers. Tiers of berths — narrow metal frames with a single piece of canvas stretched over them — lined the walls. The tiers were six and seven bunks high, each bunk barely more than eighteen inches wide.

Stephan did not stay long in steerage. When he reached the top of the stairs and moved onto the main deck, he found himself feeling relief that he was able to afford a third-class cabin.

He strolled leisurely over the main deck, noting the huge anchor chains and the boxlike frames that held the lifeboats. When he felt he had seen most of what there was to observe on the main deck, he climbed the metal stairway to the second level. He noted that the deck furniture up there was fancier than that on the main deck. Some passengers were relaxing on the furniture while others were moving about or looking out at the sea.

When he reached the third level, he was even more impressed with the deck furniture in first class. It was much nicer than what the people in second class were enjoying. He paused once again and let his eyes take it all in. For a moment, he looked at the sea and the sky. It was a beautiful day with a favorable breeze as the sun shone down from the azure blue canopy above and glistened on the surface of the Adriatic.

The scene was the same as on the other decks. A good number of passengers were relaxed on the furniture, some with their eyes closed, enjoying the breeze and the sunshine, while others were in conversation. Some strolled about the deck while many leaned on the railings, chatting, laughing, and having a good time.

Stephan decided to take a walk along the railing. He was almost to the bow when he noticed a small group up ahead of him looking down over the railing. At the same time, he caught the loud, angry voices of two men coming from somewhere below. He stopped, peered over the edge of the deck, and saw the two men on the main deck in a heated argument near the railing. He couldn't make out what they were saying, so after a couple of minutes, he moved on.

Soon he was heading toward the stern, letting his eyes take in the wealthy people in their expensive clothing. He especially noted the women with their fancy jewelry. The diamonds flashed beautifully in the sunshine.

As he continued to move along the edge of the deck, his attention was drawn to two young women who were leaning against the railing, talking. The one whose face was turned toward him was not familiar, but the back of the other one's head made him think of Andra Hardik. Her hair was the same color and style as Andra's had been that day in Baja.

When he drew up close, studying the back of the young woman's head, she happened to turn enough so he could see her profile.

A tingle slithered down his spine.

"Andra!" he called, hurrying toward her. "Andra Hardik!"

When she turned and saw his face, she recognized him immediately. She turned to her friend. "Excuse me, Alice. I know this young man."

As Stephan drew up, Andra extended her hand. "Hello, Stephan. It's so nice to see you. And quite a surprise, I might add."

Enclosing her hand in his, Stephan smiled. "It is nice to see you, Andra."

When their hands parted, Andra reached back, took hold of her friend's hand, and pulled her up close. "Stephan Varda, I want you to meet a close friend of mine, Alice Wadford."

When Alice and Stephan shook hands, he noticed that her eyes were a bit red and puffy, as if she had been crying. He was saying he was glad to meet her when the voices of the two angry men on the main deck raised in volume, then lowered again.

Andra glanced down at them, then said, "Alice, I met Stephan in Baja not long after I arrived there for Nikola's wedding."

Alice nodded. "I see. Well, speaking of the wedding, it was one of the nicest I have ever attended."

Andra looked at Stephan. "Alice and I have known each other since childhood. She was a few years ahead of me in school, but we developed a close friendship. Her father is Karl Berman, who is president of the Magyar National Bank and Savings Company. You may know that the bank has branches all over Hungary."

"I didn't know the president's name, Andra, but I'm well acquainted with Magyar National Bank. My father had his business account in the Budapest branch when he ran a tour and freight boat on the Danube." Then he said to Alice, "Are you moving to America, ma'am?"

"No. My husband, Gene, and I are on our way there to visit his parents, who immigrated a year ago and live in Chicago, Illinois." She turned to her friend. "Andra, I'm sure you would like to spend some time with Stephan. Why don't you come by the cabin a little later, and we'll finish our talk. Gene's out on the deck most of the time."

Stephan raised his hands. "Oh, I don't want to interfere with your conversation. I'll come back later and spend some time with And—"

Stephan's words were cut off when suddenly a woman's shrill scream was heard down on the main deck, followed by other men and women shouting.

Stephan, Andra, and Alice looked down and saw that one of the two men who had been arguing was now in the sea, bobbing up and down on the waves while waving his arms and crying for help.

The engines were instantly cut, and two crewmen dived into the water to rescue him. While people on the main deck swarmed that direction to see what was happening, the captain appeared on the bridge. Lifting the megaphone to his mouth, he shouted orders for other crewmen to let down a lifeboat. He handed the megaphone to a crewman who stood next to him then headed down to the main deck.

People on both upper levels were also crowding to the starboard side of the ship to watch the rescue effort. Some were hastening down the stairs to get to the main deck.

While standing with Andra and Stephan at the railing, Alice pointed down to the main deck. "Gene's down there already. I'm going to the cabin, Andra. Come see me later, and we'll finish our talk."

Down on the main level, Gene Wadford pressed his somewhat overweight body through the crowd and stopped when he was at the spot where the other man involved in the argument had picked his opponent up and thrown him overboard. The captain was giving him a tongue lashing for what he had done. The man was talking back and giving his version of the argument, trying to convince the captain that he had justification for his actions.

Abruptly, the captain told two of his crewmen to seize the man and take him to the captain's quarters, where he would deal with him later.

As the man was being dragged away, shouting at the top of his voice, the captain turned to two male passengers. "Where are those two women?"

The men pointed to two women who stood some forty feet away at the railing. The captain thanked them and hastened toward the women, threading his way among the tightly knit crowd.

Gene Wadford wanted to get closer so he

could hear the captain's conversation with the women, but he couldn't move. One of the women was a pretty redhead, whom Gene figured was in her late thirties. The other woman was much older and silver-haired. She leaned on a cane.

Though he could not hear what the captain and the two women were saying, Gene picked up from what passengers were saying: that the young woman's name was Lillian and the older woman was her mother. It was Lillian who had screamed so loudly when the man was thrown over the railing into the sea.

Gene's attention was drawn once again to the water as the two crewmen who had dived in placed the shivering victim in the lifeboat. The lifeboat was hoisted back to its place on the deck and Lillian wrapped her arms around him, weeping and smothering him with kisses.

The crowd turned and walked away, Gene Wadford included.

The captain walked up to the wheelhouse, and a few minutes later, the engines came to life. Once again, the ship was moving through the water.

Up on the third level, Andra took her eyes from the scene at the lifeboat below, sighed, and said, "I'm glad they were able to rescue that man, Stephan."

"I don't have any idea what those two were arguing about, but the other guy really took it seriously."

"That's for sure."

Stephan gazed into her dark eyes. "It sure is nice to see you again. Maybe we can get together later. I shouldn't keep you. I know Alice is expecting you at her cabin."

Andra smiled. "You don't need to hurry away. I can talk to her in a little while."

Stephan nodded. "Ah . . . Andra . . ."

"Mm-hmm?"

"I don't mean to pry, but . . . is Alice all right? When I first saw her, she looked like she had been crying."

"You're right. She had been."

"Is it something serious?"

Andra started to reply, then hesitated.

"I'm sorry. It's none of my business."

She shook her head. "It's all right, Stephan. I can tell you. Many people on this level already know about it. Alice and Gene are having marital trouble. Shortly before you appeared, the two of them were arguing right here on deck in front of forty or fifty people. Gene suddenly turned and stomped away, leaving Alice embarrassed as the crowd looked on. I was here by the railing. Alice came to me, and I let her cry on my shoulder, so to speak."

"Has their marital trouble been going on for long?"

Andra sighed. "Almost since the day they got married. You see, Gene is from a middle-class family. Alice is quite wealthy."

"Mm-hmm."

"Well, Gene has been making life miserable for Alice, always wanting to spend her money on foolish things. She is considering divorcing him. She was telling me this when you came along."

"Oh, sure. Look, if you think you should go and be with her, we can meet later."

Andra shook her head. "No. Right now, I think she needs a little time to herself. Let's go sit down. I see there are some chairs vacant right by my cabin door."

As they walked across the deck, Stephan caught the scent of Andra's perfume. He told himself how fortunate he was to be traveling on the same ship with her.

When they sat down on the chairs, Stephan said, "So, I assume Nikola's wedding went well."

"Oh yes. I'm glad I could have a part in it."

"I'm sure she really appreciated your coming all the way from America to be her maid of honor. It's a long way across the

Atlantic Ocean, the Mediterranean Sea, and the Adriatic Sea . . . let alone the distance from Memphis, Tennessee, to New York Harbor."

Andra's eyebrows arched. "Oh? You know how far it is from Memphis to New York, do you?"

"Uh-huh. I looked it up on a map not long after I met you in Baja. It's something like twelve hundred miles."

"Well, almost."

"So what took you and your family all the way from Baja to Memphis?"

"My father used to own a line of tour and freight boats that serviced the Danube River between Baja and Budapest. Both my parents grew weary with the political unrest in Hungary, so they agreed to sell the boats and go to America." She paused. "And, by the way, this means that you and I have something in common. You said your father once owned a tour and freight boat that he ran between Budapest and Vienna."

Stephan nodded. "So what's your father doing now?"

"He owns a line of eight paddle-wheel riverboats. They are called the *Hardik Line.* They travel the Mississippi River from St. Louis, Missouri, to New Orleans, Louisiana, where the Mississippi flows into the Gulf of Mexico. The company is head-quartered in Memphis. That's where we live."

"I saw on the map that Memphis is right on the Mississippi River. Tell me about Memphis. Do you like it there?"

"Very much. But enough about me. What are you doing on this ship? I never expected to see you again."

"I'm on my way to America to find my father."

She blinked her eyes. "To *find* your father? You mean like you don't know where he is?"

"Let me explain."

Stephan told her the whole story, beginning with Joseph's violent death and the events that followed. He told her about the ad his parents had put in the leading Hungarian newspapers, and how he found it in the *Szeged Daily News.*

He reached in his shirt pocket and took out the folded newspaper clipping. "Here's the ad. Take a look at it."

Andra read the ad, then looked at him and said softly, "Oh, Stephan, it is worded so beautifully."

Stephan nodded. "Yes, and as soon as I read it, I headed for home in a hurry."

Her eyes brightened. "Tell me about the reunion with your parents!"

Stephan's countenance sagged. "Well, there's something else I have to tell you."

Blinking at the tears that formed in his eyes, Stephan told Andra of his mother drowning in the flood, and that he thought his father had also drowned until he ran into his friend Janos Kudra.

Andra thumbed away her own tears. Her lips quivered as she said, "Stephan, I'm so sorry about the loss of your mother and of your little brother."

Stephan smiled. "Thank you, Andra. And thank you once again for the money you gave me in Baja." He reached for his wallet. "In fact, I want to pay you back. My uncle and aunt you saw mentioned at the bottom of the ad gave me money to make this trip. I have some extra."

Andra shook her head. "No. You're not paying me back. It wasn't a loan, Stephan. It was a gift."

"But —"

"No! You keep your money. You may need every bit of it before this trip is over."

"All right, if you insist."

"I do."

"Well, thank you again. You are quite a lady."

Andra was still holding the ad. She smiled at him, then looked down at it. "How loving it was of your parents to forgive you, Stephan, and to try to reach you so you would come home."

"I've had the same thoughts many times. Those words *undying love* mean more to me than I could ever express."

She handed the clipping back to him. "I certainly can understand why."

Gene Wadford entered his cabin on the third deck and looked around the room for his wife. She was nowhere in sight. Since the first-class cabins had two bedrooms, he walked the narrow hallway to the door of the first bedroom and saw Alice lying on the bed.

She looked at him and sat up.

He stepped into the small room. "Did you know about the man who was thrown overboard and almost drowned?"

"Yes. I was on deck when it happened. I saw the two crewmen dive in after him, and I heard the captain ordering a lifeboat into the water. I assume he was rescued."

Gene's heavy eyebrows knitted together. "You didn't stay to find out?"

"No. After our argument out there in

front of all those people, I wasn't feeling too good."

"Oh. I wish you could've seen that man's wife when he was brought back on board. She was so happy to have him alive, she kissed him over and over again, right in front of everybody. Would you have done that if I had been the man overboard?"

Alice's features hardened. "Don't put me on the spot."

Gene's face reddened. "You're not sure, eh?"

"After the way you've been acting, I'm not sure of anything. When we took our vows at the altar, I thought you loved me, Gene, but I know better now. It's my money that you love. You married me for my money."

Gene shook his head. "Not so, Alice. It's not your money that I love . . . it's you! But since your father has made so much money available to you, I figure as your husband, I should have a generous allowance so I can have the things I want."

Alice rose from the bed. "I love you, Gene, and I want our marriage to make it, but your allowance will remain the same. If you keep giving me trouble about it, we're not going to make it, no matter how much we love each other. I'm tired of money always being the theme between us. You're getting enough allowance to make any man happy."

Gene's eyes became stormy. He wheeled and stomped out of the room. She heard him open the outside door, then slam it shut.

Alice sat down on the edge of the bed and wept for several minutes. Then drying her eyes, she went back out on the deck and walked slowly alongside the railing. In her misery, she walked the entire perimeter of the deck, seeing no sign of Gene. She assumed he had gone to the main deck.

She was about to head back to the cabin when she saw Andra coming toward her. Andra focused on her swollen, red eyes. "Honey, have you been crying again?"

"Yes. Gene and I just had another argument. He stormed out of the cabin. I don't know where he went."

Andra took hold of her hand. "Let's go to my cabin and talk."

"How about mine, instead?"

"Sure. Let's go."

Moments later, Andra and Alice entered the Wadford cabin and sat down on the couch.

Andra patted her arm. "Was it the same old thing?"

"Yes. The money. Andra, I love Gene, but I can't put up with his always wanting more."

"Well, if you really love him, you'll find a way to work it out. Let me tell you what would really make things better in your life. No one's life can be right unless they know the Lord Jesus Christ as their personal Saviour."

While Alice studied her, Andra told her about having heard the gospel clearly for the first time some six months prior to leaving Hungary and going to America. She explained that she had received Jesus as her Saviour shortly after hearing the gospel in its clarity, and even though life had its hard times for anyone, everything was different since she had become a born-again child of God.

Suddenly, both women were surprised to hear heavy footsteps coming from the first bedroom. They stiffened and their eyes widened when Gene entered the room. His face was livid.

He set fiery eyes on Andra. "Didn't know I was back there, did you?"

"No, but —"

"I heard everything you said, Andra! I'm telling you right now that neither of us needs your religious stuff; you hear me?"

"I wasn't talking about religion, Gene," said Andra. "I was talking about salvation. There's a difference. A big difference."

"Well, we don't want whatever it is. Now I'd like for you to leave. I need to talk to Alice alone."

Andra looked at her friend.

Alice patted her hand. "It's best if you go, honey. I'm really not interested in what you were talking about. I love you, and we'll always be friends, but I have my own beliefs. Okay?"

Andra nodded and rose to her feet.

Alice stood up and hugged Andra.

Andra stepped out onto the deck and headed for her own cabin. Her heart was heavy for Alice and Gene.

Twenty-three

Andra Hardik's mind was still on Alice and Gene Wadford as she moved along the deck, heading for her own cabin. "Lord," she said in a whisper, "if there is anything else I can do to try to reach them for You, please show me."

Suddenly she smiled. Stephan Varda had been seated on a deck chair near the door of her cabin, and spotting her, he was rising to his feet.

Andra's heart leaped in her chest. There was something magnetic about his smile. She quickened her pace. "Hello, Stephan. I didn't know I would get to see you again so soon."

He chuckled. "I don't mean to be a pest."

She showed him her white, even teeth in a warm smile. "You could never be a pest."

Stephan let his eyes drink in her beauty.

Her hair was especially lovely, cascading like an ebony waterfall over one shoulder as the sea breeze gave it slight motion. "I . . . ah . . . I was wondering if you would honor me by allowing me to take you to dinner this evening."

Warmth washed over Andra's pounding heart. "Why, yes. That would be delightful."

"Good! Would seven o'clock be all right?"

"Of course."

"Then I'll tap on your door at seven o'clock sharp. We'll go to the dining room of your choice."

Stephan's gentleness pleased her. "I'll let you choose. Any of them is fine with me."

Stephan wondered at the turbulent emotions that were coursing through him. Andra's presence did something to him he had never felt before. "All right. We'll go to the Pine Room. That's the one closest to the bow on the port side."

"I'll be looking forward to it."

"Me too." He smiled again, then turned and walked away without looking back.

As Stephan was descending the stairs toward the main deck, his thoughts went to his dead mother and little brother. His features bunched in a spasm of grief that lasted until he forced his thoughts to Andra. There was something wonderful about Andra . . .

Andra watched Stephan walk away and kept her eyes on him till he started down the stairs and passed from view. Taking a deep breath, she turned and entered her cabin.

She made her way to the sofa and sat down. "Lord," she said, "You know I find myself very attracted to Stephan. I have never felt this way about a young man before. I know I must be very careful. When I asked him that day in Baja if he knew You as his Saviour, he said he didn't. He probably has heard the gospel, Lord, but I realize I cannot let myself get involved with him if he's not a Christian. Help me to be an effective witness to him."

While Andra and Stephan ate together in the Pine Room that evening, they talked about America for a while, then Andra looked across the table at him and said, "I keep thinking of that ad your parents put in the newspapers, Stephan. You said those words *undying love* meant so much to you."

Stephan swallowed his mouthful of fried

potatoes. "They did . . . and still do."

"I'm glad. Do you recall that after I gave you the money, I asked if you knew Jesus as your Saviour?"

He nodded. "I remember."

"And you said you didn't. My Aunt Kiraleen interrupted us, and Nikola and I were whisked away."

"Mm-hmm."

"Have you . . . have you opened your heart to Jesus by now?"

Stephan shook his head and looked away, avoiding her probing gaze. "No."

"There is another undying love I want to talk to you about, Stephan."

He met her gaze again. "You mean the undying love Jesus has for me?"

Her eyes widened. "Yes."

"My Uncle Bela and Aunt Ravina have talked to me about it many times. You see, I wasn't raised in a Christian home, but my aunt and uncle have tried over and over to get me to receive Jesus into my heart, but I've never done it."

There was compassion in Andra's eyes. "Why not, Stephan?"

He cleared his throat. "Well, all my growing up years, my parents always said what Aunt Ravina and Uncle Bela believed about being born again and washed in the

490

blood was foolishness. We had our own religion, and they didn't want me to get involved in my aunt and uncle's fanaticism, as they put it. My father was especially adamant about it."

Andra smiled. "In my family, we used to think that people like that were fanatics, too. But shortly before we left Baja for America, we heard the real gospel for the first time and opened our hearts to Jesus. My parents and I are very happy in the Lord."

A smile tugged at the corners of Stephan's mouth. "Let me tell you something that you'll like."

"All right."

"After my little brother, Joseph, was killed, my aunt and uncle told me that they had led him to Jesus a few weeks earlier. It made me feel so good when they said Joseph was now in heaven."

"Wonderful!"

"And when I arrived back home in Budapest and learned that Mama was dead, Aunt Ravina and Uncle Bela told me they had led her to Jesus shortly before she drowned. They told me that Mama and Joseph were now together in heaven."

"Oh, praise God! Stephan, they sure are. And you feel good about that, don't you?"

"I do."

"So, you no longer believe that being born again and washed in the blood is fanaticism?"

"No. I'm sure it's the true way."

Andra leaned toward him, looking him straight in the eye. "Do you want to be saved, Stephan? Do you want to meet your mother and little brother in heaven one day?"

Tears misted his eyes. "Yes, I do. But I'll need some help."

"Let's finish our dinner quickly, and we'll take care of that matter."

Moments later, Andra Hardik led Stephan Varda up to the third level of the ship. A bright lamp burned next to the door of her cabin, giving off a glow over the two deck chairs that were there. She told Stephan to sit down and she would be right back.

Andra dashed into the cabin and was back quickly with her Bible. She sat beside the young man, a bright gleam in her eyes.

"Stephan, your aunt and uncle have already told you about the Lord's undying love for you. Let me read you something."

He smiled. "I'm listening."

She opened her Bible to Jeremiah, chapter 31, then placed it so both could look on the page. Putting her finger on verse 3, she said, "Look here, Stephan. 'The LORD hath appeared of old unto me, saying, Yea, I have loved thee with an everlasting love: therefore with lovingkindness have I drawn thee.' Since it's an everlasting love, it's an undying love, isn't it?"

Tears were misting Stephan's eyes again. "Yes."

Andra told him of the undying love the Lord Jesus showed for him when He went to the cross, shed His blood, and died to provide the way of salvation and forgiveness for his sins.

Stephan wiped tears from his cheeks. "My aunt and uncle showed me this so many times, but I was so stubborn. I didn't want to make my parents angry. What a fool I've been, Andra. I know Jesus died for me. I know Mama and Joseph are up there in heaven with Him right now and that He wants me to be saved."

"Didn't He say right here that with lovingkindness He is drawing you?"

Stephan wiped more tears. "Yes."

"All right. Then if you will call on Him in repentance of your sin, Jesus will save you right now."

With Andra's help, Stephan opened his heart to Jesus.

She then showed him in the Bible that

the first step of obedience to God was to be baptized in a Bible-believing church.

There was an inner glow coming from Stephan's eyes. "I'll do that as soon as possible, Andra. I'm sure I can find one in Pennsylvania."

In the Wadford cabin, Alice's eyes flashed and her mouth was open for a hot retort when Gene snapped, "I thought when we got married that what's mine is yours and what's yours is mine! Share and share alike. But it's not that way, is it?"

Alice's face was gray. "Gene, you still don't get it, do you? If my father sees you wasting the money I give you on foolish, unnecessary things, he's liable to cut down on how much he puts in my bank account every month. Then you won't even get what I've been giving you. Is that what you want?"

"Your father doesn't need to see where my money goes. If you don't tell him, he'll never know what I do with it. So that's in your hands, Alice. And so is the amount of money I get from you each month. I'd think if you really love me as you say you do, you'd want me to be happy."

Alice drew a shaky breath. "I do love you, Gene, but all things considered, I'm keeping your allowance at the same amount."

Gene stared at her for a long moment, his eyes ugly. "And I'm supposed to believe that you love me."

"I do, but —"

Gene slammed the door behind him.

Alice shook her head. "Go ahead, Gene. Stew in your juice."

Outside, Gene huffed with anger as he made his way to the stairs. A man and woman spoke to him as they were coming up the stairs, but he ignored them. They paused, frowned down at him, then continued their climb.

When he reached the main deck, Gene found a place at the railing on the starboard side and leaned against it. There were few people on deck by then. Most were in their cabins getting ready to retire for the night.

He gazed up into the night sky that seemed to deepen the longer he looked at it. The moon was up, and its silver light danced on the waves. As he watched the moonlight on the sea, he wondered how deep it might be. How far was it to the bottom? *It would serve Alice right if I fell overboard and drowned. Then what would she do? A dead husband can't do all the little things I do for her.*

He shook his head to clear it of such a thought, but at the same time, the murmur of the sea seemed to beckon him.

"No!" he said aloud, then clamped a hand over his mouth and looked around to see if anyone had heard him.

He was quite alone.

Gene turned away from the railing, glanced back for a moment at the gently rolling sea, then hurried away, disturbed by the thoughts that had gone through his mind.

When Gene returned to the cabin, Alice had left a lantern burning, but she had gone to bed. He went to the other bedroom, undressed, and climbed into bed. He lay there for some time, trying to figure out how to get Alice to loosen up with her money. He wanted to stay married to her and he was convinced that she truly loved him. But what would he have to do to get his allowance raised?

It was almost six-thirty the next morning when Gene awakened. He went to the porthole and took in the first pink rays of the sunrise. While he was dressing, he could hear Alice moving about in the adjacent bedroom.

When he stepped out of the bedroom, he

looked down the narrow hall and saw Alice in the main part of the cabin, dressed and ready for the day. She looked at him as he entered the room. "You didn't even come in and kiss me good night."

"I figured you were asleep. Didn't want to disturb you."

"Are you ready for breakfast?"

Gene shook his head. "I'm not hungry. You go ahead. I'm just going to take a walk."

He went to the door and opened it. Before he stepped out, she said, "Darling, I love you."

"I love you, too."

The rising sun was peeking through a few vagrant white clouds as Gene made his way down to the main deck. Only a few people were moving about. He made his way along the starboard side and picked a spot where he leaned against the railing. His mind ran back to the thoughts that had assailed him last night. He stared down, pondering his situation.

Suddenly he heard Captain Wallace Knight's voice from the bridge, amplified by the megaphone, announcing to all on deck that the ship was now on the Mediterranean Sea.

Gene looked back down at the water.

"Looks the same as the Adriatic to me."

After a few minutes, he caught movement off to his left and saw a redheaded woman move up to the railing some thirty feet from him. She was alone.

He recognized her. It was the young woman named Lillian, who had screamed yesterday when the men were arguing and one was thrown into the sea. He wondered where Lillian's mother was.

It would serve Alice right if I fell overboard and drowned. He gripped the top rail. *How about if I "fell" overboard and didn't drown? If Alice almost lost me, she would be like that man's wife. She would be so happy that I was still alive that she would not only shower me with kisses, but with a little persuasion on my part, she would give me that raise I want!*

Gene gripped the rail harder and nodded. *Yes! That would do it!*

He had not been swimming since his teen years, and he was a great deal heavier now, but as fast as the crew would work to rescue him, he would be all right.

Gene looked around to see if any other passengers were close.

No one.

He inched his way closer to Lillian, who was gazing out onto the distant horizon.

When he was about ten feet from her, she turned and looked at him. He smiled and she smiled back, then turned her eyes once again to the sea.

Acting as if he were trying to see some distant object out on the water, Gene climbed up on the railing, balancing his upper body above the top rail. He looked again to see if any other passengers were near.

Still no one.

Lillian watched him balancing precariously. She frowned, then turned her attention the other direction.

Gene took a deep breath and let himself go over the rail. He let out a loud, high-pitched bellow and plunged into the cold waters of the Mediterranean.

Lillian was still looking the other way, then noticed her mother coming toward her, walking with her cane. Lillian smiled and moved toward her. As they drew near to each other, the silver-haired mother stopped, leaned the cane against her hip, and signed with both hands. Lillian nodded, and as deaf people do, answered weakly with her voice as she also made hand signals.

The sun had just gone down over the

western horizon when Captain Wallace Knight heard a tap on the door of his quarters. He opened the door and smiled. "Yes, ma'am. May I help you?"

"My name is Alice Wadford, Captain. My husband and I are in cabin fourteen on the third deck."

"Mm-hmm."

"I haven't seen Gene since early this morning. He left the cabin just before seven o'clock, saying he was going for a walk. We . . . we had a little argument, so I wasn't surprised that he hadn't come back to the cabin, even by noon. I have looked for him all over the ship right after lunch, and I can't find him."

Knight scratched his temple. "Well, give me his description, Mrs. Wadford, and I'll get some of my crew on it right away."

An hour and a half after Alice had talked to the captain, she was sitting in her cabin. The longer it went without word about Gene, the more frightened she became. She had considered going to Andra for moral support, but had decided against it. While doing her own search for Gene earlier in the day she had spotted Andra with that handsome young Stephan Varda on two occasions and didn't want to bother her.

It was dark now, and Alice was about to go back to the captain's quarters when there was a knock at her door. She jumped off the sofa and opened the door, holding her breath.

Captain Wallace Knight touched the bill of his cap. "Hello, Mrs. Wadford. I . . . I'm afraid I have bad news for you."

Alice's lips quivered. "What do you mean?"

"Well, ma'am, my crew has been all over this ship. They have searched every nook and cranny. Your husband is not on board."

"But — but how can this be?"

Knight's face was grave. "Mr. Wadford must have fallen overboard, ma'am. I have no idea how it could have happened, but to turn the ship around and make a search in the darkness would be useless. It would be impossible to see him in the water, even if he were still alive. I figure since no one reported seeing him fall overboard, it must have happened shortly after he left the cabin this morning, when there were few people on deck. If so, he's been in the water for over twelve hours. Even the best swimmer couldn't survive in that cold water that long."

Alice put a shaky hand to her mouth.

The captain helped her to the sofa, and as she settled onto it, he said, "I'm so sorry, Mrs. Wadford, but there's nothing else we can do."

She drew a shuddering breath. "I understand, Captain. Thank you for making such a thorough search for him."

"I . . . I don't like to leave you alone. Is there anyone on the ship you've become acquainted with? Someone who might come and keep you company?"

"Well, actually, I have a close friend on board. Her name is Andra Hardik. She's in cabin seven on this level."

"I'll get her for you."

Abruptly, Andra appeared at the open door with Stephan at her side. "Alice, Stephan and I were eating supper together, and we heard people talking about Gene, saying crew members had told them he had apparently fallen overboard."

Captain Knight sighed. "It's true, miss. Are you Andra Hardik?"

"Yes."

"I was about to come and get you. Mrs. Wadford told me you're her friend."

"I will stay with her as long as she needs me, Captain."

The captain thanked her, spoke his condolences to Alice, and left.

As Andra and Stephan talked to Alice, they noted that there were no tears, and soon realized that though she was shaken, she was not terribly upset about Gene's apparent drowning.

Andra tried to talk to her about the Lord, and Alice said she was not interested. She thanked Andra for the offer to stay with her, but added that it would not be necessary. She would be fine. Andra asked that Alice let her know if there was anything at all she could do for her, and Alice politely said she would. With that, Andra and Stephan left and returned to the dining room to finish their meal.

The S.S. *Friesland* was on the Atlantic Ocean a few days later, and as the days continued to pass, Andra worked at grounding Stephan stronger in his new-found faith, and they found themselves more and more attracted to each other, though neither had revealed it.

The ship pulled into New York Harbor early in the afternoon on Monday, June 26. Several sailboats were on the water, with a few fishing boats mingled among them. Andra and Stephan stood together at the railing on the third deck. Sunlight, fragmented into reflective shards by a brisk wind across the harbor, sparkled off the water's surface.

Soon the ship drew near the towering statue on Liberty Island. Everyone aboard was in awe of Miss Liberty as she cast her shadow over the harbor while holding the torch of freedom high.

Stephan fixed his gaze on the statue and smiled. "Isn't she beautiful, Andra?"

"She sure is."

"You know what? I can't help but think of the freedom and liberty I now have in Jesus from the power Satan once had over me. I was lost in sin and held in the devil's chains. But no more. Jesus went to the cross for me, and when I opened my heart to Him, He set me free. Andra, the cross is my Statue of Liberty!"

Tears filmed her eyes. "Stephan, that's beautiful!"

Before he could check himself, Stephan said, "You're beautiful, too."

She blushed and looked away.

Moments later, the S.S. *Friesland* docked in the harbor.

Alice Wadford stepped up, told Andra good-bye and rushed across a gangplank to board one of the ferryboats that would take her to Ellis Island.

While both of them watched Alice go,

Andra said, "Stephan, my heart is heavy for Alice because of her hardness toward the Lord."

Stephan thought of his father. "There are so many people in the world like that."

Andra and Stephan boarded another ferryboat, and when they stepped onto Ellis Island, they both knew that Andra would pass through a different line than Stephan would.

It was time to say good-bye.

Both were battling aching hearts. Stephan looked down at her, and his gaze seemed to be devouring her face. Andra found herself unable to take her eyes from his. She felt as if an electric storm was rising in her soul.

Stephan also felt the electric spark between them. As he ran splayed fingers through his thick hair, there was a slight tremor in his hand. "Andra . . ."

"Yes?"

"After . . . after I find my father, may I come to Memphis and see you?"

"I would love to have you come for a visit. I'd like to have you meet my parents."

She reached into her purse, took out a small slip of paper and a pencil. Writing quickly, she handed the paper to him. "Here's my address in Memphis."

A grin spread over his face. "Thank you."

As people were passing them by the hundreds, they were finding it very difficult to part.

Finally, Stephan worked up the courage. "Andra . . . I can't let you go without telling you that — well, I . . . I have fallen in love with you."

Her eyes shimmered. "I'm in love with you, too, Stephan. Very much in love with you."

Stephan's heart was in his throat. "Really?"

"Really."

He swallowed hard, trying to get his breath. "Could . . . could I hug you?"

"Oh yes! I thought you would never ask!"

As Stephan put his arms around her, she kissed his cheek. "Please do come and see me. I really do love you."

He hugged her again, then lowered his lips toward hers and paused. She closed her eyes, and their lips touched in a sweet, tender kiss.

Stephan embraced her once more, and whispered into her ear, "I'll come to Memphis as soon as I find Papa. I love you, my sweet Andra."

"I'll be waiting."

He kissed her again, and without another word, hurried away. Andra touched fingers to her lips as if to keep the kiss there and never let it go.

After nearly four hours of standing first in one line and then another, answering questions and undergoing extensive physical examination, Stephan was finally given his immigration papers by a smiling man in uniform. "There you are, Mr. Varda, and welcome to America."

Stephan's mind was on Andra as he made his way back to the Ellis Island docks and boarded a ferryboat that would carry him across the harbor to New York City.

The sun was slowly disappearing behind the horizon, shedding its golden light on the tall buildings of the city. Stephan had heard that New York City had buildings that were over twenty stories high, and he looked on in amazement.

The boat drew near the shore of this strange new land. Everything around him was unfamiliar. He frowned as panic seemed to be coming over him. But in an instant, the frown vanished. Suddenly his newfound faith was at the forefront of his mind. *Don't worry, Stephan. The Lord has brought you this far. He will lead you the rest of the way.*

The next day, Stephan arrived in Braddock, Pennsylvania. He took a room in a small hotel and asked directions to the steel mills. As he made his way toward the mills, he ran into Hungarians he had known in Budapest, but none of them had seen his father.

He was able to see executives in four of the steel mills before night fell. None of them had a Miklos Varda in their employment. Dejected, he ate supper at a café near his hotel and spent a restless night on the lumpy bed with his mind going back and forth between Andra and his father.

The next day, when he had seen his last steel mill executive, he was devastated. His father was unknown to them.

When he arrived back at his hotel room, he sat down on the bed and put his hands to his face. "Papa, where did you go? I came all this way to find you, and you're not here."

He closed his eyes and bowed his head. "Dear Father in heaven, I don't understand. Janos was so sure Papa would be here. He got a job with somebody he had known in Baja. But who? Where? You know where he is, Lord. Please lead me to him. I have no idea where to look now. Keep me from taking the wrong path. All I can do until You direct me to him is go on to Memphis and see Andra.

"I certainly don't have enough money to go back to Hungary, nor do I want to go back there. I know You brought Andra into my life. I'm so much in love with her, Lord. And she feels the same about me."

Leaving the bed, he picked up his knapsack and left the hotel, heading for the railroad station.

As he walked along the street, he said, "Lord, maybe I can get a job with Andra's father since he's in the tour boat business. Once I've got a good job, I'll ask Andra to marry me. In the meantime, please show me what to do to find Papa."

As Stephan neared the railroad station, he told himself it would be good if he could see one of Sigmund Hardik's boats and ride on it. When he approached the ticket agent, he asked if he could book him on a train to St. Louis, then on a *Hardik Lines* boat to Memphis. He was delighted when he was told it could be done and quickly purchased his tickets.

Twenty-four

Golden was the rolling land in eastern Missouri beneath the noonday sun two days later, when Stephan Varda arrived in St. Louis.

He left the depot and hired a buggy to take him to the docks on the Mississippi River. While the buggy made its way through the city, Stephan lifted his eyes toward the sky. Scattered puffy white clouds, rambunctious in the wind, billowed over the city.

The buggy driver had picked up Stephan's European accent and asked where he was from. When he learned that he was from Hungary, he knew enough about the country to ask how it was possible for the Hungarians to live with the dual monarchy that had been created by Austria. Stephan told him some of the problems the dual monarchy caused, but tried not to make

510

his country look too bad.

Soon they were approaching the Mississippi River with its broad span of twinkling waters. Stephan knew the Danube and the Tisza were beautiful rivers, but the Mississippi had a beauty all its own.

As the driver turned the buggy onto the short street that led to the docks, he pointed to a large paddle-wheel boat that was anchored at the first berth. "There it is, sir. *Hardik Lines* boat number four."

Stephan focused on the lettering on the side of the boat. "Sure enough. I've never seen a paddle-wheel boat before."

The buggy rolled to a stop. Stephan paid the driver, hopped out, and headed for the boat. According to his ticket, it would be leaving in exactly one hour. He could see crewmen moving about on the deck and a few passengers. A ticket agent stood at the top of the gangplank.

He mounted the gangplank and handed his ticket to the agent. The agent greeted him and said he hoped he had a nice trip to Memphis.

Stephan decided to look the boat over. He noticed the pilot's cabin up on the second level and three men in dark blue uniforms inside. The sun put a slight glare on the large windows, but he could tell that two of the men had caps that matched their uniforms, but the third man wore a white cap. He knew this identified him as the boat's skipper.

After walking the perimeter of the main deck, Stephan climbed the metal stairs to the second level. He wanted to get a look inside the pilot's cabin if the skipper would allow him to do it.

Just as he topped the stairs, one of the men who wore a blue cap came out of the pilot's cabin, turned, and went the other way. The other two were in conversation while they came through the door and stopped. The skipper's back was toward him, but Stephan thought that the man in the white cap was built much like his father.

Not wanting to interrupt the conversation, Stephan halted a few feet from the two men. As the conversation went on, the skipper slowly turned, showing Stephan his profile.

Stephan's heart seemed to stop in his chest, then start again, hammering his rib cage. He clamped a hand over his mouth to keep from crying out. *Papa! Oh, Papa, it's you. Thank You, Lord! You did lead me to my father!*

Just then, the crewman said a final word and walked away.

Chills ran up and down Stephan's spine as he stepped up behind the man who wore the white cap. "Hello, Papa!"

Miklos's head snapped around. His eyes bulged as he gasped. "Stephan!"

Immediately they were in each other's arms, weeping. "Oh, Stephan, my son! My son!"

When their emotions were brought under control, they stepped into the cabin.

Miklos said, "I know Janos Kudra told you that I was alive, and that he thought you would find me in Braddock."

Stephan's jaw sagged. "How do you know this?"

"Let me explain."

Miklos told Stephan how he came to know Sigmund Hardik in Baja, and how he got the job as skipper of Hardik boat number four. He then told him that when Sigmund's daughter, Andra, returned from Hungary a few days ago, Sigmund introduced him to her. She suddenly cried out that she knew his son.

Andra then told him of meeting Stephan, first in Baja, then aboard the S.S. *Friesland.* She told him what Stephan had told her about finding the ad in the Szeged newspaper, and of his returning home in a hurry. He had met Janos Kudra on the street upon his return to Budapest and was told the shocking news that his father was still alive.

While tears streamed down both their cheeks, Miklos said, "Son, Andra told me that because Janos thought I would be in Braddock, you came to America and headed there to find me. She also told me that you had promised to come and visit her in Memphis after you found me. I've been looking forward to seeing you. I sure wasn't expecting to see you on my boat, though!"

Stephan wrapped his arms around his father and hugged him tight. "It's so good to see you, Papa. I was so happy when I found out you hadn't drowned. That was the best news I've had in a long time!"

They held onto each other for a long moment, then as they eased back, Miklos said, "Andra told me that she led you to the Lord."

"Yes, she did. And I'm so glad to be saved, Papa."

A grin spread over Miklos's face. "Well, son, you'll be happy to know that your papa also got saved. I'm a child of God, too!"

Stephan was stunned. "Tell me about it!"

"Well, you remember Arpad and Sarai Fulop, don't you?"

"Sure. They rode on our boat many times."

"Well, they were on the same ship I was, coming to America. Both of them had become Christians a short time earlier, and they led me to Jesus on that ship."

"Wonderful, Papa! Wonderful!"

Father and son embraced and shed happy tears together. Then Miklos said, "The very day Andra told me that she had led you to the Lord, I mailed a letter to Bela and Ravina to let them know that both of us are now born again, and to thank them for their faithful witness to us all these years."

Stephan laughed. "I wish I could be there to see the look on their faces when they read that letter!"

"Me too." Miklos looked into his son's eyes. "I know in the newspaper ad, your mother and I asked you to forgive us for the way we treated you, but I must ask you right now for myself. Please forgive me."

Stephan smiled. "I forgive you, Papa. And I must ask you to forgive me for running away."

"You're forgiven."

"Oh, Papa, this is so wonderful! The Lord has been so good to us. Just think, Mama and Joseph are together in heaven right now, and someday we will all have a reunion up there."

"Yes, praise the Lord! We sure will."

Stephan hugged his father again. Miklos said, "Son, I have to tell you something."

Stephan eased back and looked into his father's face.

"What?"

A sly grin curved Miklos's mouth. "I think little Andra is in love with you. All she talks about is you and how much she's looking forward to your visit."

"Papa, I confess right now. I am in love with that sweet girl. And I don't *think* she's in love with me. I *know* it, because she told me she is."

"Well, great! This makes your papa very happy." Miklos glanced through the cabin window. "Well, my boy, we've got passengers boarding right now, and we're due to shove off in just a few minutes. I'd like for you to ride here in the cabin with me."

"I'd love it, Papa."

Hardik Lines boat number four pulled away from the St. Louis docks precisely on time. Stephan's heart felt lighter than it had in a long time.

Just after four o'clock that afternoon, the boat docked in Cairo, Illinois, for an hour. By that time, Miklos had introduced his son to his crewmen, and Stephan was having a good time talking to them about the tour boat business. Miklos excused himself to Stephan and his crewmen, saying he needed to leave the boat for a little while. When the hour was up, Miklos was back aboard and the boat was once again heading south on the mighty Mississippi.

Late in the afternoon on the next day, Stephan was in the pilot's cabin with his father when Memphis came into view. Pointing through the front window, Miklos said, "There it is, son. Memphis!"

Stephan's eyes widened. "Wow! Look at that huge bridge."

Miklos chuckled. "It's a big one, all right. That's West Memphis, Arkansas, on the other side."

"I see the docks, Papa."

"Well, keep your eye on them while I steer this ol' boat into port."

As Miklos was gripping the wheel and aiming the boat up to a dock where many people were looking on, he pointed through the glass and grinned. "Look right down there, son. Do you see that beautiful brunette there in the white dress?"

Stephan's heart did flip-flops when he

recognized Andra. He dashed out the cabin door and waved to Andra. She waved back, smiling.

Stephan looked back through the door. "Papa, does Andra always come to meet the Hardik boats when they arrive?" Dockworkers and the crew were anchoring the vessel to the dock with big thick ropes.

"Hardly. She's here because she knew you were on this boat."

"How'd she know that?"

Miklos's face crimsoned. "Well, remember yesterday when we docked in Cairo, I told you I had to leave the boat for a little while?"

"Yes."

"I . . . ah . . . went to the Cairo telegraph office. I sent a wire to Andra and told her I had you with me on the boat."

Stephan moved back into the cabin and playfully clipped his father on the chin. "You're a case, Papa, you know that?"

"I've been called worse."

Stephan dashed out of the pilot's cabin, down the stairs, and up to the edge of the deck. The dockworkers and crew were putting the gangplank down.

While he waited, Stephan called to Andra, "Hello, sweetheart! Can you hear me?"

"Yes, darling!"

"I love you!"

She smiled sweetly. "I love you, too!"

Miklos walked up beside his son just as the gangplank was being fastened in place. "Stephan, I wasn't going to tell you yet, but I think you need to know."

Stephan's eyes stayed fixed on the girl in the white dress. "What's that, Papa?"

"Sigmund has already told me that if you will stay in Memphis, he'll give you a job."

Stephan looked at his father and grinned. "Wild elephants couldn't drag me out of Memphis, Papa. Of course I'm staying!"

"I thought so. Just wanted to let you know."

"Thanks, Papa." He closed his eyes briefly. "And thank *You,* Lord!"

Miklos looked down at Andra and smiled as Stephan ran toward the gangplank. She smiled back, then set her eyes on the young man bounding down the gangplank. She moved through the crowd and was there to meet him when he reached the dock.

Stephan folded her in his arms and held her close for a few seconds. "Andra, I love you with an undying love. Will you marry me?"

Andra laughed happily, drew back, and looked into his eyes. "You've had me in your arms for at least ten seconds. I thought you would never ask!"